COURTESAN DUCHESS

*When it comes to seduction, there's
nothing noble about the nobility...*

JOANNA SHUPE

"Will knock your socks off!"
—Sabrina Jeffries

Wicked Deceptions

Don't miss the ne ... **ew**
Wicke ... series!

Comi
May ... *June 2012*

A LADY'S GUIDE TO SEDUCING HER LORD

"How long will it take to get there?" she asked.

"More than an hour. Torcello is the farthest lagoon island from Venice. It's also the quietest. Only a small number of people actually live there."

"What shall we do until we arrive?" She slid him a glance from beneath her lashes, and Nick felt his blood begin to heat.

"Why, I'm not sure." Turning, he nuzzled her neck just below her earlobe. He happened to know exactly how much she liked it.

She gave a long sigh, and her head fell back against the seat to allow him better access.

"What would *you* like to do until we get there?" he whispered against her throat.

"Shall we discuss politics? You haven't taken up your seat in the House of Lords, but I'm sure—"

"I would rather swim to Torcello than discuss politics. I'm afraid you'll have to do better than that, my dear." He traced the curve of her collarbone with his fingertips, the skin so soft and delicate. She rewarded him with a shiver. Leaning in, he slid his lips down the column of her throat, dropping small kisses as he went. She smelled heavenly, like soap and flowers, and he thought about tasting her everywhere.

"Hmm," she moaned. "No politics, then. What about gossip? I can tell you everything happening in London these days."

He grunted and continued kissing her neck, and she laughed. "Shall I recite poetry for you?"

"I hate poetry," he mumbled.

She laughed once more. "As it happens, so do I. Well, that leaves us only one thing." Her hand found his thigh and began slowly gliding toward his crotch. His shaft already swelling, he held his breath, waiting for her sweet touch. "To talk about ourselves."

Books by Joanna Shupe

The Courtesan Duchess

The Harlot Countess

The Lady Hellion

Published by Kensington Publishing Corporation

COURTESAN
DUCHESS

JOANNA
SHUPE

ZEBRA BOOKS
KENSINGTON PUBLISHING CORP.
http://www.kensingtonbooks.com

ZEBRA BOOKS are published by

Kensington Publishing Corp.
119 West 40th Street
New York, NY 10018

All Kensington titles, imprints, and distributed lines are
available at special quantity discounts for bulk purchases
for sales promotion, premiums, fund-raising, educational,
or institutional use.

Special book excerpts or customized printings can also be
created to fit specific needs. For details, write or phone the
office of the Kensington Sales Manager: Attn. Sales De-
partment. Kensington Publishing Corp., 119 West 40th
Street, New York, NY 10018. Phone: 1-800-221-2647.

Zebra and the Z logo Reg. U.S. Pat. & TM Off.

First Printing: April 2015
ISBN-13: 978-1-4201-3552-7
ISBN-10: 1-4201-3552-X

First Electronic Edition: April 2015
eISBN-13: 978-1-4201-3553-4
eISBN-10: 1-4201-3553-8

10 9 8 7 6 5 4 3 2 1

Printed in the United States of America

Chapter One

A smart woman may transform herself into whatever the situation requires.

—Miss Pearl Kelly to the Duchess of Colton

Venice, November 1816

The first time the Duchess of Colton saw her husband since their hasty marriage, she found him seated at a card table with a buxom woman draped across his lap, her legs dangled over the side of his chair. Julia could see them both quite clearly from across the gaming room. The woman was . . . pleasuring herself while the duke had one hand inside the woman's bodice, his fingers moving beneath the fabric to casually caress her breast. His other hand, along with his attention, remained on his cards.

The display shocked Julia. Scandalous yet strangely alluring, the performance served as a reminder that her husband's life was a world away from her own sheltered existence in London. But then, she reasoned, what else would one expect of a man dubbed the

Depraved Duke? She swallowed her embarrassment and continued to watch the scene unfold.

He was handsome, she realized. Julia had seen him briefly during the wedding ceremony, but they'd both been younger, not to mention she'd been a shy and terrified sixteen-year-old. Now he appeared older and . . . much bigger. His black hair a bit long, it fell down around his collar to frame his perfect features: a straight nose, bold cheekbones, and a full mouth. He was truly breathtaking.

Some women might be consumed with jealousy at catching their husband in such a fashion. Not Julia. The man was a stranger to her, and she felt nothing but a combination of anger and annoyance. Anger that Colton had ignored her for eight long years, and annoyance that she'd been forced to create such an elaborate ruse and travel across the Continent to carry it out.

Julia watched as the trollop on his lap began gasping for breath. The woman closed her eyes and shivered from head to toe, her head thrown back in ecstasy. Colton's expression revealed nothing about his companion or his cards, while the other players appeared nonplussed as they studied their own hands. Save Julia, no one else in the room paid a bit of attention to them. A woman was . . . finding release on his lap and no one even turned to stare. Was this a regular occurrence, then?

Once the woman caught her breath, she leaned in to whisper in Colton's ear. He smiled, politely assisted her off his lap, and gave her backside a small slap before dismissing her. His attention turned back to the game.

Julia's good friend, Simon Barrett, the Earl of

Winchester, appeared by her side. "Are you certain about this? It's not too late to back out, you know."

She shook her head. "No. I've come too far to stop now."

Simon was quite a handsome man in his own right, more so tonight with his fair hair and blue eyes contrasting nicely with his black evening clothes. He'd insisted on accompanying her to Venice, to pose as her current lover, allowing him to both escort her and protect her. Deep down, Julia was grateful for his help.

She smiled at him. "And after what we've just seen, I'd say my plan is perfect."

"I was afraid you would say that."

She sobered. This wasn't Simon's battle, and it seemed only fair to offer him the same chance of escape. "Simon, as I've said many times, I can do this on my own. Your friendship with Colton need not suffer because of your participation."

Simon glanced across the room to the duke. "I have my own reasons for helping you. I'll deal with Colt's anger, if the time comes."

She leaned up on tiptoe and placed a kiss on his cheek. "You're a good friend." Her heels came back down to the floor as she gently reminded him, "Now, I'm the incomparable Mrs. Juliet Leighton, London's most notorious courtesan. Allow me a few moments with him but no more."

"Fine. I only hope I can recognize you."

Learning of her wayward husband's preference for red-haired women, Julia had procured a dye to temporarily turn her light yellow locks to a fiery red. "What matters is catching Colton's eye."

"Oh, I shouldn't worry about that." Simon held out his arm. "Shall we?"

She nodded and accepted his escort. The card tables lined the back wall, so she and Simon were forced to amble through the clusters of guests and footmen passing glasses of champagne in order to reach their destination. Though Simon had warned her what to expect at a private party of loose morals, Julia had a hard time not staring at the goings-on around her. No wives were in attendance; instead, the women were mistresses, actresses, and prostitutes. And the men, mostly former members of the Venetian government or wealthy merchants, seemed eager to take advantage of the situation. Couples openly kissed and touched one another boldly, the air thick with smoke, lust, and sweat.

Her confidence grew as they crossed the room. No one they spoke with suspected her an imposter, and they treated her informally—as a courtesan, not a duchess.

Despite her nerves, there really was no choice in the matter. This plan *must* succeed. If Colton's odious cousin, Lord Templeton, followed through on his recent threat to further reduce her stipend, in a few months she wouldn't have enough funds to pay the servants or the rent on their small house in Mayfair. Colton's mother had made it clear Julia was unwelcome at any of the ducal properties. Which meant she and her aunt would be destitute.

Julia needed a male child, a legitimate one, to serve as the heir to the Colton estate. Only then could she thwart Templeton's designs on the dukedom.

Her plan was foolproof. Six months ago, Julia had sold off all her remaining jewelry in order to secretly hire Pearl Kelly, London's true reigning courtesan, to offer advice. Pearl had proved a veritable fount of information, telling Julia precisely how to dress, act, speak, and flirt like a Cyprian.

Pearl had even helped design Julia's gowns along with the courtesan's own modiste. The resulting wardrobe was luxurious and elegant with sumptuous fabrics and daring necklines, such as the deep emerald green gown she wore tonight. The undergarments had been ordered from Paris, and they *still* made Julia blush. Her jewelry had posed a problem, since every good piece she'd owned had been sold off over the past two years. So Pearl had graciously loaned Julia several stunning sets, which included the expensive diamond and pearl necklace now around her neck.

Julia had also learned how to use creams and paints to best enhance her features. Earlier, she'd applied a dusting of white pearl powder on her face, rose pink rouge on her lips and cheeks, and a light coating of lamp-black on her lashes and eyebrows. The enhancements combined with her red hair made her completely unrecognizable to anyone familiar with the blond and understated Duchess of Colton.

They ventured near the duke. After a moment, Colton looked up and his face registered surprise. "Winchester!" He threw his cards on the table and unfolded his lanky frame to stand before them. "I can scarcely believe it. Why didn't you write to let me know you were coming?"

Simon managed to look surprised, then slapped Colton on the back. "I'd heard a rumor you were still here, old man."

"I cannot find a reason to leave." Colton turned to Julia, focusing on her with polite interest. "I see you are not alone. Pray introduce me."

"Of course. Colton, meet the inimitable Mrs. Juliet Leighton. Juliet, this wastrel is my oldest friend, the Duke of Colton."

She dropped into a deep curtsy and watched from under her lashes as her husband took in the shockingly low neckline of her gown, where her ample bosom threatened to make an appearance at any moment. "Mrs. Leighton, your reputation precedes you," the duke said as she rose. "I've heard nothing but accolades to your beauty and wit. It is said you are the woman who holds all of London in the palm of her hand."

Julia was relieved to hear the rumors they'd started had reached her husband's ears. "Perhaps not all of London, Your Grace, but a fortunate few have indeed felt the palm of my hand."

A black eyebrow shot up, and he gave a devilish grin that would surely melt the insides of a weaker woman. "Winchester, I am beginning to envy you," Colton murmured, his smoky gray gaze never leaving hers.

"As you should. I am entirely at Mrs. Leighton's whim." Simon's intimate smile left no doubt as to the nature of their relationship.

"You flatter me," Julia said in her best coquettish voice. "Simon, darling, please leave His Grace and I alone for a few moments. Be a good lad and fetch me some champagne."

Simon flashed her a besotted glance that would've had Julia laughing under any other circumstance. "Anything for you, love." He walked away to leave

Julia alone with the husband she hadn't seen in eight years.

She should be tongue-tied, she thought, as she regarded the man who wielded enormous power over her, even from such a great distance. But considering the hot gleam of male interest in Colton's eyes, the way he studied her carefully, Julia knew the control now lay in her own hands.

"Your Grace," she started, then boldly moved closer and took his arm. "I feel as if we already know one another." Julia led him toward the terrace doors.

"Do you?" He deftly maneuvered them around other couples and placed his large hand on the small of her back as they continued outside into the cool darkness. "If we had met, Mrs. Leighton, I am quite sure I would remember."

"Oh, you must call me Juliet. All my good friends do."

"Then, by all means, you must call me Nick. I've never been fond of my title." Tall and lithe, he leaned casually against the terrace railing, the backdrop a surprisingly clean stretch of canal. He was even more handsome up close. His shoulders were broad, and power lurked beneath his finely tailored clothing. She suddenly felt so . . . alive and edgy in his wickedly alluring presence. Little wonder her husband had become such a rake and scoundrel.

"If you insist, Nick," she drawled while noticing the way he studied her lips. "Are we to be friends, then?"

"I certainly hope so." His face softened with a flirtatious smile and her knees went weak, the power of that small gesture warming her down to her toes. "Are you enjoying Venice, Juliet?"

"It is a lovely place. This is my first trip, and I must

confess it's nothing as I imagined. The food is superb and they are passionate, friendly people. And you? Have you been here long?"

"About three years. Before that Vienna, Cologne, Paris. . . ."

"And do you plan to return to our fair England one day?"

His features tightened ever so slightly. "No. I have no plans to return. There is naught there for me now."

Rage blossomed in her chest, hot and strong. How dare he. Naught there for him—even a *wife?* Although her hand itched to smack his cheek, Julia forced what she hoped was an intimate expression and dropped her voice to a husky purr. "My luck, then, in meeting you here."

"Indeed. And just when I'd thought Venice had grown boring. Have you known Winchester long?"

"No, not long. Though he's spoken of you. I understand you've been friends forever."

"It's true. Since Eton, actually. We—"

"Here you are, love." Simon appeared with a glass of champagne.

"So, Winchester," the duke began, "tell me how you've been getting on the last two years."

Two years! Julia gasped and almost choked on a mouthful of champagne. Simon had seen her husband two years ago? If Colton weren't standing here, she would give Simon a good kick in the leg for not telling her.

"I find myself remarkably well. And you?"

"I enjoy it here," Colton responded lightly. "The Venetians are quite pleasant, despite the resentment of the Austrian presence. I had thought, however, to travel to St. Petersburg next year."

"It's been eight years. Do you not think enough time has passed—"

"Do not say it." Colton's voice took on an edge and his face darkened. "After our last row, I thought you agreed to cease hounding me to return."

"But really, Colt. Your wife deserves—"

"Oh, you mean my father's pawn?" He straightened to his full height. "Cease immediately. Do not make me regret keeping you informed of my whereabouts all these years."

Pawn? What on earth? Julia could scarcely wait to get Simon alone in order to get answers.

Simon held up his hands in surrender. "I have no wish to quarrel with you. Especially in front of such a beautiful woman." He slid his arm around Julia and gave her shoulders a reassuring squeeze.

Her face a mask of polite civility, she focused on the duke. "Your Grace, we plan to attend the performance of *Tancredi* at La Fenice the evening after tomorrow. Perhaps you would care to join us?"

"I had already planned to attend, in fact," Colton replied, his posture once again relaxed. "I would be honored if you both would join the party in my box."

Julia tried to look surprised though she'd already known his plans. Simon's valet had convinced one of the duke's maids to give them information on Colton's daily social schedule. More chance meetings with Mrs. Leighton were in Colton's future. "That would be lovely, Your Grace. I shall look forward to it."

* * *

Nicholas Francis Seaton, the seventh Duke of Colton, watched covertly from his seat at the card table as Winchester and Mrs. Leighton took their leave. Since returning from the terrace, he'd hardly been able to take his eyes off his friend's companion while she charmed every other man at the party. She was good. The best, if the rumors of her superior wit, charm, intelligence, and passion were to be believed. But Nick had never placed much credit in rumors. Not after his own life had been turned upside down by gossip and innuendo, and he'd been forced to leave his home and country.

No, Nick was much more interested in discovering the woman's talents for himself.

If he had to conjure up a vision of the perfect woman, the exquisite Mrs. Leighton would be it. With alabaster skin and clear blue eyes, her fiery hair, delicate features, and lush figure were all artfully arranged and displayed to her best advantage. Bloody hell, she was a goddess in every way. The low-cut dress had barely contained her ample breasts, and Nick swore he'd caught sight of one dusky areola.

And her smile . . . With lips tilting up mysteriously at the ends, her mouth teased and tempted. Begged a man to run his tongue along the edges in the hopes it tasted half as delicious as it looked. He'd seen a woman's beckoning smile a hundred times before, but never one quite so charming as Mrs. Leighton's. It had almost seemed as if she'd been amused by him at the same time she flirted with him.

No wonder Winchester appeared so unnaturally besotted. While growing up, many a woman had hopped from his bed to Winchester's and vice versa. It had all been a game. But the tender way

Winchester looked at Mrs. Leighton tonight had been surprising. So Nick would need to gauge Winchester's feelings for the woman before making a move. Even though she had overtly flirted with him, he'd not offend one of the few men he still considered a friend.

Three-quarters of an hour later, he tossed in his hand. It had been a profitable evening and he was tired. Too many recent late nights. He collected his winnings and then departed.

Once on the street, Fitzpatrick, Nick's valet and self-appointed guard, stepped out of the gloom. "Evenin', Your Grace."

"Christ, Fitz. Stop calling me that."

"Just because you don't want to hear it don't mean it's not true," Fitz said in his raspy brogue and began leading the way to the gondola.

Nick muttered an obscene curse under his breath and Fitz chuckled. Nick knew Fitz would always use the proper title, no matter how many times he told the Irishman not to.

Seven years ago, Nick had rescued the giant man from a nasty fight in a Dublin back alley. Two ruffians had been holding Fitz down, while a third man used a knife to slice open Fitz's face. Nick had recognized them all as local thieves, so he stepped in to help even the odds. In those days, Nick had been eager for any fight he could find, and he and Fitz made short work of the three criminals. Unfortunately, Fitz had been badly cut in the fray, scars he still bore to this day.

Fitz believed Nick had saved his life. Since then, he'd attached himself to the duke, and Nick soon learned it was easier to employ Fitz than to try and get rid of him. The Irishman started as Nick's valet, but trouble followed Nick everywhere. Fitz had taken it upon himself to also look after Nick's safety and had repaid the favor with Nick's own life many times over.

They turned a corner and onto a relatively desolate street with little light. A pair of men approached, and Fitz slid a hand inside his coat, ready to produce the pistol tucked inside his waistband. The men, however, remained in deep discussion and passed without incident. Fitz relaxed and they continued walking toward the water.

"You're overly concerned," Nick told him. "We haven't had a scuffle in eight months."

"Three separate attacks in two years. Not to mention the mishap in Vienna. Perhaps you should be a little *more* concerned, Your Grace."

This was a familiar conversation, and Nick knew he wouldn't be able to dissuade Fitz from the notion that danger stalked him. He stepped into his gondola. "How many times must you save my miserable life before you realize I'm not worth it?" *Unworthy, ungrateful whelp,* his father's voice sneered. Nick beat back the memory, like so many times before. "You could be living a comfortable life in your homeland, Fitz. You're a fool to exile yourself on my account."

Fitz took a seat in the back near the gondolier. "You saved my life. Until the debt is repaid, or you no longer be needin' me, I stay."

An argument was futile, so Nick leaned back and watched the other boats float by.

"Was that your friend Lord Winchester I seen come out a few minutes before you?"

"Yes," Nick answered.

"Lovely bit o' goods on his arm."

Nick almost smiled. Mrs. Leighton was much more than your average Cyprian. "Find out where they're staying, will you? I'd like to send a note round to Winchester tomorrow." *And perhaps a small token for Mrs. Leighton as well.*

"Two years! You saw him *two years* ago and never told me?" Now inside their gondola, Julia stripped off her gloves and threw them on the seat inside the *felze.* The blinds were drawn, and the single interior lamp cast a warm yellow glow about the cabin. She was too angry to sit but had little choice in the confined space. "How could you keep that from me, Simon?"

The boat pushed off from the dock as he dropped next to her. "There was no reason to tell you. I came to Venice and tried to convince him to return with me. I told him of you. Sang your praises, really, but I failed to win him over. I worried it would hurt your feelings to learn of it."

While Julia thought on that, he continued. "The only reason I brought it up tonight was for you to be perfectly aware of what you face with Colton."

"What did he mean, calling me his father's pawn? Pawn for what, exactly?"

Simon sighed. "To him, you're the woman his father married him off to, without considering his wishes on the subject. Like I've said, he was the forgotten son 'til his brother died. And when he became the heir, Colton's father was desperate to get his only living son to fall in line, to become responsible. In Colt's eyes, you're merely another attempt by his father to bring the wayward son to heel." Simon stretched his long legs. "But you know how well that turned out. Didn't he leave for Paris directly after reciting his vows?"

Yes, and that had stung. And while she could imagine how manipulated Colton must have felt, Julia needed to stay focused on her plan—a plan Simon was not entirely privy to. "Well, he's interested in Mrs. Leighton. After I lure him in, I can spend time with him not as a wife, but as a woman. Then I shall be able to satisfy my curiosity regarding my husband," she lied.

"God save men from intelligent women," Simon muttered with a yawn. "I am not so sure this relationship with Pearl Kelly has been beneficial, Julia. You never used to be so . . . bold."

"I had no choice. I'm tired of waiting and wondering if Nick will return. I'm tired of the pity and the scorn, all the rumors. The innocent wife of the Depraved Duke—it would be laughable if only it were someone else. We've talked about this, Simon. I should have the ability to at least meet the man I am married to. To see if we suit."

"Oh, it's Nick, is it?"

The gondola stopped, and Simon rose to offer his hand. They stepped out onto the boat dock and continued toward the stairs of their rented palazzo. "He insisted," she said. "I told you he was interested."

"Of course he's interested. He'd be a fool not to be—and Colton is no fool. As I've said, I am in full approval of this plan. Colton has ignored his responsibilities for far too long."

They had procured a few local servants upon their arrival, and no one suspected the renters were not who they claimed. As far as the servants were concerned, the trio included a wealthy English lord traveling with his mistress and her companion. Julia, Simon, and her aunt, Theodora, took great pains to maintain the illusion, unless absolutely certain they were alone.

Once inside, Simon removed her cloak and handed it to the footman. Aunt Theo appeared in the parlor doorway. "Would either of you care for a sherry?" Judging by the messy riot of curls on Theo's head, Julia guessed her aunt was already on her second or third drink.

"Yes, I believe I shall. Darling?" She gave Simon a seductive smile for the benefit of the servant hovering nearby.

"Lead on, my love," he said easily, gesturing to the doorway.

"And how was your evening?" Theo asked as she settled her rounded, lush frame on the divan. Her aunt was fond of sherry and cake and hardly a day went by when she didn't indulge in at least one.

"Productive," Julia answered, closing the door behind her. "Simon, bring me a glass of whatever you're having. Sherry makes me gag." She dropped into a chair opposite her aunt.

Simon pressed a glass into her hand and Julia took a sip. Claret, she realized, and took another grateful swallow. "Oh, Aunt Theo," Julia breathed. "You would not have believed this party. *Shocking* would be a paltry description. What freedom these women have! A world away from Almack's, to be sure."

"Such freedom does not last long when your looks fade or your benefactor tires of you. And the health risks!" Theo waggled her finger at Julia. "Do not envy them. It's a hard life, full of uncertainty and scorn."

"But they do wield a certain amount of power. Pearl has had liaisons with two dukes, one earl, a viscount, and a Bavarian prince. Two lifetime annuities have been settled on her, and she's only thirty-one."

"Julia, don't be naïve," Simon said. "Not every woman could possibly be Pearl Kelly."

"Have you met her?" Julia asked him.

"Yes, once at Vauxhall Gardens. A group of us went for supper one night, and she accompanied Lord Oxley. She is intelligent and witty," he admitted. "Not only can she carry on a conversation, she listens. And Pearl makes a man feel as if everything he says is important—which in Oxley's case would've been nothing short of a miracle. But she's deuced expensive."

"Worth every banknote and gem she receives, I'd wager, if half of what she told me is true."

"I almost pity that poor husband of yours," Simon drawled.

Julia frowned. Colton deserved no pity. The man was a reprobate. And he'd left her at the mercy of his cheating, lecherous relative.

She started to argue but Simon held up a hand. "I said 'almost.' No one knows of your unhappiness these last few years better than I. Colt deserves retribution for what he's done—and more. However, it does seem as if you're well on your way to achieving your goal."

"Oh, saints be praised!" Theo slapped her thigh.

"How long, then, do you believe we must stay in Venice?"

"Not long. If I were to wager, not long at all," Julia answered with a sly smile.

"Well, I'm off." Simon rose and drained his glass. "I know of a few more parties I should like to visit this evening—without Mrs. Leighton's watchful eye, of course."

Julia held up her hand. "Say no more. We wish you luck, don't we, Aunt Theo?"

Glorious crackpot that she was, Theo nodded, her brown curls rocking back and forth. "Indeed. Here's to wine, women, and song, my lord."

Simon gave them an elaborate bow and left.

"Do you think this scheme will work?" Theo asked once they were alone.

"It must. Templeton's last visit continues to give me nightmares." After informing her—again—of the further reduction of her monthly stipend, the grotesque excuse for a man had suggested what services Julia could provide to make up the difference. And by services, he hadn't meant mending his clothes.

The thought of intimacies with Templeton—with his small black eyes, sweaty brow, and demeaning attitude—almost made her physically sick. *Damn Colton for putting me in this situation.* "Oh, how I wish my father was still alive."

"My brother would've dragged your duke home by his whirlygigs by now, that's for sure."

Julia chuckled. "Perhaps. Templeton wouldn't be a problem, in any case. I know my father believed marriage to a duke to be an unparalleled match for his only daughter, but I'd like to think he would have reconsidered if he'd known how much trouble it would bring me."

"The trouble is your duke ignoring his responsibilities at home. Leaving you to fend for yourself for eight years. With naught a word from him!" Theo sniffed in disdain. "And to wash his hands of the estate business. Does he believe all estate managers to be honest men? You know very well that Templeton is paying off Colton's man to follow his orders."

"Colton does not care. He told me himself he never plans to come back to England. So we had to do *something*. As you well know, the last of our jewelry went to pay Pearl and fund Mrs. Leighton's wardrobe. We barely have enough to carry us through until spring."

"I still say we could've asked Winchester for help. Or perhaps your Lord Wyndham."

Julia bristled. "You know we cannot ask for another man to support us indefinitely. And he is not *my* lord anything. I told you I merely flirted with Wyndham in hopes of forcing Colton back to London. But either my husband didn't hear the rumors or didn't care about being cuckolded because it failed to work."

"So if Colton does not care about being cuckolded . . ."

"I still couldn't do it. Colton would know the child was not his, and I cannot risk him telling anyone. If it were found out, my child would be an outcast. No, Colton must father my child. And when I find myself with child, we shall return to London and I'll write to my husband, explaining what I've done."

They both fell silent, contemplating the duke's reaction to such a letter, while the mantel clock ticked loud and steady throughout the room.

"Will Colton acknowledge the child, I wonder?" her aunt asked, and sipped her sherry.

Julia frowned. "Why would he not? Every man wants an heir."

"Well, what will happen if you deliver a girl?"

"Then I shall love her fiercely—from debtor's prison."

Chapter Two

To catch his eye, be both temptress and maiden. An innocent harlot is what most men desire at the end of the day.

—Miss Pearl Kelly to the Duchess of Colton

The Duke of Colton walked briskly toward Piazza San Marco, sidestepping the large puddles left over from the flooding earlier in the week. At this time of year, Venice experienced *acqua alta*, meaning the lower parts of the city were frequently submerged due to the heavy rains. Water, both in and around the city, was a natural state of affairs here.

Nick continued along the right side of the Piazza and entered Florian's. He spotted Winchester straightaway, sitting at a table near the back of the crowded coffeehouse.

Winchester stood and clapped Nick on the shoulder. "Damned glad to get your note. It's been too long."

"Indeed, my friend." The men sat, and Nick poured

himself a cup of coffee from the pot on the table. "I must confess, you took me by surprise last night."

"Did I? It does seem remarkable I've been in Venice for two weeks and not crossed paths with you before now. But then, I have been rather busy."

"Ah, your Mrs. Leighton, you mean? She's lovely." Nick knew *lovely* did not do the woman justice. *Stunning* and *enchanting* were far more apt descriptions.

"Merely temporary. No one holds on to her for long. You would not imagine what I had to promise in order to get her to come on this trip. Even still, I fear I shall be replaced the minute we dock in London—if not before."

"A shrewd business-woman, is she?"

Winchester nodded. "Shrewd and ruthless. Hardly needs the scratch anymore. A woman of her own means and can pick and choose her lovers for different reasons."

"And what were her reasons for selecting you?"

"You mean besides my reputation in bed?" Nick snorted and Winchester laughed. "I promised her Venice for as long as she wanted to stay. That, and a cache of jewelry large enough to make a princess blush."

Nick hoped Juliet would stay long enough for the two of them to become better acquainted. He'd felt the attraction last night and was sure she'd felt it, too, after the way she'd flirted with him. But it wouldn't do to offend one of his oldest friends in the process. "And if she finds someone else while in Venice?"

Winchester shrugged, took a sip of coffee. "I cannot say it would surprise me." He shot Nick a knowing glance. "Why, I do believe you are planning to outmaneuver me. Colton, how shabby of you."

Despite Winchester's teasing tone, Nick wanted to reassure his friend. "Only with your approval. You're one of only a handful of men who have stood by me all these years. Mrs. Leighton is intriguing, but not worth the ruination of a twenty-year friendship."

Winchester appeared uncomfortable for a moment, which puzzled Nick. Perhaps all these years abroad had made him more sentimental than was proper back in crusty old England.

He started to apologize, but Winchester held up a hand. "I don't mind if you set your sights on her, Colt. It wouldn't be the first woman I've lost to you. But her reasons for choosing a companion are her own. I could no more hold on to her than the wind."

"How poetic," Nick mocked. "You are becoming quite eloquent in your old age."

"Since you are a few months older than I, you should refrain from comments about age. Nevertheless, if you plan on wooing my Juliet, I daresay I should begin searching for a replacement. How are the women in Venice?"

"Plentiful," Nick answered with a grin. "Talented. Beautiful." His mind traveled back to Francesca who, up until a few months ago, had been his mistress for nearly a year. With olive skin, black hair, and long legs, she'd had a fiery temper to match his own. Bedding her had been a fierce battle for control. "Spirited. Nothing like English women."

"Do not be so quick to judge. There is one English woman in particular who is certainly all of those things."

"Mayhap I will get the chance to offer up a comparison. Is there a Mr. Leighton?"

"No. Died years ago, left the poor woman entirely

without funds. But there's some nobility in her background. Her father was a cousin to the Earl of Kilbourne, I think." Then Winchester grew serious, and Nick braced himself. "Colt, I feel compelled by my friendship with your wife to at least—"

"Enough. Did we not discuss this last evening? I have—"

"Let me speak!" Winchester set his cup down sharply. "There may come a day when you regret your poor treatment of that woman. Even now, the rakes circle her like a prized lamb. She will tire of waiting on you, and God help you when that happens, Colt."

Nick ignored the small amount of guilt produced by Winchester's words. His wife was nothing more than his father's instrument of control, Nick reminded himself. *She's the best you'll ever do, you ungrateful whelp. Do you think to do better, boy?* Nick had no intention of doing anything his father wanted, even if the arrogant whoreson was long dead.

With practiced control, he fought down the bleakness and anger inside his chest, and calmly took a sip of coffee. "If my wife finds someone else, all the better. I never want an heir, and I will not fashion myself into a proper duke and husband. Her Grace is free to do as she pleases. Hell, the woman is a bloody duchess with no husband to curtail her freedom. How could she complain?"

Winchester drummed his fingers on the table, a sure sign that Nick's answer had annoyed him. "Her name is Julia, Colt. She's a real living, breathing person and innocent in what happened. I know you blame your father, but you're making her suffer needlessly. If you do not wish to live in England, send for her. Bring her here."

A part of Nick accepted the sense of those words, but the bigger, angrier part of him wanted to punish everyone involved with his family—including the woman who'd married him. Besides, why would a gently bred lady want *him*, a man far more familiar with brothels than ballrooms? God, she'd been so young and beautiful—and so innocent—on their wedding day. How could he tarnish such a chaste *girl* when he'd driven his own brother—

Nick deliberately stifled that particular line of thinking. No, his wife was better off finding a well-titled young buck who knew how to be a careful, respectful lover. "I won't send for her, and I'll not apologize for it. If you are truly her friend, I trust you will relay what I've told you. Let her find happiness elsewhere, for none can be found with me."

Winchester leaned back and crossed his arms over his chest. "Fine. But you're making a mistake."

Nick regarded his friend thoughtfully. "Have you developed feelings for my wife? You are unusually concerned with her happiness." Winchester turned a dull red, and Nick added, "I have no tender emotions for the woman. But if *you* do, I promise it would not affect our friendship. In fact, it would explain why you are so determined to see me return to England."

"I am not mooning after Julia. That distinction belongs to Wyndham." Nick's eyebrows rose at that piece of news but he made no comment, so Winchester continued. "But don't you think you've given it enough time? The scandal, I mean. Damn, it's been eight years, Colton. And to watch Templeton act as if *he's* the duke . . . Christ, it's disgusting."

Nick shook his head. "All of London believes I seduced my sister-in-law, which caused my brother to fly into such a rage that he fell off his horse and broke his neck. That, on top of all the Depraved Duke nonsense, ensures the *ton* won't ever forget me."

"The nickname is a fair one, as I witnessed much of your youthful depravity myself. The label merely became catchy for the printmakers once you assumed the title." His voice lowered. "But Colt, we both know the true circumstances behind your brother's death."

And I bear the guilt of those circumstances every single day. "It doesn't change a thing. Not to mention, as long as my mother draws breath, you are wasting yours."

The dowager duchess deserved as much—if not more—of Nick's anger than anyone else. After all, it was she who ensured the governess brought only his brother to the drawing room for his parents' daily inspection. *Nicholas is ill-mannered and completely unworthy of the Seaton name. Only Harry may come down at the requested hour. No one else.*

From that moment on, Nick had decided he didn't need his family. And inheriting the title hadn't changed a thing.

"Animals who eat their young have more maternal instinct than that woman," Winchester muttered. "I saw her recently. Gave me the dragon's stare from across a crowded ballroom."

"Disapproval, no doubt, of our lasting friendship, when almost everyone else had the good sense to cut me. Pray fabricate the most horrifically sensational stories about me and be sure to relay them to the dowager duchess the next time you see her. I fear my current location is too far from London for my salaciousness to reach her ears otherwise."

"About this salaciousness," Winchester drawled. "If things progress with Juliet, you'll be . . . careful with her, won't you?"

"Careful?" Nick frowned. What, precisely, was Winchester worried about? If Mrs. Leighton was as talented as the rumors suggested, he suspected she could easily hold her own against any man.

Winchester waved a hand. "You know what I mean."

"No, I don't. I haven't a bloody clue what you mean."

"She may seem . . . worldly. But she's a good actress. All women in her position are, really," he amended. "I shouldn't want to see her hurt."

Something was off. Nick could feel it in his gut. Perhaps Winchester really did have feelings for Juliet—feelings Mrs. Leighton did not reciprocate. After all, his friend wouldn't be the first man to fall in love with a courtesan. Just look at Fox and his Mrs. Armistead. "If you would rather I did not—"

"No," Winchester interrupted. "I merely want her next protector to be as . . . generous with her as I have been."

"You've nothing to fear, then. I shall be all that is kind and generous, if she'll have me."

"I've yet to meet a woman who could resist you, Colt—even before you became a duke. But Mrs. Leighton will decide for herself."

The following night, Julia and Simon entered the duke's box at La Fenice. The interior of the opera house, with its noble yet simple architecture, was luxurious. Rows of private boxes surrounded the gilded interior for the wealthiest of patrons, while the floor provided ample space for those of lesser means.

Colton's large box was crowded, with at least six men and an equal number of women. The need to search for her husband, however, was rendered unnecessary as he immediately appeared at her side.

"Mrs. Leighton," the duke greeted as she curtsied. He took in her embroidered white satin dress with its silver *bandeau* and accompanying emerald green robe. "How stunning you look this evening."

She could say the same about him. The duke wore a fitted black tailcoat and breeches over a single-breasted white waistcoat, which emphasized his lean torso. His snowy cravat, folded in a complicated array of knots under his clean-shaven chin, proved a stark contrast to his dark features. When he noticed her staring, he gifted her with a smile both intimate and sly, almost as if the two of them shared a private joke. Her breath came a bit faster despite her resolution to remain unaffected. "Good evening, Your Grace."

Nick greeted Simon and then introduced the rest of the party. There were two ambassadors—one former and one current—as well as a Russian count, a Venetian painter, and a French actor. While the women were beautiful, one could discern by their dress and demeanor that there were no wives in attendance. Well, if one didn't count her, she thought.

Nick led them to their seats. Julia used the opportunity to struggle with a swatch of hair that had fallen over her forehead. Fiorella, the young girl she'd hired as a lady's maid, wasn't as proficient with hair as Meg back in London. Tonight, Fiorella had lifted Julia's thick red hair up in a series of artful curls and secured it with a silver band. But one unruly layer would not cooperate, and it drooped down to almost completely cover her right eye. With no hope of righting her coiffure on her own, Julia had little choice but to ignore it.

As they settled, she wasn't the least bit surprised to find herself seated between Nick and Simon. On Simon's other side was an empty chair, but it was soon filled with a striking Venetian actress. Nick relaxed in his seat and pressed the outside of his leg against Julia's knee. She lifted her glasses to peer into the audience and willed her heart to slow.

"Did the flowers meet with your approval, Mrs. Leighton?"

The previous day, Nick had sent her a large bouquet of white roses, artfully arranged in a colorful vase made from Murano glass. It was a stunning display. His card had been concise and clever: *To friendship.*

Part of her was so angry over the gesture she wanted to shout at him like a fishwife. He couldn't bother to send his wife of *eight years* a mere note . . . and yet rushed forward with a token of regard to a woman he'd met not even twenty-four hours earlier. Julia swallowed her outrage and bitterness in order to remember the part she played and the reason for it. Tonight, the goal was to flirt, thereby ensuring the duke's interest in her charms. "They are exquisite, Your Grace. You are too generous," she replied, giving him a teasing glance through her lashes.

"I fear you have high standards, Mrs. Leighton. After all, I heard you once sent a necklace back to Wellington because it contained an odd number of diamonds rather than even."

Julia bit her cheek to keep from laughing. That par-

ticular anecdote was one of Aunt Theo's contributions
to Mrs. Leighton's legend.

"Oh, that story is tiresome. I did no such thing."
Julia raised her glasses again to blithely peer out at
the crowd. "I sent it back because it was ugly."

Nick gave a short, genuine bark of laughter. "Well,
I shall endeavor to be more selective in my gifts."

"Are there to be more gifts, Your Grace?" She
meant for the comment to be playful and flirtatious,
but her voice betrayed her with a husky and intimate
tone.

His lids dipped and he edged closer. "Whatever
you wish for, Mrs. Leighton, shall be yours."

Julia couldn't prevent the shiver that traveled the
length of her body. Thanks to Pearl's instructions,
the sensual promise in his words was not lost on her.
While she knew exactly what he wanted from her, she
could only be grateful that Nick had no suspicion of
what *she* wanted from *him.*

The music swelled, sparing her the need to respond.

With her husband's leg tucked snugly against hers,
any effort to concentrate on Rossini's heroic opera
failed. She used the opportunity to think over her
plan.

First, gain Colton's interest. Next, stage a falling-
out with Simon in public. Colton would then pursue
her and, a few days later, she would allow him to catch
her. All that remained would be to engage in activities as old as time, as often as possible.

Julia was nervous, but not scared. Pearl had given
her the basic details of what took place, plus ways to
increase a man's pleasure. She'd also learned, despite
her initial embarrassment, about her own pleasure
since Pearl maintained that a courtesan as successful

as the mythical Mrs. Leighton would ensure both partners enjoyed the experience.

But Julia had been unprepared for what it would feel like to sit next to this compellingly handsome man, her husband, while the heat from his muscled thigh warmed her leg through layers of clothing. His well-proportioned body so near, their shoulders lightly touching, had her insides now throbbing in time with the beat of her heart. She hadn't expected to be so attracted to him. After all, he had ignored her for so long that she'd built up a sizable amount of resentment toward him. But those feelings were fast receding in the face of his wickedly powerful presence.

Struggling with the idea of actually *liking* him, Julia wondered if such a thing made her goal easier or more difficult to accomplish.

In the end, it didn't matter. Templeton must be stopped and producing the Colton heir was the only way to do it.

She decided to tempt him a bit. After all, she needed to seduce the man.

Julia let her opera glasses fall from her fingertips to the carpeted floor between them, where they landed with a thud. "Oh!" she whispered.

The duke's head turned her way, a black eyebrow raised in question.

"Your Grace, I seem to have dropped my opera glasses. Would you be so kind?"

Nick politely inclined his head before he bent over, his fingers searching in the semi-darkness for her glasses. Julia waited a beat and then lifted the hem of her skirt and petticoats up to her shins. Sliding her leg toward him a bit, she was rewarded when his fingertips brushed her stocking-covered ankle.

His shoulders tensed, as if she'd surprised him, and then she felt his hand, ever so slowly, slide up the back of her calf, his touch a white-hot charge through the silk. She couldn't prevent a gasp from escaping. When he reached the back of her knee, his fingers lingered there, drawing a delicate pattern on the soft underside. Julia closed her eyes and bit her lip while trying to maintain her composure. Something hot and needy unfurled low in her belly, a feeling she suspected was unbridled arousal for her husband.

He seemed in no hurry to remove his hand and Julia wasn't sure how much more she could take without moaning in sheer bliss. "Do you see them, Your Grace?" she breathed.

His hand fell away, and a second later he straightened. "Your glasses, Mrs. Leighton."

"Thank you," she murmured, and accepted the glasses from his hand.

"Anytime," he returned, his husky tone making the meaning quite clear.

Her cheeks flooded with heat, and she was grateful for the low light that hid her blush. She attempted to calm herself throughout the remainder of the first act.

Just before the second act began, Nick leaned over again, and his now-familiar scent of citrus and musk teased her nose. "May I escort you home later, Mrs. Leighton?"

"Simon shall escort me home. And as *helpful* as you've been this evening, I'm not currently seeking another bed partner, Your Grace."

"Oh, no. It's much too soon to become lovers." He

drew closer to her ear, his warm breath tickling her skin. "When I finally take you, Juliet, when I finally have you naked underneath me, the memory of every other man you've been with will be forgotten. You shall think of only me . . . and beg me to make you mine."

All the air left her chest in a *whoosh*. A rush of desire swept through her, so strong her knees surely would have given out if she'd been standing. He was the very devil, everything dark and forbidden and wanting in her life.

And she was way out of her depth.

She searched for something witty to say but came up empty.

Until words she'd heard spoken by Pearl months before came to mind. They tumbled out of Julia's mouth. "I wonder if you truly possess the skill to back up your arrogance."

His eyes heated to liquid silver. "If you find a private alcove, I'll happily demonstrate my abilities before the end of the performance. After all, it's only fair to know what you're getting."

The mention of the alcove was like a douse of cold water. How many alcoves and how many women were in his past? No doubt he'd trysted in buildings from Paris to Pisa. Still, she played her part. "An alcove? I hadn't thought you so unoriginal."

She'd intended to offend him, but he merely winked at her. "Then I look forward to proving exactly how creative I can be."

After the opera the entire party traveled to a nearby coffeehouse. Simon escorted her between locations, but once there, Nick deftly maneuvered the seating in order to ensure the two of them sat together. Simon ended up at the other end of the table, next to Veronica, his companion at the opera.

The after-theater crowd was lively and loud, and the smell of coffee permeated the open space. Julia ordered plain coffee, while Nick asked for *caffè corretto,* coffee with a shot of grappa.

As she chatted with the mistress of a local painter, she could feel Nick's eyes, intense and dark, watching her like his next meal. Every bit of her skin came alive, crawling and itching with awareness. Pearl Kelly had instructed Julia never to waste an opportunity to flaunt her charms, so since Nick was watching . . . She slid her fingers under the long double strand of pearls around her neck and toyed with them, dragging the smooth, creamy balls back and forth over her exposed bosom while she conversed.

She felt Nick lean in, his mouth near her ear. "Oh, to be a pearl at this very moment."

Julia looked up at him through her lashes. "Indeed? I shouldn't think you'd want to be anything so . . . small, Your Grace."

He flashed her a wicked smile, his voice a deep rumble. "I never said a word about being small."

Thankfully, their drinks arrived at that moment. Julia busied herself with adding cream and sugar to her coffee, grateful to have something to focus on other than her husband.

After the group settled with their drinks, Nick turned to Julia. "Well, Mrs. Leighton, what did you think of Rossini's work this evening?"

"Exhilarating," she answered, and all eyes turned her way. "A real maturation from his earlier pieces and the perfect essence of bel canto. The work is quite a rigorous test of his mezzo-soprano's abilities, who must possess true vocal agility and endurance in order to carry out the part. I particularly enjoyed *'Di tanti palpiti,'* although I believe the ending of the story needs work."

No one spoke. Somewhere, a spoon clattered against a saucer. Julia sipped her coffee, reveling in the surprise at her response. She'd never admit it, but she'd been arranging her thoughts since the curtain fell in the hopes of impressing the duke.

"Needs work?" someone from down the table asked.

Julia nodded. "It's too dark. Rossini would be better served to have Tancredi learn of his lover's innocence and return home in triumph. Don't you agree, Your Grace?" She snuck a glance at Simon, who gave her an encouraging wink.

"Yes." Nick leaned back in his chair. "Though such a twist would hardly be consistent with Voltaire's story on which it's based."

"Since Voltaire is dead, one can hardly worry about his disapproval with taking liberties." Julia grinned, unable to contain her enjoyment at the exchange.

"Well, taking liberties is something Colton is certainly familiar with," said the current British ambassador to Austria, Lord Lanceford, from across the table. The whole party laughed.

"Indeed. After all, how else would one earn a nickname like the Depraved Duke?" Julia wondered aloud.

"I've never taken liberties," Nick murmured only for her. "They've always been offered freely."

"I believe it," she replied. "I cannot see you ravishing innocent maidens."

"Innocent maidens bore me to tears. I much prefer

to ravish saucy, red-headed women with blue eyes as clear as the Mediterranean."

"How . . . precise your tastes are, Your Grace."

"I know what I want, Mrs. Leighton. And I want *you*. Naked. Shuddering beneath me, screaming my name."

Julia tried not to blush, but between her fair skin and his naughty words, heat crept slowly up her neck. She sipped her coffee and prayed her husband would not notice.

"My dear Mrs. Leighton," Lanceford began. "How charming to see a woman of your experience can still blush."

"Oh, I fear it's nothing but a combination of the hot coffee and the warm air," she lied. "I'll recover in a few moments."

She risked a glance at Colton and found him studying her carefully, the edges of his lips turned up into the barest hint of a smile. Embarrassed, her eyes slid away and she attempted to distract herself by listening to the other guests.

Conversation turned to politics and Julia's attention wandered. In an effort to think about anything other than Nick, she imagined the third bedchamber in her small house in Mayfair. It would make a splendid nursery for her son. How should she decorate it? Perhaps she'd have the walls painted with tales of knights and maidens—

Julia felt her skirts suddenly shift. A large foot made its way underneath the fabric to rub against her leg. Swallowing a squeak, Julia tried to move away but the foot followed. She immediately suspected Nick, but a quick glance down revealed his legs were not moving. When she looked up, Lanceford caught her eye and gave her a slippery smile.

Julia narrowed her gaze to let him know exactly what she thought of his advances. Instead of retreating, however, Lanceford daringly moved his foot even higher up her calf. So Julia did the first thing that came to mind: She kicked his stationary leg as hard as she could.

"Ooph!" Lanceford grunted and jerked his feet back to his side of the table.

Everyone stopped. "Apologies," the ambassador muttered. "Old injury acting up."

Nick's face darkened, his attention now riveted on Lanceford. Figured her husband would know what Lanceford had been up to. He'd probably played the same flirtatious game himself many times over, the cad. Though right now, Nick looked so angry, there was no telling what he might do. Julia put a hand on his arm and gave him a small shake of her head to let him know she'd handled Lanceford.

"Mrs. Leighton," Veronica began in a thick Venetian accent, "have you made the friendship with Sarah Siddons? I hear many stories of her talent on the stage."

Julia coughed to cover a gasp. If she, a duchess, associated with an actress—even the famously talented Mrs. Siddons—a horrific scandal would result. But she reminded herself that Juliet Leighton was not a duchess. She sipped her coffee and decided to answer diplomatically. "While we are not friends, I have seen her perform many times. She is truly talented."

"I hear she's retired," another woman at the table commented.

"Yes, that's true, though she's retired many times," Julia answered, and pushed the dratted wayward lock of hair out of her eye once more. "I attended her last farewell performance, and even from the seat in my box I could see not a dry eye in the house."

"Have you a box at Covent Garden?" Nick asked.

Yes, yours, she wanted to reply. "Indeed, Your Grace. How else is one to see and be seen in London?"

"Mrs. Leighton is quite the actress in her own right. I daresay I've hardly seen better," Simon drawled. Even from down the table, she could see the devilish intent in her friend's blue eyes.

"Is this true?" Veronica leaned forward. "You must tell me what parts you play."

Julia was momentarily surprised, and before she could make light of Simon's words, he answered for her. "I particularly enjoyed you in Molière's *School for Wives*."

She nearly dropped her china cup. Of course Simon would take the opportunity to poke at her lessons with Pearl. If he were closer, she would have kicked him, too. "Really? How sweet of you, my lord. Although I much preferred my role in his later play, *The Learned Ladies*."

Simon let out a sharp burst of laughter. Everyone else in the group appeared puzzled, so Julia smoothed over it nicely by turning back to Veronica. "And what parts have you enjoyed, Miss DiSano?"

Veronica began a long-winded explanation of her short acting career, and Julia used the opportunity to shoot a glare in Simon's direction and discreetly tip her chin toward the door. She'd had enough tonight. Between her bedraggled coiffure, Simon's barbs, Lanceford's foot, and Nick's powerful presence, her energies were drained. Simon gave her a slight nod in return, and they both stood.

The rest of the men came to their feet as well, and she told the group, "I have enjoyed your company, and yet I fear I am too exhausted to continue. Pray proceed with your revelry, and Lord Winchester shall see me home."

Nick watched the pair leave the coffeehouse. He'd never envied Winchester more. Damn, but Mrs. Leighton was captivating. Smart, beautiful, witty . . . What more did a man need in a woman?

After she left, the evening lost its allure. Even when Veronica sat next to him and whispered some spectacularly lurid suggestions in his ear, his mind remained focused on Juliet. "Not tonight, *cara*," he murmured to Veronica.

Not long after, Nick left as well. Fitz appeared by his side almost immediately.

"Early for you to be goin' home," his friend remarked as they set off.

"A bit." It was not yet one o'clock, and he usually didn't arrive home before three. "The night turned dull."

"When your lady left, you mean."

"Yes, though she's not my lady. Yet."

The streets of Venice were lively tonight. Soldiers, finely dressed women, prostitutes, and gentlemen all strolled along in the cool, misty evening. Fitz pointed down a side street. "Boat's down here, Your Grace."

"If I doubled your wages, could I get you to stop calling me that?"

Fitz chuckled. "No."

"Damned nuisance," Nick muttered, unsure whether he meant his title or Fitz. Likely both.

Finally, they reached the boat and both hopped aboard with ease. They were silent for a few minutes as the gondola pushed away from the landing. The gondolier navigated the tight waterway and maneuvered around the other crafts in the dark Venetian night. Nick stared into the shimmery black water and wondered how best to pursue Mrs. Leighton. He enjoyed the hunt. And he'd wooed countless women over the years so it should be easy. But it was clear Mrs. Leighton wasn't like other women.

"The lady favors you," Fitz put in.

Nick glanced over. "Why would you say so?"

He shrugged a massive shoulder. "Could see it in her eyes. I watched through the window. She studied you when you weren't payin' attention."

That was an interesting piece of news. "I must tread carefully. As you know, she came to Venice with Winchester."

"I saw them together. They're not lovers, at least not anymore."

Nick's eyebrows rose. "How can you be sure?" If this piece of information were true, he wouldn't hesitate in his efforts to seduce her.

"She kept herself apart from him, barely holdin' on to his arm. No smiles or whispers as they walked together. Friendly eyes, but not the kind of eyes she'd been givin' you."

Nick would find out for himself, but Fitz was usually right about such things.

Mrs. Leighton did not stand a chance.

Chapter Three

Never do what he expects. To surprise him is to keep him interested.

—Miss Pearl Kelly to the Duchess of Colton

The next morning, Julia and Aunt Theo were already in the breakfast room when Simon came down.

He winked at Julia, then whistled as he went to the sideboard to fill his plate with eggs and a slice of the delicious almond cake their cook made daily. Before he sat, he dismissed the servant hovering nearby.

"You are obnoxiously cheerful this morning, Simon," Julia commented when the three of them were alone. "Does this have anything to do with the lovely Veronica? I noticed you went back out last night after seeing me home."

"As a gentleman, it would be unseemly for me to discuss such a matter in the presence of ladies," Simon said evasively while he poured a cup of coffee. "But I must remember to thank Colton for making the introduction. Venetian women are everything he said—and more."

Julia's eyes narrowed and she drummed her fingers on the table. One could only imagine what Nick had to say about Venetian women, being as he'd probably fornicated with every willing woman in the vicinity. Twice.

She told herself she didn't care. There was one thing she needed from her husband, and once she got it he could go back to his life of trollops and debauchery.

"Nice of him to arrange the seating to put the two of you together," Simon said.

"Together?" Theo asked.

"At the theater as well as at the coffeehouse afterward," Julia explained. "My plan is progressing nicely."

"Excellent!" Theo clapped her hands.

Their footman, Sergio, knocked on the door, entered, and then handed Julia a card. "Signora Leighton. Flowers have been delivered for you."

"Flowers, again! Your duke is smitten," Theo declared. "Pray tell us what he wrote on the card."

Julia glanced at the note and groaned. "Thank you, Sergio. I will collect them presently." The footman left, and Julia tossed the card aside. "The flowers are from the ambassador, Lord Lanceford."

Simon chuckled. "Ah, Mrs. Leighton has another admirer."

"Stop laughing, you clod pole. This is not funny. The man tried to shove his foot up my skirts—well, Mrs. Leighton's skirts—last night at the coffeehouse."

Theo gasped. "I hope you kicked him."

Julia nodded. "I did. Hard. Colton nearly leapt across the table to strangle him."

"I suspected as much when Lanceford suddenly

howled in pain," Simon said. "But before you throw those flowers into the canal, they might be useful in making a certain someone feel jealous."

Julia sat back in her chair and sipped her tea. Was Simon right? Would Nick be jealous? "That's quite devious. Good idea. I shall display Lanceford's flowers in the front entry."

"Well, I am quite anxious to see what Colton sends today," Theo said as she buttered a piece of almond cake. "The flowers and vase yesterday were stunning, but I suspect he'll send jewelry. Rubies, perhaps?"

"Emeralds," Simon guessed.

Julia rolled her eyes. "How do either of you know he will send anything at all?"

"After seeing the two of you last night, I daresay there's naught you could demand right now that he would not agree to. So if you want a bauble to remember Colt by in those long, cold London nights"—he shrugged—"Mrs. Leighton need only drop a well-placed hint or two."

The idea had merit. Heavens, if she failed to get with child a diamond necklace could keep her and Aunt Theo supported in a modest style for quite a while. But what then? Pawning jewelry would only get her so far. No, she needed a more permanent guarantee for her future. A son would mean financial freedom and the end of Templeton's meddling.

Not to mention a part of her had already warmed to the idea of having a baby. A tiny life brought into the world in order to hold and love. There would be picnics and stories and games. . . . And since Colton would likely never act as a true father, Julia planned on loving their child so much that his absence wouldn't matter.

Later that afternoon, Julia and her aunt were reading by the fire in the second-floor sitting room. It was a cheerful space, with large windows overlooking a quiet canal. With the panes open, one could hear the bells chime from the nearby *Campanile di San Marco*.

Sergio knocked and entered. "Signora Leighton, a visitor for you."

He handed her a card. Julia assumed it would be Nick, so she was surprised upon reading the name.

"Show him up, Sergio, *per favore*." When the footman left, Julia turned to Theo. "Signore Marcellino, of Marcellino and Sons Jewelry."

Theo's eyes widened. "I knew it would be jewelry. And Marcellino's! Why, you'll be the envy of every woman in London."

"Shhh," Julia hissed. "He shall arrive at any moment."

A short, older man with gray hair was shown in. Impeccably dressed, he carried a black case, which he set on the floor to bow over Julia's hand. "Signora Leighton. A pleasure to meet you. I trust I am not interrupting, no?"

"No, signore. My aunt and I are merely spending a quiet afternoon with our books. Shall I ring for tea?"

Julia turned to call for Sergio, but Marcellino stopped her. "If you please, signora, I would like to get directly to the business at hand." He picked up his case and set it on the table, then gestured for her to take a seat on the sofa. Marcellino opened the case to reveal so many glittering stones, it almost hurt her eyes to take them all in. Julia could scarcely breathe. There were diamonds, rubies, and finely carved cameos set in gold, all fashioned into blinding necklaces, bracelets, and ear bobs.

"Signore!" she exclaimed, a hand on her heart. "What magnificence you bring."

Marcellino puffed up with pride. "I am here on behalf of His Grace, the Duke of Colton. His Grace has picked out three sets of exquisite jewelry and asked me to bring them to you so that you may have your choice. I believe he feared making a . . . misstep, as you English say."

Her aunt dropped onto the sofa and elbowed Julia to move over. "My heavens," she exclaimed, and gripped Julia's hand. "How will you ever choose? They're all splendid."

"If I may," Marcellino began. He pulled a small looking glass out of the back of his case. "Signora may try them all on and decide which she favors."

"Oh, no." Theo shook her head. "You'll need a much bigger looking glass. I'll have Sergio fetch one." Getting up, she hurried over to the bell pull.

Dazzled by the jewelry displayed in front of her, Julia could only stare. Nick was no fool to offer her choices. It was a flattering and extravagant gesture. *Yes, a gesture to a courtesan,* the wife in her reminded. But the woman in her was awed all the same.

"The diamonds first, I think," Theo put in, now back on the couch.

Julia nodded at Signore Marcellino. "Yes, let's start with the diamonds."

The jeweler smiled. He picked up a necklace dripping with diamonds. There was one large yellow teardrop stone in the middle, with smaller white stones flanking it on each side. "This necklace contains over thirty diamonds," he said as he fastened it behind her neck. "The middle stone is a yellow diamond, which is quite rare."

The weight of the piece felt sinfully outrageous, with the largest diamond settling just above her décolletage. Julia quickly slipped on the bracelet and matching ear bobs in order to see the results. Standing up, she crossed to where Sergio had placed the large looking glass brought down from her chamber.

Her breath caught at her reflection. She'd never worn something so outrageous. Even the jewelry she'd borrowed from Pearl could not rival this set. She turned slightly and studied the stones. Who was this woman, adorned in such a ridiculously luxuriant fashion? It was too much. She couldn't possibly accept these. A token of esteem was one thing, but to accept such a lavish gift made her feel tawdry.

Still, they were beautiful. She touched the stones reverently and sighed because her conscience was so loud today. "No, I am sorry, signore. These are not for me." She crossed back to the couch, where Theo's jaw had dropped open.

"Not for you? My dear, those would be suitable for a dead woman. The only requirement being the possession of a neck and two ears."

"No, Aunt Theo. The pieces are more beautiful than words can say, but they're not for me." She smiled at Marcellino. "Perhaps now the rubies?"

Almost as ostentatious as the diamonds, the ruby necklace had several large bloodred stones, surrounded by tiny diamonds that draped delicately around her neck. But the image of herself in the mirror while wearing the set gave her the same distasteful feeling in her belly. She could not accept them.

"They are beautiful, Signore Marcellino. But I fear

the rubies are not for me either." Julia didn't bother to look at Theo since a palpable shock now permeated the room.

Once the rubies had been returned to the case, Julia studied the lovely cameo pieces. "Shall we try on the last set?"

Marcellino removed the necklace so she could see the detail in the cameo. White onyx had been delicately carved to represent the head of a Roman woman. On top, a tiny flowery garland, fashioned from black onyx, was woven into her hair. The piece was set in a small diamond frame and hung from a thin gold chain. Marcellino said a very talented man named Pistrucci, who worked in Rome, had crafted the piece. "One of a kind," Marcellino said, as Pistrucci never carved the same design twice.

Once she had on both the necklace and matching earrings, Julia knew before glancing in the mirror that she wanted them. These were neither the most expensive nor the most ostentatious of the group, but they suited her. Simple, classic, and unique. And yet . . . what did it mean if she accepted them?

She touched the cameo longingly. If only the gift could be merely from a husband to his wife. Before she could change her mind, she stood and handed the necklace back. "I thank you for your time and patience this afternoon. Any woman would be honored to accept one of these fine pieces, Signore Marcellino, but I must decline His Grace's gracious offer."

Theo gasped but Julia ignored her. Marcellino's brows lifted and a fine sheen of sweat broke out on his brow. "Signora, are you sure? His Grace was quite insistent—"

Julia took pity on him. "I understand, signore, and I apologize for any unpleasantness this may cause with your customer. But I fear I must insist as well."

He bowed. "Of course, signora." He then packed up his case and retreated.

Aunt Theo shot up out of her seat with a hand on her chest as if in acute pain. "Heavens, I need a sherry." After she poured a drink at the sideboard, she shook her head. "Pearl would be quite disappointed in you."

Julia sighed. "I know. Except I have to live with myself once the choice is made."

"That is what matters, then." Theo sipped her drink and reclaimed her seat. "How will you explain your refusal to Colton? Because no Cyprian in her right mind would turn down jewelry."

She wrinkled her nose. "I'm not sure what I'll tell him. It didn't feel right to accept them. I know it's hard to understand but . . . I wouldn't be able to wear them with pride. And Colton will merely have to accept that. Honestly, he should thank me as I have just saved him a large amount of money."

"Men and their pride," her aunt warned.

"Well, I have my pride, too. Colton will learn that soon enough."

An hour later, a knock sounded just as Theo and Julia had poured tea. Sergio entered and presented Julia with a card. "A caller, signora."

Julia's stomach leapt. Could it be Colton? She glanced at the card and then frowned. "Show him up, Sergio, *per favore*."

The servant nodded and Julia turned to her aunt.

"It's Lanceford. And if you dare leave me alone with him, I will pour every drop of spirits in the palazzo out into the canal," she whispered.

Theo's eyes widened, horrified at the threat. She shifted deeper into her chair, and the two women waited silently until Lanceford appeared in the doorway. Julia stood up and gave him a proper curtsy. "My lord ambassador, what a surprise. Won't you join us for tea?"

Lanceford, a heavyset man with a whisper of brown hair combed over his balding crown, glanced anxiously at Theo. Obviously, the ambassador had hoped to catch Julia alone. "Good day, Mrs. Leighton. Thank you, I would love some tea." Julia introduced him to Theo, and Lanceford then took the chair opposite Julia's perch on the sofa.

She poured him a cup, and added milk and sugar at his request. When they were settled, he said, "I saw my violets displayed in your entryway. I am flattered you gave them such prominence."

Julia swallowed a snort. "They are beautiful and quite a thoughtful gesture. Did you enjoy the performance last evening?"

He nodded. "Indeed. Although never could I have put my thoughts into words as eloquent as yours, Mrs. Leighton. Truly, the statement has spread like fire through Venice today." Lanceford cast Theo another furtive look and cleared his throat. "Mrs. Leighton, I should like to discuss the possibility of spending time . . . alone . . . with you."

She should have been prepared for such boldness but was horribly caught off guard. Her mind raced on how best to proceed. "My lord ambassador, while the idea is flattering—"

Sergio flew through the door, interrupting their conversation. "Signora, the Duke of—"

Colton pushed past the footman, his handsome face tight and grim. With his windblown black hair and disheveled clothing, Nick looked as if he'd run the length of Venice to get to her. He drew to a sudden halt upon finding Lanceford comfortably reclined in a chair, and his eyes narrowed.

Her footman stood frozen, wringing his hands near the door, not quite sure what to do about the duke who hadn't waited to be announced. Julia took pity on him. She stood and said, "*Grazie,* Sergio. You may go."

Julia was surprised when Aunt Theo also rose from her chair. "I believe I will excuse myself as well," her aunt said, a secret smile on her cherubic face as she hurried to the door.

Nick approached, and Julia curtsied gracefully. "Your Grace. How wonderful of you to join us this afternoon."

Nick attempted a smile, though it never reached his eyes. "Mrs. Leighton." He bowed over her hand, and then turned to the ambassador. "Lanceford." The duke accepted Theo's chair and everyone sat.

"Would you care for tea, Your Grace?" He nodded and, once she had served him, an awkward silence fell. Julia wasn't quite sure what to say. Nick appeared as if he might beat Lanceford bloody at any moment, and Lanceford shifted uncomfortably under the duke's violent gaze.

"Have you been in Venice long, Lord Lanceford?" she asked, not interested in the answer but desperate to say *something*.

"Three months. I shall only stay another six weeks before I must return to Austria."

"With so little time left in Venice, then, we wouldn't want to keep you from all the important duties you surely must attend to." Nick sipped his tea and stared blithely at Lanceford.

"Yes, well," Lanceford mumbled, and set his cup on the table. "I should be going." He stood and bowed. "Mrs. Leighton, my day is indeed brighter for having seen you."

Julia ignored the snort from Nick's direction and instead rang for Sergio. "Thank you for the flowers, sir."

He opened his mouth to say more but caught Nick's menacing expression and promptly snapped his jaw shut. Sergio arrived to show Lanceford out, the door closing behind them.

It didn't take long for Nick to begin his tirade. "What madness," he began while she resumed her seat, "caused you to turn down a king's ransom in jewels? I gave you choices, by God. I sent the best pieces available in Venice. Pray tell me how I offended your delicate sensibilities with such a generous token of my esteem."

Julia sighed inwardly. How could she explain it to him? To turn down such a gift would be lunacy for any woman, much less one who traded in pleasure and avarice. "The jewels were exquisite, Colton—"

"Nick," he corrected.

"Very well, Nick. Your choices did not offend me and neither did the gesture. But we hardly know one another, and such generosity would certainly change the delicate balance of our relationship."

He blinked. "I heard every word, and yet I cannot

make sense of it. In case you are unaware, changing the delicate balance of our relationship is precisely what I am about." He huffed out a breath and crossed his arms over his chest, like a sullen little boy who had not gotten his way. "I swear, you confound me at every turn. One minute you beckon, the next you rebuff. You're worse than a fortune-hunting virgin."

He clearly meant it as a joke, so she forced out a laugh—though his observation stung. It wasn't *that* far off. "Nick, you're babbling." Julia poured herself more tea. "I'm certainly no virgin and I'm not after your fortune. You need not impress me with lavish gifts. My tastes are . . . simple."

"I've yet to meet a woman without expensive tastes."

Leaning forward to slowly refill his cup, she presented him with a long look at the tops of her breasts, which were near to spilling over of the edge of her gown. When she returned the pot to the tray, she was satisfied to see his eyes had darkened. "Perhaps you have met your match, Your Grace." Picking up her cup, she settled back against the sofa.

He gave her a sultry half smile that had her breath catching in her throat. "Perhaps I have, Mrs. Leighton." Nick relaxed as well and stretched his long legs in front of him, booted feet crossed at the ankles. "I was surprised to find you entertaining Lanceford. Is he to be another one of your friends, then?"

She barely suppressed a shudder. "No. Lord Lanceford is a fine man, but not for me."

"Are you expecting any other visitors this afternoon?"

Her brows lowered in confusion and she replaced her cup in its saucer. "No. Why?"

"Because I am thinking about locking the door,

coming over to the sofa, and kissing you senseless. In truth, I've thought of little else since I walked in this room."

She watched, mesmerized, as he carefully set his cup on the table. With an easy grace, he lifted out of his chair and shifted to the sofa, his big, lean body pressing close. He raised a hand to brush his knuckles across her cheek in a whisper-soft caress before wrapping a red curl around his finger.

The simple contact sent a shiver down her spine. Her breathing turned ragged and shallow, and she worried Nick would sense her nervousness. Only the nerves couldn't be helped. The two of them were alone in a confined space, the heat of his body rolling over her to make her light-headed. And while she portrayed a woman of experience, in truth she was a maiden.

A fact Nick must not suspect.

She needed to remain in control, to maintain her ruse . . . and flirt with him a bit more. She moistened her bottom lip, sliding the tip of her tongue from one end to the other. "I must warn you. I'm awfully hard to win."

His gaze stayed trained on her mouth for a long moment. "I prefer a challenge. And since you're financially secure, I plan to entice you in . . . other ways."

He dragged a fingertip slowly down her bare arm, her skin prickling along his finger's path. When he reached her hand, he lifted and turned it, then bent to press warm lips to her palm. He continued by fluttering soft kisses over the heel of her hand, in no hurry whatsoever. Julia's heart pounded in her chest, her insides turning liquid.

Was this how he planned to entice her? If so, he was definitely succeeding. She swallowed and tried to remain focused. "Planning to give me a few lessons in depravity, are you?"

"I must prove myself worthy of my nickname," he murmured, his eyes locking with hers as his lips glided over the sensitive skin of her inner wrist.

He pulled away but kept hold of her hand, locking their fingers together. "I find myself curious about you, Juliet. I've never seen Winchester so bewitched by a woman, at least not before I left London. And the stories circulating about you are wildly fantastic, almost as if they're fabricated. Then I meet you, and there's an air of innocence about you that is incredibly alluring."

Julia's eyes widened, but before she could respond, he continued. "I feel a . . . pull toward you that I've never experienced before with a woman. I'm intrigued."

Heavens, her husband could be charming. She fought to keep the mood light, despite the fact that her tongue felt thick with desire. "Intrigued? And here I had hoped for interested. Or better yet, infatuated."

"Oh, I am all of those things as well." He brushed his knuckles against her cheek in a tender gesture. "Our friendship won't cause you any unpleasantness with Winchester, will it?"

"No one owns me. I have the luxury of being able to control my own destiny. Lord Winchester and I do not begrudge each other from having many . . . friends."

"He's more understanding than I, then." Nick bent

forward, his mouth perilously close to hers. "Because I find I want you all to myself."

He shifted to place his lips on hers, softly, sweetly, as if testing her. When she relaxed and began kissing him back, he smiled against her mouth. His hands slid into her hair, holding her in place as he deepened the kiss. Though her insides were quivering— gads, her first real kiss!—she needed to be bold in order to convince Nick she was an experienced courtesan. If she were hesitant or shy, her plan would fail.

She brought her hands up to his shoulders and pressed closer, her breasts crushed against him. She parted her lips slightly and he took immediate advantage, wrapping his arms about her and sliding his tongue sinuously into her mouth.

It was glorious. Wild yet skillfully controlled, the kiss was more than she ever imagined. Her breasts swelled, the nipples now hardened points inside her clothing, tingling as they brushed the hard wall of his chest. Their breath mingled while tongues continued to duel, and the taste of him, tea and spice, threatened to overwhelm her. It was all so much, but somehow not enough. Before she could prevent it, Julia moaned into his mouth.

"My God. You taste better than I even imagined," he murmured and his mouth descended once more, lips claiming hers in a show of brutal possessiveness and raw need. His tongue swept inside, rubbing and stroking, teasing her. Their breath came fast and harsh in the quiet of the room as the kiss went on and on.

Pearl had explained what happened between a man and a woman in explicit detail. There was a vast difference between knowledge and experience, however. Julia hadn't realized how her pulse would pound with blinding intensity. How the area between her legs would throb and ache with a desperation unlike anything she'd ever felt. Her body moved against him restlessly, searching for more, hoping to ease the exquisite craving.

Nick palmed her swollen breast, cupping and plumping, pushing up to expose even more flesh from her low neckline. Her nipples painfully taut, she offered up no protest when he tugged her clothing down. Then his mouth was there, tongue rasping the hard bud before drawing on it with his lips. The sharp sensation traveled the length of her body, and she gasped. This caused him to suckle harder, and her nails dug into his shoulders as she clung to him.

He released her breast, raised his gaze. "If we do not stop, I'll take you right here, on this blasted couch."

Chest heaving and eyes blazing with desire, Nick looked as wild as she felt. And while she wanted him wild, this was neither the time nor the place. "An occurrence guaranteed to shock whoever chances to walk through the door." She forced herself to pull away and, with trembling hands, righted her clothing.

His head dropped back against the sofa. "Let me entertain you this evening. I need to see you."

The door flew open, and Simon appeared. "Colton! I'd heard you were here." Smiling congenially, Simon came over to kiss Julia's hand. "My dear," he said with a tender look before dropping down into an empty chair. If he knew what he'd nearly interrupted, he gave no sign.

Nick gave a terse nod. "Winchester."

Simon studied her, his face creased with concern. "Have you had a busy afternoon of callers, my dear? You look tired. I wouldn't want you too fatigued for our dinner party tonight."

"Dinner party?" Nick asked.

"Yes. Here, tonight. Did Juliet not invite you?"

Julia struggled to contain her shock. No dinner party had been planned for that evening, a fact Simon was well aware of. What was he up to?

Everyone looked at her expectantly. "Yes, Your Grace," she managed. "We would be so honored if you would join us as well."

Chapter Four

Every man believes himself irresistible. Overwhelm him with enthusiasm and he'll believe you the most competent of lovers.

—Miss Pearl Kelly to the Duchess of Colton

"Dinner party, Simon?" Julia asked as soon as the two of them were alone. "What mad scheme are you spinning?"

"Your aunt told me about your afternoon. After I recovered from the shock of your turning down jewelry, I thought we should stage our falling-out and put Colton out of his misery." He rubbed his chin thoughtfully. "Though I must say, I do like to see Colt miserable."

"How am I to plan a dinner party in"—she glanced at the clock—"three hours?"

He waved his hand. "The work's done, Jules. I invited a few guests and Theo's talked with the staff. All you need to do is continue your part as the beautiful and charming Mrs. Leighton."

"I could kill you sometimes," she grumbled. "Springing it on me like that in front of Colton."

"Keep the anger. You may yell at me later tonight in front of all our guests." He smiled and stood, turning to go.

"Wait, Simon. I need to ask you something. Where would Nick secure the funds to offer Mrs. Leighton the expensive jewels I saw today? I wouldn't have thought he'd stay in contact with the bankers for the Colton estate."

"He hasn't. Colt wants nothing from his family. Hasn't taken money from the estate since he left England. Didn't you notice his pile of winnings the other night at the card party? Colton supports himself at the tables. Does quite well, too."

"That makes sense, based on what I know of the estate finances," she said, shifting to stare out the window. A gambler as well as a reprobate. Indeed, her good fortune abounded when it came to her husband.

Simon cocked his head. "Wait, what did that mean? What is wrong with the Colton finances?"

"I'm not sure. All I know is what Templeton tells me, how my stipend has whittled down to almost nothing."

Simon's blue eyes sparked with an unholy light. "That estate is worth almost sixty thousand pounds a year. And he's whittling down *your* stipend?" His hands curled at his sides. "By God, I'll kill him."

Sixty thousand pounds? She had no idea. . . . Still, the money meant nothing if she couldn't get her hands on any of it. "Simon, what can you do? I went to see the dowager duchess, who looked at me as if I were something she'd stepped in while walking behind a horse. I suspect Templeton is paying off the ducal estate manager, but I have no proof. The only person who can do something is Nick, who has repeatedly made it clear he doesn't care what happens to me or the estate."

"I'll kill him," Simon muttered again.

"You cannot kill Templeton. Much as he deserves it."

"Not Templeton, though he will be dealt with. I meant Colton, that selfish bastard."

"Please don't. I'm handling this, Simon."

He dragged a hand down his face. "Why did you not come to me for help? You know I would have given you money."

"I cannot take your money. You know if it were merely a short loan, I would have approached you. But you cannot support Theo and me for the rest of our lives. How would it look?"

"How long has this been going on?"

She shrugged, feigning a nonchalance she didn't feel. "A little more than three years."

Simon stumbled to a chair. "I've just figured it out. This ruse, this scheme of yours. You told me it was about finding Colton, satisfying your curiosity about your husband. But it has nothing to do with that. It's about money. Forcing Templeton's hand. But how?" His brow furrowed. "If you'd hoped to get enough trinkets from Nick to sell, why turn down the jewels?"

"It's not about trinkets." She hadn't wanted to tell him like this but figured it was best to be honest. "I plan to get with child. Nick's child. The only way to gain any power for myself is to produce the Colton heir."

Simon paled and slumped into the chair. "Good God."

Julia hadn't expected this extreme of a reaction. Didn't Simon see it was the only way? "Simon—"

He held up a hand for her to quiet, so she bit off what she'd been about to say. He closed his eyes and rubbed his brow for a long minute. "I won't say anything to sabotage your plans. That's the reason you didn't tell me, correct?"

When Julia didn't answer, he shot to his feet and snarled, "Colton will be lucky if I do not punch him in the jaw before the night is over. And you can be damn sure I'll look into whatever Templeton is doing when we return to England." He sighed and scrubbed his face with both hands. Simon did not anger easily, but he tended to carry a grudge when provoked. Julia had no idea how this information would affect his friendship with Colton.

"Simon, this will work. I know it."

He appeared unconvinced. "I'm sorry you didn't trust me enough to come to me with this, Jules."

Her stomach tightened. Simon had been a good friend to her, and she never wished to hurt him. "I do trust you. But it's more than what you and I can handle alone. Nick has made much of this mess, so he should be forced to clean it up—even unwillingly."

It was the dinner party forged in hell as far as Nick was concerned.

From the moment he arrived, nothing was as it

should be. Winchester was obviously angry with him, his friend's eyes as hard as glass every time they fell on Nick. Yet Nick had no idea why. Moreover, Winchester had snarled at him all night long and, quite honestly, Nick was a bit tired of such hatred being thrown his way for no apparent reason.

The vivacious and charming Mrs. Leighton from the opera had yet to make an appearance. Instead, Juliet was restrained, her jocularity forced, as if sensing the discord between himself and Winchester. She watched them both warily, struggling to keep the conversation light during dinner. More than once, he watched her admonish Winchester with a withering glance after something his friend said.

Veronica was seated at Winchester's side, and the two flirted shamelessly throughout the evening. Nick briefly wondered if the other woman's presence had caused Juliet's strange mood. But he recalled her saying that her relationship with Winchester didn't preclude either of them from having additional partners. So what was going on?

While the other guests were familiar, none would be called friends. The prominent banker, the owner of a large shipping fleet, and the wealthy lawyer in attendance all came from a more respectable class of Venetian society than the degenerates Nick usually associated with. At least the ladies present were more to his liking: a courtesan, an actress, a ballerina, and a widow. Ah, God love the women of shameless pleasure.

Juliet's fork clattered on her plate, surprising the group. "Simon, did you hear me? Really, I am getting a little tired of repeating myself this evening."

Nick watched Winchester drag his eyes up from Veronica's décolletage to give Mrs. Leighton a bored look. "I apologize, my dear. You were saying?"

"Never mind." Juliet turned to Nick, seated on her right. "Your Grace, have you explored much of the area around Venice in your time here?"

"A bit," he murmured, fascinated by the candle-light dancing on the pink hue of her lips. He remembered kissing her this afternoon, and it was all he could do to not reach for her in the middle of dinner.

"I've heard the island of Torcello is quite wonderful," she said, sliding her bottom lip between her teeth and biting gently, as if she knew the direction of his thoughts.

His shaft began to swell, and Nick forced himself to look away from her mouth lest he embarrass himself at the table. "It is. The cathedral contains some stunning mosaics. I would be honored if you would allow me to escort you there at your earliest convenience. Perhaps tomorrow?"

"Perhaps," she answered evasively.

"My dear," Winchester spoke up from down the table. "I promised to take you shopping, if you'll recall."

"That won't be necessary, Simon." Juliet placed her knife and fork on her plate, signaling she was finished.

A little while later, the men rejoined the ladies in the sitting room. From his position on the couch, Nick enjoyed a glass of grappa and watched as Winchester pulled Juliet off to the side, near the window, for a private conversation.

Veronica slid next to him on the couch. "I believe

there is trouble in *paradiso*," she murmured, gesturing to the couple, now engaged in a rather heated, but quiet, exchange.

Winchester appeared to be pleading with Juliet, who only shook her head. Nick saw her lips form the words, *"It's over, Simon,"* and he held his breath. Could it be?

Juliet turned to leave, and Winchester put a hand on her arm to restrain her. Juliet shot him a withering glare harsh enough to shrivel a man's cock. It was a haughty, self-confident glower worthy of a duchess. Nick was impressed and damned glad he wasn't on the receiving end of such a stare. Winchester immediately released her, and Juliet gracefully crossed to the far side of the room, where she struck up a conversation with some other guests.

Winchester hurried to the couch. Ignoring Nick altogether, he held his hand out to Veronica. "Miss DiSano, would you care to come with me? It seems I am no longer needed as host tonight."

Without another word, the two of them left. Baffled, Nick wondered over both Winchester's rudeness and the fact that Juliet was no longer attached to his longtime friend. Despite his assurances to the contrary, perhaps Winchester had resented Nick's wooing of Mrs. Leighton. Had his advances driven Winchester and Juliet apart? Nick would find Winchester tomorrow and straighten it out.

But for now . . . for now he wanted to spend time with the one woman he hadn't been able to stop thinking about for days. A hot, prickly feeling broke out on the back of his neck, and he raised his head to see Juliet striding toward him, her hips gently swaying and a secret smile on her beautiful face. The low cut of her sapphire-colored dress revealed the tops of her ample breasts, the soft flesh bouncing along with her steps. Lust raced through his belly straight to his shaft. Bloody hell, she was captivating, and he couldn't wait to have her.

He stood. "It appears you have lost your host this evening."

She sighed, looking none too distraught over the idea. "Poor Simon. It is hard for some men to accept the inevitable, wouldn't you say, Your Grace?"

Nick leaned down near her ear. She smelled delicious, like gardenias and sunshine. "I could say the same about some women, Mrs. Leighton."

He heard the catch in her breath and immense satisfaction roared through him. It wouldn't be long until her legs would be wrapped around his hips as he drove inside her sweet warmth. He led her farther away from the group where they couldn't be overheard. Near the window, he shielded her from the rest of the guests. "Shall we end the game between us tonight? See what pleasure can be found together? What can I offer to entice you? Not jewels, obviously. Is it money, then? Or perhaps a fucking the likes of which you've never experienced?"

A flush crept up her neck, her delicate skin turning a pretty pink.

"Ah, could that be it? How I love to see you blush, Juliet. I wonder if your nipples are the same shade. How will they taste when I pull them in my mouth and roll them on my tongue?" The pulse at the base of her neck beat hard and fast, clear evidence of her desire. He couldn't stop tormenting them both. "Would you like to feel how hard I am, merely from standing so close to you? Hear how my cock aches at the idea of sinking into your slick, tight passage?"

Her eyes glazed over and a breathy moan escaped her lips, and Nick smiled. "Come with me, back to my palazzo, *tesorina*. Let us burn together."

She gave a short nod and then cleared her throat. "As soon as the guests leave." Before he could say anything else, she stepped around him and rejoined her party.

Unbelievably, his cock grew even stiffer. He would need to stay here, facing the window, until he could safely turn around again.

As her gondola approached the duke's palazzo, Julia found herself a bit rattled. This evening, she would seduce her husband while posing as someone else. What if he discovered her lie? If so, her plan would fail, her future would become perilous at best, and Nick would likely toss her headfirst into the nearest canal. An image of Templeton came to mind, and she took a deep breath. Julia would never, ever become that man's mistress. She'd rather starve.

There was little choice but to carry out her scheme.

A scheme more than five months in the making, during which she'd researched, planned, and listened. She'd thought of an answer for nearly every concern Aunt Theo had lodged at her.

Theo's first concern had been conception, because Nick might bring the subject up. Since Pearl said many courtesans could not bear children, the result of terminating too many unwanted pregnancies, Julia planned to tell Nick as much and hoped he wouldn't question it. However, in case he didn't believe her, or worried about disease, Julia's reticule contained a few prepared French letters, each sheath carefully pricked at the end to create a small hole for his seed to pass through.

Theo then brought up the issue of her maidenhead. How would Julia explain away the blood? Pearl believed there was a good chance, due to Julia's age, that her maidenhead had already torn—but Julia couldn't know for sure. Pearl suggested Julia use a wooden phallus on herself beforehand to ensure of its removal, but Julia hadn't the nerve.

As her boat pulled up to the dock of Nick's palazzo, she sent up a silent prayer that, if she did bleed, Nick wouldn't notice it. Too bad they couldn't make love in the canal, where the blood would wash away.

At least desire would not be an issue. There was little doubt Julia wanted him. The way he kissed her . . . the smell of him . . . even the way he walked across a room made her forget all the reasons she should hate him. Her husband was alluring, and he made her yearn for things she knew she'd never have.

And what he'd said earlier in the evening . . . Lord above, it had been all she could do not to melt into a puddle on the ground.

Stepping onto the dock, she saw a large man emerge from the shadows. "Evenin', Mrs. Leighton. I'm Fitzpatrick, His Grace's valet. The duke, he asked me t' bring you inside."

His . . . valet? Julia swallowed her shock and said, "It's nice to meet you, Mr. Fitzpatrick. Pray lead on."

"Just Fitz," he said before turning around.

As they walked toward the palazzo, she studied Colton's valet. Large and bulky, Fitz was definitely a man one would want to avoid in a back alley. Had that been a scar running down the length of his face? Her nerves, already on edge, were not calmed by Fitz's presence. Why would the duke require such a large and forbidding manservant?

Julia shook herself. A true Cyprian would be preparing to charm the duke, while silently counting the strands of pearls she planned to buy with his money—not musing about his valet. Mrs. Leighton needed to be dazzling, flirtatious, and witty. *Focus,* she admonished silently.

Fitz opened the door and stepped aside to allow her into the palazzo. She crossed the threshold and saw Nick coming down the stairs. Julia was nearly struck dumb by his handsomeness. His ebony hair was wet and slicked back from his face, emphasizing the sleek lines of his cheekbones. He wore no waistcoat, cravat, or coat; instead, a fine white linen shirt covered his lean torso, a small patch of black chest hair peeking out at the top. His trousers and evening shoes were black, making him look impossibly tall and powerful.

And the triumphant, intimate smile he gave her was full of wicked promise. Julia shivered as she handed her pelisse to Fitz.

"My dear Mrs. Leighton," Nick said, reaching the last step. He leaned in to kiss her cheek. "Your radiance steals the very breath from my lungs," he murmured, his voice husky and deep in her ear. He took her hand. "Come with me."

Nick tucked her close to his side as they went up the stairs. Her knees wobbled slightly, and it was all Julia could do not to turn around and run for the door. But she'd come too far, had too much to lose, to back out now.

They climbed another set of stairs in silence, finally reaching the top floor where Nick threw open a door to reveal his bedchamber. *I can do this. And he will not find me out.* She repeated it to herself again and again for courage as she strode inside.

Across from a small table and two chairs sat his enormous bed. Very enormous bed. Her feet stumbled a bit and he caught her elbow, steadying her.

"I thought you might like to have a drink first," he said. "Do you care for almonds? They make a flavored liqueur not far from here that is quite delicious."

Julia nodded and took a seat. Nick poured a small glass of light brown liquid for each of them and then handed one to her. He sat opposite, his gaze never wavering from her face as he settled in the chair, his long legs now stretched out in front of him. "Well?"

She took a sip, surprised at the sweet flavor. "It's nice," she said, tipping the glass for another swallow.

Though his posture was relaxed, she could sense Nick's anticipation in the clenching of his jaw, the straight set of his shoulders. He was a big jungle cat, patiently waiting to pounce on her. The thought was both terrifying and thrilling.

Half-lidded, dark gray eyes studied her face. "Are you nervous?"

Julia shook her head, though her heart was racing. "No," she lied. "Merely curious." She drained the rest of her glass, and warmth spread through her bones. The nerves began to dissipate, and the soft glow of the spirits gave her courage.

"Well, then, we must see to satisfying your curiosity." He held out his hand. She stood up and moved to stand in front of his chair, where she removed the glass from his hands and set it on the table.

Before she could do anything else, he clasped her waist and tugged her down to sit across his lap. He wrapped one arm tightly around her middle, securing her in place, while his free hand slid up to bury in her hair. Their faces were close, so close she could feel his breath, now coming every bit as ragged as hers. His erection lay beneath her, hard and urgent despite the layers of clothes between them. The proof of his desire thrilled her. Encouraged her. She stared at him boldly, her skin tingling, and waited.

His smoky gaze flicked to her lips. Unconsciously, the tip of her tongue emerged to moisten them and his grip tightened. "Witch," he murmured, and leaned down to cover her mouth with his own. The instant his lips claimed hers, the desire simmering between them exploded into something wild. Then he deepened the kiss, turning her head slightly to adjust the angle, allowing his tongue to slip inside, and the room spun. She dug her nails into Nick's shoulders in an attempt to brace herself in the onslaught of sensation.

He coaxed and stroked, his hot, wet tongue like velvet against hers, and she couldn't focus on anything but his kiss. Nothing existed but this wickedly charming man and what he was doing with his mouth. She rubbed her breasts, now swollen with need, against the hard planes of his chest in a desperate attempt to ease the ache inside her.

Nick's hand glided over her knee, under her dress, along her stockings, until he reached her bare thigh. His fingers played there, on her naked skin, dancing and teasing, while his mouth kept up the assault on her senses. Her sex burned, and she knew he would find her hot and slick if he reached a bit higher. Her own tentative explorations of her body hadn't felt anything like *this*. No, this was so much more, more than she'd ever thought possible—and still, it wasn't enough.

Her hips tilted toward his exploring fingers, searching, begging for him. Nick moved his lips to her throat, nipping and kissing the sensitive skin. "I had thought to make you beg," he whispered by her ear as his hand crept north, "but God's truth, I'll be on my knees in another few minutes, promising anything if you'll just allow me to touch you."

"Touch me, please," she said, clutching him tighter.

He reached the apex of her thighs, his fingers sliding through the wet folds to find the heat of her, and she gasped. His touch was gentle, placed exactly where she craved it most.

"So wet for me," he murmured. "Say my name. Say who has made you so warm and wet, Juliet." The tip of his finger circled the tiny sensitive nub, stroking it and sending her arousal soaring. Clothing around her waist, Julia's stocking-clad legs were splayed open on his lap, offering no resistance. She'd ceased caring how wanton she looked. "Say it, my dear," he ordered.

"Nick," she sighed, then inhaled sharply as he slid one finger into her entrance. He kissed her then, hard and deep, his tongue finding hers. Julia could hardly think, hardly breathe as he teased her, his finger moving in and out of her body to drive her higher. She broke away from his mouth, her head falling back, panting, as the pleasure built.

"My God, you're tight," he whispered against her throat. He added another finger, stretching her, preparing her. "I cannot wait a moment more." Grasping her waist, he lifted her to straddle him, the heat of her directly over his erection. Julia grabbed his shoulders, steadied herself, too mindless to do anything except fight for breath as Nick reached between them to unbutton his trousers.

Before she had time to think, his shaft sprang free and nudged her opening. He held the base with one hand and brought her hips down with the other, the pleasure mixing with pain as he worked his way in her body.

He swore through clenched teeth, a fine sheen of sweat on his brow. "So tight. So good. It's so bloody good."

The deeper he pushed, the more Julia fought to stay relaxed. She knew if she tensed up, he would not be able to enter her easily. And the last thing she wanted was for him to realize this was her first time. Inhaling steadily, she ran her hands down his chest, feeling the sinewy muscles under his light shirt to distract herself from the increasing pain between her legs.

Pearl had said to get it over with quickly, for the shaft to pierce the maidenhead as fast as possible. Then perhaps Nick wouldn't notice its presence. So gripping his shoulders and taking a deep breath for courage, Julia dropped her hips down as hard as she could, seating herself fully on him. The pain snapped through her as he filled her completely, but she tried to mask it with a groan of what she hoped sounded like pleasure.

Nick seemed not to notice. He groaned as well, his head dropping back on the chair as his fingers tightened on her hips. "Oh, hell, Juliet. What are you trying to do to me?"

God, it had *hurt*. But it was done—and he hadn't noticed. Julia felt a surge of triumph, a roar of feminine power at the success. Now the pain was receding, just as Pearl said it would, and a strange new sensation, one of delicious fullness, dawned. She flexed her hips, and lust rippled through her cleft as Nick's cock slid out and then back inside her.

"Oh, yes," he moaned, eyes closed and face taut with pleasure. "Ride me, *tesorina*."

Desperate to feel the mind-numbing desire again, Julia lifted herself up and came back down, her hips working to thrust his shaft deep. He guided her movements at first, helping her rock back and forth, and the pleasure began to build as she moved faster. His hands skated along her back to the fastenings of her dress, and he soon loosened the top enough so only her chemise covered her breasts.

Her large bosom had been a bane her whole life; dressmakers constantly complained about the re-working of patterns to amply cover her. And Julia had always envied the silhouettes of the thin, flat-chested women who looked so elegant and regal in their high-waist dresses. In comparison, she felt heavy and clumsy, constantly trying to keep a shawl around her décolletage for propriety.

But the way Nick stared at her now, as he slid her lace chemise down to reveal her bare breasts, Julia wouldn't change a thing about her body. His gaze, so reverent and full of heat, scorched her and her nipples tightened almost painfully. She arched her back as her hips flexed once more over his shaft, which caused ripples of ecstasy to travel the length of her body. His hands cupped her breasts. "You are like a goddess, straight from the depths of my dreams," he murmured before drawing one nipple into his mouth.

His lips pulled intently on one tight bud and a burst of sensation raced through her belly to settle in her womb. Her hips moved faster of their own accord, her body reveling in the pleasure caused by both his mouth and his shaft. Nick used his tongue to lave at one nipple then shifted quickly to the other in order to give it the same attention. Julia could feel her muscles tightening, every nerve straining as the pleasure increased. He continued to draw on her nipple with his lips, and she threaded her fingers through his hair to hold his head in place. Each pull of his mouth had her spiraling higher and higher, her hips thrusting harder on his cock, until she thought she would die. It was too wonderful.

Nick reached down between them and used his thumb to stroke the tiny bundle of nerves atop her sex. Once, twice, and then she exploded, a white-hot charge setting off inside her. "Nick," she moaned, his name stretched out into one long word as her body convulsed around him. She barely noticed when he grasped her hips and took over, bringing her down on him with a near-violent force. He stiffened, a groan escaping from deep in his chest, as he shuddered and poured himself into her.

Breathless and sweaty, she dropped her head onto his shoulder. Heavens, that was better than anything Pearl had described. No wonder men did this at every available opportunity.

"My God," Nick wheezed. "I hadn't thought to first take you in a chair." He pushed her hair back from her face in a gentle caress. "I don't know what came over me. You must think me a complete cad."

She almost smiled. Yes, she knew him to be a complete cad—but not for the reasons he thought. "I believe you were as caught up in what happened between us as I," she murmured. She needed to get up, to wash herself off and check for blood, but couldn't make herself move just yet. Nick was still inside her, and Julia wanted to prolong the contact as long as possible.

His large hands stroked her back, and she relaxed into him. She'd just made love to her *husband*. The idea seemed so ludicrous, Julia had to swallow a laugh. And it had been magnificent. Truthfully, she couldn't wait to repeat the performance.

He shifted, trying to get out from beneath her. "Here, *cara*. Let me get a cloth and clean you."

Julia stiffened. He could do no such thing, since he might discover blood on either of them. "No, no. Please, Your Grace," she cooed and pushed him back down into the chair. "Close your eyes and relax. Allow me to clean you." She kissed him lightly in the hopes of securing his acquiescence.

"You know I hate my title," he murmured, his lashes falling against his cheeks. "But thank God you do not want me to get up because I'm not sure I have the use of my legs just yet."

She kissed him again, unable to help herself, before getting out of the chair and pulling her dress up to cover her breasts. The washstand stood across the room, where she found a cloth and fresh water. Ensuring his eyes remained closed she turned to check the insides of her thighs. Sure enough, a small streak of blood smeared her skin. Quickly, she swiped at it to remove the evidence of her maidenhead off her body. Once that was done, she rinsed the cloth and returned to Nick.

Sprawled in the chair, still fully clothed except for his semi-flaccid manhood, he was the most handsome thing she'd ever seen. The planes of his face were slack, less guarded. His black hair tousled, he appeared roguish, more like the devil she knew him to be.

She gently washed him, fascinated by the transformation in his shaft. Pearl had shown her drawings and even insisted Julia hold a wooden phallus. But this was different. No longer as stiff as before, the smooth, pink skin was soft yet surprisingly firm. With every stroke of the cloth, it seemed to twitch under her ministrations, thickening again.

"If you continue to stare at me in such a fashion, it won't be long before we find ourselves repeating what just happened in this chair."

Standing, she smiled and strolled back to the washstand to place the cloth back in the water. Pearl had said Julia might be sore after her first time. So far, she didn't feel any ill effects from the encounter. But there was no reason to rush it, Julia thought, and decided to get him talking instead.

"Come with me to the bed," she said, holding out her hand.

Nick tucked his member back in his trousers and closed a few buttons. She watched as he stood and refilled their drinks. He handed her a glass and helped her up onto the massive four-poster bed. She settled as he reached down, gently slid off her slippers, and placed them on the floor.

"Now I know why Winchester looked so damned

besotted each time I saw the two of you together." He sipped some liqueur and stretched out. "You are a woman capable of stealing a man's soul."

She hid her smile behind her glass, taking a small swallow. "Except it is well-known you have no soul to steal."

"Is that what they say?"

"Among other things. You are still the occasional topic of conversation in London. I've heard about you for quite some time."

He set his glass on the table and then leaned up on an elbow. "So much has been said about the depraved Duke of Colton over the years. Why don't you tell me what you've heard, and I'll tell you if it's true." Nick traced a long, elegant finger down her collarbone, and she shivered.

"That you had Lady Sherbourne and her sister in bed at the same time."

He smiled, his teeth even and white. "True."

"Along with their brother."

The smile faded. "Not true."

"You kept two mistresses at once, setting them up in houses right next door to one another."

"Requiring the memorization of only one address. Quite convenient, in my opinion." Nick reached out to twirl one of her red curls around his finger.

"It was rumored you were a regular patron at Theresa Berkley's brothel, where she practiced her arts of flagellation on you."

"Not a regular customer, but I have been inside once or twice, yes. One is curious about such things, you know."

He was trying to shock her, but Julia wouldn't be

dissuaded. "Your brother's wife. Was that true as well?"

Nick's beautiful face twisted for the briefest moment before his usual insouciant expression returned. "Oh, my dear. Isn't that what everyone wants to know? Did the wicked younger brother seduce his older brother's wife, causing such despair as for the heir to have a fatal accident?"

He hooked a finger in the sleeve of her loosened gown and tugged, revealing the top of her right breast. The fabric hung precariously, where one deep breath would cause her breast to burst free from her stays and chemise. "That information, *tesorina*, comes at a price."

Chapter Five

In the beginning, they'll promise you anything.

—Miss Pearl Kelly to the Duchess of Colton

"What sort of price did you have in mind?" Juliet asked him.

As if Nick would ever tell her. Or anyone, for that matter. Fitz and Winchester both suspected the truth, but Nick had never confirmed or denied their suppositions. He smoothed a hand down over the roundness of her hip. "One higher than you could ever pay."

She smiled at him, her eyes twinkling, and his chest suddenly tightened. Determined to ignore whatever he was feeling, Nick brought them back to the matter at hand. "In our haste, we never talked about preventing conception. I almost hesitate to ask—"

"I am unable to conceive," she said quickly.

"My apologies," he replied. Though he never wanted children, Nick knew many women felt the desire for offspring.

Juliet waved her hand. "It is probably for the best."

Nick wasn't sure what to say, so he gestured to her hair. "May I take it down?"

She nodded, turning slightly in order for him to reach the pins holding up her glorious mass of red hair. Slowly, as if to torture himself, he removed each one, placing it carefully on the table before locating another. When the last pin came out, he ran his fingers through the silky strands, watching the shimmering fire slide against his skin. He wanted to feel all that smooth heat against his thighs when she took him deep into her mouth. The mere idea had desire building in his belly, his cock stirring to life.

He wanted her naked. Now. He leaned over to stroke the generous swell of breast exposed by her low neckline. Damn, but her breasts . . . they were enough to make a grown man weep in gratitude. Nick could gaze on them and touch them for hours. "Take off your clothing for me."

Confusion sparked her eyes before she lowered her lashes. Her reaction was puzzling. Surely this request had been made of her before. With such a lush body, it would be every man's fantasy to have her disrobe slowly while he watched. Juliet was a strange combination of bold and innocent—and he found both sides decidedly alluring.

She wet her lips with the tip of her pink tongue. "You want to watch while I remove my clothing?"

He allowed all the raging hot desire he was currently feeling to show in his eyes as they raked her body. "More than I've ever wanted anything in my entire life."

Juliet's lips parted and a rush of air escaped. He saw the pulse beating fast and strong at the base of her neck, and he smiled. At least he wasn't the only one affected.

She sat up and worked to the edge of the bed where she set her glass on the table, clasping the loosened gown in front of her like a shield. Her hair streamed down to the middle of her back, a cascade of red brilliance. He was already hard, his cock bursting inside his trousers, and she hadn't yet removed a single stitch.

Juliet turned and kept her eyes averted, almost as if she were shy. God, the ability of such an experienced woman to appear a novice had him in knots. In one smooth motion, she lifted her hands out to her sides and the dress fell to the floor. Nick's mouth went dry. Christ's teeth, she was a vision. Standing in a sheer petticoat, flimsy lace chemise, stockings, and short stays, he could see almost her entire form through the transparent fabric. Long, shapely legs, tiny waist, a triangle of light hair atop her thighs, flat stomach . . . and her luscious breasts framed so temptingly. He couldn't wait to taste her.

He was suddenly too hot for his own clothes. He raised himself slightly and lifted his shirt over his head, tossing it to the floor by her feet.

Juliet raised an eyebrow, her gaze now skimming his naked chest. "That is more like it."

He smirked and lay back on the pillows. "I'll show you more when you show *me* more."

She bit her lip and worked on the tiny front fastening of the petticoat. Whisper-thin, the garment slipped off her shoulders and fluttered to the ground. "I'll need help with the laces of my stays," she said, giving him her back.

Nick moved forward with a speed he hadn't known

himself capable of. He lifted her curtain of red hair, brought it to his nose, and inhaled deeply. Gardenias, he thought, breathing in the sweet fragrance once more. He knew he'd forever associate the scent with her.

Placing her hair over her shoulder, he quickly undid the laces and resumed his place at the head of the bed.

Juliet shimmied out of the stays, dropping the fabric to the floor, and Nick's whole body tensed in an effort to keep from pouncing on her. She was lovely. The lace cups of the chemise did nothing to hide the dusky areolas or rosy nipples of her breasts, the bounty barely contained by the delicate fabric. *The things they did with women's undergarments these days* . . . "Leave it on," he croaked, his throat gone dry. "Come here."

The impudent baggage shook her head, gestured to his trousers. "The trousers, Nicholas."

He groaned. Served him right for bedding such an experienced lover. Rapidly unfastening the buttons, he lifted his hips off the bed to strip off the remainder of his clothing. Naked and obviously aroused, he fell back against the bed, folding his arms behind his head.

Juliet's eyes darkened as she focused on his cock, now straining against his belly. He spread his thighs a bit and took himself in hand, stroking slowly as she watched. In only a few seconds, he was longer and thicker. His skin sensitive, the nerves responded to the slightest touch as he pumped into his fist.

Muscles tightening, Nick struggled to maintain a leisurely pace with his hand. He could come so easily, bring himself to completion while merely gazing on her beautiful body. "Climb up here, Juliet. I am dying to taste you, for you to taste me."

She leisurely crawled onto the bed, the chemise riding up to reveal her creamy thighs, and he had to stop frigging himself. If he didn't, he would explode. Juliet trailed her hands up his legs as she moved closer, drawing her fingertips over his calves, past his knees. She settled between his thighs, and Nick tensed in anticipation.

"I am dying to taste you as well, Your Grace." Silken red hair fanned over his lower half as her head dipped toward his cock.

He wanted to tell her again how much he hated his title, but all he could do was groan because she'd touched her tongue to the head of his shaft. She gave him a tentative lick that had every muscle in his body clenching to remain still. He fought the urge to surge up, to force her to take him hot and deep until he shot down her throat. His patience was rewarded when, with a firm hand on the base, she slid her mouth over the knob of his shaft, sucking him so perfectly Nick thought he might pass out.

"Oh, Jesus. Yes, *tesorina*. Suck me." He twisted his hands in the soft strands of hair that formed a fiery curtain around her face. "Take me inside your mouth."

She began to move then, earnestly and with enthusiasm. Nick couldn't breathe, couldn't think, and could only stare at her. Her lips, so rosy and plump, tightened around him, with her luscious breasts nearly spilling out of her chemise every time she lifted up and down over his cock. Over and over . . . the perfect rhythm. Watching her work him so adeptly, the pleasure built in his spine, tightening his bollocks, and he knew it wouldn't be long.

Then she shifted to gently rake her nails over his sac, and Nick was lost. He could feel the orgasm erupting from the bottom of his soul. His shout echoed off the walls as he spent deep in her mouth, his body shuddering with the force of the release. It seemed to go on and on, with her swallowing everything he gave her, until he lay back, completely drained.

She released him and moved up to stretch out beside him. "My God," he wheezed, trying to get his bearings. "I may never be the same again." If he were less of a man, he'd give in to the overpowering desire to roll over and go to sleep. But he desperately wanted to return the gesture, to taste her orgasm on his tongue.

He turned and cupped her cheek, forcing her to look at him. Her startling blue eyes were bright with arousal. He kissed her then, gentle but demanding, tasting his saltiness in her mouth. She clutched his shoulders and kissed him back fervently, her tongue now every bit as aggressive as his own. A savage satisfaction tore through him knowing that pleasuring him had heightened her desire.

Nick sat up. Juliet was on her back, her silken hair fanned out over the pillow like flames behind her head. With two hands, he clasped the edges of her thin chemise and ripped them apart, the flimsy fabric tearing easily in his hands. She gasped.

"I will buy you ten more of those," he promised and pushed the torn pieces aside. He slid her stockings and garters down, one by one, revealing the soft, creamy skin of her legs.

And then she was naked. God in heaven, she was perfect. He'd never felt possessive over a woman, but the thought of another man enjoying her as he had—as he would—filled him with what could only be jealousy. He leaned down to take a nipple, taut with arousal, deep into his mouth. She thrust her fingers into his hair to hold him in place—not that he needed her to. He cupped her other breast and slightly pinched the other peak. She rewarded him with a long, guttural moan.

Had her other lovers been rough? Gentle? Right now, Nick would be whatever she wanted. He needed to bring Juliet more pleasure than any man she'd ever been with.

His hand glided down the soft skin of her body, over her flat stomach, to her patch of intimate curls. He loved that first slide of his fingers into a woman's sex, where you could feel her arousal pooling at the entrance. And, oh . . . Juliet was wet. Wet and hot. He coated two of his fingers in her slickness and moved up slightly to circle the small nub at her apex. It was still swollen from their earlier lovemaking, begging for his touch.

"Oh, Nick. Yes," she breathed. Juliet gripped the coverlet and opened her legs wider.

He loved a woman who knew what she wanted.

But Nick had other plans. Though he longed to feel her orgasm on his tongue, screaming his name as she shuddered, he needed to draw this out, make her so mindless with lust so she would never forget him. He leaned over to pluck his glass of liqueur from the table.

A hint of apprehension flickered in Juliet's eyes. She didn't know what he was about, and Nick liked it that way. This night, he would erase the memories of all her former lovers, and if she didn't know what to expect, all the better.

"Nick, what—" she started until a small amount of liquid splashed onto her naked chest.

She gave a sharp intake of breath, and he watched, fascinated, as the amber-colored liqueur snaked down the valley between her breasts then trailed around her side. Her glorious body spread before him like a feast, he eagerly bent over and pressed his tongue to her ribs, cleaning the sweet wetness from her skin with his mouth. The almond and apricot flavor mixed with her soft skin, the taste and feel of her under the rasp of his tongue more intoxicating than any liqueur.

Onward he stroked, higher, until he licked the underside of her breast, gently bathing the plush, plump skin. Unbelievably, his cock stirred to life and thickened with a desperate desire only this one woman seemed to elicit from him. He'd never been so insatiable in his life, but Juliet made him feel as randy as a lad at his first tupping.

He began teasing the valley between her breasts by pressing wet kisses slowly up her breastbone, one after another, until she arched her back and clutched his head. He still hadn't used his hands on her, a fact he knew she was well aware of. She tried to bring his mouth to the rosy pink tip of one breast, but Nick slid away, determined to torment her.

Lifting over her, he dragged his tongue over the long length of her collarbone, cleaning away the stickiness from the liqueur as he went. She panted and shifted restlessly on the bed and he willed himself to be patient.

"Nick, please."

He nibbled the delicate column of her throat.

When she tried to meet his mouth with her own, he pulled out of her reach and studied her. Her face flushed with passion and eyes closed in sweet surrender, he'd never seen a more beautiful woman.

"Please," she breathed, and his patience cracked under her throaty plea.

He poured a long, thin thread of liqueur down her body, ending just over her mound. She jerked and shivered, and Nick absently tossed the glass on the floor, his focus entirely on her naked flesh.

He leaned down and quickly slid his tongue along the line of liqueur, not wasting time before shifting between her legs. The sweet musky scent of her arousal combined with the almond and apricots, and his shaft hardened even more.

"I want to hear you scream, Juliet. Do not hold back," he said before lowering his head, his tongue making one bold sweep through the length of her folds. Her hips lifted up in response and he smiled. He planned on enjoying this as much as she did.

Using his thumbs, he parted the glistening lips and blew gently. Then he laved the little nubbin of engorged flesh with his tongue, circling it rhythmically until she moaned beneath him, held on, and panted for breath. God, he could do this for hours. But he wanted to give her more, bring her higher, so he slipped a finger inside her warm, wet channel, then followed with another. Juliet arched up off the bed, called his name, and he knew she was close.

He continued using his tongue on her, even sucking her a bit, until her thighs began quivering. Her inner muscles clamped down on his fingers, and she stiffened. He felt her orgasm ripple through her whole body, and she shouted loud enough to be heard in Rome.

When she stopped shaking, he could think of nothing but possessing her one more time. His cock achingly hard, he rose up on his knees, gripped her thighs, and drove all the way inside her tightness with one smooth thrust of his hips. She grimaced and let out a squeak.

He froze, the haze of lust instantly clearing from his brain. "Are you in pain?"

Her lips were pressed tightly together. "A bit," she murmured. "But—"

He gently withdrew and kissed her cheek. "I am sorry, Juliet. I shouldn't be so demanding of you during our first night together. Forgive me."

"It's I who should apologize, Nick—"

"No, *tesorina*." He rolled and wrapped her in his arms until she rested atop his chest. "You owe me no apology. And I promise to let you rest if you stay with me." Nick liked the way she felt against him, all soft and warm. In fact, he couldn't remember the last time he'd felt quite this content.

In response, she snuggled into his side. Nick listened to her breathing slow while she drifted off to sleep, a small smile on his face.

The next afternoon, Sergio presented Julia with a note. "*Grazie,*" she said, taking the paper. It was from Nick.

My Dear Mrs. Leighton,

*Would you do me the honor of accompanying me
to the theater this evening? I fear I may not fully
understand the production unless you are there to
offer insight.*

*Yours,
Nick*

"Is his man awaiting a reply?" she asked her
footman.

"Yes, signora."

"Then allow me a moment." Julia got up from the
couch and went to the small desk in the corner of
the sitting room. She wrote a quick note, telling Nick
she would be delighted and he should collect her
later that evening.

When the footman left with her note, she turned
to her aunt. "I am to attend the theater tonight with
Colton."

Theo smiled. "Does that mean you shall again
spend the night elsewhere?"

"Perhaps," Julia replied, ignoring the thrill that
coursed through her when she imagined another
night with Nick. The memories of being with him,
the feel of him inside her, struck her with giddiness
at the oddest times today. And the way he'd lapped
liqueur off her bare skin . . . She sighed. The man was
deliciously wicked.

She'd crawled out of his bed early this morning,
the duke fast asleep. At the time, it had seemed
easier, but part of her wished she had stayed to experience more wickedness at his hands.

Her aunt studied her carefully. "Anyone can see

what you two were about last night. You're positively glowing today."

Julia felt heat creep up her neck. "I am not."

Theo snorted. "My dear, if you appeared any more relaxed, you'd be asleep. I guess I needn't ask if the rumors of your husband's prowess are exaggerated."

Julia frowned. She didn't want to imagine Nick bedding other women—women like Mrs. Leighton. No doubt the women in his past were far more beautiful and skilled than she, the inexperienced wife he never planned to see again. All the familiar anger she'd carried for eight years, the resentment she'd forgotten with a few passionate kisses, bubbled up.

The things he'd said—and did—last evening were so intimate and personal. Did he do and say those same things with every woman he bedded? Or was it the nature of men to act so . . . loving toward a woman one day and then turn to another the next? And they said women were fickle creatures.

Julia rubbed her brow. It would not do to become maudlin over the situation. She'd come to Venice to seduce her reprobate of a husband. That he was a reprobate only helped her achieve her goal. And she'd already succeeded. Soon she would find herself with child, whereby she would leave and never see him again. Wondering about the long line of women before her or the ones who would surely follow did no good whatsoever.

Besides, it would ruin the elation over her victory. She'd actually done it. She'd *seduced* her husband. "Just think, Aunt Theo. I could be enceinte at this very moment." Her hand found its way to her belly. "Will I make a good mother, do you wonder? I don't remember much of my own. You've been more of a mother to me than anyone else."

"You shall be an excellent mother. Loving, compassionate, and ready to fiercely protect her child. Any woman who would go to the lengths you've gone to get what you want . . . You've got spine, Julia. Your mother wasn't quite so strong."

"How so?" Theo rarely spoke of the late marchioness. She and Julia's younger sister had died in childbirth when Julia was four years old.

"You've got your father's—my brother's—stubborn streak. Your mother was content to let others make decisions for her, to obey your father's wishes. Somehow, I don't see your marriage being anything less than equal."

"What marriage? Colton won't give me a chance to be a wife."

"Perhaps what you have now is better for the both of you."

Julia smiled affectionately. "How did you get to be so wise, Aunt Theo?"

"One very short marriage of my own, with a husband who had the graciousness to die early."

Before Julia could respond, Simon strode in. "Good afternoon, ladies," he greeted, dropping into a chair. His eyes met Julia's and he paused, assessing her carefully. "Not that I want details, but please tell me Colton didn't hurt you."

"Simon!" Julia felt her face grow warm for a second time in a few short minutes.

He held up a hand. "Jules, I would ask the same of a sister, which is precisely how I feel about you."

Was the fact she no longer possessed a maidenhead so obvious? "Colton did not hurt me."

"Well, if he does, I will have to kill him." He leaned forward to pour a cup of tea. "He asked me to dinner, presumably to ascertain the reason for my hostility last night. I haven't yet decided what to say."

"Simon, you cannot stay angry at him over my financial situation. Tell him it was temporary jealousy."

"Or," Theo interjected, "a ruse to force he and Mrs. Leighton together. The battle of a common enemy."

Simon said nothing, merely stared in his cup. Julia could tell by the hard set of his jaw he was battling his anger.

"You may take solace in the idea, Simon, that my plan is working. And Nick has no suspicion of my duplicity."

Again, nothing. Julia changed the subject. "Colton and I are to attend the theater this evening. Are you coming along as well?"

"No. I will be engaged elsewhere tonight."

"With Veronica?" Theo asked, stirring her tea.

Simon rolled his eyes. "Is nothing private in a house with two women? Yes, with Veronica." He leaned forward. "Jules, has Colton said anything about the attempts made on his life?"

Julia blinked as her head swam. She gripped the arms of her chair to steady herself. "The . . . what? A-attempts on his life? To *kill* him?"

Simon nodded. "I've heard rumors. And it hasn't been only in Venice. Apparently, trouble follows Colt wherever he goes. It's one of the reasons he has that giant hulk of a man as a valet."

"But kill him? Why?" Theo asked.

"No one is sure. Colton denies it, of course. Word

is he was stabbed in Vienna. Now he never goes out at night without Fitzpatrick at his side."

Stabbed, Julia thought in horror. She hadn't noticed any evidence of a scar on his body. But then she'd been focused on other things last night.

"Regardless," Simon continued, "when you're with him, take care. Make sure Fitzpatrick is near if you're out at night. I shouldn't like it if you were hurt."

"I daresay I wouldn't like it either," she mumbled, her mind churning with this piece of news. Why would anyone want to kill Nick? Well, anyone other than the wife he'd ignored for eight years. But it wasn't her . . . so who was trying to kill the duke?

It wasn't until the middle of the play's first act that Julia realized something was amiss.

Yes, when they came in together, the legendary Depraved Duke and the infamous Mrs. Leighton, heads had turned their way. People craned their necks or stood up from their seats to get a better look inside Colton's box. Julia had found it somewhat disconcerting, but Nick seemed to take it all in stride.

What troubled her was that the stares were directed at *her* during the play. Not with hostile expressions, but rather appraising ones. The women studied and remarked to their companions behind their hands, more focused on Julia than the stage. It drove her nearly mad. *What* were the women talking about?

She found out when Veronica and Simon came into the box at the interval.

"Simon!" Julia said, standing up to greet him.

"Evening, Mrs. Leighton. Colton. You remember Veronica DiSano." With her slim figure perfectly outfitted in a luxurious blue gown, Veronica seemed to be having an issue with her coiffure. A long sweep of dark brown hair fell out and over the beautiful actress's forehead. Julia tried not to stare as she exchanged greetings with the other woman.

Julia turned to Simon. "I thought you were engaged elsewhere tonight."

Simon tipped his head toward Veronica. "We were until she heard *you* would be *here.*"

Veronica's olive skin turned a dull red. "Well . . . I cannot be the only one not talking about Mrs. Leighton's dress tomorrow." She turned to Julia and gestured to her head. "What do you think of the hairstyle? Everyone has begun to copy it. They ask their maids to 'Leighton-ize' their hair."

Julia's jaw dropped. She gave a quick glance around the theater and noticed more than one woman with such a bizarre style. Heavens, Mrs. Leighton was setting fashion trends. "I am . . . flattered," she managed, and looked at Simon, whose blue eyes sparkled with mirth.

"It appears Mrs. Leighton has some devoted followers," he said, clearly struggling not to laugh.

Nick slid his hand to cup her waist and draw her tightly against his side. With his other hand, he clasped her fingers, brought them to his lips, and placed a kiss to the tips, his intense gray eyes piercing her soul. Julia shivered. "Utterly deserved," he said. "And I find myself eager to join the ranks of just such a mob."

"Will we see you at Florian's after?" Simon asked.

Julia glanced at Nick, who looked impossibly handsome and ducal in his impeccable black evening clothes. He'd been attentive and relaxed all evening, but each time he glanced at her, the hunger in his eyes nearly knocked the breath from her chest. She suspected he had specific plans for after the theater.

"No, I don't believe so," Nick answered, his hand tightening on her hip.

"Well, we shall take our leave, then. Enjoy the rest of the performance," Simon said before whisking Veronica away.

Nick led her back to their seats. "Will you come home with me, *tesorina?*"

Desire raced down her spine. Julia remembered every moment of the night before, how his touch had driven her wild. It was almost as if some force pulled her to him, making him irresistible to her. Even if she weren't trying to conceive, Julia doubted she could refuse him. Not trusting her voice, she nodded in answer to his question.

He gave her a lazy smile full of promise. "Perhaps we should leave early."

"Nick!" she whispered, aghast. "Everyone would see us."

"Since when do either of us take notice of what people say?" The actors took the stage and the interior of the theater quieted. His lips found her ear. "I could take you, right here in the box. Slip my cock inside you and drive us both mad with pleasure. Merely say the word."

His words sent a course of heat racing through her body. Julia didn't doubt him for one minute. If she said yes, he would find a way to do it. "Behave, Nicholas," she managed.

"I find it extremely difficult to do so around you. Especially in that gown."

She'd chosen a particularly bright shade of blue

silk this evening, with a neckline bordering on scandalous. Julia had resisted such a daring dress at first, but Pearl had clapped her hands with glee upon seeing the result, insisting Julia keep it. At least Nick appreciated it as well.

"I'm pleased you noticed," she replied, unable to keep from smiling.

"How could I not? Every man in the theater is wondering just when your breasts will burst free." He took her gloved hand and placed it on his crotch, where she felt his erection, long and thick, through his breeches.

Oh, heavens. She suddenly couldn't draw a full breath—and she definitely didn't want to pull her hand away. Julia flexed her fingers, moving over him gently through the soft fabric. His shaft pulsed under her touch, and Nick groaned. "If you do not let go soon, this shall become truly embarrassing." But he made no move to stop her, and Julia took that as encouragement.

She pressed her palm against him and traveled his length a few times. "Juliet," Nick growled. His head dropped forward and he closed his eyes. One would think he was asleep if not for the muscle jumping in his jaw. Lord, he was beautiful. Julia turned toward the stage in an effort to calm her racing heart.

But all she felt was Nick, hard and hot, even through the layers of cloth . . . and she could hardly sit still for the sharp lust crawling under her skin.

"Let's go," he whispered harshly, pulling Julia to her feet.

Before she knew it, they were out of the box, headed down the stairs to the exit.

"My cape!" she protested through her laughter as he nearly dragged her along.

"I'll buy you ten more," he said before whisking her out into the cool Venetian night.

There was a hint of rain in the air and the moon cast a brilliant glow along the canal. Nick couldn't speak as he led Juliet to his gondola. Heaven help him, he could hardly think. The bewitching minx had him almost spilling his seed in his breeches.

Yes, he'd started it by playfully placing her hand on his cock, fully expecting her to pull away. But she'd surprised him by continuing to stroke him, getting him hotter than he ever thought possible.

The woman was dangerous.

Fitz had merely raised his brows when they came out of the theater, as if he'd known what prompted the precipitous exit. But Nick didn't care. He'd been partially aroused all night, from the moment he'd seen her in that gown. Small waist, creamy skin, luscious breasts . . . Juliet was sin incarnate with a hint of innocence. Something about her was so different than his previous lovers. He felt protective of her, as if she needed him somehow. Ridiculous, really, since women of her stature prided themselves on their independence. But he still couldn't shake the feeling.

He held her hand as she climbed into the boat and then jumped in himself. Fitz discreetly followed and within seconds the gondola set off, rocking gently through the water.

Nick sat next to Julia in the darkened cabin. The walk had cooled him off a bit, so he decided to hold off on undressing her until he had her in a bed.

Which served to remind him . . . "I was surprised to wake up alone this morning," he told her.

"I apologize. I assumed it would be easier if I left before you awoke. Were you disappointed?"

"Of course. And I would have been quite upset had Fitz not followed you to your palazzo and assured me of your safe return. What were you thinking, leaving unaccompanied like that? Venice can be just as unsafe as any other large city."

"Yes, I've heard how unsafe it is for *you*. Why did you not tell me there have been attempts on your life?" Even in the dim light, one could clearly see the concern in the depths of her blue eyes.

He wasn't used to having someone worry over him. Well, Fitz worried . . . but that was Fitz. He was paid to care. Juliet's interest in his safety, however, made Nick uncomfortable.

He shrugged. "Eight months ago we were set upon by some petty thieves. Fitz believes the event to be part of a more sinister plot, but I believe it bad timing."

"Bad timing?" She huffed. "Do you honestly believe that?"

The woman was intelligent, that was for certain. Nevertheless, he needn't fan any fear or anxiety over the attacks. "Yes, I do. And why are we discussing this when we could be talking about more important matters—such as how I wish to spend a week with you in my bed?"

She laughed as if he'd made a joke, and Nick frowned. Did she not believe he wanted her to himself? He'd never been more serious in his life.

"It is not a jest," he told her flatly.

Her eyebrows rose and she studied him carefully.

"Nick, the idea of a week is absurd. I could manage a few days, but I wouldn't want you to . . . tire of me."

"There is very little chance of that." He leaned forward and pressed a soft kiss on her lips. "I daresay a week would not even be enough time to discover all your secrets." His lips touched hers again, more forcefully this time.

She melted into him, opening her mouth and offering no resistance, and his shaft began to harden. The kiss turned hot, with each of them attempting to devour the other. He drank in every sigh and small moan she gave him, relishing the proof of her passion.

Neither of them noticed the boat had slowed. "Your Grace," he heard Fitz call.

Nick pulled back and swore softly. He was fully aroused again and he'd left his overcoat at the theater. *Christ.*

It was getting so he could not go out in public with her.

Fitz snickered as Nick walked by, knowing full well as to how and why Nick was uncomfortable. *The horse's arse,* he thought, shooting his friend a dark glance before helping Juliet out of the gondola.

"My dear," he said to Juliet. "What is your maid's name?"

"Fiorella. Why in heaven's name do you—"

Nick didn't bother answering her. He didn't want to give her an opportunity to contradict him. "Fitz, go see Signorina Fiorella. Mrs. Leighton needs a week's worth of clothes brought to my palazzo. She'll be our guest for the next seven days."

"Nick!" Juliet gasped. "I can't possibly—"

"Go," Nick said, ushering Mrs. Leighton toward the palazzo. "Go now, Fitz," he called over his shoulder.

Fitz nodded and Nick had complete confidence it would be handled. God, the mere thought of having Juliet at his mercy for seven days . . . He walked a bit faster.

"Please have her pack my enhancements and lotions!" Juliet called over her shoulder to Fitz before they reached the door.

"You won't need any enhancements with me, Juliet. I daresay you won't even need clothes, but I thought it better to be safe." He leaned down, hooked an arm behind her knees, and lifted her up. "Tomorrow, you can send a note round to Winchester and your aunt, letting them know you'll be with me for the next week."

"Nick, put me down!" She threw her arms around his neck and held on as he strode to the stairs.

"In seven days, Mrs. Leighton. Until then, you're mine."

Chapter Six

Allow him the upper hand, if necessary—but only for a short time. To control him is to control your destiny.

—Miss Pearl Kelly to the Duchess of Colton

Julia narrowed her eyes at the duke. "Is this a regular occurrence for you? Kidnapping women?" He had placed her on his bed and was now hastily removing his topcoat. "You cannot keep me here for seven days, Nick."

She fought down her panic. If she didn't get her hair lotion, the red color would turn back to her natural blond by week's end. At that point, Nick would know he'd been duped and likely have Fitz throw her over the nearest Venetian cliff.

Please, Fiorella.

Perhaps she could send a note to Theo, and her aunt could somehow smuggle the lotion into Nick's palazzo if necessary.

Is this what her life had come to, subterfuge for hair lotion?

She had no choice. If Nick discovered her identity,

everything she'd worked so hard for would be destroyed. There would be no baby. There would be no money. And there would be no husband, because Nick would never speak to her again.

"No, this is not a regular occurrence for me. I've never invited a woman here for one full day, let alone seven. But I know you want to be here, Juliet." Nick's waistcoat flew off. "You know it, and I know it. Why deny ourselves such wanton pleasure when it hurts no one and benefits us both?" He went to work on his cravat.

"Nick." Julia sighed, torn between arguing and giving in. Likely the latter, since she *did* want to stay with him. Not only would it make it easier for her to conceive, she liked being around him. Despite his reputation, her husband could be tender and sweet. Their previous evening together, he'd wrapped her in his arms all night long, tucking her snug against his body as if loath to let go.

But she did not care to have the choice taken away from her.

He noticed her frown while unbuttoning his falls. His hands froze and then fell to his sides. "Are you truly so unhappy with the idea of staying here?"

She sat up and swung her legs over the side of the bed. "I am not a valise, Nicholas, that can be transported and stored at your whim. It cannot always be your way."

"I know that," he snapped, black brows drawn together in apparent confusion. "Is it compensation you need? I can—"

"Absolutely not. Haven't we settled that issue already? I do not want money from you. I want you to consider my feelings along with your own. I know you are a duke, but you are not my protector. Stop dictating to me as if—"

Her jaw snapped shut. She'd almost said, "as if we are married." Thankfully, she caught herself in time. Any mention of marriage would be ridiculously out of place for so many reasons.

Nick drew near. With a finger under her chin, he tilted her head up until she met his eyes. "I would very much like you to stay with me. Not because I forced you, but because you want to." He stroked her jawbone with his thumb. "Will you stay?"

His sincerity touched her. Still, there was more at stake than her pride—hair lotion, to be precise. "Promise me you'll allow me to go home at any time during the next seven days," she said. He started to speak, and she cut him off. "Without asking me why."

Nick stepped back and dragged a hand through his hair. "If you truly do not wish to stay, you may go. I've no plans to keep you here against your will."

Julia shook her head. "I *want* to stay, Nick. But there may be a reason—a good reason—that I need to visit my palazzo. I need to know you'll let me go and not ask me why when I come back."

"You'll come back?"

"Yes, I'll come back. For seven nights and all the days I can manage." She reached for his hand and tugged him to the bed once more. "I want to be here, Nick. With you."

He grinned and bent to give her a surprisingly sweet and tender kiss.

"Thank you for understanding," she murmured against his mouth.

"You may thank me by undressing," he murmured in response.

Laughing, Julia kicked off her slippers. Nick whipped his shirt over his head. Naked from the waist up, he knelt, the bed dipping beneath his weight. "Do not take off any more, *cara*. Let me unwrap you, layer by layer, like the sweetest treat I've ever been given until I have you begging beneath me."

He leaned to kiss the sensitive skin just behind the lobe of her ear. "Where should I start, do you think?" His gray eyes were dark and hot, liquid silver as they raked over her body. He brushed his knuckles whisper-soft over the tops of her breasts. "Hmm. I believe I'll start with what I've been dreaming of all night."

Julia fell back against the coverlet and he followed, bending to slide his lips along her collarbone. She closed her eyes, reveling in the tender kisses he placed on her skin. He smelled like soap and a hint of sandal-wood.

A trail of fire erupted wherever his mouth touched. Julia could feel her breasts swell in anticipation.

"Roll over, my dear."

Julia rolled onto her stomach, hands folded under her face. She patiently waited as Nick began to loosen her gown.

And then he froze, a growl erupting from deep in his chest, and she couldn't contain her smile. He'd found her surprise.

"Is that another treat for me, you minx?"

Julia shifted onto her back, holding her loosened gown across her breasts and hiding the scarlet boned chemise. "It is. And I might let you see it if you're very, very good to me."

His eyes were fierce and bright, arousal sharpening the planes of his face. "I was already planning to be very good to you. I'm afraid you'll have to do better than that, *tesorina*."

"What if I ask you to be very, very bad instead?"

His mouth hitched into a sexy half smile. "Oh, I am entirely capable of that. Don't move. I want to get comfortable." Nick scooted until he was propped up against the headboard, arms crossed over his chest. A king about to survey all he rules, Julia thought with a laugh.

The sharp intensity of his attention made her tingle as she stood up. Once at the side of the bed, she paused—then let go of her dress. It fell to the floor with a *whoosh* and Nick's eyes went wide. "Sweet merciful heaven," he whispered.

Fashioned of bright scarlet satin, the top of the boned chemise was tight, thrusting her breasts up and out, and held up by thin red straps. Black lace covered the boning of the bodice down her rib cage, where sheer lace draped to her upper thighs. From the navel down, the thin fabric was nearly transparent.

Julia felt impossibly ridiculous in the garment. Not only was it uncomfortable, it seemed impractical. Pearl had insisted no petticoat or stays were necessary, which had added to Julia's discomfort. However, the heat in Nick's gaze made the irritation worth it. Julia felt sexy, a woman who could do anything or have anyone she wanted. Powerful.

"If you decide to seduce government secrets out of a man, I'd suggest wearing that," he said huskily.

She dragged a lazy fingertip across the swells of her breasts. "And do you have any secrets worth knowing, Your Grace?"

"I daresay I'll be babbling like a half-wit if you sit atop my cock in that." His fingers flew down the remaining buttons of his breeches, and in one deft maneuver he was completely naked.

Julia sucked in a breath. Lithe and lean, Nick was not overly muscled, but he was perfectly proportioned, with arms, legs, and chest dusted with crisp black hair. His erection was impressive, fully hard and straining against his belly. Her insides melted, moisture pooling between her thighs.

He crooked a finger. "Come here, *cara*."

Julia slid onto the bed and slowly, teasingly, crawled her way up to him. Her heart slammed in her chest, every part of her now thrumming in anticipation. There was no shyness this time; she wanted him desperately. So much that she ached with it. And considering Nick was nearly panting while watching her approach, the feeling seemed entirely mutual. She loved that she, his innocent wife, could elicit this feverish desire from such a sinful man.

When she drew close enough, his hands snatched her upper arms and he pulled her down on top of him, capturing her mouth in a blistering kiss.

Their bodies resumed where they'd left off in the gondola. Breathing hard, they drank each other in, the kisses deep and wet. Her hands, trembling with need, touched him everywhere she could reach. Under her fingers he was hard angles and taut muscles, and rough, hot male skin.

Nick brought her leg over him, so she was half on the bed and half over his body, her breasts crushed against his chest. One of his hands cupped her buttock while the other caressed a breast over the chemise.

Then his fingers slid down to her cleft, where he stroked and teased her endlessly, seemingly in no hurry to do anything more. She broke the kiss and pressed her lips to his neck, struggling to hold on as the delicious sensation coursed through her. He slipped two fingers inside her. Rocked back and forth. "Nick," she breathed, her toes curling in sweet agony. Digging her nails into his skin, she could only whimper as he mastered her body.

"You are so wet for me. Feel what I feel, *tesorina*. See how your body responds to me."

He rolled her onto her back and captured her right hand. "Feel, Juliet. Let me watch you take your passion." He guided her hand down until her fingers glided through the slickness of her cleft. She started to pull back, but he kept her hand in place. "You asked for very bad, remember? Let me watch you," he whispered, his voice low and ragged.

Julia hesitated, licking her lips nervously. Could she do something so highly improper? The wicked gleam in Nick's eyes gave her confidence, however; she knew he would enjoy it every bit as much as she did.

He leaned back and she boldly began caressing herself, lids falling shut in surrender. Ribbons of euphoria stole through her limbs, and she swept her fingers to the tiny nubbin of flesh, rolling it. She shuddered, her teeth biting her lip to keep from crying out.

Pearl had insisted Julia learn how to bring herself pleasure, to familiarize herself with her own body. But Julia never dreamed she'd ever do this in front of anyone else. It was wanton. She felt truly . . . depraved, performing for him in such a manner. And that made it all the more exciting.

She circled her clitoris, now slick and swollen,

torturing herself until her breath came in tiny pants. Nick's lips found the mound of breast exposed by the chemise, and his mouth trailed over the sensitive skin. Knowing he watched her drove her higher, made her more desperate. Her fingers moved faster, every touch adding to the marvelous pressure building inside her.

He growled, a purely male sound low in his throat. "Damn, but you are beautiful. I cannot wait." He fell onto his back and swung her on top, her legs straddling him. He lined up and, with one powerful thrust, drove inside. They both gasped, his hands locked on her hips while he took some deep breaths. She knew he was fighting for control. Only, Julia didn't want him to find control. She clenched her inner muscles around him and then wiggled a bit.

"Wait, oh God, Juliet. I—"

His hold loosened, and her hips began rocking as he'd shown her during their first time together in the chair, lifting up on his shaft and then sliding all the way down again. Harder. Faster. She set a determined rhythm, giving him no mercy as she pleasured them both, her head falling back in sheer bliss. He felt so good, the way he filled up her body and stroked her sensitive walls. It was like nothing she'd ever imagined. And now she couldn't imagine it with anyone else.

When his hands found her breasts and rubbed the nipples through the satin, a rush of heat settled directly in her womb and she was lost.

"I cannot hold back," he gritted out. "So help me, I need to come deep inside you."

Her body tightened and she could feel her release building. She looked at Nick. His eyes were closed, jaw clenched with the intense pleasure of their joining.

She had done this to him, made him completely wild for her. All of a sudden, a blinding, earth-shattering orgasm swept over her. She dug her nails into his chest, holding on, shouting, as she convulsed.

"Oh God, yes." His body strained up into hers, hips jerking furiously as he peaked as well. He tensed, every muscle taut, and she felt the pulsing of his shaft, the rush of his seed filling her.

Both of them still fighting for breath, she dropped on the bed next to him, exhausted. Was every joining between them to be like this? So frenetic, so intense?

With one arm, he dragged her closer to his side. "God, woman. You rob me of words."

Julia could only grunt in response.

"Here, *cara*. Allow me to get you out of this." She waited as he undid the laces holding her chemise together. He slid it down her body and tossed the cloth to the floor. Her stockings and garters went next. Then he pulled her to him, her back against his chest.

Surrounded by the heat of his body, she yawned. He drew a lazy pattern on her bare hip with his fingers and they stayed there, silent, for a long while, merely enjoying the simple contact.

"Tell me about Mr. Leighton," Nick said. "Were you happy with him?"

She tensed. What was there to tell about a fictional man? Julia thought about her ideal husband and decided to start there. "He was a good man. A kind man. Not selfish or cruel. And he was faithful."

"Well, not hard to see why," Nick murmured, kissing her shoulder. "It sounds as if he knew how fortunate he was."

Julia warmed under Nick's compliment. "Thank you. We were happy. I was every bit as fortunate."

"I find myself appallingly jealous of a dead man."

"I cannot imagine you jealous of any man, Your Grace."

His hand playfully slapped her buttock. "That's for using my bloody title. And it's not a circumstance I readily admit to. However, I feel as if I've known you a long time though we've just met. I feel quite . . . well, protective of you."

She smiled, the joy from his declaration gathering in her chest. And then she remembered their circumstances, the ruse she played, and the joy dimmed significantly. Was he so tender, so honest with the other women in his life?

This man was her *husband*. She felt protective of him, too, though little good that emotion served when he traipsed about Europe bedding different women every night. On the journey over, she'd been prepared to hate him. To fool him, get what she wanted, leave, and forget him when it was through. Leave him to his other women while she raised her son.

But she had not counted on his seductiveness. The way he would lull her into forgetting with pretty words and soft caresses. She would be wise to never fail to remember this was only temporary, that this was purely physical.

So she asked, "And what of your wife?"

He stiffened. "What of her?" His voice had turned brittle. "She's hardly even my wife."

"Meaning?"

"It means the marriage was never consummated. And it never will be."

Her cleft still throbbed from their lovemaking, the delicious soreness between her legs reminding her how untrue his statement was. "Is she ugly, then?"

He sighed, clearly not comfortable with the conversation. "No, she was quite beautiful as I recall. Blond, like an angel. But young. Innocent. We married when she was only sixteen, and I left as soon as the ceremony finished."

"So why not go back now? Aren't you curious about her?"

"No," he snapped, rolling over onto his back. "I am not the least bit curious. My father picked her for me, forced me to marry her with some clever blackmail. I will never, ever be a husband."

Julia didn't want to point out that he *was* a husband, whether he liked it or not. "Surely you want an heir."

Nick laughed, but it was dry and without mirth. "No, I decidedly do not want a brat. Ever. I wouldn't give my father the satisfaction. The last thing I want is for the Seaton line to continue."

"But isn't yours one of the oldest and most prestigious titles? Why—"

"A title my parents never wanted me to have. It was made quite clear to me that I was not good enough to carry on the family legacy. So no, the line ends with me."

The small bit of hope for a future together died when she heard the vehemence behind his words. He never wanted children? Heavens, Nick would truly hate her once he discovered what she'd done.

She took a deep breath and turned to face him. He stared at the ceiling, looking grim. She placed a hand on his chest. "You deserve happiness, Nick."

He didn't say anything for so long, she was sure he wouldn't answer. Then he finally whispered, "There are all kinds of happiness. What makes you think I'm not?"

Julia leaned over and kissed him softly on the cheek. She laid her head down on his shoulder and lightly stroked the soft, springy hair on his chest.

God, what had she done?

The next morning, Julia awoke, confused as to her surroundings. Then she remembered. Nick's palazzo. Stretching, she turned and saw the empty space beside her. Nick was gone, already up and about. Part of her was disappointed.

He'd awoken her sometime in the night with tender kisses and soft touches to heat her blood. Their joining had been sweet and slow, a steady, sensual climb before a dizzying burst of pleasure. Nick clung to her afterward, his head on her breast as he fell back asleep.

She had watched him for a long time as he slept, this complicated man who was so unlike what she'd pictured all these years. But she couldn't get emotionally attached. Yes, he was her husband, but he never wanted to be a proper spouse or father. The instant he learned her identity, learned she was enceinte, he would hate her forever.

And while Julia could not blame him, neither could she back down. This was the only way to secure her future.

A knock sounded at the door. Julia pulled the sheet up over her naked body. "Yes?" she called.

Fiorella poked her head inside. "Signora, are you awake?"

"Fiorella!" Julia cried, sitting up. "You're here. I didn't realize you would come as well."

The young girl walked into the room. "The duke promised to double my wages for the week if I came," she said, her face glowing with happiness. "Can you imagine? The duke, he is very generous, no?"

Julia nodded. "Yes, he is. Did you bring all my creams and lotions?"

"Yes, signora. Would you prefer to take a bath this morning?"

Julia nearly passed out with relief. Fiorella had her hair dye. "Please, Fiorella. Thank you."

An hour later, she'd eaten a light breakfast, bathed, and dressed for the day. Her hair was pulled up into a tasteful chignon and she wore a light green striped muslin day dress. Now she was ready to face Nick.

She found him fencing in the ballroom with Fitz.

It was a sight to behold. Both men were shirtless, their naked torsos gleaming with sweat as their chests heaved from the effort. They circled and parried on a large mat, the sound of their foils clanging together in the cavernous space. Fitz had both size and muscle on Nick, but the duke was fast. He managed to evade Fitz's somewhat clumsy attempts at thrusting while sneaking in quick jabs of his own.

Nick gave her his back and that's when she saw it: a rather ugly scar near his right shoulder blade, the place where he'd been stabbed in Vienna. Her stomach lurched. Dear God. Simon was right.

Someone had tried to *kill* her husband.

She must have made a small sound because both men halted and turned to the doorway. A smile broke out over Nick's handsome face, and he strolled over, the glistening muscles of his upper body rolling and shifting as he approached. "Good morning, my dear."

"Good morning. Do not let me interrupt," she said, almost shyly.

"We're nearly done. Have a seat"—he pointed his foil to a chair against the wall—"and watch me finish this great big lummox off."

Fitz snorted.

Nick gave her a quick kiss. "For luck," he said, and turned back to his opponent.

Julia relaxed into a chair, content to observe their exercise. It was a splendid display of virility and strength. Nick moved gracefully, confident in himself and his abilities, his footing sure and quick. The muscles in his arms and back worked under his damp skin. He charged, sweat running down his naked torso, black breeches clinging to his powerful thighs. . . .

Arousal hit her hard, a visceral response to his display. Her lower body warmed and tingled as she remembered sliding against his nakedness. How wonderful his hardness felt inside her, stretching her. God, she wanted to lick him from head to toe.

Even knowing how much he would hate her, how he never wanted a child, Julia couldn't stop herself from aching for him. The need for this man was like a drug, a powerful opiate she was helpless to control.

And she couldn't tear her eyes away from the magnificent sight of him. Her skin came alive, itchy and restless, while she watched him prowl and flex. Julia gripped the sides of the chair to keep from throwing herself at him.

* * *

Nick heard Juliet let out a soft sigh. He shot her a glance and instantly recognized the signs of arousal on her face. Skin flushed, her lips slightly parted, eyes bright and glassy . . . He found his own body responding accordingly, his groin tightening as blood rushed to his shaft.

She watched him with blazing intensity, clutching the sides of the armchair, and he stared, unable to—

With a whoosh of air, Nick suddenly found himself flat on his back, Fitz's foil at his throat. Damn it. Nick had let his guard down and his friend took advantage.

"Plannin' to finish me off, eh?" Fitz backed off and extended a hand.

Nick cursed and stood up with Fitz's help. He grimaced. Christ, his shoulder hurt like the devil. He must have landed on it in the fall. "I was distracted," he mumbled.

"Obviously." Fitz grinned, tipping his head in Juliet's direction. He picked up the foils along with his shirt, muttering in Gaelic, and then left.

Deliberately not putting his shirt back on, Nick strolled over to Juliet. Arms crossed, he braced his legs slightly apart and stood in front of her.

The tip of her tongue darted out to wet her lips, tempting him. "Did I distract you, Your Grace?"

She'd asked the question innocently enough, but Nick could see the knowledge in her blue eyes.

"You know very well you did, witch. Now what will you do to make it up to me?"

He was curious to see what she would do, the bold

vixen. He'd always surrounded himself with women who liked sexual pleasure as much as he did, and as wonderful as those past encounters had been, Juliet put them to shame. Her innocent enthusiasm, her intimate knowledge of the male body . . . it was like she'd been taught exactly where to touch him, how to drive him wild.

Her hands went to the buttons on his trousers and with a sly smile, she popped them slowly, taking her time, one by one, until he sprang free.

In a matter of seconds, Nick forgot all about the fencing match.

The next few days passed quickly. Nick couldn't remember a time when he felt more satisfied or content. He and Juliet were strangely compatible, even out of bed. They spent almost every minute together, and he didn't once tire of her presence as he usually did with women in the past.

She knew as much about literature as he did—if not more so. Impressive considering he'd been forced to learn the classics in school and she'd read them on her own. Juliet could also play the pianoforte, which she did for him every night after dinner.

He wanted to do something special for her before the end of their week. Remembering her desire to visit the island of Torcello, he decided to surprise her with a trip. They could spend the late morning sightseeing and then have a picnic. She'd said she needed extra time with her toilette this morning, so Nick arranged everything while he waited.

By the time she came down, the gondola was packed and ready to leave.

With her red hair piled atop her head in lush curls, and wearing a conservative light blue dress, she could be any lady strolling down The Strand. But it was the mischievous, intimate smile she gave him that had his chest tightening with emotion. He didn't want to feel tenderness for any woman, had avoided romantic entanglements for years. Juliet, however, had somehow slipped past his defenses. He felt . . . affection for her.

Could he convince her to stay longer than their agreed-upon seven days?

When she got to the bottom of the stairs, he bowed. "Madam, your carriage awaits."

"Carriage?" she asked.

Nick straightened and shrugged. "Well, gondola. It was the best I could do." He took her hand. "Today we are to be tourists, where we shall ramble about on the island of Torcello."

"Oh!" Juliet breathed, clutching at him in excitement. "Truly?"

He nodded. "I remembered how you wanted to explore it. And we'll have a picnic while we're there."

Soon they were in the water, gliding north toward the lagoon islands. He and Juliet sat in the enclosed *felze,* while Fitz and the gondolier were outside, talking softly, as the boat rocked them gently.

"How long will it take to get there?" she asked.

"More than an hour. Torcello is the farthest lagoon island from Venice. It's also the quietest. Only a small number of people actually live there."

"What shall we do until we arrive?" She slid him a

glance from beneath her lashes, and Nick felt his blood begin to stir.

"Why, I'm not sure." Turning, he nuzzled her neck just below her earlobe. He happened to know exactly how much she liked it.

She gave a long sigh, and her head fell back against the seat to allow him better access.

"What would *you* like to do until we get there?" he whispered against her throat.

"Shall we discuss politics? You haven't taken up your seat in the House of Lords, but I'm sure—"

"I would rather swim to Torcello than discuss politics. I'm afraid you'll have to do better than that, my dear." He traced the curve of her collarbone with his fingertips, the skin so soft and delicate. She rewarded him with a shiver. Leaning in, he slid his lips down the column of her throat, dropping small kisses as he went. She smelled heavenly, like soap and flowers, and he thought about tasting her everywhere.

"Hmm. No politics, then. What about gossip? I can tell you everything happening in London these days."

He grunted and continued kissing her neck, and she laughed. "Shall I recite poetry for you?"

"I hate poetry," he mumbled.

She laughed once more. "As it happens, so do I. Well, that leaves us only one thing." Her hand found his thigh and began gliding toward his crotch. His shaft rapidly swelling, he held his breath, waiting for her sweet touch. "To talk about ourselves."

Nick pulled back, aghast. "Talk about ourselves?" His hand shot out and scooped up her knees to place her legs across his lap. "I have a much better idea. Why don't you talk and I'll find a way to amuse myself with your body." He flipped up her skirts and petticoats then ran his fingers up the inside of her thigh until he found her heat.

She was deliciously wet, her body already prepared for him. He dabbled and dallied, his fingers in no hurry whatsoever to ease her torment despite her pleas. Every bit of this ride would be spent driving her wild.

Much later, when they arrived in Torcello, Nick helped Juliet off the gondola. He'd brought her to peak twice on the trip, and she said her legs were not yet steady. He couldn't contain his smile.

"You could look a little less pleased with yourself, Your Grace," she muttered as she took his arm.

"If you 'Your Grace' me once more, I'll pleasure you three times on the way home."

"Promise?" she shot back, devilment dancing in her blue eyes.

He chuckled. "Fitz," he called. "We'll return in an hour and a half for lunch." His friend nodded, and Nick led Julia down the dock toward the island. "I had no idea you would prove so insatiable, Mrs. Leighton."

"Worried you won't be able to keep up?"

"Yes," he returned with exaggerated sincerity, making her laugh. He loved to see her laugh, he realized. "Let's stop first at the Cathedral to view the mosaics." He led her toward a giant bell tower.

After they'd studied the mosaics and climbed to the top of the tower, Nick told her, "Now you need to sit on Attila's Throne." In the courtyard behind the Cathedral, he showed her a large stone chair.

"And why should I sit there?"

"Because it's what tourists do, my dear." He led her to the throne and kept hold of her hand as she sat down. "Locals say if you sit on Attila's Throne, it means you'll return to Torcello one day." He lifted her hand to his mouth and pressed a kiss on the inside of her wrist, at the edge of her glove.

She smiled at him, and he found himself smiling back, grinning like an idiot and not caring in the least.

"Someday perhaps you can bring me back," she said softly.

Nick wasn't sure how to respond to such a statement. They both knew their liaison wasn't permanent, but her voice had a strange wistful quality to it—and damn, if he didn't want to give this woman everything in his power. And that was dangerous indeed.

He decided to ignore it and brought her to her feet instead. "Now let's eat."

The rest of the trip had been quite lovely, Julia thought as they drifted back toward Venice. They'd shared a picnic inside an abandoned old palazzo, and afterward Nick had taken her gently on their soft blankets. Their lovemaking had grown less frenetic over the last few days, but certainly no less intense. Once they'd righted their clothing, they had walked a bit more, holding hands and sharing kisses as they explored. All in all, a perfect day.

Once in the gondola, Nick had stretched out in the *felze* with his head in her lap. A few minutes later, he'd fallen asleep.

Julia smoothed the hair off his forehead. After today, she had two days left with him. Yes, they could still see each other, but for now she was enjoying being at his side both day and night.

His face appeared younger and more peaceful in his sleep. Awake, there was darkness in him, a hurt from his youth that he could not, would not, allow himself to forget. It made him cold and cynical. But there was sweetness as well, the tenderness of a man who had never known love, who craved it more than he even realized.

As they ate, she'd prodded him to tell her about his childhood.

"Not much to tell, really," he'd said. "I spent it tramping about the estate, escaping my nursemaid whenever possible. I loved to be outside. Still do, whenever I can. Then I went off to Eton and only returned a handful of times in the years following. They hardly cared whether I lived or died by then."

"Who?" she'd asked.

"The duke and duchess. They washed their hands of me fairly early on. In fact, I cannot remember any tender moments with my parents. Every fond memory I have of my childhood is of my nursemaid and the head gardener, who I used to follow about every chance I got."

"What of your older brother?"

He popped an olive in his mouth. "We got on well enough, but the tutors kept him busy. 'A future duke has responsibilities,' they used to say. Made Harry fairly miserable. We were a pair: one boy with too much attention and the other with none."

"Oh, Nick," she'd said sadly.

He shrugged with a casualness she suspected he did not feel. "My parents were miserable people. In some ways, it was better to be left to my own devices, lonely as they were. Harry had to meet with our parents regularly, explain what he'd been learning, and perform like a pet monkey in a shop. I hardly saw them. In fact, one time I counted how long they avoided me. I got up to eighty-nine days."

Julia had gasped. "Eight-nine days without seeing your parents! That is terrible."

"It was a ridiculously large house," was his answer.

"And what did you do on holidays and breaks?"

"Traveled. Went home with Winchester or Quint. By the time I was old enough, I'd find a lady friend or two who did not mind an insatiable, ever-randy fourteen-year-old hanging about."

"Not much has changed, I see. You are still insatiable and ever-randy," she'd pointed out.

"Yes, I am. But only around you, it seems. And are you not glad for it?"

The moment had passed, but she began to understand why he'd run away from his family—including the wife his father had forced upon him. Guilt pressed heavily on her chest, and for one brief, insane moment she had even considered confessing her real identity. Fear held her tongue, however.

If she conceived, Julia did not believe herself capable of telling him face-to-face. She knew how devastating the news would be to her husband. He truly did not want to be a father, something he'd stated quite clearly again today.

No, a nice long letter would do the trick. Sent from somewhere far, far away.

She looked down at him, long black lashes fanning his cheeks as he slept, the hint of dark stubble on his jaw. Her heart squeezed—and the truth hit Julia like a bolt of lightning.

She was falling in love with her husband.

Oh, dear Lord, she could not allow something so ridiculously idiotic to happen. Quickly, she tried to remind herself of all the reasons she should hate him, how he'd ignored her for eight years. His reputation as a debaucher of women. Templeton. Her servants, all of whom would soon be out on the street.

But she couldn't do it any longer. She did not hate him; she *understood* him. And she could see past the façade he presented to the world: the Depraved Duke, a gambling degenerate who needed no one. No, that was not the real man. Nick had opened up to her in the last few days, sharing more of himself and showing a sweet, caring side to his personality.

In all her scheming and preparations, Julia had never thought to guard her heart. The idea of caring for him never crossed her mind. And now she was dangerously close to loving a man who would hate her forever—once he learned what she had done.

Remain strong, she told herself. You can survive two more days without sacrificing your heart.

Chapter Seven

Guard your heart. Keep it safe, for no one should ever confuse lust for love.

—Miss Pearl Kelly to the Duchess of Colton

By their last day together, they had fallen into a comfortable routine.

As he had almost every morning, Nick roused her with gentle kisses and knowing fingers, priming her body, and then sliding inside. The pace was slow and leisurely, Nick drawing out the pleasure until she was nearly mad with it. She clutched at him, begging and pleading for an end to the sweet torment.

He only chuckled in her ear. "I want to make this last, *tesorina*. Although I plan to have you at least twice more today."

Julia couldn't take it. She pushed his shoulder and rolled him onto his back. His face registered surprise as she straddled him and positioned his shaft at her entrance. "Perhaps I plan to have *you* at least twice more today as well." Bringing her hips down, his shaft rammed deep and both of them groaned.

She did it again, causing him to gasp and grip the wooden headboard. "Bloody Christ, I love when you do that." His hands found her breasts, where he pinched her nipples and rolled them with his fingertips while she continued to ride him. The friction soon had her on the edge, and Nick knew it. He leaned up and took a nipple into his mouth, alternating between suckling hard and laving the tiny bud with the flat of his tongue.

"Oh, yes, Nick. God, yes," she breathed, her hips rolling frantically.

Nick moved his hand down between them, stroked her sensitive nub with his thumb. "Come for me, *cara*. Scream my name," he murmured at her breast.

The crest was upon her, with Julia swept into a fierce orgasm, her legs shaking, body rocking through the delicious storm. Dimly, she heard herself shout his name.

When she floated back down, Nick's eyes were dark and glassy, watching her intently. "You are so beautiful when you find your pleasure. You make me feel like the most powerful man on Earth."

She barely had time to process those words before he switched positions, settled himself between her thighs, and began driving into her with a determination she'd hardly experienced from him. He was possessed, his lips pulled back in a feral snarl, chest heaving with effort. After a short minute, he stiffened and let out of a shout of his own.

He collapsed, certain to brace himself on his elbows so as to not crush her. Julia rubbed her foot along his calf and stroked his sweat-slicked shoulders, content to feel the weight of him atop her while both of them sought to regain their breath.

Eventually he shifted and pulled her against his long frame. "Perhaps we should spend the day in bed."

Twining her fingers through his black chest hair, she smiled. "Perhaps. But I should like a bath at some point."

"Will you allow me to wash you again?"

The memory of yesterday's bath, when Nick had soaped and rinsed every part of her body, warmed her face. "You may play lady's maid anytime you like, Your Grace."

He nuzzled her neck. "I live to serve you, my dear."

They ate in bed, where they shared a leisurely feast sent up by his cook, with Nick occasionally feeding her with his fingers. After, he attended to her every need in the bath, the water long cold by the time she finished.

Gray and chilly, the afternoon seemed best spent in the library in front of a fire. The two of them settled on the sofa with books, Nick's head resting in her lap while they read.

He made love to her again before dinner then helped her into an evening dress. She watched as he changed, merely content to be in the same room with him. In his black evening clothes, her husband was impossibly handsome. The arrogant set of his jaw, the width of his shoulders, those sinfully full lips curved into an intimate smile just for her. . . . Her heart sped up as their eyes met in the looking glass.

"I know that look," he murmured, finishing off his cravat. "Shall we skip dinner?"

"Indeed not. I need to keep up my strength. You take quite a lot out of a woman."

Nick chuckled and strolled toward her. "I could say

the same of you, *tesorina*." He gave her a lusty kiss then continued dressing.

"What does that mean, *tesorina*? You have called me by that name ever since I met you."

He buttoned up his waistcoat, an emerald green with white stripes. "Venetians use it as 'my darling.' Literally, however, it means 'my little treasure,' which is what I think every time I have you naked."

Her heart melted a bit further. She reminded herself to stay aloof, that she would leave on the morrow, but it was hard when he continued to be so attentive and charming.

Over dinner, they conversed easily as they ate, sharing thoughts and opinions on various topics. Surprising how much the two of them agreed upon, she thought. Under a different set of circumstances they might have even been friends.

For dessert, he arranged for her favorite treat: ices flavored with neroli, made from the blossom of a bitter orange tree. The resulting taste was sweet, sour, and fragrant, and Nick chuckled when she not only finished her bowl, but his as well.

How could such a kind and thoughtful man ignore his wife for eight years? Sorting the man she'd believed him to be from the man she now knew proved challenging—especially when he assumed her to be someone else. The deception soured in her mouth every bit as much as the dessert she'd just consumed.

No doubt about it, she'd created quite a mess.

"Tell me," she asked as they lingered at the table. "Do you harbor any regrets over the things you've done, or the way you've lived your life?"

He cocked his head, slightly frowning. "Everyone does, I suppose." He sipped his wine and gave it consideration. "I wish I'd spent more time with my brother before he died, certainly. Then there's my wife."

Julia tensed. "What do you mean, your wife?"

"Winchester is forever after me to do the right thing by the duchess, to come up to scratch. And he's correct, of course. I should. But what would I do, show up on her doorstep like a midshipman lost at sea for eight years? She'd laugh me out of London, I daresay." He sighed. "I never should have agreed to marry her. I should have stood up to my father and found a way to fight back. If I had, it would have been one less life ruined by the whole business. So yes, I regret that I was not strong enough when it counted most."

Julia swallowed hard, struggling not to show any hint of the shock streaking through her system. He actually regretted his horrible treatment of her. The revelation was staggering. *It's not too late,* she wanted to shout. *She would never laugh you out of London. She would get on her knees and thank the heavens you had returned.*

"So will you truly never return to England?" Difficult to say what response she hoped for, her emotions were so tangled. Their week together was concluding in a much different manner than she'd originally assumed.

"No—though seeing you again may be the first good reason I've had to go back." He lifted her hand and pressed his warm lips to the inside of her wrist. "Does this mean you want to see me again?"

"I am not sure," she answered honestly.

Nick's gaze turned thoughtful, almost fond, and he kept hold of her hand. "There's something so refreshing and honest about you, about us. You're a woman without guile, completely open about your affairs and lifestyle. And I'm quite single-minded in my pursuits of the fairer sex. I'd say we're evenly matched, comfortable with one another. Wouldn't you?"

Her tongue thick with guilt, all she could do was nod. *A woman without guile.* She almost laughed. Yes, she'd noticed how comfortable it was between them—she'd just been thinking the very same thing during dinner—but only because he didn't truly know her or her purpose. A pang tore through her heart.

And at that precise moment, she realized how much she wanted all of this—him—for the rest of her life.

Oh, no. No, no, no.

She *loved* him. Completely, utterly, and without shame, she loved her husband with all of her heart. Oh, *no.* She closed her eyes briefly.

"I would like for you to stay with me for the remainder of your time in Venice," he said, his thumb stroking her palm. "I have the space, and I'm sure Winchester will understand. I want you here, by my side. Every day. Every night."

Panic fluttered in her belly. She would love nothing more than to stay with him—forever, if possible—but he had no idea what she'd done. Nick would hate her for it, and she couldn't bear to see his affection poisoned when her betrayal was revealed.

And now she'd fallen in love with him—despite her resolve not to.

Oh, no.

He calmly stared at her, clearly awaiting a response.

She took a sip of wine to moisten her dry mouth. The only way to answer and not arouse his anger or suspicion would be to evade the question. "I—I will think on it, Nick. I shall need to return back to my own palazzo for a few days but then we may discuss it."

"Fine, but I shan't drop this, Juliet. I want you and I usually get what I want."

Normally, a saucy remark would have found its way out of her mouth, but she couldn't think of a thing to say. Horror had taken hold of her tongue.

"Come, my dear. I want to show you something." Clasping her hand tighter, he helped her out of her chair. She tried to relish the feel of his warm, strong skin against hers and forget the rest. He was still here, affectionate and sweet, oblivious to what she'd done.

Wordlessly, they traveled up two flights of stairs to a small door at the end of the corridor. The door opened to reveal another smaller set of stairs. "Where does this go?" she asked.

Eyes twinkling, he guided her up the steps. "You shall see. Follow me."

At the top, he pushed open another partition and Julia felt a blast of chilly air. She shivered as they stepped out onto the roof of his palazzo. Nick shrugged out of his topcoat, draped it over her shoulders, and led her to the side of the building. His chest at her back, he pulled her close, his arms enveloping her for warmth, as she blinked at the sight before them.

Lights twinkled in every direction, with the high arches of the Rialto Bridge visible in the distance. Gondolas slid silently along the black water of the canals, the glow of their soft yellow lanterns bouncing off the surface. Interior lamps inside the palazzos and restaurants made the city sparkle.

It was peaceful, and she could well imagine Nick standing here at night, watching over the city.

"This is my favorite spot in all of Venice," he murmured into her hair.

"It's breathtaking."

"I know it is a bit cold to be out tonight, but I wanted you to see this. It's the very reason I purchased this particular palazzo."

"I am glad you did. It is beautiful."

He turned her around and then tipped her chin up. "Not nearly as beautiful as you, *cara*."

His head dipped, lips claiming hers, rubbing gently, tenderly, and Julia almost melted into a puddle on the ground. Though she willed it not to, her foolish heart swelled, full of love for this man. She clung to him and poured emotion into her kiss, telling him without words how she felt. That she cared for him. What a wonderful, unexpected gift the last seven days had been. And how sorry she was for the hurt he'd feel when she eventually revealed her secret.

Because she now realized what she must do in order to protect them both.

She kissed him good-bye.

Nick found himself whistling—*whistling*, by God— as he continued the last few steps toward Florian's. He planned to meet an old friend for coffee and then he'd stop by Juliet's palazzo to surprise her.

He missed her. Though he hadn't seen her in only two days, it felt more like two years. And it was more than just the physical release. He missed waking up next to her. And the way she smelled. Everything about her, really. Bloody hell, listen to him, mooning over a woman. He never thought it would happen to him, but now that it had . . . he didn't mind. It felt right, these feelings he had for Juliet.

Though Juliet had been strangely subdued the last time he saw her, as she left his palazzo after their seven-day tryst. He wasn't sure the reason for her mood, so he'd decided to surprise her with a gift.

He'd learned from Signor Marcellino how much Juliet admired the cameo set, how wistful her face had been while she'd studied the delicate carvings. Nick knew she'd wanted the set but pride kept her from accepting such a gift. So he'd purchased it and would give it to her today.

He couldn't wait to see her face when she opened the box.

Nick entered the coffeehouse and searched the crowd for Quint. Unsurprisingly, he saw his friend near the back, scribbling madly in a small book, oblivious to a comely waitress who was attempting to get his attention.

Nick wandered over. "Quint. I see you haven't changed." Nick tipped his head toward the retreating girl.

"Colton! Damn, it is good to see you." Damien Beecham, Viscount Quint, stood up and the men slapped each other on the back.

Nick sized up his friend and concluded Quint really *hadn't* changed since the last time he'd saw him. A bit taller than Nick, Quint was his normally disheveled self, with brown hair haphazardly brushed back from his face and appallingly mismatched clothing. He was uncommonly intelligent, however, and loyal to a fault.

"It's been what, three years?" Nick asked as he took a seat.

"Something like that. I came to see you in Paris, I think. We had those two lovely women—"

"I remember," Nick said, laughing. "God, I loved Paris. Although Venice has been good to me as well."

The waitress returned and Nick ordered coffee. Then he turned to his friend. "Winchester is here, too. Did you know?" Nick, Quint, and Winchester had been close since Eton. Those boyhood friendships were the only ones to survive the scandal, and Nick was grateful to both men for standing by him.

Quint's eyes widened. "No. I've been in Rome for the last month. I can only imagine the fun you two are having."

"I have not seen much of him, I'm afraid." Not at all in the past nine days, in fact. "Where are you staying?"

"Not far from here, actually. I arrived two days ago. There's a scholar in Venice I've wanted to speak with regarding—"

"No doubt the conversation shall be riveting." Nick had learned over the course of their twenty-year friendship to cut Quint off before his friend started in on the topics of philosophy, engineering, or science. "And how have you been since I saw you last? No wife in tow, I see."

"Didn't you hear?" When Nick shook his head, Quint continued. "I was betrothed last spring. Girl ran off to Gretna Green with a stable boy a week before the ceremony. Damned good thing, too. The last thing I wanted was to be married."

Quint's troubled eyes gave away the lie. It was

obvious the girl had broken his heart. "My sympathies," Nick said in all seriousness.

Quint looked away. "Eh. I'll survive. Speaking of marriages—"

Nick groaned, causing Quint to chuckle. "I was merely going to say that I see your wife quite a bit in London. You do not know what you're missing, my friend."

"Believe me, if she's half as wonderful as Winchester says, I'm well aware of what a paragon she is. But it hardly matters."

Quint held up his hands. "I know better than to pursue that line of conversation. So . . . how are the ladies of Venice?"

Nick thought of Juliet and couldn't keep from smiling. Quint's eyes widened. "That good, eh? You're positively grinning. So who is she?"

He *was* grinning. Nick couldn't help it. "Actually I've been keeping company with Winchester's former mistress. Someone you'll know. Mrs. Juliet Leighton."

Quint cocked his head. "Who?"

"Mrs. Leighton." Quint's puzzled expression remained unchanged, so Nick elaborated. "Romanced both Wellington and the Prince Regent at the same time. Had a dinner party and served champagne from a chamber pot. Possesses a collection of diamonds rumored to rival the Crown Jewels. Surely you remember?"

"Sorry, Colt. I have no idea who you're talking about. Winchester's old mistress, you say?"

"She's from London. Juliet Leighton. You must have heard of her." Nick frowned and tried not to be annoyed at the failing of his friend's memory. But the rumors about Juliet were wildly fantastic. Any red-blooded male in London over the age of twelve would know her name. "Come on, Quint."

"No. I haven't heard of her. And she sounds like a woman I wouldn't soon forget. Maybe Winchester is pulling one over on you. You know how much he enjoyed playing pranks on us."

Quint quietly sipped his coffee while Nick struggled with that statement. Would Winchester do such a thing? What would he hope to gain? Juliet's cooperation would be required in such a scheme. Why would the two of them . . . No, such an idea was ludicrous.

Nick shook off the gnawing feeling in his gut, and their talk soon shifted to other matters. A few hours passed and Nick found himself anxious to see Juliet.

"I must go, Quint. But send round later and we'll go out this evening."

Nick departed and Fitz met him outside, the valet straightening off the side of the building as Nick came forward.

"I plan to walk over to Mrs. Leighton's palazzo. Take the gondola and meet me over there, will you?"

Fitz nodded. "Be careful."

"It's the middle of the day. I'll be fine. I need the walk to clear my head." Without another word, he spun and strode away, threading through the soldiers, shoppers, and visitors in the Piazza San Marco.

By the time he made it to Juliet's palazzo, Nick convinced himself there was no reason for concern. Quint certainly did not know everyone in London, and he'd been traveling recently. Of course there was also the possibility that Mrs. Leighton wasn't as notorious as the rumors made it seem. Nick was no stranger to the power of falsehoods and how quickly they spread.

But a small amount of doubt remained. He'd been burned before, and Nick knew better than to trust anyone.

He attempted to calm himself with a few deep breaths. It didn't work. He wouldn't be better until he saw Juliet and asked her these very questions himself. *Who are you? Have you and Winchester been making a fool of me?*

He rapped on the door, waiting in the balmy Venetian afternoon while he shifted his weight from one foot to another. He knocked once more. Where the hell was everyone?

Nick turned the handle and the door creaked open. He stepped into the entryway. "Juliet? Winchester? Is anyone about?"

No one appeared, so he continued up the stairs to the main floor. Darkness surrounded him. No lamps or candles burning, windows closed, and fear tightened his chest. "Juliet?" he called.

Rushing up another flight, Nick found his answer.

In the first chamber, drawers were opened, all ominously empty, as if the occupant left in a hurry. "Goddamn it!" he roared, charging from room to room—only each chamber looked the same.

He stumbled to the first floor, reeling. Gone? And she left without a bloody word?

The truth could no longer be denied. He'd been duped. Why else would she flee the palazzo without telling him? God, no wonder Quint had never heard of the woman.

Nick staggered into the sitting room, hoping to discover some sign of life, some proof she had not truly deserted him. Only, there was none. The furniture stood silent, the living, breathing occupants gone.

A note on the mantel caught his eye. It was addressed to him. His heart stuttered. Perhaps it was from Juliet, explaining her hasty departure. Nick lunged for it and broke the seal, expecting to read of some unforeseen event that had pulled her away from Venice.

It was not from Juliet, however. The note was from Winchester. And the words turned Nick's blood cold.

Colt,

If you're reading this, then you already know we've left.

I once told you, my friend, if you continued to ignore your wife, you would regret it. I fear that day has come.

Mrs. Juliet Leighton never existed. She was a figment of the imagination of a woman driven to desperation. A woman on the brink of despair, who was convinced she had no other hope but to invent a legendary persona in order to capture the attention of her husband. You.

Yes, Juliet Leighton is really Julia Seaton, the Duchess of Colton.

I know you may never forgive me for what I've done. I only hope you come to understand the reasons why I had compassion for the woman you've abandoned for eight years. As well, I have your best interests at heart.

We are to return to London. I do not know what transpired between you and Julia over the last few

*days, but she is frantic to leave Venice. I have no
choice but to escort her and her aunt back home.*

*I don't know when I will see you again, Colt,
but it is my fondest wish to remain friends. I hope
someday you will understand.*

Yours,
Simon

Nick stumbled to a chair, stunned. He could hear
the blood rushing in his ears. The room was spinning, so he grabbed the armrests to steady himself.

Bloody hell, was it true?

Juliet was . . . his wife?

He crumpled the note in his hand, his disbelief
shifting into white-hot rage. His muscles clenched
and he could hardly see through a haze of anger.
He'd been tricked. By his *wife*. She'd stood there,
smiling at him, laughing at him, bedding him . . . the
whole time knowing she was lying.

That *whore*.

It had all been a game. The rumors, the flirting,
the kissing. She'd merely wanted him to chase her, to
fall at her feet. And he had, goddamn nitwit that he
was. It was some sort of revenge for ignoring her for
eight years. God, and the things he'd *told* her. Nick
had revealed parts of himself to her that he hadn't
shown anyone, ever.

And she and Winchester had been laughing at him
the whole time.

The pain nearly doubled him over. Nick had never
felt this betrayed. Not even when his brother hadn't
believed him, or when his family had turned their
backs on him. No, this was a hundred times worse. He

swallowed the bile rising in his throat and shoved the note into the pocket of his coat.

Nick stalked out of the palazzo toward his gondola, his boots snapping on the stone floor. His chest felt hollow, frozen. Empty of all feeling and emotion. Fitz stood on the dock, impassively awaiting his return. "Home," Nick barked and jumped into the boat. He dropped onto the seat and put his head in his hands.

Every moment with her, every lying smile, every deceitful sigh played back in Nick's head while they floated the short distance to his palazzo. Were she and Winchester lovers? Winchester had denied having feelings for the duchess, but what man would go to such lengths to help a woman he did not care for?

Whatever he had to do, wherever he had to go, Nick vowed the two of them would regret making a fool of him.

When the gondola stopped at the dock, Nick leaped out and his hand brushed against a lump in the pocket of his greatcoat. He suddenly remembered the gift he'd bought Juliet—no, make that *his wife*. The intricately carved, unique cameo set. Simple and elegant, just as he'd once thought Juliet to be. He took the box out and held it in his trembling hand, rage coursing through him. His own stupidity mocked him.

And what of your wife? she'd asked. *Aren't you curious about her?*

With a soul-shattering roar, Nick hurled the box as far as he could into the black waters of the canal.

* * *

"Colton, what is it? What's happened?" Quint asked from the doorway.

It was early evening, and Nick was rapidly attempting to wrap up all his business in Venice. He now remembered telling Quint to come by tonight. The last thing he needed was company, but he found himself strangely unable to ask his friend to leave.

Quint lowered himself into a chair across from Nick's desk. "I can see you're angry. What is it?"

There was no reason to hide the truth from Quint. All of London would be laughing at Nick shortly, reveling in the humiliation of the Depraved Duke. Nick didn't trust his voice, so he merely tossed Winchester's note in Quint's direction and went back to writing.

A long minute went by. The room remained deathly quiet while Quint read the letter. When he finished, he folded the paper and placed it on Nick's desk.

"Beautiful, isn't she?"

Nick's head snapped up, his eyes narrowed on Quint. "Yes, for a *whore*. Quite." He refocused on the letter he was composing, barely seeing the words on the page.

"Oh, come now, Colton. So you bedded your wife. And it sounds as if you enjoyed it, if your earlier comments at the coffeehouse were any indication. While no one wants to be duped, at least you can cross 'consummate my marriage' off the items to accomplish before you die."

"That was on my list of things *not* to accomplish— ever," Nick shot back. "And the woman I bedded was no virgin, Quint. She was experienced in the arts of fornication. So with whom has she been gaining such experience? Winchester?" He realized he was shouting, so he forced himself to relax.

Quint frowned. "Well, that does seem unlikely. But you've washed your hands of her since the wedding ceremony. One can hardly blame the girl for wanting to be loved."

"Jesus, Quint. This is no time for logic." Nick dragged a hand down his face. "Fine, if what you say is true, then why come and find me? She could have any man in London. Why create this fantastic story, of a courtesan no man can resist, and then seduce me?"

"I should hate to speculate, but perhaps you have not considered the most obvious reason of all."

Other than humiliate him, or to seek revenge, Nick couldn't fathom a guess. "And what would that be?"

"Perhaps another man planted his seed in your wife, and she is trying to convince you it is yours."

His breath caught, and then a new, brighter fury raced through him, clogging his throat. The thought hadn't even crossed his mind.

Driven to desperation, Winchester had said in his note. *A woman on the brink of despair.*

And then it all made sense. The persona, the fact that she'd targeted him, Winchester's cooperation . . . The woman wanted to pass off some other man's bastard as Nick's child.

Goddamn her to hell.

"Wait," Nick suddenly said. "Her stomach exhibited no signs of rounding. At what month do women start showing?"

Quint lifted his hands and shrugged. "Damned if I know. I had heard she and Wyndham were quite close for a time. But even if she is to have another man's by-blow, do you really care? I should think you'd be relieved, considering you never planned to give her a child."

Nick rubbed his forehead. Maybe he would have felt that way before he'd met her. Before he'd held her in his arms. The thought of another man having her, losing himself inside her body . . . it made him nearly mad with jealousy. "I am *not* relieved," he said before returning to his papers. "Is that all, Quint?"

He heard Quint sigh. "I know you well enough to see you shall not let this go. So what are you planning to do?"

Nick kept his eyes on his writing. "Make them regret it, of course. I am leaving for London as fast as I can manage."

Quint sighed, heavier this time. "Well, I had better come with you, then."

Julia gripped the sides of the boat, rising from over the side where she'd just emptied her stomach into the English Channel. Again. Heavens, she'd never been so nauseated in her life.

The four-week journey from Venice had been miserable. In addition to the guilt she felt over leaving Nick so abruptly, she'd missed her monthly courses. Julia had actually achieved her goal. She was enceinte.

She pressed a hand to her abdomen, where a tiny life now grew inside her. While part of her was relieved her plan had worked, another larger part grieved for the father her baby would never know, the husband Julia would never have. For Nick.

But Julia had no time for regrets. What's done

was done, as Aunt Theo would say. Julia had to move forward and nurture the child she carried.

Once back in London, Julia planned to write him. She would apologize for leaving Venice so suddenly and tell him of her real identity. And even though he would hate her, at least she could give him the reasons behind her actions. Someday, perhaps, he could forgive her.

Lord, she missed him. That last night with him, their lovemaking had been explosive. After leaving his palazzo's roof, they had been ravenous for one another, barely making it to his chamber before tearing off each other's clothes. After, he'd held her so tightly, with something in his eyes that hadn't been there before. Julia was almost sure he had developed feelings for her.

Perhaps he had come to care for her as much as she loved him.

Which was why she'd left Venice, to put a stop to her scheme before either of them were hurt further.

"Are you feeling better?" Aunt Theo appeared at Julia's side, her cherubic face etched with concern.

"Yes," Julia answered, slowly finding her way to a deck chair. She sat down and closed her eyes, utterly exhausted. The bracing cold wind helped counteract the choppy waves and her stomach calmed. She hunched further into her ermine-lined cape and placed her hands in the matching muff.

"I am worried," Theo said, and settled into the chair next to Julia. "I've never seen you quite this bad off."

"Merely *mal de mer*. I'll be fine once we reach Dover."

"I don't mean that. Your husband, I mean. You are in love with him."

Tears gathered and Julia bit her lip in an effort to keep the moisture from falling. She didn't answer Theo, but her silence said enough.

"Oh, my dear." Theo reached into the muff to clasp her niece's hand. "You've been so unhappy on this trip and I suspected the cause. I am so sorry. To love a man who does not return the sentiment . . . it is quite painful, to be sure."

"That's the thing. I believe he did come to have feelings for me—I mean Mrs. Leighton. Perhaps he even loved her. And hurting him that way . . . I could not do it any longer. That's why we had to leave." Julia took a shaky breath. "I never expected it to go this far. I never expected to love him."

Theo sighed. "The heart loves whom it loves. We wish we could control it, but we cannot."

They sat in silence for several minutes.

"Are you going to tell him, then?" Theo asked.

Julia nodded. "As soon as we return to London. I owe him that at least."

"Are you going to tell him about the baby as well?"

Julia's head snapped to her aunt. "You knew?"

"Of course! They might be a bit bleary some nights, but I still have my eyes. Are you happy about the baby?"

She gave her aunt a tremulous smile. "I am. I'll always have a part of Nick, and even though we'll never see one another again, I'll have a son or daughter that resulted from one beautiful week together." She squeezed her aunt's hand. "Theo, will you help me raise my baby?"

"Of course!" Theo exclaimed. "Oh, my dear, I'd be honored."

"You'd be honored to do what?" Simon appeared, his hat pulled low and a heavy wool greatcoat protecting him from the stiff breeze.

"Theo," Julia said. "Would you excuse Simon and me for a moment?"

Her aunt nodded and stood up. "Pray come below and get some rest when you're finished."

"I will," Julia promised before her aunt walked away. "Please sit, Simon."

Simon looked at her warily but sat down. "Are you still ill?"

"Yes, but that's not what I have to tell you." She took a deep breath. "I am with child. Colton's child."

He smiled. "Then felicitations are in order. I am very happy for you."

"You are? I assumed you would be angry. Colton is your friend, after all. And you likely knew he did not want children."

"I'm not angry, Julia. I'm happy you got what you wanted. And who knows? Perhaps it will all turn out better than we expected."

"And what do you mean by that?"

He shrugged and turned to stare at the water.

"I plan to write to Colton as soon as we arrive in London," she told him after a bit.

"I assumed as much." Simon stretched his legs in front of him. "I am curious as to what his reply will be."

Julia's stomach clenched. Would he even send a reply? It seemed unlikely from her perspective. Nick was going to be furious. But she needed him to acknowledge the child as his own.

"How many more days until Dover, do you think?" she asked.

"Two. Why?"

"Because I do not know if I can make it that long." Julia bolted out of her chair and rushed to the side, where she promptly threw up.

Chapter Eight

Take care to be sweet and amenable, avoiding arguments when possible. An angry, vindictive lover will bring you naught but trouble.

—Miss Pearl Kelly to the Duchess of Colton

Could she stand here all night without vomiting on the floor?

Such was the thought in Julia's head as she waited at the side of the Collingswood ballroom. The heat and crowd had made her queasy, so she'd stationed herself near the terrace door in order to crack it. Drawing deep breaths of the bracing cold February air had helped to settle her stomach.

So far, carrying a child was not the joyous condition she'd imagined in her youth. She spent far more time emptying the contents of her stomach than actually eating.

"Jules!"

Julia turned and saw her best friend, Lady Sophia, approaching. "Oh, Sophie," Julia said after the two hugged. "I had heard you arrived in Town. I planned to call on you yesterday, but I've been a bit tired from my trip."

In fact, Julia was exhausted. She had skipped most of the society events since returning three weeks ago and would not have even come tonight if Aunt Theo hadn't insisted.

But she was very glad to see Sophie. Her friend was full of life, game for anything, and consequently a lot of fun. A stunning brunette with large brown eyes, Lady Sophia was the only daughter of a powerful marquess and had sworn never to marry. Julia envied her.

"And how was Paris?" Sophie asked. "I cannot wait to hear all about it. I bet you bought all sorts of fabulous things while you were there. I am so envious. Did you see Lady Morgan? She went to Paris, too. Oh, do tell!"

It was sometimes hard to get in a word whilst one was engaged in conversation with Sophie.

"I have much to tell you," Julia answered, knowing she needed to give her friend the truth about Venice. "But this isn't the best place. I'll come to call on you tomorrow."

"You had better." Her eyes dropped to Julia's black shawl. "My condolences on your mother-in-law. I suspected the old bat would live forever, but . . ." Sophie shrugged.

Julia had been of a like mind. While the dowager duchess's death had been a shock—she'd fallen down a flight of stairs and broken her neck—it was not a reason for much sadness. "Thank you. I absolutely refuse to dress in full mourning for her, but Theo would not let me out of the house without a black shawl. The accident certainly came as a surprise. She seemed quite spry the last time I saw her."

"Do you think Colton will come back, now that she is dead?"

Julia glanced away. "No, I do not. I daresay nothing could drag Colton back to England."

"Too bad. I've always wanted a glimpse of the Depraved Duke. So will you kick Lady Lambert out of Seaton Hall?" Sophie appeared positively excited at the idea. "I know she and the dowager duchess were close, but why should Colton's brother's wife get that huge estate to herself? She was only married to Colton's brother for less than a year before he died. It should be yours."

"I hadn't thought about it, to be honest. I'm not certain I have the right to kick her out, and even if I did, why would I? I have no desire to live there." Although moving to Norfolk might relieve some of her financial burden, Julia realized. She decided to discuss this idea with Theo tonight.

"Ugh. Speaking of all things ducal, here comes Lord Templeton. I expect you tomorrow, Jules." Sophie squeezed Julia's hand before disappearing into the crowd.

Julia took a much-needed breath of cold air. However, now that she thought about it, throwing up on Templeton held a strange appeal. At the very least, it would get rid of him . . . wouldn't it?

"Your Grace," Templeton greeted. She supposed he was attempting a smile, but the effort made his face resemble a small rodent in a great deal of pain. She gave the required curtsy and he bowed over her hand. Just that small contact made her flesh crawl.

"I apologize for not receiving you since returning,

my lord. We are still trying to recuperate. I'm sure
you understand."

In the last fortnight Templeton had dropped his
card on numerous occasions, but Julia left strict instructions with the servants not to admit him into the
town house. She knew he wanted to discuss the hastily
written note she'd sent him before leaving for Venice.
But Julia needed a response from Colton, recogniz-
ing the baby she carried as his, before she told Templeton and the rest of the *ton* of her condition.

"Yes, of course, my dear. I do wish to speak with
you at your earliest convenience, however. I find
myself curious about the contents of your last note."

I am sure you do, she thought. God, how she wished
her husband would come back and grind Templeton
into dust beneath his feet. Templeton would not
stand a chance against Nick.

Her heart twisted. She missed him terribly. Life was
unfair. Why did she have to fall in love with the one
person she'd never be able to have?

Then Julia's stomach turned over. She dug her
nails into her palm, attempting to forestall the casting up of her accounts on the Collingswood ballroom
floor. "I will let you know when I am receiving again,
my lord. If you'll excuse me," she said, dismissing
him. Templeton's mouth tightened but he did not
argue. He bowed, turned, and disappeared into the
crowd.

As soon as he left, Julia hurried to the French doors
and stepped out onto the terrace.

The night had turned frigid but she hardly noticed.
She walked to the edge and braced her hands on the
stone railing, inhaling deeply and closing her eyes.

If she could stay quiet and calm for a moment, the urge to vomit sometimes passed.

From the dark corner on her right, she heard the slide of a boot heel on stone. Julia spun, surprised any other guest would brave the inhospitable temperature. Then the light from a cheroot glowed, illuminating a face she'd never expected to see again.

"I much preferred you as a redhead, *Your Grace.*"

Julia gasped, then promptly vomited on the Duke of Colton's boots.

Utterly horrified, she swayed. Had he called her "Your Grace"? She tried to steady herself, her hand flailing in an effort to find the balustrade.

"Not quite the welcome I'd expected" was all Nick said before strong hands lifted her up and carried her down the steps into the garden.

Julia could barely breathe. Her head swam. It was Nick. He had come back. But . . . why? He couldn't have received her note and then traveled to England in this length of time. Which meant he hadn't yet received her letter and had no idea about the child.

She frowned. Did he come back for her?

But he addressed her as "Your Grace," so he'd learned her real identity. *Oh God.* How? Shame over what she'd done and fear over his response warred within her. What was he planning to do?

"Colton, put me down. I don't know where you think you're taking—"

His arms tightened. "If I were you, *wife,* I would not argue with me," he growled in a tone she'd not heard him use before. Sharp and cutting, like the edge of a rapier. A shiver rolled through her.

They passed through a gate and into the mews.

Colton whistled, high and shrill, and within seconds, a carriage pulled around. Fitz and a driver sat on top.

"Put her inside," Nick said and then dropped Julia into the arms of his larger-than-life manservant.

Fitz effortlessly placed Julia on the seat of Nick's carriage. She considered bolting out the opposite door but knew she wouldn't get far in her current condition.

Outside the carriage, Nick toed off his boots. He then stripped off his stockings and tossed them onto the ground. "Leave them," she heard him tell Fitz. "Let us see the duchess home, shall we? She is unwell."

He climbed into the carriage, barefoot. Even in the dim light she could see his anger. His jaw clenched tight, posture stiff, with stormy gray eyes that were cold and hard. Fury rolled off him in waves. This was not the same man who had flirted and teased her in Venice. Her heart splintered further and fresh misery oozed into her chest.

She swallowed. "My apologies for ruining your boots," she murmured.

One eyebrow lifted sardonically. "Considering all that you've done, it seems fitting, does it not?"

She felt the need to explain herself, to make him understand. Make him less angry. After all, if he hadn't abandoned her for eight years, she never would have had to resort to trickery. "Nick, I—"

He banged twice on the roof, and the carriage lurched forward.

"I did not give you leave to use my Christian name, *wife*. You may refer to me as 'Your Grace' or 'Colton.'"

Julia bristled. Her intention to establish any goodwill disappeared. "Fine, Your Grace. Why are you here? Why come back to England after all these years?"

"Can you not guess?"

"No, I cannot."

His smile was pure evil. "Why, for revenge, of course."

Julia felt it again, the bile rising in the back of her throat. It must have shown on her face because Nick shouted, "Stop!" and threw open the carriage door. She dropped to the floor and peered over the side to vomit once more.

A handkerchief appeared by her ear and she grabbed it to wipe at her mouth. "Thank you," she mumbled. After a minute or two, her stomach calmed and she felt steadier. Another deep breath and she dragged herself back to the seat.

"I can see carrying the babe agrees with you," he said acerbically.

Julia's heart stopped. "What did you say?"

"The babe. Your condition. I can see it agrees with you." He crossed his arms over his chest. "Or was I not supposed to know?"

"Colton, it's obvious you're angry with me. But you should know I sent you a letter as soon as I came back to London that explained everything."

"Instead of explaining in person, of course." He leaned forward, his gaze hard and unwavering. "If you thought, madam, to make a fool of me and then return home, patting yourself on the back, thinking you'd done the trick, you were wrong."

"Make a fool of you?" She gaped at him. "Is that what you think?"

"You wanted me, wife. Badly enough, I daresay, to lie, cheat, and steal for your purposes. Well, now you've had me. How long, I wonder, before I can make you truly regret it? And make no mistake— you *will* regret it."

Nick had never heard the main room in White's so quiet.

It had been eight years since he'd last visited the legendary gentlemen's club on St. James, but nothing ever changed here. Behind these walls, the elite males of the *ton* sought refuge—mostly from their wives. A fact to which, sadly, he could now relate.

All conversation halted when the Duke of Colton appeared. Every head turned his way. Even the staff craned their necks, curious as to the cause of the abrupt cessation of noise.

But he couldn't bother with any of that now, not when he had one very important thing to do.

Whispers started behind him as Nick traveled to the hazard tables in the back, where he'd been told he could find precisely what he was looking for.

Nick saw him right away. Simon Barrett, the Earl of Winchester, lounged against a table, his blond head bowed while counting his money, oblivious to the fact that the room had gone silent around him.

Nick kept on until he reached Winchester's side. Simon glanced up, surprise registering for a half second before Nick punched him square in the face.

The force of the blow sent Winchester to the floor. He made no effort to stand up, his cheek cradled in his hand. "*Goddamn it,* Colton. I know I deserve that, but give me fair warning next time. Christ."

Nick crouched down and snarled, "There won't be a next time, Winchester. You are nothing to me. Not a friend, not an enemy. Nothing. You chose her over me, and I'll never forgive you for it."

He rose just as Quint rushed into the room and skidded to a halt. "Damnation," Quint muttered at the sight of Winchester sprawled on the ground. "I was in the dining room. Thought I could make it in time."

Nick turned to the rest of the men in the room, straightened his cuffs. "My apologies, gentlemen, for disturbing your play."

Spinning on his heel, he left.

"Can you get up?" Quint asked.

"Yes," Simon grumbled, and rolled to his side. Hell, his face hurt. Coming up on all fours, he pushed himself upright. "Bastard snuck up on me."

Quint slapped Simon's shoulder. "Come on. Let's get a drink."

The two men strolled to the front room where they found two empty chairs in front of a fire. An order for brandy was quickly placed. Quint also asked the attendant to wet a cloth, set it outside for ten minutes, and then bring it to the table.

"What for?" Simon asked when the attendant left.

"Your face. The cold will reduce the pain and any swelling."

Simon touched his injured cheek gingerly, winced. "It's been a while, but it does seem as if Colton's punches have grown stronger over the years."

"A man is capable of remarkable feats of strength when provoked. Which begs the question . . . Why did you help her? I think your betrayal cut Colton deeper than his wife's."

Simon sighed. "I owe her. She once stopped me from doing something terribly idiotic."

"Which was?" Quint asked when Simon didn't offer more.

"I won't tell, it's so humiliating. But Julia's been a good friend to me. And while Colton has also been a good friend, his treatment of his wife has been appalling. So she asked for my help and . . ." He shrugged.

The brandy arrived and Simon took a deep, long swallow, hoping to numb the sting from where Colton's fist had connected.

"He believes you are in love with his wife," Quint explained. "I told him you weren't. You aren't, right?"

Simon nearly rolled his eyes. Hadn't he already assured Colton he was not harboring feelings for the duchess? "I'm not in love with her, though there have been days I've wished to be in Colton's shoes. She's smart, funny, and brave. If there are finer qualities in a wife, I don't know them."

"Well, I doubt he'll recover anytime soon. I've never seen him so furious. He hardly said two words the entire journey back from Venice."

"Yes, but he fell for her, Quint. I saw it happen. Colton and Julia fell in love in Venice. They were mad for each other—until the guilt overcame her. She didn't want to hurt him so she left. And it's only a matter of time before they realize how perfect they are for one another."

"Do you honestly believe that?" Quint scoffed. "I don't think Colton will ever forgive her."

"He won't have a choice. And a day will come where he'll thank me for bringing her to Venice."

* * *

And make no mistake—you will regret it.

Her husband's parting words haunted Julia the next morning. Meg had gone down to fetch a biscuit and chocolate while Julia, heartsick and nauseated, waited in her bed.

What was Colton planning? He wanted revenge, but how?

She'd been naïve to think her plan wouldn't have consequences. He hated her. The affectionate, light-hearted lover she'd known in Venice had been replaced with a hard, furious man determined to make her miserable. Her heart clenched. As much as she wished otherwise, she still loved him. That he despised her tore at her insides.

Regardless of the hurt she'd caused, their baby was not a mistake. There was a new, precious life within her, and Julia would never be sorry for her child.

She had known Nick would be angry when he discovered her identity. But the vehemence of his hatred last night had caught her off guard. He'd accused her of making a fool of him.

Heavens, did he truly believe such a thing?

The door flew open and Aunt Theo's plump frame emerged. "La, it is all over town. All over, I tell you! I've just been to the flower market and everyone stopped me to talk about it."

Fear gripped her and Julia sat up. She'd been so sure no one saw her and Nick together last night. "Talking about what?"

"Your husband is here. In London." Theo waved her arms wildly. "He punched Lord Winchester in the middle of White's last evening. It's all anyone can talk about."

Nick *punched* Simon? That didn't make any sense. Unless. . . . Nick must be furious at Simon for helping her. Julia flopped back on the bed. "Oh, it's all my fault, Aunt Theo. This whole mess. Whatever made me think finding Colton was a good idea?"

Theo sat on the edge of Julia's bed. "Winchester's no half-wit. He knew the risks when he agreed to help you. And I believe he's quite capable of holding his own against Colton. I'm worried about *you*, what Colton will do if he finds you."

"He already found me."

"*He did?* When?"

"Last night at the Collingswood ball. I went out to the terrace for some air and Colton was waiting outside."

"Did he recognize you?" Theo asked. At Julia's nod, she prompted, "Well, what happened?"

"I vomited all over him."

Theo roared with laughter, long and loud, and wiped tears of mirth from her eyes. "Oh, my dear. That is the best news I've heard all day."

"It was horribly embarrassing," Julia admitted. "He is so angry, Theo. He hates me. I asked him why he came back to London and he said for revenge. The idea makes me positively sick. What is he planning to do?"

"How did he know who you were, I wonder?"

Julia frowned. "I don't know. I didn't think to ask, I was so caught off guard. Perhaps one of our servants in Venice?"

Theo waved that off. "No, none knew your true identity, and we were careful in front of them. Perhaps the hair and makeup did not disguise you as much as we'd hoped. Then Colton saw you at the ball and recognized your face."

"Perhaps," Julia said. It seemed unlikely, but what other explanation could there be? "He knows I'm with child."

"And what did he say about the fact you're carrying his babe?"

"Nothing, other than a mocking remark about the pregnancy agreeing with me after I threw up in the carriage."

"I thought you said you threw up on Colton?"

"I did," Julia answered. "Then I was ill again on the way here."

"Oh, you poor dear," Theo crooned. "Well, get some rest. We'll be besieged with callers today." She stood up. "Or would you rather hide in your chambers all day?"

Julia shook her head. "I have to face them. If I do not, the gossip will only worsen."

A brief knock sounded and Meg poked her head in. "I have your chocolate, Your Grace."

"Come in, please, Meg. We've a long day ahead of us."

There was already a stack of cards waiting by the time Julia had dressed. Simon's was on top. She flipped it over and read his handwritten note. *I'll return in one hour.*

Continuing to the sitting room, Julia joined Aunt Theo to await the barrage of callers. She felt a bit like a woman receiving condolences on her way to the gallows.

"You look quite smart today," Theo said, taking in Julia's lilac muslin day dress. "How is your stomach?"

"Shaky. However, I'm not sure if it's the babe or Colton causing my nerves."

Theo poured her a cup of tea. "Your duke's merely feeling the sting to his pride. No man likes to be duped, no matter the reason. They wish to believe themselves superior to the whole female race, you know. Give him a few weeks to recover. He'll come around."

"I wish I shared your confidence," Julia muttered, and accepted the tea from her aunt's hand.

Their butler opened the door and announced Simon. "Please show him up," Julia said. "And turn away all other callers until Lord Winchester leaves."

A minute later, Simon bounded into the room, a dark, large bruise on his left cheek.

Julia gasped as he bowed. "Oh, Simon. It looks awful. I feel wretched. This is all my fault."

Theo squinted, holding up her quizzing glass for closer inspection. "That's a beauty of a facer. He gave it to you good, my lord."

He dropped into a chair, leaned back, and smiled. "Wouldn't have been nearly so bad if Colton hadn't snuck up on me. And I knew the consequences when I agreed to help you, Julia. I've been a friend to Colton for ages, and he's fairly predictable. Besides"—he crossed his legs—"I'm more worried about you. Has he been to see you yet?"

She nodded glumly. "He found me last night at the Collingswood ball. Scared me half to death out on the terrace."

"Tell him the best part," Theo prompted.

Simon raised an eyebrow in question, and Julia blurted, "I vomited on him."

His bark of laughter reverberated off the sitting

room walls, blue eyes sparking with delight. "Oh, how I wish I had been there to see that."

"Be relieved you did not. It was quite embarrassing, and Colton was furious. What I cannot figure out is how he knew me. Right away, he addressed me as *Your Grace.*"

Simon shifted uncomfortably in his chair. "That was my fault. I did not tell you, but I left him a note in Venice. I confessed to who you were and apologized for helping you—"

"Simon!" Julia gasped. "Why did you not tell me?"

He held up his hands. "I honestly did not expect him to follow you back to London. But I knew you would write to him in any event, explaining your side. So I wanted to . . . prepare him, I suppose. Are you angry with me?"

She gazed at her longtime friend. "How could I be angry with you? You've helped me at great expense to yourself, Simon. I will always be grateful to you. By the by, I am curious as to what Colton said after he hit you."

"Nothing of consequence," Simon answered. "He's furious, naturally, but I plan to deal with him later."

"Did you also tell him I carried his babe?"

"No. Did he know?"

"Yes, but perhaps the sickness gave me away." She sipped her tea, now blessedly tepid. It was easier on her stomach that way. "He spoke of revenge, Simon. Said I made a fool of him and that I would live to regret it. What will he do?"

Simon rolled his eyes. "Colton is getting quite dramatic in his old age. But he won't hurt you, Julia. I'll make sure of that."

"You may not be able to prevent it," Theo warned. "The man is her husband, after all."

Simon mulled that over. "If you need me, day or night, send for me. I will come. I don't believe Colton will hurt you. But he may make things . . . uncomfortable for awhile."

Just as Julia was about to ask what *uncomfortable* meant, the door slammed open and the subject of their conversation marched inside.

Dressed in an elegant royal blue frock coat with a cream-colored brocade waistcoat, tall boots over tan breeches, the Duke of Colton surveyed the room with cold gray eyes. "My, what a charming little scene this is."

Simon shot to his feet. "You are making a habit of sneaking about, Colton. You used to be much more direct."

Colton seemed to grow larger, the stark planes of his face etched in fury. "How is this for direct, then, Winchester? *Get the hell out of my wife's house,*" he snarled.

Simon's nostrils flared, and the two men stared intently at one another. Julia didn't know what to do. She glanced at Theo, whose eyes were as big as saucers. With their clenched fists and tight jaws, Simon and Nick were carrying on a silent conversation only they understood.

"Fine," Simon gritted out. "But I'll be by later to deal with you, and you had better be receiving, Colton." He turned to Julia and Theo and gave a curt bow. "Ladies."

He stalked out of the room and closed the door behind him with a snap. Colton turned to Theo.

"Lady Carville, I would like a private word with my *wife*." He gritted out the last word as if acutely painful to say.

So he'd learned Theo's identity as well. Her aunt shot a nervous glance at Julia. "Of course, Your Grace. If you'll just excuse me," she said before scurrying out of the sitting room.

Julia sat back and lifted her chin. She refused to cower in front of this man. He'd ignored her for eight years, leaving her to fend for herself. Obviously what they shared in Venice was over, and he resented her. Fine. She resented him, too.

Ignoring the pain in her heart, she steeled herself. "Well, you've scared everyone off, Colton. What is it you want?"

Her direct approach took him aback. He looked slightly confused, but only for a moment. "You didn't think you'd seen the last of me, did you, sweet wife?" Walking over, he gracefully folded himself down into a chair, flipping up the tails of his coat. "No, I plan on staying."

She didn't want to notice his handsomeness, how his silky black hair fell artlessly back away from his angular face. He was clean-shaven, but she could remember vividly the feel of his whiskers on the soft skin of her inner thighs. And at night, she still dreamed of the hard push of his erection as he first penetrated her wetness.

Julia caught herself, and her eyes flew to his. He was watching her carefully, and a spark in those gray depths told her he knew exactly what she'd been thinking. Heat broke out on her skin as a flush worked its way up her neck.

"So beautiful," he murmured. "So deceitful."

She straightened. "And does your visit have a purpose?"

"Yes. I want to know the father of your child. I plan to kill him before the day's out."

Dramatic indeed, she thought. And what did he mean? Oh God . . . he didn't believe . . .

"*You* are the father, Colton."

He tipped his head back and laughed, the sound harsh and lacking any joy whatsoever. "Christ, you must think me gullible."

She gaped at him. "Colton, you are this baby's father. I haven't . . . been with anyone else."

His whole body tensed and he leaned forward, angry. "Stop lying to me, wife. You were no virgin when I first took you."

She flinched. At least now she knew why he thought she'd made a fool of him. He believed that she'd found herself with child, whereby she came to Venice to legitimize it by bedding him.

It was tempting to tell him about Templeton, but pride stopped her. Perhaps explaining her financial troubles would reach the cold place in her husband's chest where his heart should be. But Julia found she couldn't do it. She wanted him to believe the baby was his because he trusted her.

"It's the truth, whether you want to believe it or not. I washed the blood off so you wouldn't know. I wanted you to think I was a courtesan, Colton."

"I don't believe you." He crossed his arms over his chest. "Is it Wyndham's?"

Her eyes widened. Who had told her husband about Wyndham?

"Yes, I know about your cicisbeo, madam. If Winchester hadn't already told me about him in Venice, there were a handful of people positively eager to inform me when I arrived in London."

"There was never anything other than flirtation with Lord Wyndham, which is more than I can say for *you,* Colton. How many women have you bedded since we recited our marriage vows?"

"That is immaterial," he snapped. "I don't run the risk of carrying a bastard." He gestured to her abdomen.

"This child is *not* a bastard, you dolt." Oh, he made her furious. Her blood almost boiled inside her skin. She sat up straighter. "You will acknowledge it, and then you will leave London. Go back to Venice. Or go to St. Petersburg. All I need is for this child to carry your name."

"That will never happen. I know that babe belongs to another man. Any child of yours will not carry my name."

She saw he really believed it. There would be no telling him otherwise. She was furious, yes, but also had the sudden urge to cry. With her emotions rioting, she wished to be alone. To think over how to resolve the mess she'd made. "Get out, Colton."

"If you think tears will sway me, madam, you are sorely mistaken."

Her fingers came up to her face, feeling wetness on her cheeks. She hadn't even realized she'd started crying. She took a long, shaky breath. Her morning meal threatened to make another appearance, and the last thing she wanted was to humiliate herself in front of her husband again.

She stood up. He remained seated, the arrogant arse, merely quirking a brow at her. "Good day, sir." Stepping around his chair, she moved toward the door.

In a flash, he jumped up and grabbed her arm, stopping her. "You cannot dismiss me, duchess," he gritted out, his breath hot against her ear. "And you cannot get rid of me in order to carry on with your pack of lovers here in Town." She stiffened and tried to pull away but his grip was strong. "Is it Winchester's? Are you having Simon's baby?"

Her free hand flew up and, before she could prevent it, cracked across Nick's face. She froze, shocked at what she'd done, as the sound, harsh and ugly, echoed throughout the room. He slowly turned his head back to look at her. His gray eyes glittered with hatred, rage, and—much to her surprise—desire.

He dragged her up against the hard planes of his body, her breasts crushed to his chest. Her pulse picked up, but shamefully, not out of anger. She was stunned. How could she still feel anything for this man after the hurtful things he'd said?

Then his free hand slid up the side of her rib cage to rest beneath her breast, his thumb tracing the plump underside lazily. She closed her eyes against the swift and sharp rush of need that swept through her. Her breath came fast and harsh, and it was all she could do to not push her breast into his palm. They were tender, the pregnancy making them more sensitive, and they ached, desperate for his touch.

"You were so willing to play the whore for a duke,"

he murmured, his thumb gliding higher to tease her nipple through her layers of clothing. "Would you be so willing to play one for a husband, I wonder?"

Gasping, she jerked away from him—and this time he let her go. "You bastard," she hissed before stomping out of the room.

Chapter Nine

Men are but petulant children at times. If he leaves
your bed in a fit of pique, let him go. He shall return.

—Miss Pearl Kelly to the Duchess of Colton

Nick left his wife's town house and strode to his
carriage, more shaken than he wanted to admit.

Damn her. No matter what she'd done, his body
still wanted her. Nay, *craved* her. She'd stared daggers
at him, furious and indignant, while all he could
think about was pulling her down to the carpet and
thrusting his cock into her sweet slickness, fucking
her. Hard.

After what she'd done, he should hate her. And he
did hate her. But the instant he'd grabbed her and
felt the heavy weight of her breasts on his chest, his
cock hardened to the point of pain. Bloody hell, what
a mess.

"Home, Fitz," he snapped before climbing inside
his carriage. He settled against the squabs and
watched the familiar streets of Mayfair out the
window. Eight years he'd managed to stay away, lived

in places where no one knew or cared about his reputation or the scandal. Eight blissful years of near anonymity, free from his past. Now he was back. Forced to return home by his lying, cheating wife.

His chest bursting with rage, it was all he could do to sit still as the vehicle carried him home.

She was every bit as beautiful as a blonde—perhaps more so. The golden color of her hair—rather than the bold, brassy red locks from Venice—made her seem delicate and ethereal. Though she'd been anything but delicate when he insisted he was not the father of her child. No, then she'd been a warrior queen with regal posture and snapping blue eyes, adamant the child was his.

Not that he believed her.

They turned the corner and the Seaton town house came into view. A stand-alone monstrosity made of gray stone and black ironwork, it was forbidding and cold—exactly what you'd expect from the Seaton legacy. His ancestors, including his own parents, were not exactly known for being warm, kind-hearted people.

At least his parents were dead. When he returned to London, it had been a relief to discover that his mother would not be here to torment him. The last time he'd seen her, after Harry's funeral, she'd informed him he was no longer her son.

I wish you had died instead of Harry.

She hadn't even attended Nick's wedding, as brief and forgettable as it had been. Not that one could much blame her—*he* hadn't wanted to attend his wedding, either. But his father had seen to that. Apparently, nothing worked like threats and black-mail to force your son to fall in line.

Two weeks after Harry's funeral, the duke had roused Nick out of a drunken stupor to marry Julia. When he'd refused, the old bastard cleverly threatened to reveal the true circumstances behind Harry's death. Nick felt guiltily enough over what happened. He knew Harry's memory did not deserve to be dishonored in such a way, for the world to find out he'd hung himself in the study at Seaton Hall. So Nick had gone through with the ceremony, only to leave that very night, vowing never to return or consummate his marriage.

Vows now broken because of his wife's perfidy.

Nick heaved a sigh and buried the old pain as the carriage rolled to a stop. Once on the ground, he turned to Fitz. "I want her town house watched. I want to know who goes in and when they come out."

Fitz nodded. "Round the clock?"

"Yes, definitely round the clock." If she received late-night visitors, he most assuredly wanted to know. "I want regular reports. Go find someone to start now. Take the carriage."

Fitz nodded again, and Nick headed for the house. He stomped up the steps, where the door promptly opened. Marlowe, the butler, appeared.

"Good afternoon, Your Grace. I trust your appointment went well?" Marlowe relieved Nick of his hat and greatcoat.

"Fine," Nick muttered, and started for his study. He needed a drink.

"Your Grace, you have a visitor," Marlowe called after him.

Nick froze. "Who?"

"Lord Winchester awaits in the library. Would Your

Grace care to see him now? He was quite insistent on waiting until you returned."

Instead of answering, Nick stalked to the library door, threw it open, and discovered Winchester lounging in a chair.

Winchester glanced up, a glass of claret cradled in his palm.

"Comfortable?" Nick sneered. "Somehow I do not remember offering you a drink." He braced his feet and crossed his arms over his chest. Other than his wife, Winchester was the last person he wanted to see right now. "Or allowing you inside, for that matter."

"Marlowe has better manners than you ever did," Winchester remarked. "So are you planning to hit me again, or are you ready to talk like a sane, rational person?"

Nick took a step closer. "I couldn't say. Why don't you stand up and we shall find out."

Winchester sighed. "I think I'll stay seated, then."

Nick strode to the sideboard lined with decanters. He picked up a crystal glass and poured some of his father's best brandy. A cur, his father, but a fine judge of spirits nonetheless.

Nick took a seat across from Winchester and glared at his former friend. He could almost picture him with Julia, their blond heads close together as they whispered and kissed. Plotted. A hot jealous rage bubbled in his gut. He threw back a good portion of his brandy, relieved when the fire from the liquor burned his insides instead.

"Well?" he prompted.

"You are not prepared to make this easy, are you?"

"Why should I? You're damned fortunate I haven't yet demanded your seconds."

"*My* seconds?" Winchester exploded. "You . . . idiot. I should demand *your* seconds for the shameful way you've treated Julia."

"Careful," Nick warned in a deadly soft voice. "I wouldn't threaten me, were I you. And in the future, do not address my wife using her Christian name."

Winchester shook his head at the ceiling, exasperated. "You fool. You bloody conceited, arrogant fool. You are going to owe me quite a large apology when this is over."

Nick made a derisive sound, and Winchester's eyes narrowed. "I see you don't believe me. God, I don't know why I care. If it weren't for your wife . . ."

"Yes? By all means, finish your sentence. I do so want to hear of your feelings for my wife," Nick taunted. "Have you fucked her, Winchester?"

Winchester glared at him with such indignant anger that Nick knew the answer. His friend hadn't bedded Julia. Relief cascaded through him briefly, until he remembered she'd bedded *someone* other than him.

"You know I have not. I would not dishonor you in such a fashion, and Julia has been like a sister to me. And if you do not hold your tongue and listen to reason, Colton, I shall be forced to knock your teeth back in your throat."

Nick opened his mouth to dare Winchester to try, but the other man held up a hand. "No, for God's sake, man, do not dare me to do it. What I have to say is too important. Just cease speaking until I finish."

At Nick's terse nod, Winchester began. "I've known your wife since she was seven." Nick gave a sound of impatience, and Winchester snapped, "I know this is not new information, but let me get it all out.

"Though I am almost nine years older, your wife is the sister I never had. Every holiday, I came home from school and there she was, running around with the villagers as if she wasn't the daughter of a marquess. Their title can be traced back to Charles II, but Julia wasn't snobbish or judgmental. Everyone liked her. She's one of the best people I've ever known, man or woman."

Nick shifted, uncomfortable. He didn't want to hear of his wife's virtues just now—or ever, really—but he didn't interrupt as Winchester continued.

"Now what you are unaware of is that her father had creditors banging down the door. We didn't find out until it was too late, of course, but he had quite a gambling problem. She had no dowry. And because your father and the marquess were friends, the duke paid a good deal of money for Julia. Money that was soon gone a few years later."

Winchester took a sip of claret. "This is important because of what happened when you left. Julia's father died a year after your wedding. Upon his death, she discovered everything would need to be sold off in order to pay his gaming debts. She received no inheritance from him whatsoever."

Nick cursed softly, and Winchester nodded. "Indeed. Julia had a little money of her own, left to her when her mother died many years ago, but it was not much. She did, however, receive a stipend from the Colton estate, arranged by her father at the time of the wedding. It was little more than pin money, really. Your mother did not even want Julia to have that, but could not prevent it. She did prevent Julia from living in any of the ducal properties, however. So Julia was forced to be careful and frugal, and along with whatever money her aunt had, the two of them rented their small town house in Mayfair. Remember your second cousin, Lord Templeton?"

Nick shrugged. "Barely."

"A few years after your father died, Templeton produced documents asserting his position as guardian to the Colton estate in your absentia. Your mother could have stopped him, but she didn't, and Templeton continued to wrest more and more control—and money—away for himself.

"He's been whittling down Julia's stipend for the last three years. When she realized her funds were desperately low, your wife paid a visit to your mother."

Nick winced, thinking as he swirled the brandy in his glass. Julia must have been quite desperate to see the dowager duchess. No doubt his mother would refuse help to anyone having anything to do with her least favorite son. So why hadn't Julia written to him? Winchester had known where to find him over the years. His wife could have asked for help, and he . . . might have interceded on her behalf.

Winchester said, "One can imagine how that conversation went over. Julia became desperate when your mother refused to help her. And then Templeton came to see her one more time, informing her of a further reduction in her stipend. This made her quite frantic because they were already financially strapped. When she protested, your cousin told her how she could supplement her stipend—by performing sexual favors for him. And if you dare suggest she agreed to it, I will strangle you with my bare hands."

Nick said nothing. Several theories swirled in his head but none were suitable for sharing with Winchester. The man would defend the duchess with his dying breath, apparently.

"You've left her alone for eight bloody years, Colton. She's been preyed upon, cheated, and left nearly destitute because of your family. You are the one who stood before God and promised to care and provide for her—and you've done neither. The scheme to seduce you, while unwise, was her last effort to gain a bit of control for herself. She believed if she could give birth to your child, the Colton heir, your mother would provide more financial support for her."

Nick swallowed more brandy, absorbing Winchester's words. Yes, he had promised to love and honor his wife, but it had been a vow made unwillingly. He'd never wanted to be married. But perhaps leaving her to fend for herself for eight years had been rather . . . uncharitable of him.

Still, she had no right to trick him. And the idea she'd been a virgin that first time was ludicrous. She'd ridden him in a *chair,* for God's sake. Ladies of quality were raised to undertake marital relations only while in bed, in the dark of night, under the covers with only the smallest amount of contact. He'd spilled his seed in her *mouth.* No gently bred lady would allow such a thing. No, he and Julia both knew the truth. Time would prove him right.

Winchester was watching him carefully, so Nick asked, "Are you finished?"

Winchester sighed and nodded.

"You might believe that tale, but I do not. I bedded her, and I'm telling you she was no virgin. Experienced in ways no untried lady could ever claim to be."

Winchester began to protest and Nick held up a

hand. "No, I listened to you, so now you listen to me. While the story of financial woe certainly rings true— which I will rectify at my first opportunity—I believe she found herself with child, coerced you into bringing her to Venice, and seduced me to legitimize her bastard."

"That is *preposterous!*" Winchester bellowed, claret sloshing in his glass as he flew to his feet. "She was experienced because she'd hired a courtesan to give her advice. Jesus, Colton!" He began pacing. "Must you think the worst of everyone? I know your mother ignored you and your father was an arse, but the rest of the world is not *all* like that. Julia would never trick you in such a manner. Not in a hundred years. She has too much pride."

Nick rose as well. "Well, I suppose we'll find out when the child is born, will we not? I've done the counting. If the baby is mine, it shall be born in September."

"And Julia is supposed to wait seven months for you to acknowledge the child she carries? God, you are stubborn. Do you know what the tabbies and printmakers will do to her reputation in that amount of time? I know you are angry, but to allow them to rip her apart is extraordinarily cruel—even for you. And what of your child's reputation? Think of someone other than yourself for a change, Colton."

Nick had not considered the gossip, but he wasn't about to admit it to Winchester. A small amount of guilt nagged at him. Then he came up with a solution that solved both the problem of Julia's reputation as well as whoever was cuckolding him. "Fine. I'll send her away from Town, to Seaton Hall."

Winchester chuckled. "If you think she'll agree to that, you're cracked."

"She won't have a choice."

"Nick, you should know—" Winchester started, then stopped. He shook his head and looked away.

"What?"

"No, I will not involve myself further. You are on your own and may God help you both." He tossed the rest of the claret into his mouth and placed the glass on a table, then gave Nick a hard look. "Just do not hurt her. Or I'll come after you, I swear."

Late that afternoon, a footman from Colton's staff arrived with a note. It was brief:

Pack. You leave for Seaton Hall in the morning.

N.S.

Julia's eye began twitching, so she pressed two fingers on the area, massaging.

"What is it?" Theo asked.

"I am being ordered to Seaton Hall." She looked up at the footman. "I'll need to send a reply. If you'll give me a moment."

He nodded and went to wait in the corridor while Julia showed the note to her aunt.

"Not a man of many words, is he?" Theo mumbled. "What will you say?"

"Tell him no, of course." Julia went to her writing desk where she picked up her pen. "Is *'Go to the blazes'* too harsh a reply?" she asked Theo.

"Not in my opinion, but you've got to soothe his

pride, I'm afraid. A little sweetness goes a long way with a man."

Julia muttered all sorts of horrible things about male pride under her breath before putting pen to paper. She wrote:

> *I appreciate your concern, but I believe that course of action unwise. It is much too soon for my confinement.*
>
> *J.S.*

She sent off the reply, then had a good chuckle with Theo over it. The very idea of being shipped off to his country estate . . . Why would he ever think she'd agree to such a thing? She went back to her book, satisfied the matter would be dropped.

Twenty minutes later, the duke's footman returned.

> *You are my wife, madam, and shall therefore go wherever I tell you. My carriage will arrive at eight o'clock tomorrow morning. If you are not ready and waiting, Fitz has instructions to collect you as you are.*
>
> *N.S.*

Theo clucked her tongue when she read the note. "I suppose we best get you packed."

"I have no intention of going," Julia stated emphatically. "Let Fitz come and take me, then. Colton cannot force me to do anything."

Theo raised her eyebrows. "Really, Julia. I am not sure such a battle will benefit the babe."

A twinge of guilt lodged in her chest. The last thing she wanted to do was harm her child. Could Theo be right? "How long does Colton expect me to stay there? The idea of forcing me from my home is . . . medieval."

"Well, we cannot be all doom and gloom. It will be best for the baby to be born in the country. Merely approach it as an opportunity to get settled before you're too far along."

Julia drummed her fingers on the table. She had thought to travel to the country in her sixth or seventh month. Perhaps going earlier made sense. She sighed. "If I go, please tell me you'll come with me."

"You know how I hate the country, my dear. All that fresh air and tedium. I shall make you miserable."

"Please, Aunt Theo. I need you there. Just until the baby's born."

Mentioning the baby did the trick, as Julia suspected it might. Theo's face softened and she nodded. "I cannot refuse when you put it like that. Of course I'll go with you. Lud, I had better go see to the packing right away."

Julia smiled. "Thank you, Theo. I don't know what I would do without you."

Theo came over and hugged her. "I feel the same about you. You've kept me from being a lonely old widow all these years."

Julia wiped her eyes. "Heavens, I've never cried this much in my life."

"It's the babe," Theo said, heading to the door. "It'll get better."

Julia penned a reply:

*I have decided to go, as the country air will benefit
the babe. My aunt has agreed to join me. Are you
coming as well?*

J.S.

It wasn't until dinnertime that the duke replied.
Julia and Theo were in the small dining room, enjoying turtle soup, when the duke's footman reap-
peared. She opened the note and read Colton's
response:

No.

N.S.

No explanation, no promise to visit her. One word
had been all her husband could spare. A single word
from the man who'd pursued Mrs. Leighton so ar-
dently in Venice. Angrier than she wanted to admit,
Julia crumpled the paper in her fist and dropped it in
her nearly untouched bowl of soup.

The small, childish gesture made her feel better.

"Would Your Grace care to send a reply?" Colton's
footman asked, his eyes aghast at seeing the duke's
missive float atop the turtle soup.

"No, that will not be necessary."

When she and Theo were alone again in the
dining room, Julia told her of the exchange.

"He's not coming?" Theo shrieked.

"No. I do not know whether to be furious or
relieved. Eight years that man has been gone, and the
minute he comes home, orders me to one of his
country estates. Alone! What is he thinking?"

"I fear you have your work cut out for you when it comes to your husband."

Julia sighed. "I know. He's angry and it's clear he does not want to see me. Perhaps it is for the best."

"Best, my arse. How are two people supposed to—" She sighed and picked up her spoon. "No wonder someone wants to kill that man."

"Aunt Theo!" Julia loved her aunt, but the woman sometimes said the most outrageous things.

"Well, it's true. Now, it might be the sherry, but I cannot seem to recall where Seaton Hall is located."

"Just outside Norfolk. I've only been once, when I sought help from the dowager duchess. It's a beautiful property. We'll need bread crumbs, however, to ensure we can find our way around it."

"I'll make sure to pack some," Theo said with a grin. She gestured to Julia's bowl. "Would you care for more soup, dear?"

Irritable and restless, Nick paced in his study. It was too late to deal with Templeton tonight, so he had no outlet for this burning, itchy feeling beneath his skin. Part frustration, part anger, and part something else that felt close to guilt had him unable to sit down.

Winchester's earlier words still haunted him. He didn't like contemplating the pain and suffering Julia had gone through in his absence. What had his mother been thinking? Turning the estate over to Templeton was nothing short of foolish, and his mother had always been a shrewd, calculating woman. Had it been a ploy to get her son to return to England? Now that she had died, he'd never get the chance to ask her.

So Julia and Winchester had not been lovers. Who had it been, then? Who had his wife invited to her bed? Wyndham seemed the most likely. But there could have been more than one lover in her past. After all, Julia's depth of experience would not have come from one or two quick tups in the garden during a ball. Nor did it come from a conversation or two with a courtesan. No, some man had gone to a great deal of effort to educate his wife. Taught her where to touch, how to kiss. Shown her the exact way to drive a man wild.

And Nick planned to find out exactly who it had been.

He pictured her, the last time before they parted in Venice, her luscious lips wrapped around the head of his cock, and he almost groaned. The need for her was there, simmering in his gut, despite the fact she had duped him. Unfortunately, his body did not care what his mind knew. And he wanted her so badly he feared he would go mad from it.

Well, the time had come to do something about it.

Nick strode to the door. "Marlowe," he shouted. "Have my carriage sent round."

Marlowe appeared and instructed a footman to run out to the mews. "Your coat, Your Grace?"

By the time he'd gathered his coat, hat, and cane, the carriage had pulled around to the front door, Fitz at the reins. Nick gave an address he hadn't forgotten in eight years.

The trip did not take long, and soon Nick bounded up the stairs of the unassuming three-story house. One would never guess from the outside that this was the most elite brothel in London, a place Nick remembered quite well. A man nearly Fitz's size opened the door, and Nick sauntered inside.

Madame Hartley rushed over. "Your Grace. I heard you had returned. I so hoped you would come and see me."

With her delicate features and graceful manners, Madame Hartley was a beautiful woman. Nick took in her tasteful lemon-colored silk evening dress and gloves. If one saw her on the streets of London, one would never know she was the abbess of the most exclusive nunnery in the city.

"How could I stay away?" Nick murmured as a footman offered a drink on a salver. Whisky. She had remembered. "I see little has changed in eight years."

In the main salon off to the right, richly patterned red wallpaper surrounded elegant furniture, where the fashionable men of the *ton* socialized with Madame's girls. Right now, business was brisk. No fewer than six men relaxed around the room with drinks in hand, settled in for an evening of civilized debauchery.

Nick inhaled deeply, the familiar scent of cheap, cloying perfume mixed with sex like a balm to his lascivious soul. For him, this was home. He'd spent more nights here than he could count.

A fact his brother had thrown in Nick's face that one fateful night. *You've treated my wife no better than one of Hartley's whores. Perhaps Father is right. Perhaps you don't know the difference between a whore and a lady.*

"Do you have any specific requests this evening, Your Grace? Or would you care to wait and see if anyone strikes your fancy?" Madame Hartley started to lead him toward the main salon but Nick stopped her.

"I trust you, Madame. We know each other well enough."

Her lips tilted upward. "Yes, we do, Your Grace. A redhead this evening, I think." She turned and whispered to a girl nearby. Nick almost called her back to say under no circumstances did he want a redhead. But God, he did. He wanted one redhead in particular.

Maybe tonight he could forget her.

A few minutes later, Nick was led to what he knew to be the largest and plushest of the second-floor rooms. Having once been a regular customer had its benefits, he realized. The bed was large and a nice-sized marble fireplace rested on one wall, a cheerful fire blazing in the grate. The room was masculine, done in dark greens, blues, and heavy wooden furniture. Erotic drawings adorned the walls.

Nick was left alone to wait—but not for long.

When the door opened, a girl appeared and his heart almost stopped. It was uncanny. She looked so much like Juliet, he could scarcely breathe. Luscious, bountiful breasts, a small waist, fiery red hair piled on top of her head. Then his eyes flicked to her face and he immediately saw the differences. This woman didn't have Juliet's fine features or creamy white skin. No, she was coarser, less refined. And her eyes were brown where Juliet's were the clearest blue you'd ever hope to see. . . .

Nick shook himself. He *would* forget her.

Lifting a finger, he beckoned the girl toward him. She moved forward with a saucy swing to her hips then bobbed a curtsy. "Your Grace. Would you like to have a drink first?"

Nick shook his head. "No, that won't be necessary."

The tip of her tongue came out to trace her upper lip. "Shall I undress you, then?"

"God, yes," he murmured. "But first, take down your hair."

The girl smiled at him and began removing the pins from her hair. Bit by bit, the long red strands fell down to the middle of her back. She shook it out and he reached forward to run his fingers through it. Her hair wasn't quite as soft as—

Jesus. What was wrong with him?

He took her hands and placed them on the buttons to his trousers. As her nimble fingers went to work, Nick shrugged out of his coat and tossed it across the room to a chair. He'd started unbuttoning his waistcoat when her hand found his naked shaft.

He groaned and let his lids fall shut. Within seconds, he was fully hard. His hips rocked forward to thrust into her tightened fist. The girl freed him from his clothing and then dropped to her knees. Nick barely had time to comprehend what was happening before she brought him into her mouth.

"Yes," he hissed as she teased the underside with her tongue.

Sliding her lips over him, she took him deep, the tip of his shaft reaching the back of her throat. He tunneled his fingers in her hair, and let himself remember another time, another place.

She moved faster, sucking him harder, stroking him, and his chest began heaving with the effort to breathe. Lust rushed down his spine, and he felt himself grow even harder.

"Oh, yes, Juliet. Suck me, *cara.*"

The mouth suddenly withdrew, releasing him with a wet pop. Nick blinked and looked down.

"Will you be wanting to call me Juliet, then?" a strange face asked. It wasn't the face he'd been thinking of.

Disappointment crashed through him, and he struggled to maintain his composure. "Pardon?"

"You called me Juliet. Name's Sarah, but I don't mind what you call me."

"I did?" Embarrassment and frustration had Nick pulling away. He didn't want this woman. He wanted one particular woman, the one who'd left him in Venice.

Cursing himself a pathetic fool, he buttoned up his trousers. Would he ever be able to escape the memory of her?

"My apologies," he said. "I'll see you're paid for the whole night." He pulled on his coat, not bothering to button it, before striding into the corridor.

Chapter Ten

A little rivalry does a man good.

—Miss Pearl Kelly to the Duchess of Colton

At precisely quarter past eight the next morning, Julia and her aunt were loaded into the opulent ducal traveling coach, headed for Norfolk. The frigid February air had them huddling with warming bricks and thick blankets inside, while Fitz and the driver bundled up in gloves, coats, and furs outside.

Before they departed, Fitz had instructed Julia to bang on the roof if she needed to stop for any reason. Apparently he hadn't forgotten how she'd vomited over the side of the carriage the other night. Grateful, she thanked him, and then he added, "His Grace said not to push you too hard today, though he probably wouldn't want me repeatin' it." He winked and then got up on top of the perch.

"That man is quite scary," Theo whispered as they clattered away. "Where did Colton find him?"

"I don't know. Perhaps we can find out when we stop for lunch."

Theo shifted unhappily in her seat. "Heavens, I hate traveling. I can never get comfortable in one of these things. How do you feel? Did you eat this morning?"

Julia held up the satchel their cook had prepared for her. "I did, and I've got plenty of muffins, macaroons, and rolls to keep my stomach settled along the way."

"Good. I wonder if Colton has let his sister-in-law know we're to arrive tomorrow."

"Oh!" Julia exclaimed. "I had completely forgotten about her. How will she receive us? I can only imagine she won't be very happy to have guests."

"I do not know, but one would assume her to be quite lonely." Theo shifted again on her seat and muttered under her breath about long distances in carriages. "Have you ever wondered what really happened between her and Colton?"

Julia sighed. "I try not to think about it. Colton never denied seducing her—but never confirmed it, either. When I asked him about it in Venice, I sensed there was more to the story. It's . . . painful for him."

"Well, I would imagine so. Because of his actions, his brother died."

"I suppose. Although I think we can safely assume the Seatons were never a close family."

Theo grunted and closed her eyes. "Wake me for lunch, my dear. The only way I'll get through this horrendous ordeal is to sleep." Pulling the thick blankets up to her chest, she yawned. Ten minutes later, she began snoring.

* * *

The morning after Julia left, Nick and his newly hired solicitor presented themselves at his cousin's town house. Templeton's butler promptly ushered them inside to the study to await the arrival of the master of the house.

Templeton certainly lived well, Nick noted. It was a small house on the outskirts of Mayfair, but the furniture all looked fairly new. Nothing shabby or worn. Fresh flowers artfully arranged throughout— including tulips, which did not come cheap. Large Turkish rugs scattered on the floors and paintings littered the walls. A large number of crystal de- canters were displayed in the study, each brimming with spirits. Yes, Templeton lived well for a man who supposedly collected less than three hundred pounds per year.

While Nick didn't care about the Seaton legacy, or much about the Colton estate, really, he *did* care about being swindled. And he really, *really* cared about Templeton stealing his wife's money in hopes of forcing her to his bed.

Had Templeton succeeded? Had his cousin fa- thered Julia's baby?

The door opened and a man who Nick assumed to be Lord Templeton stepped inside. Thinning black hair and a high forehead, Templeton had a sharp nose and pointed chin. Nick recognized him imme- diately from the Collingswood ball. Nick had been outside on the terrace watching his wife, and this man had addressed her just before she came outside. To vomit.

Her reaction to him had not been favorable. In

fact, she'd been revolted. If this man and the duchess were lovers, Nick was the Archbishop of Canterbury.

Which meant Winchester had told the truth. Templeton had blackmailed the duchess in order to get under her skirts.

A new rush of fury whipped through Nick. Oh, he planned to enjoy this.

"Your Grace, what a pleasant surprise," Templeton said, his small opaque eyes shifting between the two visitors. "Welcome back to London."

"Thank you. May I present my new solicitor, Mr. Barnaby Young. He will be handling all of the Colton estate business from this point forward." Nick took a seat and brushed a piece of imaginary lint from his breeches while letting Templeton absorb the meaning of those words.

"I—I don't understand, Your Grace. I'm sure you don't want to handle the estate business in your short sojourn here in London." Templeton sat and Nick could see sweat beading on the man's upper lip.

"You're right, I do not. That is why I have hired Mr. Young. He will in turn hire a competent estate manager and the two of them will oversee my interests. So no matter how long my sojourn, you no longer need be involved."

Templeton's mouth worked as if he wanted to speak but couldn't find the words.

Nick gave him a smile that held no warmth. "No, do not thank me, Templeton. I know this news comes as a relief to you, how trying the duties have been for you these past few years." He gestured to Mr. Young. "Now if you don't mind, Mr. Young requires your signature on some papers I've had drawn up."

The solicitor produced a stack of papers from his

satchel and handed them to Templeton, who accepted them begrudgingly.

Nick stood and strolled over to the desk while Templeton read the contents. He heard Templeton gasp. "Keep reading," he told his cousin. "It gets better." On the surface of the desk, Nick saw stacks of bills from various shopkeepers and tradesmen.

"Your Grace," Templeton squeaked. "This is preposterous. It says here that if any funds are discovered to have been misappropriated in the last eight years, I will be required to pay those funds back to the estate."

"That is correct. Which won't be a problem, will it, cousin?"

Templeton's hand shook as he set the papers down on an end table, "But the estate manager had control of the funds as well. Why should I be made to cover any funds he may have misused? This is highly improper and entirely unfair."

"You may rest assured that Mr. Young and I will be speaking with my father's man today." He picked up the quill and twirled it in his fingers. "If he has cheated the estate of funds, he will be dealt with accordingly. In the meantime, it's in your best interest to sign these documents."

Templeton gestured toward the papers. "I'm not certain I should sign anything yet. Perhaps my own solicitor should review them."

"Mr. Young, please wait in the corridor for a moment."

Without a word, Nick's solicitor left the room, closing the door softly behind him.

Nick's smile faded. God, he wanted to pound Templeton into the ground. The man was obviously guilty, though he'd likely deny it until his dying breath.

Which, considering what he'd done to Julia, might be sooner rather than later.

The anger Nick had tried to control now erupted into a blistering fury. Standing in front of Templeton, he brought his foot up to the edge of the chair—and pushed. The chair rocked back on two legs and with one more nudge, it and Templeton smacked against the floor.

Nick quickly placed his boot heel atop Templeton's throat. The man's eyes went wide with fear, his face turning red, so Nick added a bit more pressure.

Templeton's eyes bulged and Nick knew he now had his cousin's full attention.

"If you thought," he snarled, "I would allow you to rob me blind and proposition my wife, you were wrong. If you ever, *ever* speak to the duchess again for any reason—or even look in her bloody direction— I won't bother to meet you at dawn like a gentleman. No, I will find you on a dark street one night, drag you into a back alley, and rip the beating heart from your chest with my bare hands."

With Templeton's skin gone purple, Nick lifted his foot, allowing the man to breathe. He stepped back and straightened his coat, satisfied when Templeton scurried up and away from him.

"Your involvement in my affairs is over, Templeton. Now you can sign those papers of your own free will and suffer the consequences, or you can look over your shoulder every night for the rest of your life, wondering and waiting to see what I might do."

Templeton swallowed and nodded.

"Excellent," Nick said, and then called Mr. Young back into the room.

If the solicitor was surprised to see a chair overturned and Templeton struggling to breathe, he showed no evidence of it.

The papers signed and witnessed, Mr. Young quickly put them away. "Now we require any account ledgers or paperwork you have pertaining to the Colton estate, Templeton." Nick crossed his arms over his chest and waited.

Five minutes later, Nick and his solicitor walked out. Templeton had claimed the old estate manager possessed the ledgers and they'd had no choice but to believe him.

"Mr. Young, take my carriage and go see my father's man. Let him know of the termination of his services and remove any paperwork and books we may need. I don't believe he'll give you any trouble, but if he does, my footman may fetch me."

"Yes, Your Grace."

"Take Mr. Young wherever he needs to go," Nick shouted to his coachman.

One of his footmen jumped down from the carriage. "Beg your pardon, Your Grace, but Mr. Fitzpatrick said I was to follow you wherever you went as long as he's away."

Nick heaved a sigh. It was like having a damn nursemaid. "Stay with Mr. Young, David. He may need your assistance more than I." When the boy started to protest, Nick held up a hand. "I'm walking over to my club and it isn't far. And we're in Mayfair, for God's sake. Nothing will happen to me."

"Fitz won't like it," the boy muttered.

"Yes, but I pay your wages," Nick snapped, and strode off down the street.

Only, he wasn't headed to White's. He'd lied. There was one more unpleasant task this morning, one he needed to do alone.

On the far side of Grosvenor Square lived one Lord Robert Wyndham.

Though it had been some time, Nick remembered Wyndham from the clubs and about town. Wyndham was a few years younger and seemed rather reserved. Bookish, if Nick had to guess. He looked the type. What Julia saw in the man, Nick could not fathom.

Ten minutes later, Nick gave his card to Wyndham's butler. Though an odd hour to make calls, no one left a duke dawdling on one's doorstep, especially not one as notorious as the Depraved Duke. As predicted, Nick was immediately shown into the sitting room and the servant left to ascertain his lordship's availability.

Nick had no doubt Wyndham would present himself.

Not long after, the door opened. Wyndham, who had clearly been dragged out of bed, hurried in. He had rather plain features, with short brown hair and brown eyes, and a thin beard that did nothing to contain the flush to the man's skin. Good. Wyndham knew why Nick was here.

"Your Grace," Wyndham greeted warily as both men sat down. "Welcome home."

"Thank you, Wyndham. I apologize for the early hour. This is a visit I'd rather no one took notice of."

Wyndham swallowed. "Was there something you needed, Your Grace?"

Nick regarded the other man thoughtfully, letting the moment linger. When Wyndham shifted uncomfortably in his chair, Nick asked, "Is there anything you should care to tell me, Wyndham?"

"I—I don't know what you mean." He cleared his throat. "What would I need to . . . tell you?"

"One hears things. Although I've lived away from London, you would be surprised how eager people are to speak of what happens here in Town." Nick leaned back and rested his ankle atop the opposite knee. While he may appear cool on the outside, inside he pulsed with uncertainty and anger. It was all he could do to keep from leaping forward, wrapping his hands around the man's throat, and forcing Wyndham to admit whether he'd bedded Julia. "So I'm quite current on all the latest *on dits.*"

"Well, if you've heard anything regarding me," Wyndham blurted, "there is no truth to the rumor. Absolutely none." He looked Nick straight in the eyes, unblinking.

The man might be an excellent liar, but Nick found himself believing Wyndham. Still, he wasn't absolutely sure—and he wouldn't be until September.

"That is good to know. Because if I thought certain rumors were true, I would be forced to deal with it. And you know, of course, I never bother following convention. Not to mention that I do not like to get up at dawn. No, I much prefer the element of surprise, of having my enemy wonder and wait. The anticipation of when I might retaliate. Not very sporting of me, I know, but infinitely more amusing. Do you understand, Wyndham?"

Wyndham nodded emphatically. "Oh, yes, Your Grace. Indeed I do."

"Excellent," Nick announced, and rose to his feet. "Then I believe we're done here."

Not long after arriving at Seaton Hall, Julia found herself wandering about the large, rambling structure. Nick's man, Fitz, had returned to London shortly after dropping them off, and Theo had ordered Julia to rest for two full days after the trip. Now that she felt better, Julia itched to explore her new home . . . at least her home for the next several months.

The house itself was enormous. With the weather still too cold to be outdoors, she walked the neverending maze of corridors as a way to keep her mind off the ever-present nausea, not to mention the anger and heartache over Nick's recent cruelty.

If only she hadn't ever met the sweet, tender man who'd wooed her so fervently in Venice. Such lovely memories—memories now tarnished with the knowledge that her husband thought the worst of her. He actually believed she came to Venice in order to legitimize another man's baby. Had called her a whore. Accused her of being intimate with both Simon and Wyndham.

And now he'd sent her away.

"Your Grace?"

Julia's head snapped up. Lady Lambert, the wife of Colton's late brother, stood a short distance away. She had greeted them warmly upon arrival, much to Theo and Julia's relief. "Good morning, Lady Lambert."

"Oh, please. Call me Angela." She smiled tentatively and gestured to the otherwise empty room behind her. "Would you mind if we sat for a moment? I wish to speak with you."

Julia nodded and followed into what turned out to be the music room. A large pianoforte rested in the corner, chairs surrounding it, while various stringed instruments and horns adorned the walls. Angela took a seat and motioned for Julia to do the same.

"I hope you do not think me forward," Angela began before smoothing her skirts. She cleared her throat. "But I should very much like us to be friends. I realize there are . . . reasons why you may not be interested in pursuing a friendship with me. Many things have been said, about me, about . . . your husband. So I wanted to assure you that any rumors you might have heard are false."

Julia started to speak and Angela held up a hand. "No, wait. Let me say everything I need to say. I loved my husband. I was devastated when he died. Many people believed the rumors about your husband and me, and I . . . didn't have many friends after that. Most of society turned their backs, except for the dowager duchess. Oh, they were polite to my face, of course, but said horrible things about me when they thought I couldn't hear. Invitations dried up as well. The dowager duchess was very . . . kind to me, and I will always be grateful to her for giving me a home when no one else would."

Angela's gaze fell, and Julia could see tears swimming in the woman's eyes. She reached forward and clasped Angela's hand, giving it a brief squeeze.

"I am so glad you are here," Angela whispered, squeezing back. "I have not had any friends near my own age in many years. It's been rather lonely, in fact.

It would mean everything to me if you could forget what you've heard and . . . please give me a chance to be your friend."

"Of course!" Julia exclaimed. "I should like that very much, Angela."

Angela visibly relaxed. "Good." She wiped her eyes and took a deep breath. "Now, how do you feel today?"

"Better, thank you. Every day, less and less nauseated." While Angela knew the baby was Nick's, Julia hadn't divulged the circumstances by which she'd gotten with child. She didn't plan on revealing that to anyone . . . ever.

"Well, since you're feeling better, perhaps you care to join me on my morning walks. I don't travel far and it would be nice to have company."

Julia nodded at Angela. "I'd love to. The fresh air and exercise will do me a world of good."

"Excellent! I have to ask again—are you certain you wouldn't rather I move out to the dower house? I feel awkward staying here, when it rightfully belongs to you. The dower house isn't far, and we could still see each other."

"Heavens, no," Julia answered. "The house is large enough for the three of us. I daresay we could invite thirty more guests and never bump into one another except at meals."

"Oh, thank you. I am so grateful. After being here with the dowager duchess for so many years, I find myself starved for talk of parties and fashion . . . and scandals that do not involve myself."

"Well, Theo is certainly an expert on all of that." Julia chuckled. "So you no longer have family of your own?"

"No. My mother died a few months after Harry. My father was killed in a carriage accident when I was small, and I never had any brothers or sisters."

"That sounds familiar," Julia murmured. "Except for Theo, I have no family left."

"You have the duke," Angela said, as if such information should be a comfort.

Julia made a noncommittal sound and stared at the pianoforte. She didn't want to discuss her husband. Her heart was still too raw, her anger at his mistrust too fresh.

They sat in silence for a long moment. Then Angela asked, "Will he come and visit you, do you think?"

Julia could hear a note of something in Angela's voice but couldn't quite place it. Hope? Eagerness? Fear? "I honestly do not know."

"Well, Theo and I can keep you amused in the meantime." Angela stood. "I believe I'll spend some time in front of the pianoforte. I'll see you this afternoon, Your Grace."

"Please, call me Julia. We are sisters-in-law, after all."

Angela grinned. "Thank you, Julia."

With a wave of farewell, Julia took her leave and continued her wanderings about the Hall. Something about the conversation with Angela left her a bit uneasy. Did Angela have designs on Nick? If they truly had been intimate at one time, she may be eager to renew the affair. So would Nick refuse her? Better not to know the answer to that question.

A month went by, and Julia had to accept that Nick wasn't coming to visit her. He hadn't written, either.

There'd been no word from him of any kind since the terse exchange in London. Once again, she'd been left to fend for herself.

Only, she wasn't exactly alone. A precious little life now grew inside her. Nick's baby. Some days, Julia could scarcely believe that in a few short months, she would be a mother.

In the last two weeks, the sickness had begun to abate. Now she felt ill only first thing in the morning, before she filled her stomach. The remainder of the day Julia found herself constantly hungry, eating everything in sight. Instead of hanging off her frame, her dresses were finally becoming snug.

Julia and Angela had taken to walking together each morning. Aunt Theo refused to join them, saying there was only so much nature an old woman could take.

The two young women talked easily as they tramped about the estate. The vastness of the Seaton property amazed Julia. There were endless hills and fields, spectacular gardens, a dense forest, and the River Wensum even ran through at one point. She could almost imagine Nick as a precocious little black-haired boy, running all about and causing trouble.

This particular morning, Angela suggested they walk through the forest, on a path that led from the pond out to the dower house. They set off, wearing multiple petticoats and heavy pelisses to ward off the April chill. The fog had swept in the previous night and one couldn't see far into the distance, but this was a path they'd taken a few times before.

Angela chattered on incessantly and Julia found herself listening with half an ear. The grounds were lovely, fresh grass sprinkled with delicate purple, white, and yellow crocuses. Regardless of how she felt about her husband, one could not deny the beauty of the ducal family seat. The last time Julia visited, she'd been treated as an interloper. An outcast. This time she was the lady of the house. Everyone deferred to her in Colton's absence, and no one contradicted her wishes here. And likely there never would be, since her husband clearly had no plans to visit.

They trudged deeper into the forest, where the birds and insects echoed loudly in the morning stillness. Here, the ground sloped dramatically alongside the narrow path. Due to the sparse light under the dense canopy of trees, the leaves and moss remained slippery, forcing Julia to pick her way carefully along the path.

She wondered again how Nick was spending his time in London. Pride kept her from writing him or anyone else to ask. She'd written to Sophie, but only to tell her friend of her extended stay at Seaton Hall. Sophie had replied with plans for a visit, but no news of the duke.

Had he a mistress? Seemed likely, as the idea of the Depraved Duke remaining celibate was laughable at best.

She told herself she was still angry with him and therefore didn't care if he bedded other women. And yet, she did. Quite a lot. The memory of his clever hands and hot mouth haunted her. Her body, lush and ripe with pregnancy, remembered him, ached for him in the lonely darkness of her chamber.

Not to mention her foolish heart, which refused to let go of the tender memories from their glorious week together in Venice. The way he'd smiled at her. His laugh. How he'd made her feel like the most beautiful, most desirable woman in the world. Had she been mad to believe he'd felt more than lust for her?

"Don't you think, Julia?" Angela asked, breaking into Julia's reverie.

"I beg your pardon. What did you ask?" Julia tripped over a stone and winced. "I was not paying attention."

"Obviously." Angela chuckled and moved ahead to step over a root lying on the path. "I suggested the nursery be redecorated. Perhaps—"

As Julia stepped over the root, she must have misjudged its placement because her toe caught and she lost her balance. Instead of righting, she pitched sideways, the ground shifting beneath her feet, and she fell—only to slide in the wet leaves and grass along the steep embankment. Before she could find purchase, Julia felt herself tumble down the side of the slope.

"Angela!" she screamed as she clawed at the dense underbrush. But everything was too slick to grasp, and her horror mounted.

She rolled and bounced toward the bottom of the embankment, her hands covering her belly to protect the babe in the tumultuous descent. Her leg snagged on a branch, followed by a sharp bite of pain in her ankle.

Then her head collided with a tree trunk, and a burst of agony exploded in her skull before everything went black.

* * *

The light hurt her eyes. Julia closed her lids tightly and struggled to remember. Heavens, her head ached along with her ankle. She moved her hands, touching leaves, sticks, and grass. Yes, she'd tripped and fallen along the steep part of the forest path. So where was Angela?

Taking a few steadying breaths, she cracked her lids and saw no one about. Perhaps Angela had gone to fetch help. Julia gingerly tested her limbs to assess the extent of her injuries. She was better off than she feared. Other than her ankle and a nasty headache, she could likely climb to the path. There was no sense in waiting for someone to come drag her up.

Carefully, she crawled toward the path, using roots and fallen branches to assist her. The ground was slick and a few times she slid down a short distance until she could find footing enough to keep climbing. Her sore ankle hampered her some, but sheer will got her back up to the path. Once on level ground, she located a tall, thick branch to serve as a walking stick and used it to make her way back to the hall.

It felt like hours, and she nearly dropped in exhaustion by the time she entered the house. Gasping for breath, she allowed the butler to bring a chair over just inside the door. He then sent a footman to fetch the physician from the village.

Just then, Angela came around the corner, Theo and another footman right behind her. The three of them stopped in their tracks when they saw Julia, dirty and bedraggled, on a chair in the entryway.

"Julia!" Angela flew to her side, relief etched on her face. "I raced back to the house to get help.

I didn't know what else to do. How badly are you hurt?"

"John, carry Her Grace up the stairs," Theo ordered. "Angela, send for the doctor and then ask the cook for something to eat. I'll fetch the brandy."

"Doctor's already been sent for," Julia said wearily as the footman lifted her out of the chair. "And I do not need food. Just help me upstairs."

Soon Julia found herself tucked in bed, surrounded by pillows and a room full of worried faces.

"I am fine," she told them. Theo and Angela sat on the end of her bed, their brows creased with concern. "Really, I'm fine. I have a headache and my ankle hurts like the blazes. But I shall live."

"But what about the baby?" Angela asked in a panicked, hushed tone. "Heavens, I'll feel wretched if something happens to your baby. I never should have taken you out on that path today. It was too misty and wet."

"Hush, girl," Theo snapped. "It's not your fault and we won't know about the baby until the doctor gets here. No sense in making anyone hysterical."

Julia took another sip of brandy. "I'm merely tired. I feel as if I could sleep for days." As if to prove it, she yawned.

"Do not sleep," Theo told her. "Not until the doctor gets here and has a chance to look you over."

The doctor arrived half an hour later. A nice, older man, he took his time examining her. He was gentle and respectful, and talked the whole time both to relax her and keep her awake.

When he finished, Theo and Angela came back into her room to hear the results.

"Her Grace has a slight concussion, which should resolve itself in a few days with some rest. I'll leave laudanum for the pain, but I would advise against using it unless absolutely necessary. The ankle is sprained and should be elevated for a few days. In a week or so, Your Grace should be fine."

He cleared his throat. "With regards to the babe, I couldn't say whether Your Grace will lose it or not. Falls have been known to precipitate a miscarriage. So if Your Grace does not begin bleeding in the next day or so, I'd say it likely the pregnancy will keep. However, if Your Grace begins cramping or bleeding, send for the midwife. I am happy to come as well, but Mrs. Popper has plenty of experience when it comes to both losing and birthing babies. She might be able to give you something to help stop the process."

The room fell silent. *Falls have been known to precipitate a miscarriage.* The words rang in Julia's ears. Her chest constricted, every bit as painful as her ankle.

Angela showed the doctor out while Theo came over to sit on Julia's bed. "Do not cry, my dear," her aunt said, and stroked Julia's hair. "Everything will be fine. You'll see."

"But you don't know that," Julia whispered, tears now falling in earnest. "No one knows. Oh, Theo. What will I do if I lose this baby? I shall never forgive myself." A sob escaped from her chest, and Theo's arms enveloped her.

"Shhhhh, it is not your fault. It was an accident. Nothing more." Her aunt rubbed her back, rocking her, as Julia cried and cried.

"That is enough," Theo finally told her. Her aunt gently forced her back on the pillows. "You will lose the baby if you do not save your strength. Be strong, Julia. That little one needs you. Crying and carrying on won't help—but getting some rest and eating *will.*"

Julia dried her eyes with the edge of her coverlet. "You're right. I must force myself to stay calm and get well."

"Sleep, my dear. I'll return to check on you in a little bit."

That day and night were foggy. Sore and tired, all Julia wanted to do was sleep. Theo came in every few hours to check on her, waking her to give her food and drink when necessary. She helped Julia relieve herself, which caused Julia no end of embarrassment. But Theo was so matter-of-fact about it that Julia was grateful.

In the morning, she slept late but felt remarkably better. As of yet, she had no bleeding or cramping—a very good sign all would be well with the babe. She planned to follow the doctor's advice while doing her best not to worry. Theo was right: Julia needed to save her strength.

After breakfast, Theo brought a few old copies of *La Belle Assemblée* for them to read while Julia remained in bed. Then Angela visited for a short while in the afternoon to give Theo a break.

"I do not require constant supervision," Julia told her sister-in-law. "You and Theo should enjoy the day, not sit here with me. Go." She motioned to the door. "Besides, I want to nap."

Convinced Julia told the truth, Angela left. Julia snuggled down in her pillows and went back to sleep.

The rest of the day was spent much in the same manner, resting and assuring the two other women of her improved condition.

Meg had just taken away her dinner tray when the outer door burst open.

Her husband, looking as haggard and disheveled as Julia had ever seen him, flew into the room. At least a day's worth of stubble peppered his jaw, and his eyes were rimmed red and surrounded by dark circles. Cravat askew, his rumpled clothing was covered with dust from the road.

Mouth agape, Julia blurted, "Colton! Whatever are you doing here?"

He cleared his throat and clasped his hands behind his back. "One of the footmen brought news of your accident, madam. I wanted to assess the extent of your injuries for myself."

Had he been . . . worried about her? He must have ridden like the devil to make it here this quickly. Joy blossomed in Julia's chest, and she tried not to smile.

"Tell me what happened. You were walking in the woods? Were you alone?"

She shook her head. "No. Lady Lambert was with me."

"And you tripped?"

"Yes, on an exposed root. I must have misjudged the distance. Then I could not catch my balance and tumbled down an embankment. But I am fine, really. A slight concussion and a twisted ankle, both mending nicely since Theo won't let me out of bed."

"And the babe?"

She paused, searching Nick's eyes to find some emotion other than concern. Hope? She noticed he didn't say *my* babe but rather *the* babe. Had he hoped she would miscarry?

God in heaven, that must be why he had raced to her side. The joy she experienced only a moment ago withered like a flower in the hot sun. He'd rushed here in hopes she would lose the baby, offering a tidy solution to all his problems.

She took a deep breath, fighting the despair weighing on her heart. The situation was futile. She would never change his mind. Nick would never believe her or accept their child. "I am sorry to disappoint you, husband," she said softly, "but I did not lose the babe. At least, not yet."

He frowned. "Regardless of how I feel about the child, I do not wish you harm, Julia."

Julia couldn't bring herself to answer. A miscarriage *would* harm her. She would never recover from it. Her body, yes; but there would never be a child conceived under similar circumstances, with such passion and affection. Now existed only cold mistrust between them, and Julia had not the energy for the battle any longer.

She turned her head, averted her gaze, and willed him to go away.

After a moment, he sighed. "I plan to stay a few days, until you are back on your feet," he told her quietly. "When I return to London, Fitz will remain here to watch over you."

Her gaze snapped to his. "I hardly think a guard necessary, Colton. I merely stumbled."

"I am not so sure. And until I am, Fitz stays." He gestured to the small chamber she had appropriated upon arriving almost two months ago. "Why are you not in the duchess's chambers?"

Julia shrugged. "Angela appropriated those rooms when your mother died. I did not think it fair to ask her to move out. Besides, this room is sufficient enough for me."

Nick spun on his heel and strode to the door. "Fetch Lady Lambert at once," he told a footman lingering in the hall.

"Colton, really—" Julia began, only to stop when he held up a hand.

"You are mistress of this house and deserve to be treated as such. Not to mention, you'll sleep where I tell you to sleep."

"Not after eight years I won't," she tossed back. Did he honestly believe he could order her about after ignoring her for so long? "You cannot selectively choose when to exert your rights as a husband, Colton."

His lids dropped and he gave her a lazy, smug smile. "I think we both know I'd never need to resort to *husbandly rights*, Juliet."

Chapter Eleven

Men like to offer protection, even when we do not need it. It is generally best to agree in order not to wound his ego.

—Miss Pearl Kelly to the Duchess of Colton

Julia gasped at the use of the name, which had certainly not been a slip of the tongue. Oh, if only she could wipe that smirk off his face. Just as she was about to tell him to go to the devil, the door opened.

"Your Grace!" Angela exclaimed, her expression one of surprise. "We did not know you had arrived." Theo came in right behind her, both of them staring curiously at Colton.

"I know. I came up here first." He placed his hands on his hips. "I would like my wife to have the chambers adjoining mine, as is her rightful place in this household. Please clear your belongings out tonight."

Angela's cheeks flushed. "Oh, of course," she breathed. "I never meant any disrespect to Julia. I offered to move and she told me—"

"Well, now *I'm* telling you," Nick said, his voice edged with hard steel.

"Of course. Right away. If you will excuse me." Angela turned and left.

"Colton, that was unnecessary," Julia protested.

"No, he is right," Theo put in from the doorway. "She should have given up those chambers without being asked. Good evening, Your Grace." She curtsied.

Nick gave Theo a small bow. "Lady Carville."

"Will you be staying with us a few days?"

"Yes, until my wife is back on her feet."

Theo shot Julia a brief glance. "How interesting," she murmured. "Well, I shall see both chambers are cleaned and readied." She left the room, closing the door behind her.

Julia shut her eyes and rubbed her temples. Heavens, she was exhausted, confused, and angry. Colton had been nothing but a nuisance since coming to England. Had he truly been *disappointed* she hadn't miscarried? Was he so cruel? Tears pooled behind her lids, both for their child and the man she'd fallen in love with in Venice—a man she knew she'd never see again.

"You need to rest," Nick said, his tone flat. "I shall return to help move you to your new chamber."

She nodded and heard him leave the room. Rolling over, she unleashed her tears into her pillow.

Nick closed his wife's door and strode down the hall. Emotion churned in his gut and he desperately needed a drink. He'd ridden half the night and all day, hardly leaving the saddle except to change horses, the fear over Julia's health nearly driving him mad.

And seeing her so pale and tired, it had been all he could do to stop from wrapping his arms around her and never letting go.

What was wrong with him?

She had likely tricked him in the worst way a woman could deceive a man. Yet, he couldn't get her out of his mind. For six weeks, he'd tried to forget her—and failed. Nights were the worst, when the smell of her . . . the feel of her . . . the taste of her haunted him. And after what happened at Madame Hartley's, Nick hadn't the desire to try again with another woman. So he was trapped, desperate for the one woman he could not allow himself to have.

He'd vowed to stay away from Seaton Hall, hoping the terrible need would dissipate. Then in September, when he learned whether the babe was his or not, Nick could leave without regrets. After all, she hadn't wanted a husband—she'd wanted a baby born under the protection of the Seaton name. Julia had said herself that he should leave and go back to Venice.

Clearly the woman did not yearn for him.

So why was he so bewitched by her?

He found Thorton, the butler. The man had been at Seaton Hall for as long as Nick could remember. Although in his late sixties or early seventies, Thorton was remarkably spry for a man of advanced years. When Nick and Fitz had arrived earlier in the evening, Thorton had almost sprinted in an effort to alert the staff of the duke's presence.

"Have Mr. Fitzpatrick located and sent to the study," Nick ordered.

"Yes, Your Grace," Thorton returned in his raspy baritone.

Nick strode into the opulent study, a room used by his brother, his father, and the rest of the bloody Colton dukes. If that wasn't depressing enough, the room held especially dark memories for Nick since he'd discovered his brother's body here.

He went to the sideboard and was grateful to find it well stocked. He poured a healthy glass of his father's best whisky. At least he didn't have his mother to contend with any longer. He could still remember many of the scoldings she'd given him—in front of his father, of course—in this very room. Her favorite topic had always been the disappointment that was her second son.

Then, the night after his brother's funeral, he'd stood here with both his parents, hate and blame in their eyes as they stared at their only surviving child. Nick had tried to explain, but no one believed him. So he'd stopped explaining.

He tossed back a mouthful of spirits, chasing away the bitter memories with the oak and peat-flavored whisky. Christ, he hated this place.

Instead of sitting behind the large desk, Nick chose a small chair by the fireplace. A brief knock sounded before Fitz lumbered into the room.

"Good evening, Your G—"

"Do not say it," Nick snapped. "I've been *Your Grace*'d to death since returning to this damned pile of rocks." He stood and returned to the sideboard, where he poured Fitz a whisky as well. "Sit, Fitz."

Nick handed Fitz the glass and retook his own seat. "Tomorrow, I want to ride out to the forest path and look at where my wife fell. I want to verify for myself it was an accident."

"You suspect otherwise?"

Something about it gnawed at Nick. Two mysterious falls in such a short period of time, if one considered his mother's death. Could it be coincidence?

When first told of the dowager duchess's death, he'd assumed Satan had grown tired of waiting for the harpy and arrived to collect her. But now he wondered over the circumstances. Had she tripped or had it been . . . something else? Seemed unlikely. Sheer evil was deuced difficult to kill, after all. And who would've wanted to do her in? A disgruntled staff member weary of being berated?

Yet with his own share of scrapes, Nick had learned to trust his instincts. And right now, two falls appeared too much to brush off—at least not until he checked Julia's accident site for himself.

He shrugged. "I confess I do not know. But to trip and fall at the precise point where the path steepens? You of all people know the danger in assuming that tragic events are mere coincidence. So until my curiosity has been satisfied, I want her protected. In fact, when I go back to London, I want you to remain here in my absence."

Fitz scowled, the scar on his face twisting viciously. "Why?"

"It appears my wife needs more watching over than I do."

Fitz shook his head. "No. Why will you be goin' back to London?"

Because I cannot stay here and not touch her. "It is better if I leave."

"Better for who?" Fitz gulped some whisky, the

small, delicate glass almost comical in his large hands. "I never picked you for a coward."

Nick started to deny it, but Fitz knew him too well. So he said nothing, merely stared into the fire.

"How long will you be stayin', then?" Fitz asked.

"Until she's mended. Perhaps two or three days."

"Aye, I'll watch over her, but you'd best take heed in London. If somethin' happens to you whilst I am here, I'll never forgive you."

"You needn't worry. Quint hardly leaves my side as it is. He's taken your warnings regarding my safety to heart."

"When will you be forgivin' Lord Winchester, then?"

Nick's shoulders tightened. "When I bloody feel like it, Fitz." He hadn't spoken to Winchester since the day in his study, when his friend told him of Julia's financial troubles. "And why do you care?"

"I don't. Seems a shame, though, to throw away an old friendship because Winchester did the gentlemanly thing."

"The gentlemanly thing?" Nick growled through a clenched jaw. "Helping my wife pose as a *whore* to trick me? Making a fool out of me? Lying to my face? Is this what gentlemen do where you're from?"

Fitz shook his head. "No. Where I'm from, if a man ignored his wife for eight years, leavin' her to almost starve, her family would be meetin' him in a back alley with a fist or two."

"Yes, her *family*. Not her husband's best friend."

"Winchester considers her family, though." He drained his glass and rose to his feet where he towered over Nick. "And you know it. You just don't want to admit you're wrong. You never do, you bloody stubborn duke."

Nick's eyes narrowed. "Yes, and this stubborn duke can have you sleeping in the stables if you aren't careful."

Fitz threw his head back and chuckled. "I've slept in worse spots than your stables, Your Grace. In fact, it's a palace compared to some of the Dublin alleys I've found myself in. I'm off to bed, unless you'll be needin' anything else."

"No. You've done enough for one night."

Thorton came in next. "Your Grace, the main chambers have been readied for yourself and Her Grace."

"Thank you. I will see to settling my wife in her new room. Have her maid move Her Grace's things in the morning."

"Very well, Your Grace. Good night."

"Good night, Thorton." Nick finished his whisky and stretched. He was exhausted. The sooner he got Julia settled, the sooner he could find his own bed.

When he knocked softly on his wife's door, there was no answer. He peeked in—only to see she was fast asleep. Moving silently, he came forward, intent on scooping her up. Instead, he found himself pausing by her bed.

Her breathing even and deep, she looked peaceful. Innocent. Her long blond hair swirled around a face carved by angels, and while the covers hid her body from his view, Nick remembered every luscious bit. Dreamed of her curves each night. Merely being in the same room with her made him ache.

Hard to say why, but he wanted her in the room

directly next to his. *Because you're a fool,* a voice whispered in the back of his head.

He pulled back the bedclothes and sucked in a breath. Her night rail had crept up her legs, revealing creamy, smooth thighs, while her breasts, now even larger with pregnancy, strained at the bodice. Desire punched Nick in the gut, and he closed his eyes, fighting to regain control.

He tried not to think about sliding into her bed, naked, and making love to her.

When he felt more himself again, he lifted his lids—and that's when he spotted the gentle swell of her belly. It wasn't much but he could see a bump under the thin cotton. Christ, it was truly a baby. Nick dragged a hand down his face, emotions cascading though him.

The plan was solid, he reminded himself. When it was proven the child wasn't his, he could leave the country without giving the boy or girl the protection of his name. If he happened to be wrong and it *was* his . . . Well, he'd never wanted to be a father—he didn't know how, really—and he didn't want to stay in England.

But it wasn't really his child . . . was it?

The possibility was too much to think about. Nick slid his arms underneath Julia, one behind her neck and one under her knees. She sighed as he lifted her, her arms winding around his neck. Nick smothered a groan. Not only were her breasts crushed against his chest, but also her scent—gardenias, so sweet and familiar—enveloped him. It made him long for those innocent nights in Venice, before he knew of her deceit.

Nick slowly traveled the long corridor and turned

the corner. The duchess's chambers adjoined his at the far end of the east wing, though he'd never slept in the master suite. The last time he'd been at Seaton Hall, his father had still been alive. It had been Harry's funeral.

Nick nudged open the door with his boot and stepped inside Julia's new apartments. The rooms were large, decorated with his mother's heavy hand. Nick made a mental note to tell his wife to redecorate at her leisure. Now that he'd gone though the estate finances, he knew they could well afford any changes she wanted to make to Seaton Hall.

Hell, she could burn the place down and start over for all he cared.

He leaned over and gently placed Julia on the bed. When he tried to pull away, she tightened her arms. "Nick," she breathed against his throat.

He froze. Indecision gripped him, anger and pride battling the raging lust in his groin. How easy it would be to give in, he thought. To sink into her softness and slake his need for her. Only, what then?

A quick glance at her face convinced him she was asleep. Relieved, he untangled her arms from around his neck and lifted the bedclothes to cover her. He stood for another minute, watching and wanting her. Torturing himself.

Before he could prevent it, Nick bent to place a soft kiss on her forehead. Her skin was cool and supple, and it was hell to pull back. Sighing, he went to the adjoining chamber and fell into bed, clothes and all.

* * *

The next morning, the two women were already seated in the breakfast room when Nick arrived.

"Good morning, Your Grace," Lady Lambert and Lady Carville both called cheerfully.

"Good morning, ladies," he answered. After a restless night, he'd been up for hours, having already broken his fast and gone for a morning ride. "Lady Lambert, would you be so kind as to ride out with me this morning? I should like to see the exact place in the path where my wife fell."

His brother's wife nodded. "Certainly, Your Grace. I would be happy to accompany you. I'll change and meet you in about twenty minutes." She stood and hurried from the room.

Lady Carville gave him a shrewd glance. "Why, if you don't mind my asking?"

"I don't know yet. It may be nothing," he answered honestly. "But my years abroad have taught me to be cautious about accidents."

"Yes, I had heard you met with a few supposed accidents yourself. Do you believe Julia is in danger?"

"I hope not. In any case, I will leave Fitz here to watch out for the three of you when I leave."

"Do you think it necessary? Perhaps you should stay until your son or daughter is born."

Nick's spine straightened. It was on the tip of his tongue to insist the child wasn't his, but he refrained. Time would prove him right. "No, I must leave. But if the babe is not born before September, I will return."

Understanding dawned in Lady Carville's eyes, and she sighed. "Have you thought as to the consequences of your mistrust, Your Grace? She'll likely never forgive you."

"Then we shall be even. If you'll excuse me, madam."

His mood decidedly sour, Nick found Fitz readying three mounts in the stables. There was a small mare for Lady Lambert, a massive hunter for Fitz, and Nick's new stallion, Charon. Purchased three weeks prior at Tattersall's, Charon was sixteen hands high and solid black. Spirited and stubborn, Nick had enjoyed turning him loose on the grounds earlier this morning.

"You sure to be wantin' me along?" Fitz asked as Nick approached.

"Definitely. I would rather not be alone with Lady Lambert. Besides, I want your opinion on the spot where my wife supposedly fell."

"Worried she'll throw herself at you, eh?"

Nick remembered several uncomfortable exchanges with his brother's wife while Harry had been alive. She'd taken every opportunity to flirt with him, even in front of Harry. He'd never encouraged her, but she had been persistent, surprised that the Depraved Duke would balk at cuckolding his brother.

And then there had been the fateful night, the one where it all turned to hell.

"Just stay close," Nick muttered, and grabbed Charon's reins. In one fluid motion, he vaulted into the saddle.

"Well, here she comes now." Fitz motioned toward the house and Nick turned to see Lady Lambert, looking cheerful as she sauntered out to the stables in a brown riding habit.

When she reached them, Nick could see her displeasure as she absorbed the fact that there were three mounts, not two. "Fitz will ride along," he announced.

She nodded and moved to the mounting block. A

nearby groom held her mount while she seated herself on the mare.

Nick made an impatient gesture toward Fitz, so his friend quickly swung himself onto the hunter. "Let's go," Nick said, and led Charon toward the forest.

The three of them took off at a steady clip. It was a clear, crisp spring morning and the familiar sights and smells reminded Nick of his boyhood, tramping about the estate. He could still recall the head gardener, a grizzled Mr. Thompkins, who never minded a small boy following him about. Because of Mr. Thompkins, Nick knew the name of almost every flower and tree on the property. As if that knowledge would ever do him any good.

Nick wondered when Lady Lambert would begin talking. She was never one to remain quiet, and he suspected she had quite a bit to say to him after eight years.

He didn't have to wait long. As soon as they passed the pond, Lady Lambert maneuvered her horse next to Nick's, Fitz trailing behind.

"Your Grace," she began, her voice no louder than a murmur. "Should we not at least discuss what happened that night?"

"No, we should not." That night was the last thing he wanted to think about. He kept his eyes forward, his concentration on the path.

"But you must allow me to apologize."

Nick said nothing. Apologies wouldn't bring his brother back. Or repair the damage to Nick's reputation. And then there was the matter of his guilt, which no apology would ever eliminate.

"I am different now, you should know," she continued. "I see how foolish I was then. Oh, Nick—"

His eyes, narrowed in warning, flew to hers.

"I mean, Your Grace." She blushed and looked away. "I merely wanted you to know how much I regret what happened. And I hope one day we can be friends."

He couldn't form a response polite enough for a lady's ears, so he kept quiet. He prayed she would do the same.

Fitz called, "How much farther, Lady Lambert, if you don't mind me askin'?"

"About ten more minutes, I think. It was right before the big bend in the path." She shifted in her saddle and smoothed her skirts. "Have you been to visit your mother's grave, Your Grace?"

He sighed. The unpleasantness of this journey knew no bounds, apparently. "No, I have not. But do not worry. I plan to dance a jig on it before I leave."

Lady Lambert's jaw snapped shut. He had a blessed moment of silence before she blurted, "Your wife is quite lovely. She and I have become fast friends."

"Have you?"

"Indeed. She is smart and—"

"Why have you stayed, Lady Lambert?" he cut in to ask. Her eyes widened in surprise but he pressed on. "Why did you cozy up to the dowager duchess for all those years? Why have you not moved back home with your family?"

She squared her shoulders. "I have no family. There is nowhere for me to go. Your mother was my family for the last eight years."

"Then allow me to give you a settlement. You can have the dower house. Take your pick of the cottages.

Go and buy a town house in London and send me the bill."

"Are you *forcing* me to leave, Your Grace?"

"Do not put me in that position. I would rather not force you to leave, but I cannot understand your insistence on remaining here." He tapped Charon's sides, and the horse cantered ahead of the others.

A few minutes later, they arrived at the spot where Julia fell. Nick dismounted, throwing the reins over a low branch. The area around the path was dense with foliage and there was a steep embankment on one side.

"Her foot caught on that root there," Lady Lambert said, pointing. "It was quite misty that morning, and I fear she slipped in trying to regain her balance."

Nick nodded. He wanted to investigate but didn't need her incessant chattering to do it. "Thank you for your assistance this morning, madam. Would you like Fitz to escort you back to the house?"

Something flashed in her eyes, likely surprise at being dismissed, he thought. "No, that is unnecessary. I am able to find my way back. Good day, Your Grace."

Turning her horse, she cantered away. When she was out of earshot, Fitz smiled and imitated in a high voice, "'And I hope one day we can be friends.'"

"Bugger off, Fitz," Nick growled. "And get off that damned horse and come down here."

Chuckling, Fitz swung his long leg over the hunter and jumped to the ground. "What are we lookin' for, then?"

"I do not know. Nevertheless, something feels strange about it. She trips and goes tumbling off down the side of a hill? Perhaps she is clumsy now that she is . . ."

"With child?" Fitz finally filled in, an eyebrow raised in disbelief. "Can you not even be sayin' it?"

"I can say it," Nick shot back. He stomped over to the root, moved it with his toe. "Seems rather loose, wouldn't you say?"

"More like a rope than a root." Fitz lifted it easily as Nick moved toward the embankment. Fitz pulled on the thick root until he held the end in his hand. "Look at this," Fitz called.

Nick hurried back to where Fitz stood. "Don't it seem as if somethin' has been tied to this end? Perhaps a rope?"

Nick wasn't sure. The end crimped at odd angles, suggesting it had been wrapped around something else. But that something else could have been another root. "See if you can find what it may have been tied to." Fitz nodded and headed off to the other side of the path, into the trees.

At the embankment, Nick glanced around at the mass of leaves on the ground. There were a lot of them and Lady Lambert had said it was misty that morning. He skated his boot over the leaves to test their slipperiness. Hmmm. . . .

He peered over the side. Stepping gingerly, he made his way down the slope, holding on to tree trunks and branches to keep from falling. When he neared the bottom, he could see the path in the leaves where Julia's body had slid to a stop. It made his blood turn cold.

Jesus, had she rolled all the way down there? It was a bloody miracle she hadn't broken her neck.

He climbed back up and found Fitz waiting for him. "Well?"

"Ground's too wet to hold footprints, if there ever were any. Might be some rope marks against a far tree, but they're too faint to know for sure."

"Damn," Nick muttered. "I had hoped we would learn one way or the other."

Fitz grabbed the reins of his hunter. "Still want me to stay when you return to Town?"

"Yes." Nick didn't have any evidence, but something about the fall seemed off. And even though he didn't want to admit it, he didn't like leaving Julia unprotected. The idea of something happening to her . . .

He pushed those thoughts from his mind and swung onto Charon's back. The big stallion shifted and pranced under the additional weight and Nick tightened his hold on the reins. "Do not let my wife out of your sight. Stay with her, Fitz. Meals, walks, tea . . . whatever it is she chooses to do with her time."

"Of course, although it would be better if you—"

"Do not say it," Nick growled, and kicked his boot heels into Charon's sides.

Julia didn't see her husband for three days. She knew he was still about, however, because she heard his footsteps in the adjoining chamber each night as he came to bed. That she actually looked forward to any sign of his presence said quite a bit about the tedium of her days.

Theo also kept her updated regarding the duke's whereabouts. Not surprisingly, he spent most of his time on horseback with Fitz in tow. Dinners were apparently awkward affairs, with Nick, Theo, and Angela having exhausted every available topic of conversation on the first evening.

Tonight, she decided to join them. Her ankle felt remarkably better, and the idea of spending one more day in bed was too much for her to take.

Julia rang for Meg and tried not to think about why Nick had stayed away the past few days. Since that first night, he hadn't visited her or checked on her at all. Was he awaiting news on whether she miscarried or not?

Well, she thought with a stubborn lift of her chin, he would be disappointed. According to the midwife today, all was well with the babe. It had been a relief to hear. In fact, both Julia and Theo had cried tears of joy at the news.

Meg came in and the two of them discussed what to wear to dinner. "You still have one or two of those gowns from Venice that should fit for another week or so," Meg suggested. "That'll get His Grace's attention."

"I'm not so certain I want his attention," Julia mumbled. She was still angry and hurt. He'd said such hateful things, so quick to believe the worst of her.

Not that Meg would know that. But servants talked, and Meg was obviously aware that the duke and duchess had not spent time together since his arrival.

"Let's do the rose gown, Your Grace. I'll fetch it straightaway."

Nearly an hour later, Julia viewed herself in the mirror. "Well, Meg. What do you think?"

"I think you'll knock His Grace on his arse, if Your Grace don't mind me sayin' so."

Julia chuckled. She'd had to forgo stays to get in the thing, but the result was worth it. The rose silk hugged her torso, the low bodice thrusting her breasts high and out. The whisper-soft fabric fell gracefully to the floor, skimming her thighs and calves over her lightest petticoat. The cap sleeves accentuated her shoulders and neck, the color of the gown highlighting the creaminess of her skin.

Too bad she'd sold her grandmother's pearls.

"That was the gong. Your Grace had best hurry."

"On a sore ankle? I'll be lucky if I make it there before dessert," Julia scoffed. "Wish me luck, Meg."

"That dress is all the luck Your Grace needs."

Julia laughed and began a slow descent to the first floor. By the time she reached the dining room, everyone had started the first course. They all stood and rushed forward to help her, and she was surprised to see Nick arrive first.

"My dear," Theo greeted as Julia took her husband's arm. He was warm and strong under her hand and her stomach fluttered. "Are you certain you should be out of bed?"

"I'm fine, Aunt Theo." Nick began to walk to the other end of the table, to her customary seat. "Colton, pray don't make me walk all the way down there. If you don't mind, I shall just sit here on the end, next to you."

She saw his eyes dart to her neckline and he cleared his throat. "Whatever you wish, madam."

Chapter Twelve

Men do not share their feelings as we would expect. In fact, you may discover more from what he does not say.

—Miss Pearl Kelly to the Duchess of Colton

Nick hardly glanced in her direction all evening. The courses dragged on with Angela and Theo chatting incessantly, while her husband focused intently on his food and barely participated in the conversation. In the end, Julia almost wished she'd stayed in bed.

Finally, dessert arrived and Julia stifled a yawn.

"My dear," Theo said to Julia. "No doubt you are tired. If you should care to retire, I'm certain Colton would be happy to walk you to your chambers."

Nick's head snapped up, and he glanced from Theo to Julia. "Of course. Merely say the word."

"Thank you, but I'm sure I can manage on my own."

"Nonsense," Theo put in. "Allow your husband to escort you. We would hate for you to fall again."

Julia couldn't very well argue, especially since

Colton had already risen, his tall and sinewy frame graceful as he moved to help with her chair. She sighed and resigned herself. "Good night, Theo. Angela."

He took her arm. "Lean against me," he said, supporting her weight while she limped from the dining room.

They didn't speak. Merely touching him had her body heating, a fact that bothered her, considering how awful he'd been. How could she still be attracted to a man who had been so cruel? It was maddening.

When they reached the stairs, she mistakenly put her bad foot on the first step, causing her to wince.

"You shouldn't even be out of bed," Nick grumbled before bending down and scooping her up into his arms.

"Put me down. I am perfectly capable of walking."

"I have no doubt, but I'd like to get there before Michaelmas."

He took the stairs easily, muscles bunching and shifting under her fingertips as he moved. He smelled exactly as he had in Venice, of citrus and musk, and she had the absurd urge to rest her head against him. In fact, if he turned to look at her, she would barely need to lean forward in order to kiss him.

She gave herself a mental shake. Why was she thinking about kissing him?

But, oh heavens, she was. Tucked snugly against him, Julia remembered that one glorious week in Venice. Rather, her body remembered. Her heart pumped hard and fast, her nipples beading inside her dress as the need she'd tried to deny threatened to overwhelm her.

If only things weren't so complicated between them.

Nick pushed open her door and entered her chambers. As if he couldn't stand touching her any longer, he immediately set her on the carpet. He stepped away and crossed his arms over his chest. Cleared his throat.

"Fitz and I rode out to where you fell and, while it seems suspicious, there is no obvious evidence to suggest something sinister. Nevertheless, you need to be more careful. Fitz will accompany you wherever you go."

"Sinister? Really, Colton, you are so dramatic. I told you it was naught but a simple tumble."

"A simple tumble that could have killed you, madam."

She resisted the urge to roll her eyes. "If there is no evidence, then why do I need Fitz following me about?"

One black eyebrow rose. "Because I said so."

Julia's jaw dropped. The man's arrogance astounded her. "Is that all, Colton?" she asked peevishly.

"I don't know. Is it?" he drawled, as his eyes raked her from head to toe. "After all, one could not help but notice how artfully your charms are displayed this evening. Perhaps you are attempting to gain my attention."

Julia resented the thrill that rushed through her at his inspection, so her voice dripped with venom. "My charms, as you so aptly put it, hardly fit into anything nowadays. This"—she gestured to her dress—"was not done for your benefit."

"And I would believe you if I did not already know

what a clever little liar you are." He moved closer but Julia held her ground.

"I would not have been forced to lie if you had not ignored your duties for eight years," she tossed back at him. "You have no idea what I've been through with your family. Why, Templeton—"

She snapped her mouth shut, unwilling to tell him how bad it had truly been. Not that Colton would even care.

"Templeton has been dealt with, madam. Not only has your financial situation been sorted out, my cousin will never utter one single word to you again in this lifetime."

Hope and horror warred within her as she contemplated Nick's words. "Did you . . . kill him?"

Nick threw his head back and laughed, the first actual smile she'd seen from him since Venice. "No, I did not. I should have, considering he propositioned you like a . . ."

"Whore," she finished when he trailed off. "But is that not what you believe me to be, husband?"

Myriad emotions crossed his face. Before she could discern them, he closed the distance between their bodies. One hand slid up to cup the back of her neck while the other pressed into the small of her back, keeping her in place. "And yet I cannot keep from wanting you." Something wild and dark flared in his storm gray eyes. "Every minute, every second of every day," he whispered before he bent his head and captured her mouth with his own.

The instant their lips met, everything else was forgotten. Lust burned fierce and hot between them as his tongue invaded to taste and torment. She clutched his shoulders, nails digging into cloth, bracing herself during the onslaught of glorious sensation.

Their breathing fast and harsh, their mouths continued to slant over each other frantically, each of them fighting for control. It wasn't a gentle kiss; instead it was hard and angry, resentment and suspicion flavoring the wildness between them. Julia didn't care. In fact, she thought she might die if he stopped kissing her. And when he rocked his arousal, large and hard, against her, she moaned into his mouth.

He broke away to slide his lips down her throat, his tongue flicking over her skin in an erotic trail. When he reached the base of her neck, he bit the curve of her shoulder, his teeth sinking gently into the muscles and tendons there. Julia shivered, the pain and pleasure combining to send a white-hot rush of fire between her legs.

His warm palm covered her breast and pushed up to allow his lips to tease the generous curve of flesh exposed by her dress. She arched her back, desperate for more, her breasts tender and sore and . . . aching for him.

Suddenly, he reached under her, cupped her buttocks, and lifted her. Julia instinctively wrapped her legs around his waist, and before she knew it, the wall pressed into her back. His mouth found hers once more in a drugging kiss, and his arousal, hard and rigid, nestled perfectly into the cradle of her thighs. She couldn't resist rubbing her bare cleft against his length, and he growled, a low and thrilling sound. So she did it again.

He took over, rolling his hips to tease her most sensitive flesh. Each brush made her gasp, the pleasure spreading down to her toes, but it wasn't enough. She burned, her skin both hot and cool at the same time, and she'd never felt so empty. So desperate. It had been too long, but her body well remembered the sensation of having him inside her. "Nick," she breathed, moving her hips in time with his.

He pressed closer, crushing her to the wall, his mouth hot and urgent on her throat. She panted and clutched his shoulders, delirious with the intense pleasure that removed any last reservations about what they were doing. She needed this. She wanted everything he could give her and more.

The desire to please him, to join his body to hers, took over. She reached between them, intent on undoing the buttons on his breeches.

When her hands reached his waistband, he froze and immediately stepped back. Confused and off balance, Julia collapsed against the wall and attempted to stay on her feet.

What had just happened?

Her husband appeared as dazed as she felt. A hand went through his black hair, disheveling it. "I—" He blew out a breath and wouldn't meet her eyes. "I beg your pardon, madam. Good-bye."

"Colton, wait," she called, unable to do anything but watch as he hurried toward the door.

He stopped but didn't turn around. She remembered how he'd said he would only stay until she was back on her feet. And he'd just said *good-bye* instead of *good night.* "Are you leaving for London, then?"

"Yes," he answered, turning his head slightly to give her his profile. "I think it best."

He was *leaving.* She could scarcely believe it. His hands had been up her dress not even one minute ago, and now he was leaving? That she still burned for him, had not wanted him to stop, made her even angrier. How could she hate him and yet desire him so much?

Furious, she spat, "So you can continue to ignore me? Is that it? You must have been quite disappointed to rush here only to find out I had not lost our baby."

Nick spun to face her, his expression every bit as livid as she felt. "I never wished for you to lose the babe." He took a step toward her. "I was sick with worry when I heard you'd had an accident."

"I sincerely doubt that. Especially when you do not believe the child is yours."

"I have never lied to you."

"Ah, a clever reminder that *I* have lied to *you*. Yes, I lied, Nick. I lied because I had no choice! Theo and I sold off everything we could. I went to your mother—who would have gladly seen me thrown out on the street. My options were you or Templeton. Perhaps I was a fool, but I chose you."

"And if that were true," he sneered, gray eyes gone cold and flat, "you would have written to me, explaining your problem. I could have helped you, taken it up with the solicitors. Instead, you had to seduce me. I wonder why, Julia."

Her head twisted wildly as she searched for something to throw at him. Seeing nothing within reach, she clenched her fists. "Would you, Colton? Would you have really come to my rescue, a woman you never wanted to marry, part of the family you hate with every breath you take? Simon had warned me again and again. I *knew* how you felt about me. And I waited *eight years* for you! Something had to be done."

He smirked and opened his mouth, so she held up

a hand. "Do not say it. I was a virgin that first night with you. I have been with no one else. If you choose not to believe me, then there is nothing more to say."

"A virgin does not ride her husband in a chair." He prowled closer, his voice low and menacing. "A virgin does not suck her husband's cock. A virgin does not strip off her clothes, stroke herself, or beg me to lick her."

Julia felt the heat on her face, unsure whether it was from embarrassment or the rush of desire at his coarse words. She remembered those seven nights so clearly, had relived them in her mind many times. Perhaps proper ladies did not act in such a fashion, but the Duchess of Colton had—and enjoyed it.

"I knew your reputation. You would've run screaming if you suspected I was a virgin—let alone your *wife!*—so I paid Pearl Kelly to teach me the ways of a courtesan. I am sorry for duping you, Colton, but I truly believed there was no choice."

Nick towered over her, over six feet of outraged man. Only, she refused to back down, her heart beating wildly as she boldly stared at him.

"Yes, you certainly gave me no choice in the matter," he growled.

She wanted to laugh. His insistence on always being the injured party, making her out to be some kind of monster, was too much. "You pursued me. You seduced *me* every bit as much as I seduced *you.* And God knew you were not concerned about *conception* when we were together. You made no effort whatsoever to prevent a child from our union. Tell me, how many bastards have you sired over the years?"

His nostrils flared, and he stepped back. "You told

me you *couldn't* have children and I believed you. I thought you were trustworthy. You were with one of my closest friends, for God's sake! How was I to know what you truly were?"

"And what was I, Colton? Besides a wife driven to desperation because her husband had ignored her for *eight years?*"

He gave her a patronizing, self-righteous smile. "You don't truly want me to say it, do you?"

She gasped, heat suffusing her entire body. Blood rushed through her veins, a steady hum of outrage in her ears. At that moment, she hated him with a vehemence she hadn't thought herself capable of before now. Julia wanted to hit him, insult him—anything to make him hurt as much as she did.

"You are a coward and a hypocrite," she said. "I wish I'd never gone to Venice."

"That makes two of us."

They faced each other, barely an arm's length between their bodies, for a long moment. His breathing rasped every bit as fast as hers as they stared at each other. The air in the room was thick with tension and emotion, like a long-overdue thunderstorm.

Then the atmosphere shifted, became intimate, as the familiar current jumped between them. Nick's gaze grew hooded, filled with a blatant carnality that never failed to turn her knees to jelly. He focused intently on her, as if he wanted to eat her alive. She fully expected him to surge forward and kiss her once more.

A tingling awareness spread over her body, and her lips parted in anticipation.

Nick glanced at her mouth, where the tip of her

tongue slid out to moisten her dry lips. He blinked then straightened. "I leave at first light." Spinning, he strode to the door.

"Why? Why are you so determined to ignore me?" She hadn't meant to say anything but couldn't prevent the words from tumbling out.

Hand poised on the latch, Nick dropped his forehead to the door. "Because it's killing me to stay away from you. And if I let myself have you, I'll hate us both when it's over." He opened the partition and disappeared.

Colton departed in the morning before the rest of the household awoke. Julia heard him leave but did not get out of bed. Her emotions were conflicted, and she didn't know whether she wanted to strangle him or strip him down the next time she saw him.

Probably best not to find out, she reasoned.

So she determinedly put her husband out of her mind. She had her health and her baby to focus on.

True to his word, Colton instructed Fitz to follow her everywhere. The large man even joined the group each night for dinner, which had Angela and Theo in quite a dither at first. Julia could understand since Fitz did pose a rather stark and forbidding presence about the house. But as she got to know him, she found him funny and sweet. It was clear he would do anything for Colton, and Julia wondered not for the first time what had transpired between the two men to inspire such loyalty.

A week after Colton left, Simon arrived.

They were in the middle of dinner when Lord Winchester's tall, rangy frame strode into the dining room. "Simon!" Julia sprung up from her chair.

He enveloped her in a hug. "Evening, Jules." Stepping back, he held her at arm's length. "You look radiant. Truly." He turned to the other women and Fitz, greeting them as well.

Theo signaled for another place setting and two footmen rushed forward with the necessary items, placing Simon on Julia's right. When they were all seated, Julia asked, "Is Parliament still in session, or have you finished?"

Simon selected some roast mutton from the platter closest to him. "Still going on, I'm afraid, which means I cannot stay long. However, I heard from Quint, who heard from Colton, that you'd been injured. Wanted to come see for myself."

"And why would the duke not tell you himself?" Theo asked, scooping more French beans onto her plate.

When he didn't answer, Julia blurted, "He's still not speaking to you?"

Simon said nothing, merely attacked his dinner, which gave Julia the answer she needed. "If Colton were here I'd box his ears," she swore.

"I would love to see that," Simon said with all seriousness.

"As would I," Fitz put in from down the table.

Everyone chuckled and Simon continued. "Yes, Colton is still angry with me. But I anticipate an apology coming soon. Oh"—He looked down at Julia's stomach—"about September."

"I must have missed something," Angela commented. "Why September?"

"You haven't told her?" Simon asked Julia, who just shook her head. "Because that is when Julia's baby is due."

"And once Colton sees his child," Theo said in a rush, "all will be forgiven. Now, tell us what news you have of Town, Lord Winchester."

Julia noticed how smoothly her aunt answered Angela's question. While she liked Angela, Julia was not comfortable with having the entire story spread far and wide. The fewer people who knew what she'd done in Venice, the better.

Simon proceeded to regale them with stories from the various balls, parties, and events he'd attended over the last month. Theo, who missed Town life more than she let on, hung on Simon's every word. Julia felt a pang of guilt but wasn't about to let her aunt leave now. Not until the baby arrived.

After dinner, Simon turned to Julia. "Walk with me?"

She nodded. "Fitz, Lord Winchester and I are going for a walk. I am quite confident he can safely guard my person during that time. Feel free to retire."

Fitz frowned, the scar on his face turning white. "The duke wouldn't—"

"The duke is not here," she snapped, and then sighed. "I apologize, Fitz. I do not mean to be cross with you, since none of this is your fault. Simon, can you ensure my safety for the next hour?"

Simon grinned, the dimples in his cheeks deepening. "I shall protect thee, fair maiden."

Fitz didn't appear to like it, but he agreed. Simon

helped Julia out of her chair and they set off for the lawn to the west side of the house.

It was unusually warm for an early May evening. The lilac bushes were just beginning to show promises of blossoms, as were the lily of the valley plants. Everything was green and hearty, a new beginning after the cold, wet winter. She sat down on a nearby stone bench.

"Are you well? Truly? When I heard you fell, I swear I lost a year off my life." The soft glow of the lights from the house illuminated his concerned face.

Julia smiled up at her friend. "A sprained ankle and a headache. Nothing more. I was quite fortunate."

"Thank heavens. I hear Colton couldn't find evidence of a cause."

"That is true, though I'm not sure why he suspected something to be amiss in the first place. Regardless, he left Fitz behind to serve as bodyguard."

"Why the hell didn't Colton stay, if he was so worried?"

Julia shrugged. "He said it was best if he went back to London. I do not think he's planning to return."

"He'll come around, Jules. Give him time."

"How much time, Simon?" She stood and moved away stiffly to stare out into the darkness surrounding the hall. "I've waited eight years for him. And you should hear the hateful things he says to me when we're together." A tear slipped from her eye and she swatted it off her cheek. Lord, she was tired of crying over that man. "Why does Colton deserve any more time?"

Because you love him, a voice inside her whispered.

Simon came forward to squeeze her hand. "Because

he's stubborn and cynical and anyone he's ever loved has turned their backs on him. He deserves to have one or two of us hang about. He will come around, I promise."

She leaned her head against his arm. "And if he doesn't?"

"He will. I know him almost as well as I know myself. And if I were in his shoes, I'd be scared to death."

"Scared? Colton isn't scared."

Simon laughed. "Surely, you jest. Colton is downright terrified."

"Of *what?*"

"Of you, silly."

Simon entertained the household over the next few days. He played cards—usually piquet or speculation—in the afternoons with Julia, went riding with Angela and Fitz every morning, and drank spirits with Theo in the evenings.

Julia felt invigorated. Her body grew a little more each day and she had a great amount of energy. Theo suggested a transformation of the nursery might be in order, so one morning Julia and the housekeeper, Mrs. Gibbons, went to the third floor to assess it.

The room was dusty and in disrepair, which was hardly a surprise since it hadn't seen the light of day in thirty years. The large windows were covered in grime, casting a grayish pallor to the dirty walls.

"The dowager duchess said not to bother with this room," Mrs. Gibbons said defensively at Julia's side. With her gray hair pulled back into a serviceable bun, Mrs. Gibbons was not a woman used to frills. As Theo said, this housekeeper was more of the no-nonsense variety. Julia could only imagine how terrified the maids would be of making a mistake under Mrs. Gibbons's watchful eye.

"Of course," Julia reassured her. "I would not blame you or your staff for the neglect in here, Mrs. Gibbons. But I should like to see it cleaned now."

"And what shall we do with the furniture and the toys, Your Grace?" She gestured to the two small beds at one end of the room.

Julia smiled and imagined Nick snuggling in his bed. Growing closer, she noticed writing of some kind on one of the headboards. Taking her hand, she smoothed away the dust and saw the initials *N.S.* carved into the wood. Something rolled over in her chest as she traced the letters with a fingertip. "Can we clean and store them? We might use them someday."

Mrs. Gibbons's eyes twinkled. "A rapscallion, that one." She motioned to the bed where Nick had carved his initials. "Cutest little boy you'd like to see, your husband, but a devil all the same."

None of which had changed now that he was a grown man, Julia thought.

"What was his brother like? Harry?"

"Proper. Full of responsibility. The opposite of your husband in every way." Mrs. Gibbons shook her head. "It was a shame what happened."

"Indeed," Julia muttered, although she had no idea what exactly had happened. She made a mental note to ask Simon this afternoon. "Let's get the place cleared out, Mrs. Gibbons. Donate the toys to the children in the village and get the beds stored away.

The mattresses should be burned. When it's clean, we'll talk about paint colors and curtains."

"Very good, Your Grace."

That afternoon, she and Simon sat down for a game of piquet.

"Are you ready for a trouncing today, Duchess?" Simon grinned and deftly shuffled the deck.

"Considering the outcome of our game yesterday, sir, I should be asking you that question."

"Perhaps we should up the ante?"

She shrugged. "If you are ready to part with more than the two pounds I won off you yesterday."

Simon laughed and shook his head. "Your arrogance matches your husband's." He handed her the deck and sat back. "I'll even let you deal first."

Julia rubbed her hands together. "You may well regret that." Soon they each had twelve cards. Silence descended as they studied their hands.

"Simon, what happened with Colton's brother? The scandal, I mean."

He rubbed his chin thoughtfully. "What has Colton told you?"

"Not a word. He wouldn't answer when I questioned him about it."

"Well, no one knows what exactly happened because Colton has never said. I've hinted at a few things and he hasn't corrected me, so I can only assume I am correct. But you should really hear it from him."

"Were he and Angela . . . ?"

"Lovers?" Simon finished. "No. I know the rumors but Colton never would have done such a thing to Harry. He loved Harry. Nearly destroyed him when his brother died." He put three cards down on the table and selected the same number from the talon.

"How so?" She discarded two cards and then picked up two more.

"Colton was drunk and angry. I sensed he and his brother had some sort of falling-out, with Harry siding against Colton, right before Harry died. And his parents blamed Colton for Harry's death." Simon made his declaration, the best possible combination in his hand.

Julia responded, acknowledging his hand could be scored. "That must have been terrible for him."

"I think the falling-out with Harry hurt Colton far worse than with his parents. He'd given up on winning their approval years ago."

"How did his father ever get him to agree to the marriage?"

Simon led a card, a jack of hearts. "I think I know, but I cannot tell you."

"Can't or won't?"

"Won't, then. Colton is already angry with me for meddling. I'm sorry but I really cannot say anything more. And stop trying to distract me."

The door opened and Angela appeared. Simon stood up to greet her, and Julia noticed he was reserved, not his natural flirtatious self.

"This just arrived for you." She handed Julia a note. "I told Thorton I'd bring it in."

Julia ripped open the seal and read the letter. The contents had her grinning. "Oh! It's from Sophie. She's coming to visit."

"Sophie?" Angela asked.

"Lady Sophia Barnes," Simon answered, his eyes

on his cards. "Otherwise known as the Marquess of Ardington's daughter and Julia's partner in hell-raising."

"Oh, how fun!" Angela returned. "The house is positively brimming in jocularity. The more, the merrier I always say. When is she to arrive?"

"Tomorrow," Julia said. "She and her stepmother are to stay for three weeks."

Simon grunted and Julia looked at him sharply. "What?"

"An unmarried maiden and her mama. Lord help me."

Julia and Angela laughed. "Sophie has sworn never to marry, Simon. So you're safe."

"So I've heard but I still cannot see how she plans to avoid it."

"She's the only daughter and the marquess dotes on her every whim. He's richer than Croesus and has promised to let Sophie find her own husband. I'm quite jealous of her, actually."

Simon gave her a gaze full of pity, and she held up a hand. "Do not say it."

Angela's eyes rounded. "B—but you're a duchess!" she sputtered. "Almost every woman in the kingdom would love to trade places with you."

"Yes, almost," Julia mumbled, staring at the cards in her hand. "Simon, do get on with it. I've got ten pounds to win yet."

They all went out to meet the carriage as it lumbered into the drive.

It took forever for her friend to descend but when

Sophie finally appeared, Julia rushed forward. The two women laughed and embraced, then Sophie pulled back sharply. She glanced down. "Julia! The rumor is true. You're . . ."

"Yes, I know. I have a lot to tell you, but not until you come inside. Good afternoon, Lady Ardington," she said to Sophie's stepmother.

"Greetings, Your Grace. I do hope our visit is not an inconvenience."

"Nonsense. We're glad for the company." Introductions were made all around and the entire party moved indoors while the Colton footmen took the visitors' trunks up the stairs.

Sophie looked ready to burst from curiosity. "I know I am dirty and covered with the smell of horses, but I cannot stand another minute more. Please come and walk with me," she said to Julia.

The two women went to the back of the house, toward the gardens. Fitz appeared out of nowhere, ready to follow them outside. Julia stopped him by lifting her hand. "We are merely going to sit in the gardens, Fitz. No need to come along."

"Yes, Your Grace. But no farther, if you please."

Sophie's jaw dropped, her brown eyes round, as she watched Fitz walk away. "What in the blazes is going on?"

Julia laughed. "Let us go outside and I'll tell you everything."

Once they found a bench in the gardens, Julia blurted, "Yes, it's Colton's."

"The baby, you mean?" When Julia nodded, Sophie rolled her eyes. "Well, of course. I never imagined you would be carrying another man's child. So when you said you were in Paris, you really went . . ."

"To find Colton in Venice. And I succeeded." She gestured to her belly.

"Why now after eight years?"

Julia proceeded to tell her friend everything, including Templeton, hiring Pearl Kelly and what transpired in Venice, concluding with Colton's most recent visit to Seaton Hall.

"A courtesan?" Sophie repeated. "I do not believe it! You must tell me everything she said. And Lord Winchester helped you, you say? I can see why Colton is furious."

"You are supposed to be on my side!" There were times when her friend's insistence on speaking her mind grated on Julia's nerves.

"I am sorry, Julia, but you know I would never sugarcoat anything, not even for you. I may not be married, but it's clear any man would not appreciate being tricked. However, I can see how you felt there was no other choice."

"He does not believe he is the father. Colton is convinced I traveled to Venice with another man's babe in my belly, intent on seducing him so the child would be legitimate."

"Well, time will tell on that," Sophie said. "Nine months is nine months, Julia. Tell me of the time you spent with him in Venice. Was he . . . kind?"

Julia's heart softened as she recalled that one magnificent week. "Yes, he was kind. And attentive and sweet. It was truly wonderful."

"Oh, heavens. You fell in love with him. It's right there on your face."

Julia sighed, not bothering to deny it. "I do not

want to love him. He's been deliberately cruel since he returned. I understand he is angry, but what if he never forgives me?"

Sophie hugged her. "Then he's a bigger fool than we thought," she said softly. "You are so brave and strong, Julia. If Colton refuses to love you back, then we shall just ignore him. You have many friends who love you and who care about you. Though I do wish you had come to me about Templeton. Perhaps my father—"

"Oh, Sophie. No one could have stopped Templeton save Colton or the dowager duchess. But thank you. I'm fortunate to have you, and I apologize I did not confess all before now."

"Well, I forgive you, of course. It took forever to convince Stepmama to leave Town to come visit you. The Season is winding down but she positively would not leave before now. If I hadn't begged Papa—"

"Ah, so that's how you managed it. And how is the marquess?"

"Desperate for grandchildren. He told me I have one more year to find a husband or he will find one for me."

Julia gasped. "Oh, no!"

Her friend laughed and waved her hand. "I do not believe he truly means it. It is not the first time he's made some sort of threat."

"Well, is there anyone who has caught your eye? What about Simon?"

"No, definitely not. I know you adore him, Jules, but he doesn't make my toes tingle. Do you know what I mean?"

"Yes, unfortunately I do. In fact, I could do with a little less tingling around Colton."

Sophie eyes turned speculative. "So will you let me read the advice Pearl gave you? If it worked on Colton . . ."

"The woman is a veritable genius, Sophie. When you find the man you want to capture, I'll give you what she wrote. And he won't stand a chance."

Chapter Thirteen

Never mind what others say. If you are being well cared for, let them talk.

—Miss Pearl Kelly to the Duchess of Colton

Nick threw down Fitz's letter. Bloody Winchester. He should've guessed her knight in shining armor would run to her side. One of these days, Nick would get the story of what good deed she'd performed in order for Winchester to hold her in such high esteem.

Nick hated feeling jealous. Especially since he'd never, ever experienced anything similar in his life. But this burning rage and uncertainty in his gut could not be denied.

Not that he thought the two of them had been intimate. No, he hated the closeness they shared, the friendship and affection she readily gave to a man who was not her husband. Why it bothered Nick, he couldn't say. After all, she'd played him for a fool.

But the memory of seeing her hurt, so pale and

fragile, haunted him. He wanted to protect her, to be her gallant knight—not Winchester. And feeling so deeply for a woman who'd betrayed him made him the worst kind of idiot.

He was pouring himself a drink when Marlowe announced Quint. His friend came in, as disheveled and poorly dressed as always, and so Nick asked Marlowe to bring tea. Quint never touched spirits.

His friend dropped into a chair. "I came round to see if you wanted to go to White's for dinner. Then the theater, perhaps? There's a new play at Covent Garden."

Nick sighed. A night on the town sounded tedious and unappealing. "I do not think so."

"You've hardly been out in weeks. What happened during your last visit to Seaton Hall?"

The truth roared through his brain, humbling him. *I nearly bedded my wife, who likely carries another man's child, because I can no longer control myself.* Afraid the humiliating thought would slip out if he opened his mouth, he merely shook his head in response.

"I will not take no for an answer, Colton."

Nick knew he would not make for good company tonight. Perhaps if Quint learned that for himself, he would stop pestering Nick to go out all the time. He threw back the brandy. "Fine. Let's go. We'll play some hazard first."

When they arrived at White's, Nick could sense by the avid stares thrown his way that something had transpired. Undaunted, he and Quint made their way to the hazard tables in back. They elbowed in at a nearly full table and began betting. Over the course of the next few minutes, however, the other players started to drop out until only he and Quint remained.

They played a bit longer and then ambled to the dining room. The chatter dropped down to whispers as he and Quint were seated. Nick sighed. What now?

Turning in his chair, he tapped the man behind him. "St. John, what the devil is everyone blithering about?"

St. John's gaze bounced to Quint and then back to Nick. "Uh, I take it you haven't seen the betting book?"

Nick's stomach dropped but he kept his voice steady and calm. "No, I haven't. Is there a reason I should?"

"Your . . . wife is mentioned in it." St. John cleared his throat. "It's—"

Nick pushed back his chair and strode from the dining room. No one dared stop him as he made his way to where the betting book was displayed.

It wasn't hard to find. Last entry, made anonymously.

Fifty pounds to who can guess when the Duchess of C. will give birth.

Nick grabbed the page and ripped it out in one smooth motion. Crumpling the paper in his hand, he stalked to the main room and tossed it into the nearest fire. He returned to the dining room and reclaimed his seat. Dinner had arrived, but Nick hardly tasted the baked sole, rage and humiliation nearly choking him.

That damned betting book. He still remembered the numerous bets placed during the scandal, such as whether Nick had seduced his brother's wife, or whether he'd killed his brother. Numb at the time, Nick had been able to ignore it all. Not to mention the reality had been so much worse than what the idiots at White's could imagine.

Speculation had followed him wherever he went in those days. And now, thanks to his wife, nothing had changed.

They were betting on the legitimacy of his wife's child. Hell.

Quint leaned over. "Dare I ask what it said?"

Nick repeated it and Quint frowned. "There are rumors, but no one knows for certain that your wife is enceinte. More likely they are betting on when you'll get her with child, now that you're back in England."

Nick hadn't considered that. The knot in his stomach eased somewhat. "Then why the whispers? Why is everyone here acting like a frightened rabbit in my presence?"

Quint's face registered stupefied surprise, as if the answer were completely obvious. "Because you punched a man in the face the last time you were here. Or had you forgotten?"

Nick had, in fact, forgotten. He dragged a hand across his jaw. "Regardless, I do not want my wife's name in that book. No matter the reason."

"Well, if you still harbor doubts, Winchester swears the baby is yours."

"And he would know," Nick drawled.

Their dinner was cleared, and the two of them lingered with their drinks, port for Nick and tea for Quint. The conversation in the dining room had picked up a bit, so Nick could only assume they were no longer whispering about him and Julia.

His wife. Would he ever be free of her, of this all-consuming desire for her? These obsessive feelings surely had to fade at some point. Then he'd move on with his life. So why was it taking so blasted long?

Because he'd never been so bloody miserable.

Not after his brother's death, nor when his parents turned their backs on him. Even his lonely childhood paled in comparison to finding this perfect woman in Venice, then discovering it had all been a lie.

A clever deception. He'd never suspected a thing.

I knew your reputation . . . so I paid Pearl Kelly to teach me the ways of a courtesan.

Nick frowned and sipped his brandy. Though he hadn't been back in London long, even he had heard of Pearl Kelly. Had Julia really hired the legendary courtesan to learn the tricks of the trade, so to speak?

He'd been so sure another man had introduced his wife to the arts of the flesh. After all, she'd been so . . . skilled. Like the night he'd told her he couldn't possibly perform a fourth time, which she'd taken as a direct challenge and proved him wrong. The memory of the way she'd used her tongue caused a bolt of desire to shoot down to his groin. Could he have been mistaken this entire time?

Quint tossed his napkin. "Shall we go? The performance starts in less than an hour."

He'd forgotten about the theater, but the idea of leaving the club had never sounded better. Nick nodded and the two men soon found their way to Covent Garden. They ended up in the Colton box, one of the largest in the center of the theater. When they'd taken their seats, Quint elbowed him and whispered, "Don't look now, but Pearl Kelly is with Burston, two boxes to your left."

Immediately, he glanced over and locked eyes with a slight brunette. She gave a brief twitch of her lips and then leaned over to speak to Lord Burston. Nick watched as Burston nodded, then rose.

"I believe you are about to be invited to request an introduction," Quint mumbled.

"More like summoned," Nick said under his breath.

Quint chuckled as Burston entered the box. A rotund, balding man, Burston had enough money that a woman like Pearl Kelly would overlook his appearance. "Your Grace," Burston greeted with a bow. "I had heard you returned. How were your travels?"

"Surprising," Nick hedged. "Not what I expected."

"Do you know Miss Kelly?" Burston waved a hand toward his box.

"I have heard of her."

"Come, allow me to introduce you, won't you? We've a few minutes before the performance starts."

Curiosity and politeness had Nick following down the corridor, through the curtains, and into the box. Miss Kelly did not turn around until they reached her side.

"My darling," Burston began, and a very lovely, expensively attired woman stood to greet them. With her bright smile accented by a rope of diamonds woven in her coiffure, Pearl Kelly was nothing like Nick imagined. Small in stature and not particularly curvy, her delicate face was surrounded by thick chestnut curls. Diamonds graced her ears as well as her neck, and rings adorned almost every finger. Clearly, a woman who appreciated jewelry.

Burston quickly made the introduction. Her curtsy was proper and polite. "Your Grace!" she exclaimed. "What a treat you've come to visit." Her eyes were brown with green flecks in them. Intelligent, knowing eyes that appraised him carefully. "Shall we sit? I like to be comfortable when entertaining."

Nick nearly laughed. He'd been so busy measuring her, he'd forgotten his manners. "Forgive me." He settled into the seat beside her and noted with mild curiosity that Burston had disappeared.

"You are every bit as handsome as rumored." She raked him from head to toe, causing him to lean back in amusement.

"And you are every bit as lovely as I'd heard."

"I admit, I feel a bit giddy. It's quite a coup to lure the Depraved Duke into my box." Her mouth tilted up. "You know, I feel you and I might have met under very different circumstances, if not for your wife."

"And here I thought most women in your position would not care a fig for the existence of a wife." He was curious to see how this line of conversation progressed. Would she confirm taking Julia under her wing, teaching her all the tricks a Cyprian had at her disposal?

"But, then, I'm not most women. Speaking of wives, you are a fortunate man. Her Grace is quite beautiful." Miss Kelly's expression revealed nothing, and Nick found himself more confused. Before he could respond, she asked, "Wouldn't you agree?"

"Indeed, she is. And quite clever."

"Most women are. You males tend to not notice

such things. Call it an obsession with our more obvious assets." She smoothed her skirts and didn't meet his eye. "But a woman will do whatever she feels necessary to get what she wants."

"And what is it a woman wants, Miss Kelly?"

"Oh, you must call me Pearl. All my good friends do—"

He straightened, remembering a very similar exchange with Mrs. Leighton in Venice.

"—and I want for very little, Your Grace. These days, I hardly do a thing unless it amuses me."

Was she referring to helping Julia? Confound women and their abilities to talk in circles. "A fine habit, if such amusement does not hurt others." *Like a husband,* he wanted to add.

"Oh, I doubt I have ever caused harm. My amusements tend to stray more toward the pursuits of pleasure. Surely, a man with your reputation appreciates such efforts."

Ah, now they were getting to the heart of the matter. He crossed his arms over his chest. "Yes, I appreciate the pursuit of pleasure, but only when solicited honestly and openly. I've never been one for duplicity."

She laughed, a low, husky sound, and briefly touched his arm. "Oh, Your Grace. Even a bit of duplicity can be a good thing. Life is not a Greek tragedy. Life is to be enjoyed! To be relished. To be lived without regret. I heard you were a serious, brooding fellow, but you really must adopt more *joie de vivre.*"

He found himself amused despite himself. "Are you always this obnoxiously optimistic?"

"Only in the company of handsome men. And why would I not be? While it is true I did not have a pleasant childhood, look at all that I've accomplished, all that I have now. If we were but slaves to our doubts and failings, life would be dull indeed."

What could he say to such a statement? It was a mirror of his life, and he didn't like it, not one little bit. Since returning to London, he'd spent many dull nights in the town house, brooding and alone.

"Your friend—Viscount Quint, I believe." She tipped her diamond-wrapped head toward the Colton box. "Has he always had such dreadful fashion sense?"

Nick chuckled. "Yes, as long as I've known him. We try not to hold it against him."

She nodded her understanding. "It is what's on the *inside* that counts, is it not?" Relaxing back in her chair, she glanced at Quint again. "He suffered a near miss with that dreadful Pepperton girl. The stupid chit ran off with a groom, of all things. Ridiculous."

Nick only knew what Quint had told him, which wasn't much. "'*Love looks not with the eyes, but with the mind,*'" he quoted.

"'*And therefore is winged Cupid painted blind,*'" she finished. "Do you believe that to be true, Your Grace? Did you fall in love with your wife's beauty or her brains?"

He resisted the urge to laugh. In *love?* With Julia? The idea was preposterous.

Wasn't it?

"You look as if you've sucked on a rotten egg." She laughed. "You men are so predictable. Oh, here comes Burston." Pearl stood and Nick rose as well. "It seems our time together is at an end, Your Grace."

"It was truly a pleasure, Miss Kelly." He picked up her gloved hand and then brought it to his lips. Her eyes twinkled, and he regarded her carefully. "I get the sense I have served my purpose, that I have amused you this evening."

"Indeed, you have. This exchange has been memorable for many, many reasons." She leaned closer. "Please give your wife my best. I do hold her in the highest esteem."

Nick stared intently into the courtesan's eyes and the answer he'd been searching for was there. It was true—Julia *had* hired Pearl so she could learn how to seduce him. He swallowed the questions clogging his throat. "You may depend upon it."

He took his leave and walked back to his box, dazed. The performance passed, but he paid little attention. Instead, his mind reeled from the exchange and what he'd learned.

Nick had been so certain Julia had lied, that another man had been responsible for her intimate knowledge of physical activities. She'd been too . . . talented for him to believe otherwise. The idea that he'd been her first lover seemed laughable.

He thought back to that first time, when she'd straddled him in a chair. He'd been too consumed with lust to notice any sign of a maidenhead, but he did remember the force with which she'd ridden him. She'd instantly taken him deep and hard. Had it been out of frenzied lust, as he'd assumed, or to pierce her membrane without calling attention to it?

Afterward, she'd immediately risen to clean both

herself and him—the only time she'd done so in the time they spent together.

A sickening feeling blossomed in his stomach.

Had his wife really remained a virgin for *eight years?*

The idea seemed ludicrous. With her body, wit, and intelligence, she could have any man at her fingertips. Why in the world would she save herself for him—a man she didn't know and would likely never meet? It didn't make any sense.

He rubbed the back of his neck. If Julia had truly been a virgin in Venice, then the baby . . . Dear God. A sharp stab of pain exploded in his chest. Had he been wrong this entire time?

He took a deep breath and attempted to keep a level head. There was no use getting hysterical. Time would tell whether the child was his or not. And just because Julia had hired Pearl Kelly didn't mean she'd been a virgin in Venice. If she'd been desperate to trick him into believing her bastard child was his, then gaining advice from Pearl would have guaranteed her success by making her irresistible in his eyes, maiden or not.

Again, time would tell. He merely needed to be patient in order to get the answer he needed.

But the seeds of doubt had sprouted, leaving him shaken and unsure.

Simon left Seaton Hall after Lady Sophia and her stepmother arrived. Julia was sad to see him go, but he promised to visit again once the baby was born.

Over the next two weeks, she and Sophie began working on the nursery in earnest. New rugs were laid on the floor and the room had a fresh coat of cheery yellow paint. They purchased curtains and furniture, and Sophie drew an exact replica of the Seaton Hall pond on one of the walls.

They were unpacking a box of toys purchased in the village when Julia felt a light flutter inside her abdomen. When it happened again, she gasped. "Sophie! The baby. He just moved. I felt it!" She grabbed her friend's hand and placed it on the hard bump of her belly.

It took five minutes, but the baby did it again. "Did you feel it?"

Sophie's eyes were huge. "No. But I believe you. Is it strange?"

Julia nodded. "Strange and wonderful. I must go find Theo. I'll see you later."

She dashed down to the second floor and hurried to Theo's chambers, where her aunt was resting this afternoon. Julia couldn't wait to tell Theo about finally feeling the baby move.

When she turned the corner, Theo's door cracked. Fitz, appearing somewhat disheveled, stepped out of her aunt's bedchamber. Julia stopped in midstride. Perhaps he had been bringing Theo—

A feminine hand Julia recognized as Theo's shot out to grab at Fitz's shirtfront, and the huge man was pulled down at the waist. His head disappeared into the room and Julia heard . . . kissing.

Fascinated, Julia pressed herself into the shallow alcove of a closed doorway in order to remain invisible. She studied her shoes and waited.

Theo . . . and Fitz.

She suppressed a hysterical giggle.

Heavy footsteps sounded. She peeked out to see Fitz sauntering down the corridor in the opposite direction. Theo, who had watched him go, spun to return to her room—and spotted Julia.

Eyes wide, her aunt clutched her dressing gown closed. "How long have you been standing there?"

Julia hurried over, pushing her aunt back inside the bedchamber. "Long enough. Aunt Theo, I cannot believe you! He's so . . ."

"Big. I know." She gave Julia a conspiratorial elbow in the ribs.

Julia couldn't hold back a laugh. "Theo! I was going to say *young*. He's got to be half your age."

"Not quite, my dear. I'm not that old, either. And I like him. He's sweet."

"Well, I'm happy for you. How long has this romance been going on?" Julia went to sit on Theo's bed, and then thought better of it when she remembered what had just transpired there.

"A few weeks." Theo's cherubic face fairly beamed, and Julia could see how much joy the affair brought her. "I wanted to tell you, but I wasn't sure how you would feel about it."

Julia stood up and hugged her aunt. "If he makes you happy, Aunt Theo, then it makes me happy." Feeling the hard swell of her belly against her aunt made her recall the original purpose for her visit.

"Oh, I came to tell you I felt the baby move. Here"—she held her aunt's hand on the mound— "let's see if he'll do it again."

A few minutes went by and nothing happened.

"Oh," Julia muttered. "I really wanted you to feel it with me."

Theo patted her arm. "There is plenty of time ahead for that, my dear. In only a few more months, we'll be holding that precious love in our arms. But why do you always refer to the baby as a 'he'? It might be a girl, you know."

"True. But since this is the only child Colton and I will produce together, I am hopeful it will be a boy. Then I'll know I've done my duty."

"And who gives a flying fig about your duty? If Colton truly does not wish for an heir, then no one need be concerned with the sex of your child."

"I suppose that is true, although Colton could change his mind someday. Well, whatever it is, this child will be *mine,* and I shall raise him or her how I see fit."

"Fitz says Colton is miserable in London." Theo kept her voice low, even though no one else could hear them.

Julia leaned forward to grip Theo's hand. "He is? Oh, what else did Fitz tell you?"

"Says the duke hardly goes out, merely sits and broods in the London town house by himself."

"By himself? Oh, I hardly believe that. Surely Nick has found companionship there. I wouldn't be surprised if he already had a mistress—or two."

Theo shook her head. "According to Fitz, the duke hasn't entertained any lady friends. Said they went to a brothel one night, but Colton came out a few minutes later looking scared out of his wits."

Julia didn't know what to make of that information. While she was glad her husband hadn't taken a lover, she found herself confused as to why he would rather be alone than here at Seaton Hall. "He'd rather ignore me and be miserable in London than be here, together."

"That's what Fitz thinks. Says Colton is punishing himself and you by staying away."

"Well, at least I have you and Angela to keep me company."

"And soon you'll have a baby as well," Theo reminded her.

Chapter Fourteen

A man, especially a stubborn one, may often anger you. Only you can decide if it's of a benefit to forgive him.

—Miss Pearl Kelly to the Duchess of Colton

It was a lovely summer. Julia became larger and larger as the weeks went on. She took long walks, read by the pond, and clipped fresh flowers from the garden. Theo and Fitz were constant companions on her outdoor excursions, the result of wanting to be together as much as guarding over Julia. Angela was also about, chatting incessantly as always.

When the August heat finally rolled into September, Julia expected Nick to arrive at any moment. Surely he had realized his error, that this baby was not a bastard but his own flesh and blood. Shouldn't he be groveling at her feet for forgiveness?

His absence hurt. When the baby kicked, she wanted to share it with him. At night, she longed for his touch to soothe her backaches and sore feet. She felt alone and scared, preparing for the birth of their first child in just a few short weeks. Was he still so angry that the truth no longer mattered? The small amount of hope she'd harbored to salvage her marriage wilted along with the summer blossoms.

As the second week in September became the third, Julia no longer cared about anything other than giving birth. She was miserable . . . and huge. Walking—even breathing—became uncomfortable, and she could hardly eat anything because she felt full all the time. She no longer even cared about Nick. He'd obviously washed his hands of her, and she couldn't muster up enough energy to be hurt any longer.

The midwife said it would be any day. She told Julia to walk as much as possible and send for her at the first sign of labor.

And just when Julia was sure she would not survive another day, it happened. At nuncheon, she'd been complaining to Theo how much her back hurt. The ache was more powerful than in days past and she wondered if she shouldn't return to bed. Theo urged her not to, repeating the midwife's words to keep walking. So it was that afternoon, while strolling out on the terrace, when fluid gushed from between her legs.

Fitz, who'd been watching her closely the past few days, quickly ran for Theo, who immediately sent a footman for the midwife, Mrs. Popper. The two of them then helped Julia up to her bedchamber, where Theo dismissed Fitz and changed Julia in a clean night rail. The pains started not long after, light and mildly irritating at first. By the time Mrs. Popper arrived thirty minutes later, however, the pain had increased significantly.

Four hours into it, Julia thought the agony could not possibly get worse. The midwife had Julia on her feet, moving slowly about the room, in an effort to hurry the babe. The pain, when it came, ripped from behind her back all the way across her belly for what seemed an eternity each time. During those moments, she clutched Theo's hand and every unlady-like word in her vocabulary came pouring out of her mouth.

"How much longer?" She gripped the bedpost and held on, panting for breath.

"I'll check you again in another thirty minutes, Your Grace. The last time I looked, the babe was not ready to come out." Mrs. Popper was a kindly older lady, but Julia was not thinking particularly kind thoughts about her at this time.

A knock sounded at the door. Theo went over to deal with whoever it was, and Julia doubled over as another pain seized her. When Julia could breathe again, Theo took her hand. "Colton is at the door, my dear. Shall I let him in?"

"Colton? How in heaven's name did he get here so quickly?"

Theo shifted uncomfortably. "He's been staying at the inn in the village for the past three weeks."

"*Three weeks!*" He'd been in the village for almost a month. Why had he not come to stay at Seaton Hall? Or at least visit? "Why did you not tell me?"

Theo wrung her hands. "Fitz asked me not to.

Apparently, Colton did not want you to know of his presence."

God, did he hate her so very much, then? She'd proven she hadn't cuckolded him, and he still didn't want to see her. She was having their baby and he couldn't even bother to stay in the same house.

A pain that had nothing to do with the baby ripped through her chest. "Send him away."

"Are you sure—"

"Send. Him. Away," she snarled as another pain came upon her. Nodding slowly, her aunt turned to the door.

Six more hours dragged by. Angela arrived to sit for a bit in order to give Theo a break. Julia was now in the bed, resting between the pains. The periods of rest between pains were becoming shorter and shorter, and the amount of pain was increasing, too. Mrs. Popper warned her not to expect the baby for another hour or so.

Julia did not know if she could last much longer. She was exhausted and nearly delirious with pain. Angela and Theo mopped the sweat off her brow and gave her sips of barley water, neither of which did anything to alleviate the feeling of being ripped apart from the inside.

An hour and a half later, Mrs. Popper declared it time to push. The room became a flurry of activity in preparation for the baby, though Julia hardly noticed. She was so tired, she hadn't the slightest clue where the required strength to push would come from. Her limbs already felt like jelly and she could barely keep her eyes open.

Her mind drifted as an escape from the pain. She

thought of Venice, of running her fingers through her husband's silky black hair as his head lay in her lap. Nick, holding her hand and teasing her through Torcello. Nick, smiling softly at her right before he kissed her. She wanted to feel that way again. "Nick," she moaned. "Please, I need my husband. Someone—"

A pain clutched at her insides and Julia screamed. Mrs. Popper began directing Theo on how to help hold Julia now that she needed to push. "Nick!" Julia shouted when she caught her breath. It no longer mattered that he'd stayed in the village, away from her. She needed his strength, his reassurance that all would be well. She wanted the Nick from Venice.

In agony, her head thrashed wildly on the pillow, sweat poured off her. "I need Nick. Here with me. Now." She dimly heard Angela tell Theo she would take care of it before leaving the room.

Nick couldn't sit still. He'd nearly worn a hole in the Aubusson carpet from pacing. Almost twelve hours had gone by. Was this normal? Should there not be a baby by now? He'd heard the screams from outside Julia's rooms. The awful feeling that something was wrong gnawed at him. Christ, if he lost her—

The library door opened and Lady Lambert walked in. "Well?" he breathed.

Angela shook her head. "Not yet. She asked that you to go back to the inn. We shall send word if she needs you."

A wave of disappointment rolled through him. "She does not want to see me at all?"

Angela's eyes were full of pity. "I'm sorry, Your Grace. We'll send for you if you're needed before morning." She turned and left.

It was exactly as he feared. Julia did not want him or need him. He'd been so wrong, so stupid, in assuming she'd been having another man's child. The things he'd said to her . . . He worried if she would ever forgive him. God knew he would never forgive himself.

It was why he'd kept his distance these past few weeks. Based on the timing, no doubt the child was his. How could he face its mother, knowing what he'd said? She had every right to hate him, and apparently she did.

"Mayhap we should stay, regardless of what Lady Lambert says." Fitz was in the chair by the fire, flipping through a biography on Jonathan Swift.

Nick dropped into a chair, put his elbows on his knees, and cradled his head in his hands. He'd gone to her door earlier, had asked to see her. It had been terrible, standing in the corridor and listening to her shouts of pain. His only thought had been to offer whatever small amount of comfort he could. But Theo said Julia did not want to see him right then. That he should wait in the library, and his wife might change her mind.

Apparently she hadn't.

The house seemed to mock him. He hadn't been wanted here when his parents were alive, and nothing had changed now that they were dead. His wife didn't want him here, either.

Not that he could blame her. The guilt over what he'd done had been eating at him the last few weeks.

He could hardly sleep or eat, knowing the day would soon come when he'd have to face Julia. What could he possibly ever say to her in order to apologize enough?

And now she'd sent him away. His chest constricted, and he cursed himself a fool for the hundredth time. "I'll be at the inn. Send me word when . . ."

Fitz nodded. "I will. Have a care on your ride back."

"I'm carrying a loaded pistol, Fitz. I'll be fine." With a heavy heart, Nick stood and walked toward the front door. Thorton appeared out of nowhere. "My horse, Thorton."

"Very good, Your Grace." He disappeared down the hall, leaving Nick to look around one more time.

Perhaps it was for the best. After all, what would he know to do with a baby?

As he left, the Duke of Colton had but one objective in mind: to get blinding, stinking drunk.

The world tilted and flipped. Something was wrong. The fog in Nick's mind cleared ever so slightly, just enough for him to realize his feet weren't on the ground. And yet he was moving. He could feel the jostling of footsteps but they weren't his own. He tried to open his eyes, couldn't, and started laughing instead.

"Christ." The voice was deep and somewhat familiar.

"Fish?" Nick tried and failed once again to make his eyelids cooperate.

"It's me, Your Grace. And apologies for what I'm about to do."

Nick didn't understand, the words hopelessly jumbled in his skull. So he relaxed. . . .

Icy cold water splashed on the back of his head, jolting him out of his stupor. He tried to move out of the way but his arms wouldn't lift. All he could do was shake in order to tell the water to stop. Only, the cold water kept coming, gushing over him until he almost couldn't breathe.

He didn't know how long it went on—it seemed forever—but he finally staggered away, soaked to the skin, and forced his eyes open. "Damn it! Stop." He pushed the wet hair back out of his face.

Fitz let go of the inn's pump handle and the water trickled to a stop. "I haven't seen you this foxed in a good number of years. Facedown on the floor of your room, you were, when I found you."

Ah, it was coming back. Seaton Hall. The inn. Julia and the—"Did she . . . have the baby?"

Fitz grinned. "She did. A baby girl. Congratulations, Your Grace."

A baby girl. His daughter. Nick's knees gave out and he crumpled to the ground. Bloody hell. He was a *father.*

Though his brain was still muddled, the horror and fear sank in. He didn't know how to be a father. It was obvious he didn't even know how to be a husband. How was he supposed to act? What should he do?

"Lady Carville said to fetch you. We best be headin' back to the hall."

Nick sat in the dirt of the inn's yard. He was a mess and, despite the cold bath, half-sprung. "I need to make myself presentable first. Help me up, will you, Fitz?"

An hour and a half later, Nick had sobered considerably. He'd bathed, shaved, and dressed, all the while allowing Fitz to ply him with strong tea. He felt wretched. His head pounded a rhythm directly behind his eyes and his stomach rolled at the mere idea of food. But he was anxious to return to the hall, so Nick soon found himself on Charon's back, riding toward his ancestral home.

"Have you seen her?"

"Your daughter?" Fitz asked. When Nick nodded, Fitz smiled. "I have. A head full of black hair and a set of healthy lungs, that one. Takes after her father, I'd say."

Nick's stomach clenched. He should have been there, should have waited at the Hall to see his daughter. Not even a day into fatherhood and he'd already failed her.

And what of his wife? How would Julia react to his presence? Fitz said Theo had sent for Nick. So did that mean Julia wanted him there? Or, would she tell him to leave again?

God, he'd made a hash of it.

One thing for certain, if Julia couldn't forgive him then he'd leave for the Continent as quickly as possible. It made sense. Julia had made it clear she didn't need him, and he'd already straightened out the estate finances. She'd never want for anything ever again. So what more could he do by staying in England?

When he finally knocked on his wife's door, he was not sure what to expect. Would she even see him?

The door cracked an inch and Theo's round face appeared. "Come in, Your Grace," she whispered, holding a finger up to her lips.

Nick stepped inside and saw a tiny bundle in Lady Carville's arms. His breath hitched. Fuzzy black hair covered the baby's head. He couldn't look away from the small delicate face, with long dark lashes resting on her cheeks as she slept.

Theo took his arm and led him past Julia's bed, where his wife was currently sleeping. There were hollows under Julia's eyes, her skin a ghostly white. She appeared exhausted.

They entered Julia's sitting room, and Theo closed the door.

"Pardon me for asking, but where the devil have you been?" Theo gave him a hard glare though her voice remained soft. "She needed you, Your Grace."

Nick frowned. "What are you talking about? She told me to leave. I went back to the inn last night."

Theo sighed heavily and rolled her eyes. "She called for you. For *hours*. She had a rough time of it and wanted to see you."

He must have more alcohol left in his system than he thought because none of this made sense. "Lady Lambert said—" And then it hit him. Nick pinched the bridge of his nose. Why had he assumed Angela spoke the truth? He, of all people, should know how deceitful she could be, despite her assurances that she had changed.

"I am an idiot," he mumbled.

"Yes, you are. Now sit down and I'll give you your daughter."

Nick froze. "Oh, no. I—"

"Nonsense." Theo steered him to a rocking chair that had been placed by the window. "Sit down."

He did as she bade, though he could hardly breathe. Surely he would hurt such a small thing with his big hands. How did one even hold a baby?

Theo gave him a few directions on the placement of his arms, then leaned over and gently transferred the tiny bundle to him. God in heaven, she was small. And *bellissima,* as the Venetians would say. His daughter shifted, snuggling further into him, and emotion clogged his throat.

"Her name is Olivia," Theo whispered.

He nodded, unable to speak or look anywhere but at his daughter's adorable pink face. Her perfect features, from a tiny nose to the delicate bow of her upper lip, reminded him of Julia. The hair, however, was his.

Regret clogged his lungs. Julia had needed him. Called for him for hours, apparently. He should have been here last night for her—and for Olivia. And here he'd been hopeful that she would forgive him. She ought to have him horsewhipped. How could he have been so stupid?

Lady Lambert would be dealt with today.

Theo patted his shoulder. "I shall be back, Your Grace. I need to check on my niece. Just keep doing what you are doing."

Nick continued rocking while watching his daughter's chest rise and fall. His eyes grew suspiciously watery. It seemed surreal to think this perfect creature was a part of him. What had he ever done to deserve anything this precious?

If he'd known Julia had wanted him last night, nothing would have driven him from the Hall. He planned to tell her so, to apologize every minute, every hour until his wife forgave him. They might not get back what they once had in Venice, but they were tied together for life, both through marriage and their child. He would make her understand.

Right now, however, he was content to sit here with his daughter and hold her while she slept.

After about twenty minutes, Theo returned. "Your wife is awake, if you'd like to see her." She bent and removed Olivia from his arms, leaving Nick little choice but to go face Julia.

He crossed through the adjoining door and into his wife's bedchamber. She looked tired, propped up on pillows and sipping tea. Her blond hair had been pulled up into a hasty knot, and her eyes raked over him as he entered.

"You look as if you've been dragged behind a team of horses, Colton. Did you have an amusing evening out, then?" Her voice was rough and scratchy.

"No," he said quietly, shutting the door behind him to give them privacy. "I did not. I—I was told you didn't want me here, Julia."

"It hardly matters now, does it?"

"It matters to me. It matters a great deal." He shifted on his feet, waiting for her to say something else.

When she didn't, he moved closer to the bed. "I fear I owe you a greater apology than I could ever make. I cannot blame you for your anger or resentment. Obviously, I never should have doubted your word."

She gave him a bland stare devoid of all emotion. "Is that all? I should like to feed Olivia if you're through."

He almost winced at the lack of feeling in her voice but determinedly pushed on. "She's beautiful."

Julia smiled, a real smile that softened her face and reminded him of the enchanting woman from Venice. "Thank you."

An awkward silence descended. Nick clasped his hands behind his back. "I plan on having my things brought over from the inn."

"You are moving back into the Hall?" She frowned. "For how long?"

He shrugged. The idea had just come to him, actually. At some point while holding his daughter, Nick had decided to stay and fight. But he would not tell Julia his plans. Not yet. "It's my home, you know. And the food's better here."

"Which didn't seem to be a problem during the past three weeks while you were in hiding."

So she knew. "I was not hiding. I did not want to upset you or the babe before the birth. It was out of consideration for you that I stayed away."

She snorted. "Consideration? You must think me dense. Pray just save us all the aggravation and go back to London, Colton."

"Not just yet," he replied. At least the exchange had brought some color back to her cheeks. "Occasionally, the aggravating things are the ones most worth pursuing." With that, he bowed and continued on to his bedchamber.

Let his wife think on that.

He rang for Fitz, and then went to the looking glass. Team of horses, indeed. He splashed cold water on his face and dried off with a towel.

When Fitz arrived a few minutes later, Nick instructed him to have his things brought over from the inn.

"So you'll be stayin' here?"

Nick nodded. "I am."

"About damned time, if you don't mind me sayin' so."

"When have you not said precisely what you wanted, Fitz?" he muttered, dryly. "Before you go, however, I need you to do one very important task."

Chapter Fifteen

There are times when avoidance is necessary in order to teach him a lesson.

—Miss Pearl Kelly to the Duchess of Colton

Nick was flipping through the pages of a book when Lady Lambert entered the library. "Have a seat," he said, not even bothering to stand.

No, he would not show her respect or kindness. In fact, he wanted her as uncomfortable as possible, so he intentionally let the silence stretch for a few moments. Finally closing the book, he set it on a side table and met her eyes.

"I cannot fathom what game you played last night, madam. In fact, I doubt there is any explanation you could offer that I would believe or excuse. I do not yet know the reasons why, but you used the birth of my daughter to exact some small measure of revenge against me."

She produced a sly smile. "Even if Julia had a moment of weakness where she called for you, I know she does not truly want you. I've heard her say so upon many occasions."

"While that may be true, it was not for you to decide. I will not have you interfering in my marriage."

"Your marriage?" she said, adding a laugh. "Your marriage is a farce, Your Grace." She stood up and moved slowly toward him. "Come now," she purred, and the hair on the back of Nick's neck stood up. "There's nothing standing in our way now. Harry is dead and your wife cannot stand you. We can finally be together, as we always planned."

Bloody hell. Nick slipped out of his chair and stood behind it, the wood serving as a barrier between him and his sister-in-law. "We planned nothing of the kind, madam. I told you nine years ago I did not want you. Nothing has changed that—not even Harry's death."

"I do not believe you. Even Harry knew there was something between us."

Nick clenched his fists, his muscles tightening. The guilt over his brother's death was a black shadow on Nick's soul. "There was never anything between us, and anything Harry believed were lies from your lips."

"Don't you see? It's not too late for us."

"I want you out of the house, Angela." He strode to the pull and rang for Thorton. "I will not have you spreading more lies."

Thorton appeared. "Yes, Your Grace?"

"Have Fitz come and escort Lady Lambert to the dower house."

Angela gasped as Thorton closed the door. "You cannot be serious."

"I am. And if I did not hold my brother in such high regard, I would toss you out on the street after what you have done. So be grateful I'm permitting you to stay at the dower house. Your maid will pack up your things and send them over."

"Colton, be reasonable—"

"I am being more than reasonable," he snapped. "But if you *ever* interfere with my family again, I'll cut you off without a farthing. You'll be out on the street to fend for yourself."

Her lips tightened. "You wouldn't dare."

"I more than dare, madam. I promise to ruin you if you cause more trouble in this house."

A knock sounded and Nick bellowed, "Enter."

Fitz came in, his expression positively forbidding. "You wanted me, Your Grace?"

"Escort Lady Lambert to the dower house, Fitz."

"Very well." Fitz crossed his arms across his massive chest and waited.

"Nick, please—"

He held up his hand. "It is 'Your Grace.' And I want you to leave this house, madam, and never come back." Nick looked at Fitz. "If she refuses to go or gives you a whit of trouble, you have my permission to throw her over your shoulder and carry her out of here."

"He *what?*" Julia leaned forward, anxious to hear more while she gently patted Olivia's back.

Theo nodded. "Threw her out of the house. Told Fitz to carry her out like a sack of flour, if need be. Fitz said she was spitting mad. Seethed all the way the dower house."

It was hard to muster up sympathy for Angela, Julia thought. Not when she'd purposely lied. Julia was every bit as furious as Nick at the woman's deception and intended to get answers as to why at her first opportunity. It would need to wait, however, until she'd recovered from the birth. She placed a soft kiss on Olivia's head and settled into the pillows behind her.

"Has Colton come back to see you?"

"No. Not since yesterday." Truthfully, she didn't expect to see much of her husband whether he was in the house or not. She was bedridden for at least the next few days, and dinners would be taken in her room.

One question nagged at her, however. Why was Colton here? He'd lurked in the village weeks before the birth, unwilling to even sleep under the same roof as his wife, so why not return to London now that their daughter had been born?

Julia gazed down at Olivia, sleeping peacefully on her chest. Her heart swelled with love and pride. No, she hadn't given Colton an heir, not that her husband wanted one. But Olivia was precious all the same. Her daughter would always be a reminder of those glorious seven days in Venice.

Before it had all gone horribly wrong.

There was no hope of fixing their marriage. Forgiveness would never come, at least not from her. Things had gone too far. He'd been cruel and then ignored her when she'd needed him most. The man was rude, arrogant, and utterly self-absorbed. No matter how much her heart yearned for him by day—and her body ached for him by night—she could not forget the past months. No, he'd broken her heart once. She would not risk that happening again.

A knock sounded. Mrs. Larkman poked her head in. "Oh, the little lamb," Olivia's nursemaid said softly and drew near the bed. "Let me take her up, Your Grace, and get her settled." She reached out and carefully took the sleeping baby away from Julia.

"Thank you, Mrs. Larkman," Julia whispered, and blew a kiss toward her beautiful little girl.

"The woman seems very capable," Theo commented when Mrs. Larkman had left the room.

"Indeed, she is. I like her tremendously and she seems to truly adore little Olivia." She picked up her cup of tea and regarded her aunt. "I swear, Theo, I have never seen you look so well. You are positively glowing. And you've stopped drinking so much over the last few weeks." Her aunt's eyes widened, and Julia smiled. "Of course I noticed, silly. I suppose I don't need to ask how goes your affair with Fitz."

Theo grinned. "I am happy. He is a good man. In fact, if you do not need me . . ."

"Go," Julia ordered with a smile of her own. "I plan to take a short nap anyhow."

"Very well, my dear. Get some rest and I will come by later." She patted Julia's arm and then departed.

Not long after, Julia was almost asleep when the adjoining door to her husband's chambers opened.

Her lids flew open in time to see Colton stroll inside, all beautiful male arrogance. Instantly, her shoulders stiffened. "Do you not knock, husband?"

One black brow shot up, the hint of a smile tugging at his lips. "No."

Annoyed, she settled farther down in bed and shut

her eyes. "I am taking a nap, Colton. So if you do not mind . . ."

"I do not plan to stay. I merely wished to inquire after your health and bring you something to read."

Julia peeked and saw a small book in his hands. Colton . . . being thoughtful? Well, it was a waste of his time. She let her lids fall. "I am fine. And leave it on the nightstand on your way out."

His footfalls drew closer and she heard a soft thump. "It's one of my favorites," he said. "I found it in the library." Then she felt his large hand pass over her forehead in a gentle caress, and the familiar scent of his soap filled her senses. Julia had to fight to remain still.

What was he about?

Without another word he retreated, and the door snicked shut behind him. Since sleep was no longer an option, she stared at the ceiling, wondering over his actions. Curiosity had her reaching for the book. It was Voltaire's *Tancrède,* the play on which Rossini had based *Tancredi*—a not-entirely-subtle reminder of the first opera they'd attended together in Venice.

She softened for a moment, her heart giving a silly stutter. No doubt Colton could be charming when he chose. Yet she must strive to remain unaffected; she would not risk loving a man so undeserving of the emotion.

Even if she still craved him with every breath.

The clock struck one, the lonely sound echoing in the darkness of Julia's chamber. She blinked, exhausted yet unable to sleep. It had been three weeks since she'd given birth to Olivia. She loved every precious minute of being a mother, from holding and feeding her daughter to just looking at Olivia's perfect little face as her daughter slept. The moments when she wasn't with Olivia, Julia ached until she could hold her baby again.

But it wasn't the yearning for her daughter keeping her awake tonight. No, someone else was responsible for the anxiety that had her tossing and turning.

Her husband was driving her to distraction.

Every time she found herself alone, Nick appeared. He inquired after her health, asked about Olivia, brought her treats from the kitchens, even produced another book for her to read. Today, he'd brought her a flower—a dahlia, he'd called it. A fairly new addition to the Seaton Hall gardens, its dramatic round shape made up of deep red, pointed petals.

She didn't know what to make of his attention. He never tried anything physical or touched her in any way, not since he'd run a hand over her hair. Rather, he seemed content to spend time with her, almost as if he were *wooing* her. Whatever the reason for it, she found his presence disconcerting.

In fact, Julia could have resumed taking dinners in the dining room each evening, but she'd continued to eat in her own room. It was cowardice, pure and simple—a desire to spend as little time with her husband as possible.

Since she was awake, she decided to go up to the nursery to see Olivia. Donning a wrapper and grabbing a taper, she slipped into the corridor. The house was quiet, everyone long abed. She took the stairs quickly and made her way to the room she and Sophie had so carefully decorated.

A soft yellow glow streamed from the open nursery

door, a sign Mrs. Larkman must already be there. As Julia drew near, she was surprised to hear a deep male voice carry into the corridor. It was . . . Nick. What in heaven's name was he doing in the nursery? Julia quickly blew out her candle, stopped just outside the door, and peeked in.

Her husband relaxed in a rocking chair near the fire, a sleeping Olivia in his big arms. Their daughter was cradled against his chest while he rocked gently. He'd removed his coat, leaving him in a white linen shirt, cravat, and ruby red waistcoat. Seeing his dark head bent so close to their daughter, emotion gripped Julia and tears suddenly sprang to her eyes. She stepped away from the door to avoid being noticed and held still, listening.

"—and on the east side of the house are the roses, Livvie."

Livvie? He already had a pet name for their daughter?

"All different colors. Pink, white, red. But you must mind the thorns if you decide to pick one. Now, your mother favors gardenias, at least in her perfume. We have those out in the greenhouse. I'll show them to you one day."

Julia smiled at the mention of her perfume. She hadn't thought Nick would notice something so trivial.

"And I *will* show them to you. I shall do my best not to ever let you down," her husband said softly. "I'm not quite sure what kind of father I'll be. My father . . . he wasn't much of an example. I saw him only a few times a year, and even those were unpleasant encounters. My brother used to say I was fortunate because I didn't have to endure the endless instructions on such things as duty and honor. I was free to run about and do as I pleased, which I guess was true.

"You would have liked my brother, Harry. He would have made a much better duke, that's for certain. Harry always did precisely the correct thing."

He proceeded to tell their daughter about the time his brother had saved him from drowning in the pond one winter. Nick had been determined to cross the ice, even though Harry had tried to talk him out of it. When the ice cracked open and Nick fell in, Harry found a tree branch and pulled Nick out of the freezing water, yelling at him the entire time for being an irresponsible half-wit.

Julia smiled and realized her cheeks were wet. This was a side of her husband he rarely let anyone see, and he was sharing it here, in the middle of the night, with Olivia. Julia swiped at her tears, drying her face, and a hand gently touched her shoulder.

Startled, she covered her mouth to smother a gasp. Relief flooded her when she saw the nursemaid, Mrs. Larkman, by her side.

"Comes every night about this time," Mrs. Larkman whispered with a nod to the nursery. "His Grace sits with her for an hour or so to give me a break, he says." She elbowed Julia's arm. "Can you imagine, Your Grace? The duke, wanting to give me a break? I keep it to myself, though. I wouldn't want any of the staff talking."

They both peeked inside. Now awake, Olivia had wrapped a miniature pink hand around one of Nick's large fingers and he was grinning down at her. Julia's heart melted. Here she thought he hadn't any interest in their daughter, while he was actually spending time with her each night.

"Have you ever seen anything so precious?" Mrs. Larkman murmured.

"No. Indeed I haven't," Julia answered, her mind spinning. She needed time to think about what she'd seen and heard. Nick was . . . puzzling. She backed away from the door. "I think it's best if I went back to bed. Good night, Mrs. Larkman."

Julia relit her taper from a sconce before creeping back toward the stairs.

She was still mulling the changes in her husband the following day over breakfast. Sleep hadn't arrived until early in the morning. Every time she closed her eyes, she pictured Nick holding and smiling tenderly at Olivia. She wanted to hate him, but that image kept playing in her mind and the anger she'd nursed for so long began to dissipate.

But could she afford to let it go completely? How could she ever trust him after what he'd said and done?

She'd trusted him once—and he'd thrown that love and trust back in her face, called her horrible names, and cast her out from his life. He'd broken her heart. She didn't want to give someone the power to hurt her like that ever again. It had been too painful.

Heavens, how she wished he would go away. It would be much simpler if she didn't have to see him every day.

Since he clearly had no plans to leave, it was past time to find out what he was doing here.

Later that morning, Julia rang for Thorton to ascertain the whereabouts of her husband.

"His Grace and Mr. Fitzpatrick are fencing in the ballroom," the butler informed her.

A flash of a sweaty, half-naked Nick fencing in Venice went through her mind. She remembered the way his muscles had bulged and dipped as his feet shuffled around the floor. Her breath quickened at the memory. The urge to see him that way again was strong—stronger than she even realized.

Which meant it was a dangerous idea.

"Thorton, please ask His Grace to join me in the library when he is finished."

"Very well, Your Grace. Shall I send for tea as well?"

"No," she blurted, her voice sharp. This would not be a social visit. "Thank you, Thorton," she added in a gentler tone, "but that will not be necessary. I do not plan on taking up too much of His Grace's time."

Julia went to the library to wait. She chose a book of poetry to distract herself, only to remember how much she detested poetry. Casting the book aside, she'd just selected a novel instead when the door opened.

Nick strode into the room, bone-deep confidence in every step of his long-legged gait. Black hair swept away from his rugged face, he wore only a fine linen shirt and breeches—both now damp with perspiration and sticking to his lithe frame. Heaven above, he was delicious. She swallowed and willed herself not to notice.

"I apologize for coming in without bathing first, but Thorton said you wanted to see me?" Was she imagining it, or was that hope in his eyes?

Julia cleared her throat. "Yes, I do. Shall we sit?" She resumed her seat on the sofa and he dropped into a chair.

She hesitated, deciding the best way to proceed. When the moment stretched, he quirked an arrogant brow. Annoyance rushed through her. "Why are you still here?"

"Because you've not yet told me what you need."

She rolled her eyes. "Do not be deliberately obtuse. You know perfectly well what I meant. At Seaton Hall, Colton. Why are you still here?"

Nick seemed caught off guard by her forthright question. He shifted and rubbed his chin. "It is *my* home. Am I not welcome here?"

She fought the urge to tap her foot. "You have three other properties scattered about England, plus the town house in London. There is a reason you are *here* and I should like to know what it is."

A long moment ticked by. By the muscle jumping in his jaw, she could tell he wrestled with his answer. But she remained silent, curious as to what he would say.

"I don't know," he finally replied, his voice low and soft. "Perhaps I am here for you. For Olivia."

Emotion welled in her chest, but she forced it back down. This was all weeks too late. She stood and began to pace. "In your unreasonable anger, you ordered me here and then ignored me for *seven* months. Did you honestly believe I would welcome you with open arms whenever you decided to return? While I will not deny you contact with your daughter, I will *never* forgive you for what has transpired between us."

His gray gaze was dark and solemn. "I have apologized for my part in what has happened, Julia. If I could go back and do things differently, I would."

"And while I am sorry for duping you, I do not

regret what I have done." How could she, when she had Olivia as a result?

"Would you rather I left, then?"

Yes, she wanted to tell him. *Go before my resolve deserts me.* But she recalled his nightly visits with Olivia. It would be unnecessarily cruel to take that time away from both of them. "No. But I wanted you to know how I feel. We shall see each other at dinner, obviously, and I should like our relationship to be . . . cordial. For Olivia's sake," she hurried to add. "But pray, cease your attentions during the day. I do not want to spend time—alone—with you."

A mask of civility, his face revealed nothing of his inner thoughts. "Very well. As you wish, madam. If that is all?"

Julia nodded, remembering that this was for the best. Her husband rose, offered her a polite bow, and walked out of the room.

Nick stomped up the main stairs. Rage and frustration clogged his throat and he spun around to return to the ground floor. A bath, where he would do nothing but think, was not what he needed at this moment. No, dark emotions were strangling his insides and they needed to be purged or else he would go mad. He strode toward the rear of the house, headed for the stables.

He passed Fitz along the way. His friend must have seen something in Nick's face because he changed direction and fell into step.

"Go away," Nick snarled.

"Are you certain about that?"

"Quite."

Fitz ignored him, as usual, and kept pace until the stables, where Nick found a groom and ordered Charon saddled.

Fitz disappeared for a moment into a stall while Nick paced in the dirt, awaiting his mount, blood pounding in his ears. The October weather was a bit brisk and he wore nothing but a thin shirt, but he hardly noticed. He needed to escape. To feel the wind on his face. To drive himself to exhaustion.

After Nick swung onto Charon's back, Fitz handed up a satchel. "Strongest Irish whisky you'd ever like to find, Your Grace. And if you don't return in two hours' time, I'll be comin' to find you."

Too numb to argue, Nick nodded, tied the satchel to the saddle, and kicked his heels into the sides of the horse. Charon shot off into the rolling country-side.

The air stung his skin as the powerful horse tore up the ground with its massive hooves. Nick leaned down over Charon's neck and gripped the sides of the animal with his thighs, his mind solely focused on staying seated.

Both he and Charon were covered with sweat by the time he slowed near the river. He walked the horse to the water and then dismounted, dropping the reins to the ground.

Satchel in hand, Nick threw himself down on the sandy bank. He dug into the bag and withdrew the bottle, uncorked it. When the first swallow hit his throat, liquid fire trailed down to his stomach. He sucked in a breath. Damn, Fitz had been as serious as a parson on Sunday, Nick thought, his eyes watering slightly. This was the strongest drink he'd had in some time.

And exactly what he needed. He took another long pull from the bottle.

I will never forgive you for what has transpired between us.

For three weeks he'd been trying to melt the ice between them, attempting to be a proper, kind, and respectful husband—and he'd failed. All along, he'd hoped to make her understand how truly sorry he was.

He'd been a fool to try. Those words—*proper, kind, respectful*—had never been applied to him in his whole life. Hadn't his parents said it time and time again? Nick hadn't the first clue on how to be a husband. So why the devil had he believed he could pull it off after all this time?

He flopped back into the soft dirt. The tightness in his chest had now dulled to an ache. He stared up at the gray clouds floating in the sky, listened to the river gurgle softly.

He could well understand Julia's anger. He'd treated her horribly. The shame of what he'd done in Venice to the mother of his child, a proper lady who'd never been with another man . . . it nearly made him sick. The things he'd said, made her do, and did to her in return, not to mention his accusations and vitriol once back in London. Little wonder she didn't want him around. He hated himself every bit as much as she did.

And even if she did want him, he could never be the husband she needed, who came to her in the cover of night, touched her only as much as necessary before politely taking her under the sheets. The mere idea was laughable.

But he also couldn't treat her like Mrs. Leighton.

She was his wife, not a whore—even if she had acted one for a short period of time—and he could not expose her to his baser nature as he had in Venice. He could not disrespect her in such a fashion.

The rather alarming problem, however, was that he couldn't forget Mrs. Leighton—Julia. Wanted her with every beat of his salacious heart. He'd pleasured himself to the memories of her so often in the last seven months that she should be purged from his mind by now. Only, the need continued to grow stronger.

Tilting the bottle up to his mouth, he took a few gulps, a trickle of whisky sliding down his cheek and into the ground.

When would this torture end, for God's sake? When would he lose interest in her, as he'd done with countless women before?

Some inexplicable force drew him to her, made her entirely irresistible. Perhaps it was her fire and bravery, or that she said what she thought and had stood up to him from the start. If he were a better man, they would be perfect together.

The whisky turned sour in his stomach. Was he . . . *in love* with her? He took another swallow, hoping the idea would disappear. When it didn't, Nick groaned. No wonder he hadn't been able to have another woman since Venice. He'd gone and fallen in love, damn it. And with the one woman he'd never have.

Bloody hell.

God, wouldn't his father love the irony. He'd told Nick over and over how no respectable woman would ever have him, title or no. Even the night of Nick's wedding, his father had berated him, saying, "I had to pay a king's ransom for her, you ungrateful whelp.

You'd best get a couple of brats on her quickly, before she learns what a terrible bargain you are and locks the door to her bedchamber."

And he was a terrible bargain. Coarse, stubborn, and angry, he'd spent nearly all of his life alone. Harry had been the only person Nick felt affection for, yet their relationship had poisoned soon after Harry's marriage. Despite Nick's vehement denials, Harry had been convinced Nick was trying to seduce Angela, and the despair over it had driven his brother to take his own life.

The guilt, the horror of finding his brother's body . . . Nick would never be able forget it—or forgive himself. Bottle at his lips, he poured the whisky down his throat in one long guzzle.

So now he'd made it all worse by falling in love with his respectable, beautiful, paragon of a wife—who happened to loathe his very existence. *Christ, what a mess,* he thought, his surroundings starting to blur a bit. Good. Mayhap he'd stay here and drink all day. God knew there was nothing awaiting him at the Hall.

A thought of Olivia went through his mind, and emotion swelled around his heart. Sweet and perfect, his daughter was more precious to him than anything. He'd never imagined feeling love like this for his child, and it nearly overwhelmed him. In his experience, children were ignored—but he could never see doing that to Livvie. She needed to grow up knowing that her father loved her.

Maybe that was why he didn't want to leave, not just yet. He didn't want to repeat the sins of his own parents. Olivia should never be made to feel unworthy or unloved. Un-bloody-anything. He may not have wanted a child, but he'd be damned if anyone took Livvie from him at this point.

So he'd keep his distance from his wife and continue to visit his daughter at night, when the two of them could be alone. They didn't need anyone else. He had Livvie and that was enough.

The decision should have made him feel better, but oddly, it did not. Perhaps another drink would help.

Chapter Sixteen

Just remember, a man can only be pushed so far.

—Miss Pearl Kelly to the Duchess of Colton

A month went by and Julia saw her husband a mere handful of times. He no longer dined with them in the evenings and kept to himself during the day. She knew from Mrs. Larkman he continued to visit the nursery each night to spend time with their daughter, but he never sought Julia out. In fact, she wondered where he slept because she never heard him in the adjoining chamber.

She tried not to be hurt. After all, she had *asked* him to leave her be. Yet she hadn't expected him to disappear altogether. At the very least, she had assumed he would continue to attend dinners. So what was he doing with his time?

To find out would require pursuing him, which Julia refused to do. Instead, she spent her afternoons with Olivia and Aunt Theo. Her body now completely recovered from the birth, she could take long daily walks about the estate, which she did each morning.

This particular morning, she had agreed to visit Angela. Yesterday, Lady Lambert had written Julia a note, where she'd apologized for sending Nick away on the night of Olivia's birth and begged for Julia to come visit her.

It had been two months since Colton had ordered Angela to the dower house, and Julia's confusion and anger over the night of Olivia's birth had not diminished a bit. How could this woman, one Julia had considered a friend, turn on her at such a crucial moment? It made no sense. Julia never would have suspected Angela capable of such cruelty. And while nothing Angela could say would excuse her behavior, Julia needed to hear straight from the woman's mouth on *why* she'd done it.

In the kitchens, Julia was overseeing the preparation of a basket with various treats and foods when she heard the jangle of keys.

"Good morning, Your Grace. Off for a picnic?" Mrs. Gibbons, the housekeeper, smiled politely from across the room.

"Good morning, Mrs. Gibbons. I am off to see Lady Lambert and thought she might appreciate some of Cook's treats."

The housekeeper frowned. "A far way to walk alone, Your Grace, if you don't mind my saying so. Shall I have one of the footmen go with you?"

"No, that is not necessary. I traveled nearly as far the other morning. I'll be fine."

"If you insist, Your Grace. It's quite chilly, so take care with your warmest cloak."

Julia nodded. "I will. Thank you, Mrs. Gibbons."

Twenty minutes later, she set off, wearing a thick cloak, hat, mittens, and scarf. The weather was indeed cold, the late-autumn wind blowing through nearly bare trees. Leaves of all shapes, sizes, and colors swirled on the ground like a pagan carpet, crunching under her sturdy half boots as she walked.

The forest closed in around her, and she tried not to think of her accident. True, she hadn't ventured along this path since, but there was no cause for concern. It had been a strange incident, surely caused by her lack of balance due to pregnancy.

Through the other side of the thick trees, she could see the dower house on the rise of the hill. It was a sturdy, brick two-story structure, with green ivy snaking up the façade. Since no one had lived there in quite a number of years, Julia was unsurprised to see the grounds a bit unkempt. Angela had taken a servant or two with her, but it would take time to bring the property up to snuff.

She came up the walk and noticed a horse resting nearby. Did Angela have a visitor?

Before she could get to the door, a sharp pain exploded behind her head, the force of a blow sending her forward, the ground rising up to meet her. Cool dirt beneath her cheek was the last thing to register before blackness engulfed her.

Nick stood in the ballroom, stripped to the waist, waiting for Fitz to ready himself. His friend had requested a quick break to catch his breath.

"If you were not so busy with nocturnal activities, perhaps you would have more stamina for our morning exercise," he called out.

"And if you found a bit of nocturnal activity for

yourself, you wouldn't feel the need to drive us both to bleedin' exhaustion each day," Fitz grumbled.

Probably true, Nick admitted. His body frustrated to distraction, these daily workouts were all that kept him sane. But he wasn't about to tell Fitz that.

"And how is the lovely Lady Carville?"

Fitz reddened, a sight Nick had never thought to see. Bloody hell, Fitz was in love.

"Lovely," the big man replied. "And gentle. Sweet as—"

"Enough." Nick held up a hand. "I'd prefer to hold on to my morning meal, if you don't mind."

Fitz smiled knowingly, a look that had Nick's fingers tightening on his foil. "You could be under a particular woman's spell, too, if you'd but let yourself fall."

He'd already fallen, but didn't bother correcting Fitz. "Get up, you lazy ox. You talk more than a woman."

Right then, the door opened and one of the footmen came in. "This just arrived, Your Grace."

Nick tossed down his foil, took the note, and tore it open. All the air left his lungs. Blood pounding in his ears, he murmured, "My God."

"What is it?" Fitz rushed over and Nick handed him the note.

Colton—

I have your wife. An exchange can be made for the right price. Come _alone_ to the crofter's cottage just outside the forest's edge. If you bring anyone, your wife dies.

"Who do you suppose this is from?" Fitz asked.

Nick shook his head, his mind frozen with fear. Someone had Julia. *Kidnapped* her. How in the blazes had that happened?

He grabbed his shirt and ran out of the room. "Thorton!" he shouted as he pulled on his shirt and thundered down the stairs two at a time. "Thorton!"

"Yes, Your Grace?" Thorton appeared at the bottom of the stairs, his eyes wide with concern.

"My wife. Where is she?"

"I believe Her Grace went on a walk this morning. She planned to visit Lady Lambert at the dower house."

"*Alone?* No one went with her?"

When Thorton shook his head, anger and guilt tore through Nick, and he slammed a fist against his thigh. *Damn it.* He should have kept a closer eye on her, but his bloody pride had prevented him from doing so. She'd told him to stay away and, like a fool, he'd done exactly that.

Jesus. If anything happened to her, he'd never forgive himself.

"Fitz!" he called loudly.

"Here, Your Grace." Nick whirled and saw Fitz looming on the stairs, his scarred face showing concern. "What do you want to do?"

"I don't know yet. But grab the pistols and let's discuss it on the way."

Julia roused slowly, the pain in her head excruciating. Everything hurt. Confused, she twisted slightly and realized with no small amount of alarm that her hands were tied behind her. She blinked in the dim light and glanced around. It was a small cottage of some sort, one she did not recognize, though it appeared to have gone unused for a good number of years, if the cobwebs were any indication. What had happened?

She took some deep breaths in an attempt to ease the pounding in her skull. The walls and floor were bare wood, with very little furniture inside the room. A small wooden table with a few chairs and a cot. A fire burned brightly in the fireplace, warding off the cold air.

Who lived here? And what did they want with her?

Moving her arms, she tested the strength of her bindings. Perhaps she could wriggle free. With a soft grunt, she gave up. Escape would not come easy. The ropes were too tight for her to get any slack.

The door opened and a man came inside, his arms loaded with firewood. He looked up—

Templeton.

Oh, for God's sake, she should have known. Julia's eyes narrowed on her husband's cousin. Instead of fear, white-hot anger flooded her. This man had plagued her for far too long.

"Good. You're awake. I did not want you sleeping the afternoon away." He strode to the fireplace and dropped the wood next to the wall.

"I would not have slept at all if you hadn't clobbered me, you dolt. Untie me."

"Shouting at me won't do you any good, Your Grace. And I don't take orders from you."

She sighed. "Have you lost your mind, Templeton? Why have you brought me here?"

"You shall see," he said, removing his overcoat. "First I must deal with your husband when he arrives."

Oh, no. She swallowed the panicked hysteria welling up inside her. Why had he hit her over the head? What was he planning to do to Nick?

"How do you know Colton will even come?"

Templeton took a chair and placed it against the wall, facing both her and the door. "I sent a note. He'll come."

Julia wasn't so sure. After all, she and Nick weren't exactly on friendly terms. In their last conversation, she told him to leave her alone, and he'd been only too happy to do so. She seriously doubted the man would rush off to rescue her. "And if he doesn't?"

"Oh, he will." Templeton withdrew a pistol from inside his pocket. "But no more talking. I want to be ready for him."

"You're planning to kill him." Suddenly it became clear. If Nick were out of the way, with no Colton heir, Templeton stood to claim the title for himself.

"Yes, that is the general plan. The degenerate never should have come back. And if it weren't for *you* he wouldn't have."

"So why kidnap me?"

"When the authorities find the gun in your hand instead of mine, Colton's death will appear as a lover's quarrel gone bad. After all, everyone knows of the lack of affection between the two of you."

Her stomach rolled. "Templeton, even for you, that is disgusting."

He smiled, his sharp, pinched features twisting in evil merriment. "Thank you."

A loaded silence descended. The hiss and crackle of the fire was deafening, and every second that passed was torture. Her muscles tensed in dreaded anticipation of the moment Nick came through the door. Perhaps she could convince him to give her more slack in the bindings. If so, she might be able to escape.

"The ropes are a bit tight, Templeton. My arms are quite sore. Would you mind loosening them?"

He shot her a withering glare. "Not a chance. I cannot risk having you escape. Now cease your chattering, harpy, or I will gag you."

The minutes crept by. How long had she been here? Hours? Her anxiety grew, since she had no idea if Nick would come for her. And if he did, how would he stay alive?

She imagined Nick rushing in the door and Templeton shooting her husband dead right in front of her. Pain gripped her chest and she had to close her eyes. No, no, Nick couldn't *die*. Yes, she was angry with him, but the idea of losing him filled her with a despair she would not have expected.

She still loved that infuriating man—and he was not allowed to die before Julia had a chance to tell him. Only Nick had the ability to turn her emotions inside out. He could make her spitting mad one second and burn with lust in the next. He'd hurt her, no question about that, but Julia needed him. Olivia needed him.

The thought of her daughter caused moisture to gather in her eyes. Would she ever see little Olivia again? If Templeton made good on his threat, both she and Nick would die today.

Which meant Olivia would be dependent on the kindness of relatives. While Julia loved Theo, her aunt had never wanted children. So would she take Olivia in? They had never talked about it, but if Theo didn't raise Olivia, who would?

Julia hated the idea of a distant relative or a stranger caring for her daughter. Who would kiss Olivia's scrapes and smooth her hair? Who would help her pick out dresses and present her at court? Would they tell Olivia about her real parents, how much she was loved? Tears slid down Julia's face and she muffled a sob.

Templeton shot her a strange look, then stood and threw the last of the logs onto the fire. "I'm going out for more wood." With that, he pulled on his greatcoat and hat, and stomped out of the cottage.

She almost smiled. If she'd known crying would get rid of Templeton so quickly, she would have produced a few tears a long time ago.

Pulling frantically with all her might, Julia attempted to loosen her bindings. She used her fingernails to pull at whatever section of the rope she could reach. With even a bit of slack, she might be able to squirm free. She knew from the sharp sting of pain in her hands that her fingers were bleeding, but that hardly mattered. Templeton would not win.

The door bounced open. She froze, expecting Templeton, but instead saw her husband. Braced for battle, his face was hard and angry, a pistol in his right hand. "Nick," she breathed, her shoulders sagging in relief. "Thank God."

Nick rushed forward, glancing around to confirm they were alone. "Are you hurt?" He touched her cheek gently with his free hand, his face softening.

She nodded. "I'm fine. It's Templeton. He means to kill you."

"Indeed I do," Templeton said from behind them, his pistol trained on Nick. "And if Colton will turn around, I shall claim what should be rightfully mine."

Julia found Nick's gaze. There was determination and savage ferocity in the gray depths of his eyes, but also fear. He was scared for her. "Do not dare," she told him quietly. "Do not sacrifice yourself for me."

"Drop the pistol, Colton." Templeton stepped farther inside. "On the floor. Now."

Nick's stare never wavered from hers. A loud *thud* reverberated as the pistol hit the wood floor. "No, Nick," she whispered, a tear sliding free and cascading down her cheek.

He lifted his hand to gently brush the wetness with his thumb. "Do not cry, *tesorina*," he murmured.

Julia swallowed, the endearment warming her heart even as panic threatened to smother her. Surely he planned to stop Templeton, didn't he?

"Turn around. Slowly." Templeton kept his weapon pointed at Nick.

With a grim set of his lips, Nick straightened and faced Templeton. "You do not honestly believe you'll walk away from this, do you?" His voice like steel, the duke crossed his arms over his chest. "And even if you do, no one will believe you."

"They won't be able to prove a thing," Templeton sneered. "The gun will be found in your wife's hand and you'll both be dead. All I have to do is shoot you from the front, to make it appear as a lover's quarrel gone bad."

"You mean the same way no one was able to prove you rigged a root in the forest to trip my wife?"

Julia gasped, and the look on Templeton's face confirmed the accusation. "I wanted her to lose the brat," her husband's cousin snarled. "I couldn't risk her producing an heir. When she did not die, I had to think of something else. This is far better because now both of you will be out of the way. Now move!"

Nick held up his hands. "Templeton, this is madness. You do not want to kill us."

"Yes, I do. And you're first. Stand in the middle of the room."

Nick carefully stepped to the center of the floor, perfectly still, and Templeton lifted his pistol to aim it directly at the duke's chest.

Julia couldn't believe this was happening. Was Nick truly going to let Templeton shoot him without fighting back? "Nick, no!" She worked frantically at her bindings again, desperate to reach Nick's abandoned gun on the floor by her feet.

Templeton pulled the hammer back and—

A shot exploded. Time stopped, with her eyes trained on Nick while waiting to see him recoil from the wound. Only, he remained upright, his eyes on Templeton . . . who crumpled to the ground with nary a whimper.

Fitz appeared in the doorway, a smoking pistol in his hand.

"Nicely done, Fitz," Nick called, turning toward Julia. "Make sure he's dead, will you?" Fitz nodded and went over to inspect Templeton's wound.

Nick smiled at her. "Are you certain you're unharmed? He didn't touch you, did he?"

Julia shook her head, too relieved to speak.

Her husband lowered to his haunches behind her chair. Within seconds, her wrists were freed. The blood rushed back into her arms in sharp tingles, and she squeaked in pain. His large hands on her shoulders, Nick began kneading all the way down until he reached her wrists. When feeling finally returned, she stood up, turned, and threw her arms around his neck, squeezing him as hard as she could.

She never wanted to let him go.

"I thought he was going to kill you," she murmured against his throat.

His strong arms slid around her and pressed her close. "I was sorry to worry you, but I could not alert him to Fitz's presence." He pressed a soft kiss to the top of her head, holding on to her tightly.

Neither of them noticed a shadowy figure in the doorway. Julia heard a shout and saw Fitz sprinting toward the exit just as another shot rang out. In horror, she watched Fitz crumple to the ground.

Angela crossed the threshold, small pistol in each of her hands. "Damn. That bullet was for you, Colton." She threw the empty weapon to the ground, quickly lifted the second pistol and pulled the hammer back.

"Angela, what in God's name are you doing? Put the gun down." Nick shifted to stand in front of Julia, his hand wrapped around her forearm to keep her in place. She peeked around his shoulder to keep an eye on Angela.

"Not before I kill you first. That fool"—Angela threw a look at Templeton—"never could be trusted to do anything right."

"You . . . and Templeton?" Nick's voice indicated his disbelief.

"Do not sound so surprised. We had mutual interests. Eight years I've been grooming that idiot to take over the dukedom, urging him to take more and more control for us. And he's failed at every turn."

"Allow me to guess. He's the one responsible for the attacks on me over the years."

Angela threw her head back and laughed. "Him? Please. No, that was *me*. It took forever to save enough pin money to hire someone to find and then try to kill you. But you always managed to stay alive, and I'd have to start squirreling money away once more. Well, not this time, Your Grace."

"Why?" he asked, his voice calm and steady. "Why are you doing this?"

She took a step forward, her hands trembling. "I should be a *duchess*. I should be the one in control of the Colton fortune—not begging for scraps like a dog. Forced to put up with that evil witch for *eight years,* listening to her berate me and everyone else for hours. The only reason I didn't kill her sooner was because I had convinced her to let Templeton control the estate."

Julia's head swam. Angela had killed Nick's mother? The woman was clearly mad.

Leaning around Nick once more, Julia glanced down at Fitz, who still hadn't moved. A large red stain bloomed on his side but she could make out the faint rise and fall of his chest, which meant he was still alive, thank goodness.

Remembering the gun on the floor, Julia eased down in the chair and used her foot to slowly drag it under her skirts.

"But Harry died and you sent me away. And now I'm *nothing*," Angela spat, her nostrils flaring.

"Harry didn't just die, Angela. He hung himself because you arranged for him to find us together. An innocent encounter where you conveniently threw yourself at me as Harry walked in. The whole business was cleverly timed. And when Harry gave you a chance to explain, instead of telling him the truth, you proceeded to fill his head with lies," Nick said. "Harry actually loved you. It broke him to learn you never felt the same. He refused to believe me and died thinking I'd dishonored him by carrying on a secret affair with his wife. All of this is your doing."

Shocked, Julia straightened in her chair. His brother . . . took his own life? Oh God. Poor Nick. How guilty he must feel. No wonder his father had been able to blackmail him into marriage all those years ago. Nick never would have wanted anyone to find out the truth over his brother's death, to have Harry's memory tarnished in such a way.

"Harry did not kill himself, you fool. I knew finding us together would drive him over the edge. He was already so jealous of you, of the way I felt about you. I saw the way you looked at me, Nick. I knew how much you wanted me. And I loved *you*. We would have been perfect together. Only, you *ruined* everything!"

Julia felt Nick stiffen. "What do you mean, he didn't kill himself?" he asked.

Angela's voice softened, turned husky. "Come, Nick. Do not pretend with me. I am the one woman who understood you, who could have given you what you need. And I know how much you wanted me, how you stared at me."

"Angela, did you kill Harry?"

"I had to. He locked himself in the study and drank until he nearly passed out," she explained. "It was easy to fasten the rope on the study's upper railing. I only had to guide him to the chair, slip the noose over his neck, and then pull the chair away. He never felt a thing. But you had to ruin it. You left me and married *her*, and I was *nothing*."

Angela crept closer, the gun still pointed at Nick's chest. Eyes wild, her lips curved into a malevolent smile, Angela had truly become unhinged. At any minute, her sister-in-law could shoot Nick dead.

Very slowly, with Nick still blocking her from view, Julia began reaching down to the gun hidden underneath her skirts.

"You do not want to do this, Angela. You'll swing for it."

"Oh, I definitely want to do this. I've been waiting to do this for eight years. And after I kill you, I'm going to kill your wife."

"There are two of us, and you have but one remaining shot. Do not be stupid."

How Nick remained calm boggled Julia's mind. Panic coursed through her, down to the very tips of her toes. Regardless, she had to do something. She would not allow Nick to be killed. A bit farther to the side and she was able to touch the cool ivory handle of the pistol.

With the gun now in her hand, she stood and moved to Nick's side. She aimed the weapon at the other woman and cocked the hammer with her free hand. "Lower the gun, or I will shoot you."

"Have you ever fired a gun, you stupid cow?" Angela sneered. "I'm a crack shot. You don't stand a chance. But perhaps I'll merely shoot you first."

Her eyes burning with an unholy light, Angela adjusted her aim right at Julia's chest.

It seemed to all happen at once. Angela and Julia both fired their pistols at the same time, the harsh sound exploding in the small space. She heard a shout—Nick's—half an instant before he threw himself in front of her.

As Nick fell to the ground at her feet, Julia barely registered the fact Angela had collapsed as well. Nick—had he been shot? She dropped to her knees, not daring to breathe. *No. Please, no.*

She rolled him gently and saw the red stain on his shoulder. "Nick! Oh God, you're hurt."

His eyes fluttered. "I'm fine. Help me stand."

"No, don't move." She nudged him back down when he tried to get up.

"Julia, be reasonable. I have to see that Angela is dead and help get Fitz back to the Hall." Though his jaw tightened in pain, she knew that stubborn look in his eyes.

"Fine. But if you bleed out and die on our way back to the Hall, I'll never forgive you."

A small smile twisted his lips. "I would expect nothing less, wife."

Chapter Seventeen

*From time to time, a man may think to make decisions
for you. It is our duty to dissuade them of this illusion.*

—Miss Pearl Kelly to the Duchess of Colton

"What are you doing out of bed?" Julia gripped the
doorframe, watching as her husband struggled to
dress himself with one arm.

While Nick's wound hadn't been serious, the
doctor had recommended rest in order to reduce
the chance of fever. So far, he'd stayed in bed for a
total of twenty minutes.

She closed the door behind her. "Nick, it's obvious
you are in pain. The doctor said you should rest."

He continued to wrestle with his cravat, trying to
knot it with one hand. "I need to see Fitz."

Julia took pity on him and strode forward to help.
She pushed his hands out of the way and began tying
the white linen. "I already told you. The bullet shat-
tered his rib and he suffered a concussion when he
hit the floor. Other than pain when he breathes, your
friend will be fine. At least he will be because he is still

abed, following the doctor's orders, unlike the *other* men in the house with bullet wounds."

She tried not to look at the bare skin of his throat or the silky black hair of his chest so close to her fingertips. Being this near to him had her pulse racing. If she tilted her head up, would he kiss her? The idea made her gown suddenly feel too tight.

"I should think you'd be glad to be rid of me," he murmured as she finished.

Surprised, her eyes snapped to his, only for him to glance away. Did he really believe such a thing? Of course he did. There'd be no reason for him to assume she'd changed her mind. There was much to say, so many things he needed to know, but her tongue felt thick and awkward. "Nick, I—"

A knock sounded at the door. "Enter," the duke barked.

Thorton appeared. "Your Grace, the constable is below and wishes to speak with you. Shall I send a footman up to assist you with your clothing?"

"No, I'll manage. Tell the constable I'll be down directly."

The butler nodded and disappeared. Nick began stuffing his long, crisp linen shirt into his trousers with his good hand. "Help me with the waistcoat, will you?"

Julia held out the blue waistcoat he'd selected from the wardrobe, and he shrugged it on slowly, favoring his injured shoulder. He turned and Julia did the buttons. She tried not to think about the hard planes of his abdomen directly under her fingertips . . . how she'd kissed his flat stomach in Venice before working farther down—

"Thank you." He reached for his topcoat and after she helped him into it, he began to walk away.

"I do not wish to be rid of you," she blurted before he could get to the door. He stopped but did not turn around. She continued. "I sat, terrified, for hours while thinking Templeton would shoot you. And then when Angela *did* shoot you—" Her voice broke and she took a deep breath. "I need you, Nick. If you'd been killed today, I do not know how I would've survived it."

He didn't move, merely stared at the wall, his posture stiff. "You would find a way. You've done quite well all these years without me. I daresay you'll be fine no matter what happens."

"How could you possibly think that? I cannot contemplate a future without you."

"I do not know why, when I've failed you in every way imaginable."

She blinked. Failed her? "I think you are woozy from the loss of blood. You are not making sense."

He faced her, his injured arm tucked against his side. "Because of me, you were kidnapped and nearly *killed* today. How could you live with the man responsible for that?"

"What happened was not your fault, Nick. Angela had gone barking mad."

"Nevertheless, you've suffered enough for my stupidity." He shook his head and dragged his good hand through his hair. "I knew Angela to be a bit cracked, yet I did nothing to prevent her presence in this house. I allowed her to cozy up to you; meanwhile she and Templeton were scheming to rid you of Olivia. It is unforgivable."

"Maybe so, but I don't blame you for what she—"

"It does not matter because I blame *myself!* I lost ten years off my life racing to that cottage, knowing someone had hurt you. And to watch Angela turn and fire on you . . . I'll relive that moment in my nightmares for the rest of my days."

She'd never seen Nick so distraught, so pale and shaky. The events of the day had clearly rattled him. She had to make him see reason, to make him understand it wasn't entirely his fault. "Angela duped both of us, Nick. And I was foolish enough to walk to the dower house alone. If I'd taken someone with me, this whole thing might have been avoided."

"Or someone else may have been harmed." He slid his hand to the back of his neck and squeezed. "And it's more than Angela, as you very well know. Can you honestly tell me that you can forgive me, can forget all I have said and done? I cannot see how that is possible, or how we could build a life together after so much hurt and mistrust."

Hadn't she recently been pondering those very questions? There was no easy answer, other than they must get past it because the alternative was not to be borne. "I share the blame for all that's happened between us. I came to Venice to seduce you, to get with child—even *after* learning your wishes on the subject. And then—"

"Do not try and make excuses for me, Julia. I do not deserve it."

"Have you forgiven me for my duplicity, then? For what I did to you?"

"I forgave you months ago, only I wouldn't admit it. The truth is that tricking me would not have been necessary had I not washed my hands of my responsibilities. You have my sincerest apologies for all you've been through."

"Nick, please—"

"No, let me say this. When I look at you, I see such beautiful innocence—only to remember how I've tarnished it. God, I deflowered you in a chair!" Nick shook his head, pinched the bridge of his nose. "I'll never be able to make it up to you, to feel as if I've atoned for the hurt I've caused. I've been the worst kind of husband—God knows you'd be better off with any man other than me. I've ignored you, treated you shamefully, and said and done all manner of unforgivable things to you."

Julia knew this was not merely about her virginity. "You have not *tarnished* me. Our week in Venice . . . I'll never regret it. How could I, when it was the most wondrous, amazing, beautiful experience of my life?"

He closed his eyes briefly then turned away. "I am not what you need, Julia. I cannot be a proper husband. In fact, I wouldn't know where to even begin. And after today, that should be glaringly apparent."

Quite the opposite, she realized. Today, he'd proven *exactly* what kind of husband he'd be: brave, caring, and protective. She crossed the floor to stand before him and stroked his whisker-roughened jaw with her fingers. "But you saved me. Do not forget that part, husband."

He leaned in to her touch for a brief instant, then pulled away. "A fact that does not change anything, nor does it change who I am. I cannot be what you need—a proper society husband who asks for permission before entering his wife's bedchamber to touch her in the dark. The title, this house . . . they were never meant for me. And I never wanted any of it.

Trying to become the husband you deserve will only serve to turn us both miserable, Julia."

Her mind spun. This was much worse than she originally feared. He truly believed himself unworthy of everything he'd been given—including her. "I deserve a husband here with me, by my side. That husband is *you*, Nick. I do not want anyone else."

He walked around her, farther into the room. "You don't know what you are saying. I was broken a long time ago and any hope of leading a normal life has long eluded me. Winchester has accused me many times of being selfish, of only thinking of myself. Well, I learned to be selfish because there's never been anyone else to give a damn. I cannot change, and it is better if I do not stay."

"You can change. You *have* changed. Would a selfish man have raced to save his wife from kidnappers? Would a selfish man have thrown himself in front of a bullet meant for someone else? Would a selfish man spend his nights rocking his daughter in his arms, telling her stories instead of sleeping?"

His eyes widened. "You knew?"

"I knew. And a man who would do those things is more than good enough for me."

He said nothing and his expression, bleaker than she'd ever seen it, seemed to grow even more desolate. How could this be possible? She'd finally realized she loved him and he was slipping away, unwilling to fight for a future together. Did he not feel anything for her, anything at all?

She did not want anyone else. Nick was certainly not perfect, but neither was she. And, deep down, he was a good man. She knew it with certainty, had seen many examples of it—including earlier today. There would be no other man for her. Ever.

Her stomach clenching, she felt true fear for the second time that day. Did he really hate himself that much, feel so unworthy of genuine love and affection that he refused to even try? He'd walked away from his life eight years ago, unable to come to terms with himself and his past, and it seemed he was determined to escape once more.

"Please, Nick. We can put this behind us and move on. Ours would not be the first marriage started on such rocky ground."

He pressed his lips together in a stubborn expression she recognized. "I cannot see how it's possible."

"Why not?" Anger and sadness, frustration and disappointment all warred within her, and she could scarcely reason which emotion to voice first. "Can you not accept that I want you?" It was on the tip of her tongue to tell him she loved him, but something held her back. Perhaps the fear over what he'd said, the fear the sentiment would not be returned.

He moved to the window, leaned his good arm against the panes, and gazed down at the gardens for a moment. "You never even answered my question," he said quietly, his voice thick with emotion. "Which is an answer unto itself, don't you think? I'll never be able to forget what I've done and you'll never be able to forgive me for it."

Julia opened her mouth to deny it . . . but couldn't get the words past her lips. Had she forgiven him? She didn't want to lose him, certainly, but could she honestly say she'd absolved him of his hurtful words and deeds since returning from Venice?

When she hesitated, he pushed off the window

and went to the door. "So what happens now?" she choked out.

He paused with his hand on the latch. "I leave." Then he opened the door and disappeared.

The next morning, Julia lay in bed, exhausted. She'd spent the night tossing and turning until the purple wisps of dawn broke out across the sky. Nick was leaving. His mind had been made up, his self-loathing and fear too strong for Julia to overcome.

After Meg had delivered her morning chocolate, Mrs. Larkman brought Olivia down for a bit. Holding her daughter only served to remind Julia of Colton's decision not to be a part of her life. Did that extend to Olivia as well? The idea of their daughter growing up without a father broke Julia's heart all over again. Yes, when the idea to have Colton's child first took root, she had assumed to be the sole parent in her husband's absence. But Colton had seen their daughter, held her in his arms. How could he not want to watch her grow?

Theo arrived and found Julia on the brink of tears. "Oh, heavens—whatever is wrong?" She strode to the bell pull, giving it a firm tug.

Mrs. Larkman was sent for and Olivia returned to the nursery. Theo then sat on the bed and reached to clasp Julia's hand. "Now, my dear. What is the matter?"

Julia took a shuddering breath. "I apologize. I cannot seem to stop crying."

"Is it Colton?" When Julia nodded, Theo sighed. "I suspected as much. From what Thorton tells me, he's been locked away in the study since last evening. So what happened?"

"I told him I needed him, that I wanted a future together. Almost losing him yesterday nearly scared the life out of me. I love him, Theo." The tears she'd been trying to hold back slid down her cheeks.

"And what did Colton say to this revelation, I'm afraid to ask?"

Julia related the conversation for Theo, of Nick's insistence he could never be the husband she needed. Theo clucked and shook her head. "If his mother were still alive, I would give her a good tongue-lashing over the way she raised that boy. There is no cause for a mother to be so cruel, even if the child was not conceived under ideal conditions."

"What do you mean, not ideal conditions?"

"Did Angela not tell you? She suspected, based on conversations with the dowager duchess, that Colton's father forced himself on his wife when she refused him. When your husband resulted from the encounter, the duchess could never forgive or forget what had been done and took her anger out on the boy."

Julia gasped. "How terrible! I wonder if Colton knows."

"If he doesn't, he should be told. It could go quite a long way to helping him understand that her lack of motherly devotion was not *his* fault, but hers."

Julia made a mental note to tell Nick of this new information—if she got the chance. "What am I to do, Theo? I know he cares for me. How can I prove how much I love him? I want to get back what we had in Venice."

"How far are you willing to go to convince your husband to stay?"

"I'll do whatever is necessary. I want to fight for him, but I do not know how."

Theo smiled. "Then leave it to me. I know precisely what you must do."

Nick watched Fitz's chest rise and fall. Fitz's breathing was even and deep, and the doctor had assured Nick his friend would recover.

Even still, guilt threatened to choke him. Fitz and Julia had nearly been killed because of Nick's stupidity. How could he not have seen the madness within Angela? He'd learned eight years ago that she would lie and scheme to get whatever she wanted. So why did he not do anything to stop her then?

Nothing had gone as planned since he'd returned to England. He'd made a complete hash of it, not thinking clearly. First he'd been consumed with fury at Winchester and Julia, and then he'd been blinded by an unshakable lust for his wife. And even now, after Olivia's birth, peace and happiness continued to elude him.

Mayhap it would always elude him here, where the memories and heartache were too powerful. The farther away from England he went, the better. Julia deserved more than the life she'd had thrust upon her, with a husband who could never be what she needed. Divorce was not a possibility, but he could at least give her a measure of freedom by returning to his life abroad.

God, he loved her so much, his teeth ached. He longed for his wife in a way he'd never experienced with any other woman, and to be near her and not have her was unimaginable torture. Distance would benefit them both, in his opinion.

Fitz snorted in his sleep and shifted, regaining Nick's attention. Though Nick would resume his travels, Fitz would not join him this time. His friend was in love with Lady Carville and Nick would not dare deny Fitz a minute of happiness with the woman. Besides, now that Angela had claimed responsibility for the attacks over the years, Nick hardly needed a bodyguard. No, he would go alone. Tomorrow, before Fitz had fully recovered. Before Fitz could try and talk him out of it.

Nick sighed and rubbed his eyes with his good hand. Hell, he was tired. Last night had been awful. The day's events combined with Julia's revelations about her feelings ensured he hadn't slept a wink. Even visiting Olivia in the early hours of the morning hadn't bolstered his spirits. It had only depressed him more, had him wishing for things that he could never have.

The door creaked open and Lady Carville stepped in. "Is he awake yet?"

He stood. "Still asleep, I'm afraid. Is this usual? Should he be sleeping this long?"

"Sleep is the best thing for him, Your Grace," she assured him. "I woke him every few hours last night because of the head injury. It's likely he will sleep the rest of the day away."

Lady Carville smiled at Fitz, love shining unabashedly in her eyes. Sensing the need for privacy, Nick started for the door. "Will you fetch me if he awakens? I need to thank him."

"He knows, Your Grace. That is the way with those

we love, is it not? We want to protect them from harm—whether they need us to or not." Clear and steady, her eyes were full of meaning, and Nick realized they were no longer discussing Fitz.

"Nevertheless, if you wouldn't mind, have one of the footmen fetch me if he awakens today."

Hours later, after a long ride and a bath, Nick settled in the study. Many things remained to be done before he departed, such as letters to his solicitor and estate manager, as well as finishing his will.

And then there was Olivia. She deserved a written explanation as to why he hadn't stayed, lest she feel abandoned when she grew older. The one thing he never wanted his daughter to believe was that he didn't love her—because he did. Fiercely. The few hours he spent with her each night would be the best memories of his life.

Along with Venice, he thought ruefully.

He hadn't the faintest idea how to say farewell to his wife. Sentimentality was a skill Nick did not possess, and baring his feelings would only make them both more miserable. Nevertheless, he had to say *something* and the devil only knew what it would be.

By the time he'd finished the instructions to both the solicitor and estate manager, the gray afternoon had long darkened into night. He rubbed the back of his neck, stretching a bit to ease the pain in his wounded shoulder, and continued his writing.

A knock sounded. Likely Thorton again, ready to badger him about food. "Enter," he shouted, not even bothering to look up.

He heard the heavy wood swing open. "Thorton, I asked not to be disturbed. What is so pressing this time?"

The faint scent of gardenias suddenly stole through him, invading his senses, and Nick's head snapped up.

Julia.

His wife stood there, so beautiful and untouchable that he wanted to howl at the unfairness of it. She wore a dressing gown, her feet bare, and even that small hint of bare skin had his heart hammering. Damn, but the woman tempted him at every turn.

Her face gave nothing away as she closed the door behind her. When the click of the lock echoed throughout the room, he shot to his feet, almost knocking over the chair. "Is something amiss?" he heard himself ask, his voice a mere croak as she sauntered forward.

Instead of answering, she lifted her arms and removed a pin from her hair. Six pins later and a curtain of blond curls swirled down her back. He froze, transfixed, unable to speak. Part of him couldn't wait to see what she would do next. Another part of him wanted to flee, posthaste.

She ambled toward him, hips swaying and the tops of her breasts peeking out from the lapels of the dressing gown. . . . He could scarcely believe this was not a dream. When he met her sultry blue gaze—one he hadn't seen since Venice—he clutched the edge of the desk to keep from pouncing on her.

"What are you about, Julia?"

Her hands reached for the sash at her waist, slowly untied it. "Showing you what you're missing when you leave. Would you care to see?" She parted the layer of thin silk and began slipping it down over her shoulders. His mouth went dry.

The creamy skin of her neck and shoulders appeared, followed by the graceful ridges of her collarbones. Then the dressing gown fluttered to the floor, and Nick's jaw fell. Jesus Christ . . . It was the boned red chemise from Venice.

Comprised of satin and lace, the garment did little to cover the beauty she'd been born with. The black lace bodice hugged her tightly, her breasts held up and out in a deliciously tempting offering. Her lower body . . . was on full, glorious display. The transparent red fabric stopped just above her mons in the front and dipped down to brush her buttocks in the back. His body responded instantly, hardening, until his stiff cock pushed painfully against the inside of his trousers.

She glided toward him, and he couldn't make his feet work—or his arms, for that matter. He couldn't do anything but watch, helpless to stop whatever she planned. "Julia," he breathed. At least he still had control over his voice.

His wife shook her head, her lips curved into a secret smile. "Not tonight, my darling. Tonight, you may call me Juliet."

She'd never forget the look on her husband's face. The hesitation, the hope . . . and the bone-melting lust. His eyes glittered hot as they raked over her, and he appeared a hairbreadth away from leaping on her. Any nerves completely disintegrated, replaced with a surge of feminine power she'd not experienced since Mrs. Leighton packed up her powders and flimsy petticoats.

"Why?" he wheezed.

She trailed a finger over the tops of her breasts. "You profess to know what sort of man I need. But never once have you asked me what sort of man I *want*." Once they were an arm's length apart, she said, "I do not want a husband who asks permission before coming to my bed, groping me in the dark like an untried schoolboy. No, I want a man. A wicked man who enjoys my wickedness as well."

Leaning in, she placed her hands on his chest, rose up on her toes, and whispered in his ear, "Because I quite enjoyed being wicked with you, Nicholas." Her breasts grazed his hard chest, and she was satisfied to hear him groan.

His breath sharp and fast, he held himself utterly rigid. He was trying so hard to resist her, the poor man. A very good thing she had not yet used up all her tricks.

Her hand slid down his stomach until she reached the thick ridge of erection in his trousers. Tracing the outline with her fingertips, she watched as his lids fluttered closed, black lashes fanning his cheeks.

"Shall I tell you of all the wicked things I'd like to do with my hands?" she murmured, then moved closer until their lips almost touched. "With my mouth?"

That did it. With his good arm, he crushed her against him, his mouth crashing down to devour hers. The kiss was hard. Unrelenting. Desperate. There was no air to be had and their teeth clicked together, tongues stroking. It was everything she remembered from Venice and more.

His lips slanted over hers again and again, and she replied in kind, throwing her arms around his neck and kissing him back feverishly. Then her hands began touching him everywhere, relearning the taut planes of his shoulders and chest. She tried to get closer, nearly writhing in an effort to ease the insane craving deep inside her.

He moved to kiss her throat and murmured, "Let me take you to bed."

Julia shook her head. "No. Right here." She scooted her bottom up onto his desk. Perched on the edge, her bare legs dangled over the side. "I want you to take me right here."

"We shouldn't—"

She clasped his crumpled cravat and pulled him in close. He stepped between her knees, the heat of him pressed directly against her bare cleft. She gasped at the rough sensation, yet still needed more. "Nick, *please.*"

His hand moved between them, and he found her entrance, fingers sliding easily through the slickness gathered there. He teased her, stroking and caressing, and she had to bite her lip to keep from crying out.

"Christ, woman," he panted. "You have the power to make me daft. If I don't get inside you—"

Her fingers flew to the fall of his trousers, unfastening the buttons as quickly as she could manage. A few tore in her haste and dropped to the carpet. "Now, Nick. I need you now."

When his shaft sprang free, he wasted no time before lining up and driving deep. They both moaned. His hardness stretched her, filled her, and she wrapped her legs around his waist to hold him in place. He withdrew with an agonizing slowness and then drove forward once more, burying himself inside her.

"I've been dreaming about this every night since Venice," he said before thrusting with enough force to drive her back on the desk. He slid his good hand under her buttocks to hold her in place. "Embarrassing, but I'm afraid I won't last."

Julia couldn't respond for the unbelievable intensity of it. He fit her perfectly, snug into the cradle of her hips while he drove them higher. She loved that he was so wild for her, both of them nearly mad with lust.

He kissed her again, panting into her mouth as he thrust, and then slid her bottom lip between his teeth. Bit down. The exquisite pain and pleasure raced down her spine, through her groin, straight to her channel, which clenched around his penis in sheer bliss.

"Oh, hell," Nick breathed. He began slamming into her, his head thrown back, their bodies meeting in a frenzied rhythm.

She felt it building, the sensuous ribbons of exhilaration pulling her limbs taut. Her hands clutched at him and her nails sank into the muscles of his forearms. "Yes, faster. Oh God, Nick." His fingers located the bundle of nerves between her legs, which he expertly rolled. Higher and higher she climbed . . . until her body exploded into a thousand tiny pieces. Light sparkled behind her lids and a long moan tore from her throat, the orgasm stealing through every bit of her, turning her body inside out with the force of her pleasure. She shook and trembled, only vaguely aware that Nick began shuddering as well, his hips stuttering, muscles clenched in ecstasy.

Limp and spent, she clung to him and sucked in air. There were no words to describe how wonderful that had been. Nick didn't speak either, merely leaned over to rest his forehead against hers. They stayed there a long moment, his shaft still buried in her.

When he caught his breath, he withdrew, awkwardly tucking himself back in his trousers with one hand while avoiding her eyes. "My apologies," he mumbled.

She grabbed his arm. "Do not apologize to me. We both wanted this, Nick."

"No, you don't understand. This is . . ."

Julia took a deep breath for courage. "I love you." His surprised gaze flew to hers, so she repeated it. "I love you. I fell in love with you in Venice and I don't want anyone else. I certainly don't want a husband who comes to me only in the darkness, touching me under the covers. I want a husband who will ravage me on the desk in his study."

His brow furrowed. "You love me?"

"I love you," she declared again with a nod. "And if you leave me, I'll follow you, Nicholas. I swear it. If you do not want to live in England, Olivia and I will come with you wherever you want to go."

He blew out a long breath. "You do not know what you're saying—"

"Look at me." When his stormy gray gaze met hers, she continued. "You will never be free of me, husband, just as I will never be free of you. I chased you down once, and I'm prepared to do it again. I know exactly what I want, and he's standing right in front of me."

"I'm . . ." His eyes slid away as he trailed off.

"You are what?"

He cleared his throat. "I do not know if I can be what you need."

"You are *exactly* what I need." She cupped his face in her hands. "Do you love me?"

He nodded. "I love you. God, I think I fell in love with you the minute I met you. I am miserable without you."

She grinned. "Say it again, husband."

Nick leaned forward, his mouth a whisper from hers. "I love you, wife. But what happens if you are wrong? What if I make you miserable?"

"No doubt you will make me miserable some days, just as I will do the same to you. There will be ups and downs in our marriage. But you cannot run any longer, Nick. Stay with me and let's start the life we both want. The life we both deserve."

He seemed to grapple with that, trying to understand, and a hint of hope appeared in his expression. "No under the covers in the dark?"

"Absolutely not. If you try it, I'll box your ears." Her hand came up to caress his cheek. "I fell in love with the Depraved Duke in Venice, after all. You cannot go back now."

Dark clouds lifted from his eyes, and a sly grin slowly spread over his face. That smile warmed her in all the very best places. "Well, if you can be Mrs. Leighton every now and then, I suppose it's only fair if I am the Depraved Duke in exchange."

"Indeed, it is only fair," she said with mock seriousness.

"If you truly want me, *tesorina*, I'm yours. I'm uncertain if I can be a good husband and father, but I will die trying because to be without you would kill me." He gave her a kiss then, long and deep.

"How many more outfits of this sort does Mrs. Leighton own?" he asked when they broke apart. His hand skimmed across the lace covering her breast, and she shivered.

"A few. Why?"

"Because this wicked husband has the urge to rip it off and ravage you once more—this time on the floor of his study."

Chapter Eighteen

'Tis a rare—and lucky—woman who experiences the gift of true love.

—Miss Pearl Kelly to the Duchess of Colton

One month later

Nick gently bounced Olivia on his lap, his heart turning over in his chest as she smiled up at him. His daughter had the ability to make him feel like the most powerful man on earth. She readily gave him her unconditional love and trust, and he vowed never to squander that gift.

And then there was his wife, who had her own way of making him feel quite powerful. He'd been unsure at first of her insistence to want him exactly as he was, flaws and all. It seemed much too good to be true. But she'd proven in a hundred ways over the past month how perfectly suited they were. In fact, there were a few nights when her depravity had out-matched even his own. He made a mental note to send a generous token of gratitude to Pearl Kelly.

They had decided to live at Seaton Hall. His wife

had taken it upon herself to redecorate, and workmen were ever present on the estate. Most of the Seaton family portraits had been removed and stored in the attic. While Nick now understood the reason for his mother's resentment, he could do without the daily reminders of his family.

Except for Julia and Olivia, of course. "Livvie, your papa promises to spoil you. No matter what your mama says, *bellissima.*"

His daughter smiled as if she understood every word. And if she was half as smart as her mother, she likely did.

"Are you spoiling her again, Nicholas?"

He turned and caught sight of his wife striding into the room. So beautiful and strong willed, and she belonged to him. Loved him, even. Some days, he still couldn't believe it.

"Shhhh." He leaned down and whispered to his daughter, "Do not tell your mother."

Julia laughed, long and loud, her joy filling the room, as it did everywhere she went. She reached for Olivia. "I'll take her. You have a visitor."

"A visitor? Who?"

"You shall find out soon enough. Run along, Nick." Julia lifted their daughter, giving him no choice but to stand up.

He left, but not before giving his wife a lusty kiss.

When he finally entered the study, a blond-haired man spun around, a man Nick would know anywhere. "Winchester!" he greeted. "I wasn't expecting you." Nick closed the door. "Did you receive my letter?"

Winchester nodded, his expression smug. "I did, but I came to hear it in person."

Nick rolled his eyes. "I already groveled. What more do you want from me?"

"To hear it once more. And again every day for the rest of my life."

Nick chuckled. "Fine. You were right. I was a self-ish bastard who treated her unfairly. I am grateful to you for helping when she asked, and for bringing her to Venice to find me. I apologize for hitting you and for questioning your pure, unselfish motives. Was that all of it, or did I forget anything?"

"I think that was all. And you're both happy?"

"Appallingly so, yes."

"Excellent," Winchester said, and clapped Nick on his uninjured shoulder. "Then let's have a drink and you can tell me all about what changed your mind."

A few minutes later, both men settled in armchairs, brandy glasses in hand. "So," Winchester began, rest-ing a booted foot upon the opposite knee. "Hard to tell your wife 'no,' is it not?"

"Indeed. I daresay she's the most stubborn person I've ever met. Did you see her already?"

"For a few minutes when I first arrived. I told her I was here for you. For a second, I didn't think she'd leave us alone, afraid we'd come to blows again. I had to tell her that you'd written to me, begging my eter-nal forgiveness, before she'd agree to find you."

"Eternal forgiveness? And you say *I'm* the dra-matic one."

"Oh, you've had your moments. The crowd at White's still talk about the day you came in and laid me out in front of the hazard table."

Nick sipped his brandy and refrained from com-menting. "How's Quint?"

"Still heartbroken, though the man professes otherwise. I keep telling him that if the Depraved Duke can find happiness with a woman, so can we all."

"Speaking of happiness, how did you know? How did you know Julia and I were so well suited?" Nick set down his glass. "There was every chance I would turn her away in Venice and your trip would've been for naught."

Winchester shrugged. "I've known both of you for a long time, and it was clear there would be a spark. How could there not be with two such passionate people? When you married her, do you remember what I told you?"

Nick searched his brain for a memory of that time more than nine years ago. Only, he'd been too drunk after his brother's death to remember much. "No, I don't."

"I told you she was as fiery and stubborn as you are, and that you were lucky to have her. If anyone could bring you to your knees, I knew it would be Julia." He set the glass carefully on the desk. "Do you remember what else I told you that day?"

Nick shook his head, watching as his friend stood and removed his coat. Now in his shirtsleeves, Winchester moved to the center of the room.

"I told you that if you ever hurt her, I'd break your jaw." He motioned for Nick to stand up. "Come now, Colton. Get up and take it like a man."

Nick choked on a laugh. "You don't think I'll stand there and allow you to pummel me, do you?"

"It's no more than I allowed when you returned to England. I let you get one in and didn't bother fighting back because I knew I deserved it. Up, Colt. Let's go." Winchester clenched his fists and raised them into a fighting stance.

A shot in the face was no less than he deserved, so Nick got to his feet. "I cannot wait for you to fall in love, Winchester. I vow to make your life a living hell."

"Cease your squawking, old man, and come closer." Winchester raised his fist, drew back his arm, and—

"*Simon!*"

Their heads spun toward the door, where Julia stood, horrified. Winchester quickly dropped his arms, his expression sheepish as the duchess marched into the room.

"Were you going to *hit* him, Simon? You promised me you wouldn't!"

Winchester clasped his hands behind his back, the picture of innocence. Nick almost snorted. "No, of course not. I merely wanted to show him some moves from a boxing match I attended recently in London. Why in the world should I want to hit Colton?"

This time Nick really did snort. His wife narrowed her eyes on both of them. "I don't know what is between you two," she snapped, "but you need to make up. *Now.* Let bygones be bygones. Both of you. You're acting like children."

Nick raised his hands in surrender. "I apologized."

They both looked at Winchester, who heaved a sigh and shook his head. "Fine. But if he causes you any trouble again, promise to contact me, madam duchess."

She smiled at him affectionately. "I will, Simon. Now, if you'd like to come up and see your god-daughter . . ."

"I'd love to." Winchester started to follow but stopped when Nick put a hand on his arm.

"We'll be along in a few minutes. I want to have another word with Winchester."

"A word that does not involve striking one another?" she asked.

He nodded. "Yes. We'll come to the nursery in a bit." Julia gave them both glares of warning before leaving. Nick motioned for Winchester to sit. "Tell me how you and Julia came to be so close. I've never known why you seemed determined to protect her."

"Ah." Winchester shifted in his chair, a flush creeping up his neck. The reaction intrigued Nick even more. "Did you ask Julia?"

"Yes," Nick replied. "She told me to ask you."

"It's not a story I care to recount, so let's just say your wife once stopped me from doing something incredibly stupid."

When Winchester did not elaborate, Nick prompted, "And? You don't think you can stop there, do you?"

His friend chuckled softly. "And have you mock me for the rest of my life? You must think me a veritable half-wit, Colt. No, I've told you all you need to know."

"We've been friends for more than twenty years, and you won't tell me?"

"It's not an event I share proudly. But I can say this: When I marry, it shan't be because I fancy myself in love."

"I don't know, Winchester. Love has its benefits."

Winchester rose. "All this happiness would be bloody revolting if I weren't so disgustingly fond of you both. Let's go see your daughter, Colton. I'm told she possesses her father's temper."

When they walked into the nursery, they found Julia cradling Olivia, singing to her softly. Nick couldn't remember a more beautiful sight. He leaned a shoulder against the doorjamb, perfectly content to watch the two females he loved above all else.

Winchester slapped him on the back. "You are incredibly fortunate for a degenerate."

Nick's grin nearly split his face. "I know."

When Julia spotted them, she beamed at Nick, happiness and love shining in her eyes, and Nick's heart stuttered. Damn, she could get him every time, simply knock him down with a look.

"Olivia, come meet Uncle Simon," she cooed, and Winchester scooped up the child, handling Olivia with sure but careful hands. He swung her around, and the infant smiled broadly.

Julia sauntered over to where Nick stood and laced her arm through his. They watched Winchester and Olivia together. "You have the oddest expression on your face," she murmured. "What are you thinking?"

He pulled her tight to his side and pressed gentle lips to her temple. "I know Winchester has just arrived, but I had plans for this afternoon. Mayhap we could sneak away for a bit?"

She looked up, her eyes twinkling. "Hoping for a visit with Mrs. Leighton, are you?"

Leaning down, he whispered, "I only need you, sweetheart. Preferably without clothing and in my bed."

"Why, Nick. How positively boring," she teased. "You shall never retain your nickname with habits such as those."

"Nothing is ever boring with you, wife. I daresay you'll be leading me in circles until the day I drop dead."

"That is the plan, husband. That is the plan. . . ."

Keep reading for a special sneak peek at
The Harlot Countess,
coming next month . . .

Lady Maggie Hawkins's debut was something she'd
rather forget—along with her first marriage.
Today, the political cartoonist is a new woman.
A thoroughly modern *woman. So much so that her*
clamoring public believes she's a man . . .

FACT: Drawing under a male pseudonym, Maggie is known as Lemarc. Her (his!) favorite object of ridicule: Simon Barrett, Earl of Winchester. He's a rising star in Parliament—and a former confidant and love interest of Maggie's, who believed a rumor that vexes her to this day.

FICTION: Maggie is the Half-Irish Harlot who seduced her best friend's husband on the eve of their wedding. She is to be feared and loathed as she will lift her skirts for anything in breeches.

Still crushed by Simon's betrayal, Maggie has no intention of letting the *ton* crush her as well. In fact, Lemarc's cartoons have made Simon a laughing-stock . . . but now it appears that Maggie may have been wrong about what happened years ago, and that Simon has been secretly yearning for her since . . . forever. Could it be that the heart is mightier than the pen *and* the sword after all?

Spring, 1809, London

Silence rippled throughout the ballroom the moment her slipper hit the top step.

Before Lady Margaret Neeley had a chance to comment on this odd reaction, her mother began tugging her down the stairs. Only then did the impending doom become apparent: the way each person avoided her gaze, the hushed tones sallied around the room, dancers paused midturn.

And she realized at once that they knew.

They *knew.*

Somehow, despite her best efforts, stories of what happened the night before had circulated through the streets of London this afternoon. On morning calls, rides in Hyde Park, and promenades down Rotten Row, the *ton* had spread the tale of what had happened hither and yon.

With Maggie's younger sister ill today, Mama hadn't wanted to go on calls. Relieved, Maggie had spent the time drawing, grateful that they hadn't received any callers. Now it was clear why.

She hadn't done anything wrong, she wanted to shout. In fact, she had tried very hard during her debut to appear a proper English girl. With the black hair and fiery temper of her Irish father, it had been a constant battle. She neither looked nor acted like all the other girls, and the *ton* seemed to enjoy casting her in the role of outsider despite that she'd spent most of her life in London.

"Why has everyone gone quiet?" Mama hissed in her ear. "What have you done, Margaret?"

Of course Mama would pick up on the disquiet. Also unsurprising she would place the blame for the uneasiness squarely at Maggie's feet. Even still, Maggie couldn't answer. A lump had lodged in her throat and even breathing proved a challenge.

Escape, her mind cried. Just run away and pretend this whole evening never happened. But she'd done nothing wrong. Surely someone would believe her. All she had to do was explain what occurred in the Lockheed gardens.

Lifting her chin, she continued down toward the glittering candlelight. Stubbornness had long been a defect in her character, so everyone said. Mama lamented that Maggie would argue long after the point had been made. So she would not turn tail and run, though her stomach had tied itself into knots. No, she would face them, if only to prove she could do it.

When they reached the bottom of the steps, the quiet was deafening. Their hosts did not bustle forth to greet them. Not one of her few friends rushed over to share gossip or compliment her dress. No young buck approached to request a spot on her dance card.

Instead, the crowd swelled backward as if an untamed beast had wandered inside and might run amok at any moment.

"Come," her mother ordered, taking Maggie's elbow. "Let us return home."

"No," Maggie whispered emphatically. What happened was not her fault, and she would not allow anyone to bully her. Someone would believe—

A blur of blue silk sharpened into the flushed features of Lady Amelia. "I cannot believe you are so foolish as to show your face," the girl hissed.

Maggie straightened her shoulders and focused on her friend. "Whatever you have heard—"

"He told me. Did you think he would not? My betrothed confided in me of your . . . your *wickedness*, Margaret. You tried to steal him from me but you failed."

The entire room was now avidly watching and listening to this conversation. Even the orchestra had quieted. "Amelia, why would I—"

"You were always jealous. I've had three offers this Season and you haven't had a one. It comes as no surprise that you would try to steal Mr. Davenport for yourself." The heir to Viscount Cranford, Mr. Davenport was widely considered the most eligible young man in London. He had proposed to Amelia more than a month ago and Maggie had been nothing but pleased for the other girl.

So Maggie ignored her mother's gasp and kept her eyes trained on Amelia. "You are wrong."

"Amelia." Lady Rockland appeared and tugged on her daughter's arm. "Come away this instant. You will ruin yourself by even speaking to that . . ." She did not finish, did not add the hateful word before spinning away in a flurry of obvious revulsion. Maggie could well imagine what Lady Rockland had been about to say, however.

Whore. Harlot. Strumpet.

Is that what she'd become in their eyes? It seemed incomprehensible, especially since Mr. Davenport had lied. Maggie had agreed to meet him to, as he said, discuss Amelia. Yet once on the edge of the gardens, it had become apparent the young man had something else in mind. He'd grabbed her, tried to pull her close, and put his mouth on her. He'd ripped her dress. Maggie struck back in the one place it counted on a man and he'd released her. When she hurried back to the house, the couple arriving on the terrace must have drawn their own conclusions about her dishabille.

Mr. Davenport had tricked her. Tried to seduce her. Then he compounded the sin by lying about it to Amelia, one of the few girls Maggie had befriended. The unfairness of it tore at her insides. Did no one care for the truth?

As she swept the room with her gaze, the hatred staring back at her made it undeniably clear that the truth did not matter. The *ton* had passed judgment. She wanted to scream with the unfairness of it. Would no one come to her aid? Surely one of the other unmarried young girls or the man she thought—

More than a little desperately, she searched the room, this time for a tall, blond-haired man. He had been her safe harbor this Season, the one person who truly knew her, who would believe she'd never do anything so reckless. Likely he'd heard what happened by now. So why had Simon not stepped forward to defend her?

There, in the back of the ballroom. Her eyes locked with the brilliant blue gaze she knew so well, a gaze that had sparkled down at her for more nights than she could count. His eyes were not sparkling now, however; they were flat, completely devoid of any emotion whatsoever. A flush slowly spread over his cheeks, almost as if he was . . . angry or perhaps embarrassed—which made no sense at all.

She clasped her gloved hands together tightly, silently imploring him to come rescue her. Yet he made no move toward the stairs. Without glancing away, he raised his champagne glass and drained it.

Hope bloomed when Simon shifted—only to be quashed when she realized what was happening. He'd presented her with his back.

Simon had turned away.

No one stirred. No one spoke. It seemed as if they were all waiting to see what she would do. Hysteria bubbled up in Maggie's chest, a portentous weight crushing her lungs.

Dear God. What was to become of her?

3/18 (11) 10/17

GREAT BOOKS, GREAT SAVINGS!

When You Visit Our Website:
www.kensingtonbooks.com
You Can Save Money Off The Retail Price
Of Any Book You Purchase!